The Weathercock

George Manville Fenn

Illustrated by A. W. Cooper

ESPRIOS DIGITAL PUBLISHING

The Weathercock

Chapter One.

Toadstools!

"Oh, I say, here's a game! What's he up to now?"

"Hi! Vane! Old weathercock! Hold hard!"

"Do you hear? Which way does the wind blow?"

Three salutations shouted at a lad of about sixteen, who had just shown himself at the edge of a wood on the sunny slope of the Southwolds, one glorious September morning, when the spider-webs were still glittering with iridescent colours, as if every tiny strand were strung with diamonds, emeralds and amethysts, and the thick green moss that clothed the nut stubbs was one glorious sheen of topaz, sapphire and gold. Down in the valley the mist still hung in thick patches, but the sun's rays were piercing it in many directions, and there was every promise of a hot day, such as would make the shade of the great forest with its acorn-laden oaks welcome, and the whole place tempting to one who cared to fill pocket or basket with the bearded hazelnuts, already beginning to show colour in the pale green husks, while the acorns, too, were changing tint slightly, and growing too big for their cups.

The boy, who stood with his feet deep in moss, was framed by the long lithe hazel stems, and his sun-browned face looked darker in the shade as, bareheaded, his cap being tucked in the band of his Norfolk jacket, he passed one hand through his short curly hair, to remove a dead leaf or two, while the other held a little basket full of something of a bright orange gold; and as he glanced at the three youths in the road, he hurriedly bent down to rub a little loam from the knees of his knickerbockers—loam freshly gathered from some bank in the wood.

"Morning," he said, as the momentary annoyance caused by the encounter passed off. "How is it you chaps are out so early?"

"Searching after you, of course," said the first speaker. "What have you got there?"

"These," said the lad, holding up his basket, as he stepped down amongst the dewy grass at the side of the road. "Have some?"

"Have some? Toadstools?"

"Toad's grandmothers!" cried the lad. "They're all chanterelles—for breakfast. Delicious."

The first of the three well-dressed youths, all pupils reading with the Reverend Morton Syme, at the Rectory, Mavis Greythorpe, Lincolnshire, gave a sidelong glance at his companions and advanced a step.

"Let's look," he said.

The bearer of the basket raised his left hand with his fungoid booty, frankly trusting, and his fellow-pupil delivered a sharp kick at the bottom of the wicker receptacle—a kick intended to send the golden chalice-like fungi flying scattered in the air. But George Vane Lee was as quick in defence as the other was in attack, and his parry was made in the easiest and most effortless way.

It was just this:—

He let the basket swing down and just passed his right hand forward, seeming only to brush the assailant's ankle—in fact it was the merest touch, but sufficient to upset the equilibrium of a kicker on one leg, and the next moment Lance Distin was lying on his back in a perfect tangle of brambles, out of which he scrambled, scratched and furious, amidst a roar of laughter from his companions.

"You beggar!" he cried, with his dark eyes flashing, and a red spot in each of his sallow cheeks.

"Keep off!" cried the mushroom bearer, backing away. "Lay hold of him, Gilmore—Aleck!"

The lads addressed had already caught at the irate boy's arms.

"Let go, will you!" he yelled. "I'll let him know."

"Be quiet, or we'll all sit on you and make you."

"I'll half kill him—I'll nearly break his neck."

"No, don't," said the boy with the basket, laughing. "Do you want your leave stopped? Nice you'd look with a pair of black eyes."

"You can't give them to me," roared the lad, passionately, as he still struggled with those who held him, but giving them little trouble in keeping him back.

"Don't want to. Served you right. Shouldn't have tried to kick over my basket. There, don't be in such a temper about that."

"I'll pay you for it, you miserable cad!"

"Don't call names, Distie," said the lad coolly. "Those who play at bowls must expect rubbers. Let him go, boys; he won't hurt me."

It was a mere form that holding; but as the detaining pair loosened their hold, Lance Distin gave himself a violent wrench, as if he were wresting himself free, and then coloured to the roots of his hair, as he saw the laugh in his adversary's eyes.

"Distie's got no end of Trinidad sun in him yet.—What a passionate fellow you are, Cocoa. I say, these are good, really. Come home with me and have breakfast."

Lance Distin, son of a wealthy planter in the West Indies, turned away scornfully, and the others laughed.

"Likely," said Fred Gilmore, showing his white teeth. "Why, I wouldn't poison a cat with them."

"No," said Aleck Macey; "I know."

"Know what?"

"It's a dodge to make a job for his uncle, because the doctor can't get any practice."

"Don't want any," said the lad, good-humouredly. "If he did, he'd go back to Savile Row."

"Not he," snarled Distin, pausing in his occupation of removing thorns from his jacket. "Killed all his patients, and was obliged to run away into the country."

"That's it!" said Vane Lee, with a laugh. "What a clever chap you are, Distie; at least you would be if your tongue wasn't quite so sharp. There, shake hands, I didn't mean to hurt you."

He stretched out rather a dirty hand, at which the young Creole gave a contemptuous glance, looked at his own white fingers, and thrust them into his pockets.

"Ah, well, they are dirty," said Vane, laughing. "No, they're not. It's only good old English soil. Come on. Uncle will be glad to see you, and then we'll all walk up to the Rectory together."

Crick!

Distin struck a match, and, with a very haughty look on his thin face, began to puff at a cigarette which he had taken from a little silver case, Vane watching him scornfully the while, but only to explode with mirth the next moment, for the young West Indian, though he came from where his father's plantations produced acres of the pungent weed, was not to the manner born, and at the third draw inhaled so much acrid smoke that he choked, and stood coughing violently till Vane gave him a hearty slap on his back.

Down went the cigarette, as Distin made a bound forward.

"You boor!" he coughed out; and, giving the lad a malevolent look, he turned haughtily to the others.

"Are you fellows coming home to breakfast?"

He did not pause for an answer, but walked off sharply in the direction of the Rectory, a quarter of a mile from the little sleepy town.

"Oh, I say," cried Vane, in a tone full of remorse, "what an old pepper-pot he is! I didn't mean to upset him. He began it,—now, didn't he?"

"Yes, of course," said Gilmore. "Never mind. He'll soon come round."

"Oh, yes," said Macey. "I shouldn't take any notice. He'll forget it all before night."

"But it seems so queer," said the lad, taking out and examining one of his mushrooms. "I just came out for a walk, and to pick some of these to have cooked for breakfast; and just as I've got a nice basketful, I come upon you fellows, and you begin to chaff and play larks, and the next moment I might have been knocking all the skin off my knuckles against Distin's face, if I hadn't backed out—like a coward," he added, after a pause.

"Oh, never mind," said the others.

"But I do mind," cried the lad. "I want to be friends with everyone. I hate fighting and quarrelling, and yet I'm always getting into hot-water."

"Better go and get your hands in now—with soap," said Macey, staring at the soil-marks.

"Pooh! a rinse in the water-cress stream would take that off. Never mind Distin: come home, you two."

"No, not this morning," said Gilmore.

"I won't ask you to taste the mushrooms: honour bright."

"Wouldn't come if you did," said Macey, with a merry laugh on his handsome face. "Old Distie would never forgive us if we came home with you now."

"No," said Gilmore; "he'd keep us awake half the night preaching at you. Oh! here's old Syme."

"Ah, gentlemen, good-morning," said a plump, florid clergyman with glittering glasses. "That's right, walk before breakfast. Good for stamina. Must be breakfast time though. What have you got there, Lee?"

"Fungi, sir."

"Hum! ha!" said the rector bending over the basket. "Which? Fungi, soft as you pronounce it, or Fungi—Funghi, hard, eh?"

"Uncle says soft, sir," said Vane.

"Hum—ha—yes," said the rector, poking at one of the vegetable growths with the forefinger of his gloved hand. "He ought to know. But, *vulgo*, toadstools. You're not going to eat those, are you?"

"Yes, sir. Will you try a few?"

"Eh? Try a few, Lee? Thanks, no. Too much respect for my gastric region. And look here; hadn't you better try experiments on Jamby's donkey? It's very old."

"Wouldn't be any good, sir. Nothing would hurt him," said Vane, laughing.

"Hum! ha! Suppose not. Well, don't poison one of my pupils—yourself. Breakfast, gentlemen, breakfast. The matutinal coffee and one of Brader's rolls, not like the London French, but passably good; and there is some cold stuffed chine."

"Cold stuffed chine!" said Vane, as he walked in the other direction. "Why, these will be twice as good—if Martha will cook 'em. Nasty prejudiced old thing!"

Ten minutes later he reached a gate where the remains of a fine old avenue leading up to a low mossy-looking stone house, built many generations back; and as he neared it, a pleasant odour, suggestive of breakfast, saluted his nostrils, and he went round and entered the kitchen, to be encountered directly by quite an eager look from its occupant, as he made his petition.

"No, Master Vane, I'll not."

Chapter Two.

Aunt and Uncle.

"No, Master Vane, I'll not," cried cook, bridling up, and looking as if an insult had been offered to her stately person; "and if master and missus won't speak, it's time someone else did."

"But I only want them just plainly stewed with a little butter, pepper, and salt," said Vane, with the basket in his hand.

"A little butter and pepper and salt, sir!" cried cook reproachfully; "a little rhubar' and magneshire, you mean, to keep the nasty pysonous thinks from hurting of you. Really I do wonder at you, sir, a-going about picking up such rubbish."

"But they're good food—good to eat."

"Yes, sir; for toads and frogs. Don't tell me, sir. Do you think I don't know what's good Christian food when I see it, and what isn't?"

"I know you think they're no good, but I want to try them as an experiment."

"Life isn't long enough, sir, to try sperrymens, and I'd sooner go and give warning at once than be the means of laying you on a bed of agony and pain."

"Oh, well, never mind, cook, let me do them myself."

"What?" cried the stout lady in such a tone of indignant surprise that the lad felt as if he had been guilty of a horrible breach of etiquette, and made his retreat, basket and all, toward the door.

But he had roused Martha, who, on the strength of many years' service with the doctor and his lady in London, had swollen much in mind as well as grown stout in body, and she followed him to the kitchen-door where he paused without opening it, for fear of the dispute reaching the ears of aunt and uncle in the breakfast-room.

"Look here, Martha," he said, "don't be cross. Never mind. I'm sorry I asked you."

"Cross? Cross, Master Vane? Is it likely I should make myself cross about a basketful of rubbishing toadstools that you've wasted your time in fetching out of the woods?"

"No, no, you are not cross, and I beg your pardon."

"And I wouldn't have thought it of you, sir. The idee, indeed, of you wanting to come and meddle here in my kitchen!"

"But I don't want to, I tell you, so don't say any more about it."

But before Vane could grasp the woman's intention, she had snatched the basket from his hand and borne it back to the table, upon which she thumped it with so much vigour that several of the golden chalice-like fungi leaped out.

"Here, what are you going to do?" cried Vane.

"What you told me, sir," said cook austerely, and with a great hardening of her face. "I don't forget my dooties, sir, if other people do."

"Oh, but never mind, cook," cried Vane. "I'm sorry I asked you."

"Pray don't say any more about it, sir. The things shall be cooked and sent to table, and it's very thankful you ought to be, I'm sure, that master's a doctor and on the spot ready, for so sure as you eat that mess in the parlour, you'll all be on a bed of sickness before night."

"Now, Martha," cried Vane; "that's just what you said when I asked you to cook the parasol mushrooms."

"Paragrandmother mushrooms, sir; you might just as well call them by their proper name, umberrella toadstools, and I don't believe any one ate them."

"Yes; uncle and I ate them, and they were delicious. Cook these the same way."

"I know how to cook them, sir, only it's an insult to proper mushrooms to dress them in the same way as good wholesome food."

"That's good wholesome food," said Vane, "only people don't know it. I wanted to bring you some big puff balls to fry for me, but you turn so cross about it."

"And enough to make anyone turn cross, sir. There, that will do now. I've said that I'd cook them, and that's enough."

Vane Lee felt that there was nothing to be done now but make a retreat, and he went into the hall where Eliza Jane, the doctor's housemaid, was whisking a feather-brush about, over picture-frames, and ornaments, curiosities from different parts of the world, and polishing the hall table. From this she flew to the stand and caught up the hat brush with which she attacked the different hats on the pegs, speaking over her shoulder at Vane in a rapid way as she went on.

"Now, don't you ask me to do anything, Master Vane, because I'm all behind, and your aunt's made the tea and waiting for you, and your uncle will be back directly, for he has only gone down the garden for a walk, and to pick up the fallen peaches."

"Wasn't going to ask you to do anything," was the reply.

"But you've been asking cook to do something, and a nice fantigue she'll be in. She was bad enough before. I wouldn't have such a temper for all the money in the Bank of England. What have you been asking her to do?—Bother the hat!"

Eliza was brushing so vigorously that she sent Vane's hard felt hat, which she had just snatched up from where he had placed it, flying to the other end of the hall just as Doctor Lee, a tall, pleasant-looking grey-haired man, came in from the garden with a basket of his gleanings from beneath the south wall.

"That meant for me?" he said, staring down at the hat and then at Vane.

"Which I beg your pardon, sir," said the maid, hurriedly. "I was brushing it, and it flew out of my hand."

"Ah! You should hold it tight," said the doctor, picking up the hat, and looking at a dint in the crown. "It will require an operation to remove that depression of the brain-pan on the *dura mater*. I mean on the lining, eh, Vane?"

"Oh, I can soon put that right," said the boy merrily, as he gave it a punch with his fist and restored the crown to its smooth dome-like shape.

"Yes," said the doctor, "but you see we cannot do that with a man who has a fractured skull. Been out I see?" he continued, looking down at the lad's discoloured, dust-stained boots.

"Oh, yes, uncle, I was out at six. Glorious morning. Found quite a basketful of young chanterelles."

"Indeed? What have you done with them?"

"Been fighting Martha to get her to cook them."

"And failed?" said the doctor quietly, as he peered into the basket, and turned over the soft, downy, red-cheeked peaches he had brought in.

"No, uncle,—won."

"Now, you good people, it's nearly half-past eight. Breakfast—breakfast. Bring in the ham, Eliza."

"Good-morning, my dear," said the doctor, bending down to kiss the pleasantly plump elderly lady who had just opened the dining-room door, and keeping up the fiction of its being their first meeting that morning.

"Good-morning, dear."

"Come, Vane, my boy," cried the doctor, "breakfast, breakfast. Here's aunt in one of her furious tempers because you are so late."

"Don't you believe him, my dear," said the lady. "It's too bad. And really, Thomas, you should not get in the habit of telling such dreadful fibs even in fun. Had a nice walk, Vane?"

"Yes, aunt, and collected a capital lot of edible fungi."

"The word fungi's enough to make any one feel that they are not edible, my dear," said Aunt Hannah. "What sort did you get? Not those nasty, tall, long-legged things you brought before?"

"No, aunt; beautiful golden chanterelles. I wanted to have them cooked for breakfast."

"And I have told him it would be high treason," said the doctor. "Martha would give warning."

"No, no, my dear, not quite so bad as that, but leave them to me, and I'll cook them for lunch myself."

"No need, aunt; Martha came down from her indignant perch."

"I'm glad of that," said the lady smiling; "but, one minute, before we go in the dining-room: there's a beautiful *souvenir* rosebud over the window where I cannot reach it. Cut it and bring it in."

"At your peril, sir," said the doctor fiercely. "The last rose of summer! I will not have it touched."

"Now, my dear Tom, don't be so absurd," cried the lady. "What is the use of your growing roses to waste—waste—waste themselves all over the place."

"You hear that, Vane? There's quoting poetry. Waste their sweetness on the desert air, I suppose you mean, madam?"

"Yes: it's all the same," said the lady. "Thank you, my dear," she continued, as Vane handed the rose in through the window.

"My poor cut-down bloom," sighed the doctor; but Vane did not hear him, for he was setting his hat down again in the museum-like hall, close by the fishing-tackle and curiosities of many lands just as a door was opened and a fresh, maddening odour of fried ham saluted his nostrils.

"Oh, murder!" cried the lad; and he rushed upstairs, three steps at a time, to begin washing his hands, thinking the while over his encounter with his Creole fellow-pupil.

"Glad I didn't fight him," he muttered, as he dried his knuckles, and looked at them curiously. "Better than having to ask uncle for his sticking-plaster."

He stopped short, turning and gazing out of the bedroom window, which looked over the back garden toward the field with their Jersey cows; and just then a handsome game-cock flapped his bronzed wings and sent forth his defiant call.

"Cock-a-doodle-doo! indeed," muttered Vane; "and he thinks me a regular coward. I suppose it will have to come to a set-to some day. I feel sure I can lick him, and perhaps, after all, he'll lick me."

"Oh, Vane, my dear boy, don't!" cried Mrs Lee, as the lad rushed down again, his feet finding the steps so rapidly that the wonder was that he did not go headlong, and a few seconds later, he was in his place at the dining-room table, tastily arranged with its plate, china, and flowers.

A walk before breakfast is a wonderful thing for the appetite, and Vane soon began with a sixteen-year-old growing appetite upon the white bread, home-made golden butter, and the other pleasant products of the doctor's tiny homestead, including brahma eggs, whose brown shells suggested that they must have been boiled in coffee.

The doctor kept the basket he had brought in beside him on the cloth, and had to get up four times over to throw great fat wood-lice out of the window, after scooping them up with a silver tablespoon, the dark grey creatures having escaped from between the interstices of the basket, and being busily making their way in search of some dry, dark corner.

"It is astonishing what a predilection for peaches the wood-louse has," said the doctor, resuming his seat.

"All your fault, uncle," said Vane, with his mouth full.

"Mine! why?"

"You see you catch them stealing, and then you forgive them and let them go to find their way back to the south wall, so that they can begin again."

"Humph! yes," said the doctor; "they have plenty of enemies to shorten their lives without my help. Well, so you found some mushrooms, did you?"

"Yes, uncle, just in perfection."

"Some more tea, dear?" said Vane's aunt. "I hope you didn't bring many to worry cook with."

"Only a basket full, aunty," said Vane merrily.

"What!" cried the lady, holding the teapot in air.

"But she is going to cook them for dinner."

"Really, my dear, I must protest," said the lady. "Vane cannot know enough about such things to be trusted to bring them home and eat them. I declare I was in fear and trembling over that last dish."

"You married a doctor, my dear," said Vane's uncle quietly; "and you saw me partake of the dish without fear. Someone must experimentalise, somebody had to eat the first potato, and the first bunch of grapes. Nature never labelled them wholesome food."

"Then let somebody else try them first," said the lady. "I do not feel disposed to be made ill to try whether this or that is good for food. I am not ambitious."

"Then you must forgive us: we are," said the doctor dipping into his basket. "Come, you will not refuse to experimentalise on a peach, my dear. There is one just fully ripe, and—dear me! There are two wood-lice in this one. Eaten their way right in and living there."

He laid one lovely looking peach on a plate, and made another dip.

"That must have fallen quite early in the night," said Vane, sharply, "slugs have been all over it."

"So they have," said the doctor, readjusting his spectacles. "Here is a splendid one. No: a blackbird has been digging his beak into that. And into this one too. Really, my dear, I'm afraid that my garden friends and foes have been tasting them all. No, here is one with nothing the matter, save the contusion consequent from its fall from the mother tree."

"On to mother earth," said Vane laughing. "I say, uncle, wouldn't it be a good plan to get a lot of that narrow old fishing net, and spread it out hanging from the wall, so as to catch all the peaches that fall?"

"Excellent," said the doctor.

"I'll do it," said Vane, wrinkling up his brow, as he began to puzzle his brains about the best way to suspend the net for the purpose.

Soon after, the lad was in the doctor's study, going over some papers he had written, ready for his morning visit to the rectory; and this put him in mind of the encounter with his fellow-pupil, Distin, and made him thoughtful.

"He doesn't like me," the boy said to himself; "and somehow I feel as if I do not like him. I don't want to quarrel, and it always seems as if one was getting into hot-water with him. He's hot-blooded, I suppose, from being born in the West Indies. Well, if that's it," mused Vane, "he can't help it any more than I can help being cool because I was born in England. I won't quarrel with him. There."

And taking up his books and papers, he strapped them together, and set off for the rectory, passing out of the swing-gate, going along the road toward the little town above which the tall grey-stone tower stood up in the clear autumn air with its flagstaff at the corner of the battlements, its secondary tower at the other corner, holding within it the narrow spiral staircase which led from the floor to the leads; and about it a little flock of jackdaws sailing round and round before settling on the corner stones, and the top.

"Wish I could invent something to fly with," thought Vane, as he reached the turning some distance short of the first houses of the town. "It does seem so easy. Those birds just spread out their wings, and float about wherever they please with hardly a beat. There must be a way, if one could only find it out."

He went off into the pleasant lane to the left, and caught sight of a bunch of blackberries apparently within reach, and he was about to cross the dewy band of grass which bordered the road, when he recollected that he had just put on clean boots, and the result of a scramble through and among brambles would be unsatisfactory for their appearance in the rector's prim study. So the berries hung in their place, left to ripen, and he went on till a great dragon-fly came sailing along the moist lane to pause in the sunny openings, and poise itself in the clear air where its wings vibrated so rapidly that they looked like a patch of clear gauze.

Vane's thoughts were back in an instant to the problem that has puzzled so many minds; and as he watched the dragon-fly, a couple of swallows skimmed by him, darted over the wall, and were gone. Then, flopping idly along in its clumsy flight, came a white butterfly, and directly after a bee—one of the great, dark, golden-banded fellows, with a soft, velvety coat.

"And all fly in a different way," said Vane to himself, thoughtfully. "They all use wings, but all differently; and they have so much command over them, darting here and there, just as they please. I wonder whether I could make a pair of wings and a machine to work them. It doesn't seem impossible. People float up in balloons, but that isn't enough. I think I could do it, and—oh, hang it, there goes ten, and the rector will be waiting. I wonder whether I can recollect all he said about those Greek verbs."

Chapter Three.

In the Study.

Vane reached the rectory gate and turned in with his brains in the air, dashing here and there like a dragon-fly, skimming after the fashion of a swallow, flying steadily, bumble-bee-fashion, and flopping faintly as the butterfly did whose wings were so much out of proportion to the size of its body. Either way would do, he thought, or better still, if he could fly by a wide-spread membrane stretched upon steel or whalebone ribs or fingers like a bat. Why not? he mused. There could be no reason; and he was beginning to wonder why he had never thought of making some flying machine before, when he was brought back to earth from his imaginary soarings by a voice saying,—

"Hullo! here's old Weathercock!" and this was followed by a laugh which brought the colour into his cheeks.

"I don't care," he thought. "Let him laugh. Better be a weathercock and change about, than be always sticking fast. Uncle says we can't help learning something for one's trouble."

By this time he was at the porch, which he entered just as the footman was carrying out the breakfast things.

"Rector isn't in the study then, Joseph?" said Vane.

"No, sir; just coming in out of the garden. Young gents is in there together."

Vane felt disposed to wait and go in with the rector, but, feeling that it would be cowardly, he walked straight in at the study door to find Distin, Gilmore, and Macey seated at the table, all hard at work, but apparently not over their studies.

"Why, gracious!" cried Macey.

"Alive?" said Gilmore.

"Used to it," sneered Distin. "That sort of creature takes a deal of killing."

"What's the matter?" said Vane, good-humouredly, taking a seat.

"Why," said Gilmore, "we were all thinking of writing to our tailors to send us suits of mourning out of respect for you—believe it or not as you please."

"Thankye," said Vane quietly. "Then I will not believe it, because Distin wouldn't order black if I were drowned."

"Who said a word about drowned? I said poisoned," cried Gilmore.

"Not a word about it. But why?"

"Because you went home and ate those toadstools."

"Wrong," said Vane quietly, "I haven't eaten them yet."

"Then three cheers for the tailors; there's a chance for them yet," cried Macey.

"Why didn't you eat them?" asked Gilmore. "Afraid?"

"I don't think so. They'll be ready by dinner time, will you come?"

Grimaces followed, as Vane quietly opened his books, and glanced round the rector's room with its handsome book-cases all well filled, chimney-piece ornamented with classic looking bronzes; and the whole place with its subdued lights and heavily curtained windows suggestive of repose for the mind and uninterrupted thought and study.

Books and newly-written papers lay on the table, ready for application, but the rector's pupils did not seem to care about work in their tutor's absence, for Macey, who was in the act of handing round a tin box when Vane entered, now passed it on to the latter.

"Lay hold, old chap," he said. Vane opened it, and took out a piece of crisp dark brown stickiness generally known as "jumble," and transferred it to his mouth, while four lower jaws were now seen at work, giving the pupils the aspect of being members of that portion of the quadrupedal animal kingdom known as ruminants.

"Worst of this stuff is," said Macey, "that you get your teeth stuck together. Oh, I say, Gil, what hooks! A whole dozen?"

Gilmore nodded as he opened a ring of fine silkworm gut, and began to examine the points and backs of the twelve bright blue steel hooks at the ends of the gut lengths, and the carefully-tied loops at the other.

"Where did you buy them?" continued Macey, as he gloated over the bright hookah.

No answer.

"Where did you buy them, Gil?" said Macey again.

"Cuoz—duoz—ooze."

"What!" cried Macey; and Distin and Vane both looked wonderingly at their fellow-pupil, who had made a peculiar incoherent guttural noise, faintly represented by the above words.

Then Vane began to laugh.

"What's the matter, Gil?" he said.

Gilmore gave his neck a peculiar writhe, and his jaws a wrench.

"I wish you fellows wouldn't bother," he cried. "You, Macey, ought to know better: you give a chap that stickjaw stuff of yours, and then worry him to speak. Come by post, I said. From London."

Distin gave vent to a contemptuous sniff, and it was seen that he was busily spreading tobacco on thin pieces of paper, and rolling them up into cigarettes with the nonchalant air of one used to such feats of dexterity, though, truth to tell, he fumbled over the task; and as he noticed that Vane was observing him with a quiet look of good-humoured contempt, his fingers grew hot and moist, and he nervously blundered over his task.

"Well," he said with a vicious twang in his tones, "what are you staring at?"

"You," replied Vane, with his hand holding open a Greek Lexicon.

"Then mind your lessons, schoolboy," retorted Distin sharply. "Did you never see a gentleman roll a cigarette before?"

"No," said Vane quietly, and then, feeling a little nettled by the other's tone, he continued, "and I can't see one now."

Distin half rose from the table, crushing a partly formed cigarette in his hand.

"Did you mean that for another insult, sir?" he cried in a loud, angry voice.

"Oh, I say, Distie," said Gilmore, rising too, and catching his arm, "don't be such a pepper-pot. Old Weathercock didn't mean any harm."

"Mind your own business," said Distin, fiercely wrenching his arm free.

"That is my business—to sit on you when you go off like a firework," said Gilmore merrily. "I say, does your father grow much ginger on his plantation?"

"I was speaking to the doctor's boy, and I'll thank you to be silent," cried Distin.

"Oh, I say, don't, don't, don't!" cried Macey, apostrophising all three. "What's the good of kicking up rows about nothing! Here, Distie," he continued, holding out his box; "have some more jumble."

Distin waved the tin box away majestically, and turned to Vane.

"I said, sir, goo—gloo—goog—"

He stepped from his place to the window in a rage, for his voice had suddenly become most peculiar; and as the others saw him thrust a white finger into his mouth and tear out something which he tried to throw away but which refused to be cast off, they burst into a simultaneous roar of laughter, which increased as they saw the angry lad suck his finger, and wipe it impatiently on his handkerchief.

"Don't you give me any of your filthy stuff again, you. Macey," he cried.

"All right," said the culprit, wiping the tears out of his eyes, and taking the tin box from his pocket. "Have a bit more?"

Distin struck the tin box up furiously, sending it flying open, as it performed an arc in the air, and distributing fragments of the hard-baked saccharine sweet.

"Oh, I say!" cried Macey, hastily stooping to gather up the pieces. "Here, help, Gil, or we shall have Syme in to find out one of them by sitting on it."

"Look here, sir," cried Distin, across the table to Vane, who sat, as last comer, between him and the door, "I said did you mean that as an insult?"

"Oh, rubbish!" replied Vane, a little warmly now; "don't talk in that manner, as if you were somebody very big, and going to fight a duel."

"I asked you, sir, if you meant that remark as an insult," cried Distin, "and you evade answering, in the meanest and most shuffling way. I was under the impression when I came down to Greythorpe it was to read with English gentlemen, and I find—"

"Never mind what you find," said Vane; "I'll tell you what you do."

"Oh, you will condescend to tell me that," sneered Distin. "Pray what do I do?"

"Don't tell him, Lee," said Gilmore; "and stop it, both of you. Mr Syme will be here directly, and we don't want him to hear us squabbling over such a piece of idiotic nonsense."

"And you call my resenting an insult of the most grave nature a piece of idiocy, do you, Mr Gilmore?"

"No, Mr Distin; but I call the beginning of this silly row a piece of idiocy."

"Of course you fellows will hang together," said Distin, with a contemptuous look. "I might have known that you were not fit to trust as a friend."

"Look here, Dis," said Gilmore, in a low, angry voice, "don't you talk to me like that."

"And pray why, sir?" said Distin, in a tone full of contempt.

"Because I'm not Vane, sir, and—"

"I say, old chaps, don't, please don't," cried Macey, earnestly. "Look here; I've got a tip from home by this morning's post, and I'll be a good feed to set all square. Come: that's enough." Then, imitating the rector's thick, unctuous voice, "Hum—ha!—silence, gentlemen, if you please."

"Silence yourself, buffoon!" retorted Distin, sharply, and poor Macey sank down in his chair, startled, or assuming to be.

"No, Mr Gilmore," said Distin, haughtily, "you are not Vane Lee, you said, and—and what?"

"I'll tell you," cried the lad, with his brow lowering. "I will not sit still and let you bully me. He may not think it worth his while to hit out at a foreign-bred fellow who snaps and snarls like an angry dog, but I do; and if you speak to me again as you did just now, I'll show you how English-bred fellows behave. I'll punch your head."

"No, you will not, Gil," said Vane, half rising in his seat. "I don't want to quarrel, but if there must be one, it's mine. So look here, Distin: you've done everything you could for months past to put me out of temper."

"He—aw!—he—aw!" cried Macey, in parliamentary style.

"Be quiet, jackass," cried Distin; and Macey began to lower himself, in much dread, under the table.

"I say," continued Vane, "you have done everything you could to put me out of temper, and I've put up with it patiently, and behaved like a coward."

"He—aw, he—aw!" said Macey again; and Vane shook his fist at him good-humouredly.

"Amen. That's all, then," cried Macey; and then, imitating the rector again, "Now, gentlemen, let us resume our studies."

"Be quiet, Aleck," said Gilmore, angrily; "I—"

He did not go on, for he saw Distin's hand stealing toward a heavy dictionary, and, at that moment, Vane said firmly:—

"I felt it was time to show you that I am not quite a coward. I did mean it as an insult, as you call it. What then?"

"That!" cried Distin, hurling the dictionary he had picked up with all his might at his fellow-pupil, across the table, but without effect. Vane, like most manly British lads, knew how to take care of himself, and a quick movement to one side was sufficient to allow the big book to pass close to his ear, and strike with a heavy bang against the door panel just as the handle rattled, and a loud "Hum—ha!" told that the rector was coming into the room for the morning's reading.

"That!" cried Distin, hurling the dictionary.

Chapter Four.

Martha's mistake.

As quickly as if he were fielding a ball, Vane caught up the volume from where it fell, and was half-way back to his seat as the rector came in, looking very much astonished, partly at the noise of the thump on the door, partly from an idea that the dictionary had been thrown as an insult to him.

Macey was generally rather a heavy, slow fellow, but on this occasion he was quick as lightning, and, turning sharply to Distin, who looked pale and nervous at the result of his passionate act.

"You might have given the dictionary to him, Distin," he said, in a reproachful tone. "Don't do books any good to throw 'em."

"Quite right, Mr Macey, quite right," said the rector, blandly, as he moved slowly to the arm-chair at the end of the table. "Really, gentlemen, you startled me. I was afraid that the book was intended for me, hum—ha! in disgust because I was so late."

"Oh, no, sir," cried Distin, with nervous eagerness.

"Of course not, my dear Distin, of course not. An accident—an error—of judgment. Good for the binders, no doubt, but not for the books. And I have an affection for books—our best friends."

He subsided into his chair as he spoke.

"Pray forgive me for being so late. A little deputation from the town, Mr Rounds, my churchwarden; Mr Dodge, the people's. A little question of dispute calling for a gentle policy on my part, and—but, no matter; it will not interest you, neither does it interest me now, in the face of our studies. Mr Macey, shall I run over your paper now?"

Macey made a grimace at Vane, as he passed his paper to the rector; and, as it was taken, Vane glanced at Distin, and saw that his lips were moving as he bent over his Greek. Vane saw a red spot in each of his sallow cheeks, and a peculiar twitching about the corners of his eyes, giving the lad a nervous, excitable look, and making Vane remark,—

"What a pity it all is. Wish he couldn't be so easily put out. He can't help it, I suppose, and I suppose I can. There, he shan't quarrel with me again. I suppose I ought to pitch into him for throwing the book at my head, but I could fight him easily, and beat him, and, if I did, what would be the good? I should only make him hate me instead of disliking me as he does. Bother! I want to go on with my Greek."

He rested his head upon his hands determinedly, and, after a great deal of effort, managed to condense his thoughts upon the study he had in hand; and when, after a long morning's work, the rector smilingly complimented him upon his work, he looked up at him as if he thought it was meant in irony.

"Most creditable, sir, most creditable; and I wish I could say the same to you, my dear Macey. A little more patient assiduity—a little more solid work for your own sake, and for mine. Don't let me feel uncomfortable when the Alderman, your respected father, sends me his customary cheque, and make me say to myself, 'We have not earned this honourably and well.'"

The rector nodded to all in turn, and went out first, while, as books were being put together, Macey said sharply:—

"Here, Vane; I'm going to walk home with you. Come on!"

Vane glanced at Distin, who stood by the table with his eyes half-closed, and his hand resting upon the dictionary he had turned into a missile.

"He's waiting to hear what I say," thought Vane, quickly. Then aloud:—"All right, then, you shall. I see through you, though. You want to be asked to lunch on the toadstools."

In spite of himself, Vane could not help stealing another glance at Distin, and read in the contempt which curled his upper lip that he was accusing him mentally of being a coward, and eager to sneak away.

"Well, let him," he thought. "As I am not afraid of him, I can afford it."

Then he glanced at Gilmore who was standing sidewise to the window with his hands in his pockets; and he frowned as he encountered Vane's eyes, but his face softened directly.

"I won't ask you to come with us, Gil," said Vane frankly.

"All right, old Weathercock," cried Gilmore; and his face lit up now with satisfaction.

"He doesn't think I'm afraid," said Vane to himself.

"Am I to wait all day for you?" cried Macey.

"No; all right, I'm coming," said Vane, finishing the strapping together of his books.—"Ready now."

But he was not, for he hesitated for a moment, coloured, and then his face, too, lit up, and he turned to Distin, and held out his hand.

"I'm afraid I lost my temper a bit, Distie," he said; "but that's all over now. Shake hands."

Distin raised the lids of his half-closed eyes, and gazed full at the speaker, but his hand did not stir from where it rested upon the book.

And the two lads stood for some moments gazing into each other's eyes, till the blue-veined lids dropped slowly over Distin's, and without word or further look, he took his cigarette case out of his pocket, walked deliberately out of the study, and through the porch on to the gravel drive, where, directly after, they heard the sharp *crick-crack* of a match.

"It's all going to end in smoke," said Macey, wrinkling up his forehead. "I say, it isn't nice to wish it, because I may be in the same condition some day; but I do hope that cigarette will make him feel queer."

"I wouldn't have his temper for anything," cried Gilmore, angrily. "It isn't English to go on like that."

"Oh, never mind," said Vane; "he'll soon cool down."

"Yes; but when he does, you feel as if it's only a crust," cried Gilmore.

"And that the jam underneath isn't nice," added Macey. "Never mind. It's nothing fresh. We always knew that our West India possessions were rather hot. Come on, Vane. I don't know though. I don't want to go now."

"Not want to come? Why?"

"Because I only wanted to keep you two from dogs delighting again."

"You behaved very well, Vane, old fellow," said Gilmore, ignoring Macey's attempts to be facetious. "He thinks you're afraid of him, and if he don't mind he'll someday find out that he has made a mistake."

"I hope not," said Vane quietly. "I hate fighting."

"You didn't seem to when you licked that gipsy chap last year."

Vane turned red.

"No: that's the worst of it. I always feel shrinky till I start; and then, as soon as I get hurt, I begin to want to knock the other fellow's head off—oh, I say, don't let us talk about that sort of thing; one has got so much to do."

"You have, you mean," said Gilmore, clapping him on the shoulder. "What's in the wind now, Weathercock?"

"He's making a balloon," said Macey, laughing.

Vane gave quite a start, as he recalled his thoughts about flight that morning.

"Told you so," cried Macey merrily; "and he's going to coax pepper-pot Distin to go up with him, and pitch him out when they reach the first lake."

"No, he isn't," said Gilmore; "he's going to be on the look-out, for Distie's sure to want to serve him out on the sly if he can."

"Coming with us?" said Vane.

"No, not this time, old chap," said Gilmore, smiling. "I'm going to be merciful to your aunt and spare her."

"What do you mean?"

"I'll come when Aleck Macey stops away. He does eat at such a frightful rate, that if two of us came your people would never have us in at the Little Manor again."

Macey made an offer as if to throw something, but Gilmore did not see it, for he had stepped close up to Vane and laid his hand upon his shoulder.

"I'm going to stop with Distie. Don't take any notice of his temper. I'm afraid he cannot help it. I'll stay and go about with him, as if nothing had happened."

Vane nodded and went off with Macey, feeling as if he had never liked Gilmore so much before; and then the little unpleasantry was forgotten as they walked along from the rectory gates, passing, as they reached the main road, a party of gipsies on their way to the next town with their van and cart, both drawn by the most miserable specimens of the four-legged creature known as horse imaginable, and followed by about seven or eight more horses and ponies, all of which found time to crop a little grass by the roadside as cart and van were dragged slowly along.

It was not an attractive-looking procession, but the gipsies themselves seemed active and well, and the children riding or playing about the vehicles appeared to be happy enough, and the swarthy, dark-eyed women, both old and young, good-looking.

Just in front of the van, a big dark man of forty slouched along, with a whip under his arm, and a black pipe in his mouth; and every now and then he seemed to remember that he had the said whip, and took it in hand, to give it a crack which sounded like a pistol shot, with the result that the horse in the van threw up its head, which had hung down toward the road, and the other skeleton-like creature in the cart threw up its tail with a sharp whisk that disturbed the flies which appeared to have already begun to make a meal upon its body, while the scattered drove of ragged ponies and horses ceased cropping the roadside herbage, and trotted on a few yards before beginning to eat again.

"They're going on to some fair," said Macey, as he looked curiously at the horses. "I say, you wouldn't think anyone would buy such animals as those."

"Want to buy a pony, young gentlemen?" said the man with the pipe, sidling up to them.

"Look at them, banging that poor pony about."

"What for?" said Macey sharply. "Scarecrow? We're not farmers."

The man grinned.

"And we don't keep dogs," continued Macey. "Oh, I say, George, you have got a pretty lot to-day."

The gipsy frowned and gave his whip a crack.

"Only want cleaning up, master," he said.

"Going to the fair?"

The man nodded and went on, for all this was said without the two lads stopping; and directly after, driving a miserable halting pony which could hardly get over the ground, a couple of big hulking lads of sixteen or seventeen appeared some fifty yards away.

"Oh, I say, Vane," cried Macey; "there's that chap you licked last year. You'll see how he'll smile at you."

"I should like to do it again," said Vane. "Look at them banging that poor pony about. What a shame it seems!"

"Yes. You ought to invent a machine for doing away with such chaps as these. They're no good," said Macey.

"Oh, you brute!—I say, don't the poor beggar's sides sound hollow!"

"Hollow! Yes," cried Vane indignantly; "they never feed them, and that poor thing can't find time to graze."

"No. It will be a blessing for it when it's turned into leather and glue."

"Go that side, and do as I do," whispered Vane; and they separated, and took opposite sides of the road, as the two gipsy lads stared hard at them, and as if to rouse their ire shouted at the wretched pony, and banged its ribs.

What followed was quickly done. Vane snatched at one stick and twisted it out of the lad's hand nearest to him Macey followed suit, and the boys stared.

"It would serve you precious well right if I laid the stick about your shoulders," cried Vane, breaking the ash sapling across his knee.

"Ditto, ditto," cried Macey doing the same, and expecting an attack.

The lads looked astonished for the moment, but instead of resenting the act, trotted on after the pony, which had continued to advance; and, as soon as they were at a safe distance, one of them turned, put his hand to his mouth and shouted "yah!" while the other took out his knife and flourished it.

"Soon cut two more," he cried.

"There!" said Macey, "deal of good you've done. The pony will only get it worse, and that's another notch they've got against you."

"Pish!" said Vane, contemptuously.

"Yes, it's all very well to say pish; but suppose you come upon them some day when I'm not with you. Gipsies never forget, and you see if they don't serve you out."

Vane gave him a merry look, and Macey grinned.

"I hope you will always be with me to take care of me," said Vane.

"Do my best, old fellow—do my best, little man. I say, though, do you mean me to come and have lunch?"

"It'll be dinner to-day," said Vane.

"But won't your people mind?"

"Mind! no. Uncle and aunt both said I was to ask you to come as often as I liked. Uncle likes you."

"No; does he?"

"Yes; says you're such a rum fellow."

"Oh!"

Macey was silent after that "oh," and the silence lasted till they reached the manor, for Vane was thinking deeply about the quarrel that morning; but, as the former approached the house, he felt no misgivings about his being welcome, the doctor, who was in the garden, coming forward to welcome him warmly, and Mrs Lee, who heard the voices, hastening out to join them.

Ten minutes later they were at table, where Macey proved himself a pretty good trencherman till the plates were changed and Eliza brought in a dish and placed it before her mistress.

"Hum!" said the doctor, "only one pudding and no sweets. Why, Macey, they're behaving shabbily to you to-day."

Aunt Hannah looked puzzled, and Vane stared.

"Is there no tart or custard, Eliza?" asked the doctor.

"Yes, sir; both coming, sir," said the maid, who was very red in the face.

"Then what have you there?"

Eliza made an unspellable noise in her throat, snatched off the cover from the dish, and hurried out of the room.

"Dear me!" said the doctor putting on his glasses, and looking at the dish in which, in the midst of a quantity of brownish sauce, there was a little island of blackish scraps, at which Aunt Hannah gazed blankly, spoon in hand.

"What is it, my dear?" continued the doctor.

"I'm afraid, dear, it is a dish of those fungi that Vane brought in this morning."

"Oh, I see. You will try them, Macey?"

"Well, sir, I—"

"Of course he will, uncle. Have a taste, Aleck. Give him some, aunt."

Aunt Hannah placed a portion upon their visitor's plate, and Macey was wonderfully polite—waiting for other people to be served before he began.

"Oh, I say, aunt, take some too," cried Vane.

"Do you wish it, my dear? Well, I will;" and Aunt Hannah helped herself, as the doctor began to turn his portion over; and Macey thought of poisoning, doctors, and narrow escapes, as he trifled with the contents of his plate.

"Humph!" said the doctor breaking a painful silence. "I'm afraid, Vane, that cook has made a mistake."

"Mistake, sir?" cried Macey, eagerly; "then you think they are not wholesome?"

"Decidedly not," said the doctor. "I suppose these are your chanterelles, Vane."

"Don't look like 'em, uncle."

"No, my boy, they do not. I can't find any though," said the doctor, as he turned over his portion with his fork. "No: I was wrong."

"They are not the chanterelles then, uncle?"

"Oh, yes, my boy, they are. I was afraid that Martha had had an accident with the fungi, and had prepared a substitute from my old shooting boots, but I can't see either eyelet or nail. Can you?"

"Oh, my dear!" cried Aunt Hannah to her nephew; "do, pray, ring, and have them taken away. You really should not bring in such things to be cooked."

"No, no: stop a moment," said the doctor, as Macey grinned with delight; "let's see first whether there is anything eatable."

"It's all like bits of shrivelled crackling," said Vane, "only harder."

"Yes," said the doctor, "much. I'm afraid Martha did not like her job, and she has cooked these too much. No," he added, after tasting, "this is certainly not a success. Now for the tart—that is, if our young friend Macey has quite finished his portion."

"I haven't begun, sir," said the visitor.

"Then we will wait."

"No, no, please sir, don't. I feel as if I couldn't eat a bit."

"And I as if they were not meant to eat," said the doctor, smiling. "Never mind, Vane; we'll get aunt to cook the rest, or else you and I will experimentalise over a spirit lamp in the workshop, eh?"

"Yes, uncle, and we'll have Macey there, and make him do all the tasting for being so malicious."

"Tell me when it's to be," said Macey, grinning with delight at getting rid of his plate; "and I'll arrange to be fetched home for a holiday."

Chapter Five.

The Miller's Boat.

Vane so frequently got into hot-water with his experiments that he more than once made vows. But his promises were as unstable as water, and he soon forgot them. He had vowed that he would be contented with things as they were, but his active mind was soon at work contriving.

He and Macey had borrowed Rounds the miller's boat one day for a row. They were out having a desultory wander down by the river, when they came upon the bluff churchwarden himself, and he gave them a friendly nod as he stood by the roadside talking to Chakes about something connected with the church; and, as the boys went on, Macey said, laughing, "I say, Weathercock, you're such a fellow for making improvements, why don't you take Chakes in hand, and make him look like the miller?"

"They are a contrast, certainly," said Vane, glancing back at the gloomy, bent form of the sexton, as he stood looking up sidewise at the big, squarely-built, wholesome-looking miller. "But I couldn't improve him. I say, what shall we do this afternoon?"

"I don't know," said Macey. "Two can't play cricket comfortably. It's stupid to bowl and field."

"Well, and it's dull work to bat, and be kept waiting while the ball is fetched. Let's go to my place. I want to try an experiment."

"No, thank you," cried Macey. "Don't catch me holding wires, or being set to pound something in a mortar. I know your little games, Vane Lee. You've caught me once or twice before."

"Well, let's do something. I hate wasting time."

"Come and tease old Gil; or, let's go and sit down somewhere near Distie. He's in the meadows, and it will make him mad as mad if you go near him."

"Try something better," said Vane.

"Oh, I don't know. We might go blackberrying, only one seems to be getting too old for that sort of thing. Let's hire two nags, and have a ride."

"Well, young gents, going my way?" cried the miller, from behind them, as he strode along in their rear.

"Where are you going?" said Vane.

"Down to the mill. The wind won't blow, so I'm obliged to make up for it at the river mill, only the water is getting short. That's the best of having two strings to your bow, my lads. By the time the water gets low, perhaps the wind may rise, and turn one's sails again. When I can't get wind or water there's no flour, and if there's no flour there'll be no bread."

"That's cheerful," cried Macey.

"Yes; keeps one back, my lad. Two strings to one's bow arn't enough. Say, Master Lee, you're a clever sort of chap, and make all kinds of 'ventions; can't you set me going with a steam engine thing as 'll make my stones run, when there's no water?"

"I think I could," said Vane, eagerly.

"I thowt you'd say that, lad," cried the miller, laughing; "but I've heard say as there's blowings-up—explosions—over your works sometimes, eh?"

"Oh, that was an accident," cried Vane.

"And accidents happen in the best regulated families, they say," cried the miller. "Well, I must think about it. Cost a mint o' money to do that."

By this time they had reached the long, low, weather-boarded, wooden building, which spanned the river like a bridge, and looked curiously picturesque among the ancient willows growing on the banks, and with their roots laving in the water.

It was a singular-looking place, built principally on a narrow island in the centre of the stream, and its floodgates and dam on either side of the island; while heavy wheels, all green with slimy growth, and looking grim and dangerous as they turned beneath the mill on either side, kept up a curious rumbling and splashing sound that was full of suggestions of what the consequences would be should anyone be swept over them by the sluggish current in the dam, and down into the dark pool below.

"Haven't seen you, gents, lately, for a day's fishing," said the miller, as he entered the swing-gate, and held it open for the lads to follow, which, having nothing else to do, they did, as a matter of course.

"No," said Macey; "been too busy over our books."

The churchwarden laughed.

"Oh, yes, I suppose so, sir. You look just the sort of boy who would work himself to death over his learning. Tired of fishing?"

"I'm not," said Vane. "Have there been many up here lately?"

"Swarms," said the miller. "Pool's alive with roach and chub sometimes, and up in the dam for hundreds of yards you may hear the big tench sucking and smacking their lips among the weeds, as if they was waiting for a bit of paste or a fat worm."

"You'll give us a day's fishing any time we like to come then, Mr Rounds?" said Vane.

"Two, if you like, my lads. Sorry I can't fit you up with tackle, or you might have a turn now."

"Oh, I shan't come and fish that way," cried Macey. "I've tried too often. You make all kinds of preparations, and then you come, and the fish won't bite. They never will when I try."

"Don't try enough, do he, Master Lee?"

"Yes, I do," cried Macey. "I like fishing with a net, or I should like to have a try if you ran all the water out of the dam, so that we could see what fish were in."

"Yes, I suppose you'd like that."

"Hi! Look there, Vane," cried Macey, pointing to a newly-painted boat fastened by its chain to one of the willows. "I'm ready for a row if Mr Rounds would lend us the boat."

"Nay, you'd go and drown yourself and Master Vane too."

"Pooh! as if we couldn't row. I say, Mr Rounds, do lend us the boat."

"Oh, well, I don't mind, my lads, if you'll promise to be steady, and not get playing any games."

"Oh, I'll promise, and there's no need to ask Lee. He's as steady as you are."

"All right, lads; you can have her. Oars is inside the mill. I'll show you. Want to go up or down?"

"I don't care," said Macey.

"If you want to go down stream, I shall have to slide the boat down the overshoot. Better go up, and then you'll have the stream with you coming back. Hello, here's some more of you."

This was on his seeing Distin and Gilmore coming in the other direction, and Macey shouted directly:

"Hi! We've got the boat. Come and have a row."

Gilmore was willing at once, but Distin held off for a few moments, but the sight of the newly-painted boat, the clear water of the sunlit river, and the glowing tints of the trees up where the stream wound along near the edge of the wood, were too much for him, and he took the lead at once, and began to unfasten the chain.

"You can fasten her up again when you bring her back," said the miller, as he led the way into the mill.

"I do like the smell of the freshly-ground flour," cried Macey, as they passed the door. "But, I say, Vane Lee, hadn't we better have gone alone? You see if those two don't monopolise the oars till they're tired, and then we shall have to row them just where they please."

"Never mind," said Vane; "we shall be on the water."

"I'll help you pitch them in, if they turn nasty, as people call it, down here."

"There you are, young gents, and the boat-hook, too," said the miller, opening his office door, and pointing to the oars. "Brand noo uns I've just had made, so don't break 'em."

"All right, we'll take care," said Macey; and, after a few words of thanks, the two lads bore out the oars, and crossed a narrow plank gangway in front of the mill to the island, where Distin and Gilmore were seated in the boat.

"Who's going to row?" said Macey.

"We are," replied Distin, quietly taking off his jacket, Gilmore following suit, and Macey gave Vane a look, which plainly said, "Told you so," as he settled himself down in the stern.

The start was not brilliant, for, on pushing off, Distin did not take his time from Gilmore, who was before him, and consequently gave him a tremendous thump on the back with both fists.

"I say," roared Gilmore, "we haven't come out crab-catching."

Whereupon Macey burst into a roar of laughter, and Vane smiled.

Distin, who was exceedingly nervous and excited, looked up sharply, ignored Macey, and addressed Vane.

"Idiot!" he cried. "I suppose you never had an accident in rowing."

"Lots," said Vane, with his face flushing, but he kept his temper.

"Perhaps you had better take the oar yourself."

"Try the other way, Mr Distin, sir," cried the miller, in his big, bluff voice; and, looking up, they could see his big, jolly face at a little trap-like window high up in the mill.

"Eh! Oh, thank you," said Distin, in a hurried, nervous way, and, rising in his seat, he was in the act of turning round to sit down with his back to Gilmore, when a fresh roar of laughter from Macey showed him that the miller was having a grin at his expense.

Just then the little window shut with a sharp clap, and Distin hesitated, and glanced at the shore as if, had it been closer, he would have leaped out of the boat, and walked off. But they were a good boat's length distant, and he sat down again with an angry scowl on his face, and began to pull.

"In for a row again," said Gilmore to himself. "Why cannot a fellow bear a bit of banter like that!"

To make things go more easily, Gilmore reversed the regular order of rowing, and took his time, as well as he could, from Distin, and the boat went on, the latter tugging viciously at the scull he held. The consequence was, that, as there was no rudder and the river was not straight, there was a tendency on the part of the boat to run its nose into the bank, in spite of all that Gilmore could do to prevent it; and at last Macey seized the boat-hook, and put it over the stern.

"Look here," he cried, "I daresay I can steer you a bit with this."

But his act only increased the annoyance of Distin, who had been nursing his rage, and trying to fit the cause in some way upon Vane.

"Put that thing down, idiot!" he cried, fiercely, "and sit still in the boat. Do you think I am going to be made the laughing-stock of everybody by your insane antics?"

"Oh, all right, Colonist," said Macey, good-humouredly; "only some people would put the pole down on your head for calling 'em idiots."

"What!" roared Distin; "do you dare to threaten me?"

"Oh, dear, no, sir. I beg your pardon, sir. I'm very sorry, sir. I didn't come for to go for to—"

"Clown!" cried Distin, contemptuously.

"Oh, I say, Vane, we are having a jolly ride," whispered Macey, but loud enough for Distin to hear, and the Creole's dark eyes flashed at them.

"I say, Distin," said Gilmore in a remonstrant growl, "don't be so precious peppery about nothing. Aleck didn't mean any harm."

"That's right! Take his part," cried Distin, making the water foam, as he pulled hard. "You fellows form a regular cabal, and make a dead set at me. But I'm not afraid. You've got the wrong man to deal with, and—confound the wretched boat!"

The Boating Party.

He jumped up, and raising the scull, made a sharp dig with it at the shore, and would have broken it, had not Gilmore checked him.

"Don't!" he cried, "you will snap the blade."

For, having nearly stopped rowing as he turned to protest, the natural result was that the boat's nose was dragged round, and the sharp prow ran right into the soft overhanging bank and stuck fast.

Vane tried to check himself, but a hearty fit of laughter would come, one which proved contagious, for Macey and Gilmore both joined in, the former rolling about and giving vent to such a peculiar set of grunts and squeaks of delight, as increased the others' mirth, and made Distin throw down his scull, and jump ashore, stamping with rage.

"No, no, Distie, don't do that," cried Gilmore, wiping his eyes. "Come back."

"I won't ride with such a set of fools," panted Distin, hoarsely. "You did it on purpose to annoy me."

He took a few sharp steps away, biting his upper lip with rage, and the laughter ceased in the boat.

"I say, Distin," cried Vane; and the lad faced round instantly with a vindictive look at the speaker as he walked sharply back to the boat, and sprang in.

"No, I will not go," he cried. "That's what you want—to get rid of me, but you've found your match."

He sprang in so sharply that the boat gave a lurch and freed itself from the bank, gliding off into deep water again; and as Distin resumed his scull, Gilmore waited for it to dip, and then pulled, so that solely by his skill—for Distin was very inexperienced as an oarsman—the boat was kept pretty straight, and they went on up stream in silence.

Macey gazed at Gilmore, who was of course facing him, but he could not look at his friend without seeing Distin too, and to look at the latter meant drawing upon himself a savage glare. So he turned his eyes to Vane, with the result that Distin watched him as if he were certain that he was going to detect some fresh conspiracy.

Macey sighed, and gazed dolefully at the bank, as if he wished that he were ashore.

Vane gazed at the bank too, and thought of his ill luck in being at odds with Distin, and of the many walks he had had along there with his uncle. These memories brought up plenty of pleasant thoughts, and he began to search for different water-plants and chat about them to Macey, who listened eagerly this time for the sake of having something to do.

"Look!" said Vane pointing; "there's the Stratiotes."

"What?"

"Stratiotes. The water-soldier."

"Then he's a deserter," said Macey. "Hold hard you two, and let's arrest him."

"No, no; go on rowing," said Vane.

"Don't take any notice of the buffoon, Gilmore," cried Distin sharply. "Pull!"

"I say, old cock of the weather," whispered Macey, leaning over the side, "I'd give something to be as strong as you are."

"Why?" asked Vane in the same low tone.

"Because my left fist wants to punch Distie's nose, and I haven't got muscle enough—what do you call it, biceps—to do it."

"Let dogs delight to bark and bite," said Vane, laughing.

"Don't," whispered Macey; "you're making Distie mad again. He feels we're talking about him. Go on about the vegetables."

"All right. There you are then. That's all branched bur-reed."

"What, that thing with the little spikey horse-chestnuts on it?"

"That's it."

"Good to eat?"

"I never tried it. There's something that isn't," continued Vane, pointing at some vivid green, deeply-cut and ornamental leaves.

"What is it? Looks as if it would make a good salad."

"Water hemlock. Very poisonous."

"Do not chew the hemlock rank—growing on the weedy bank," quoted Macey. "I wish you wouldn't begin nursery rhymes. You've started me off now. I should like some of those bulrushes," and he pointed to a cluster of the brown poker-like growth rising from the water, well out of reach from the bank.

"Those are not bulrushes."

"What are they, then?"

"It is the reed-mace."

"They'll do just as well by that name. I say, Distie, I want to cut some of them."

"Go on rowing," said Distin, haughtily, to Gilmore, without glancing at Macey.

"All right, my lord," muttered Macey. "Halloo! What was that? a big fish?"

"No; it was a water-rat jumped in."

"All right again," said Macey good-humouredly. "I don't know anything at all. There never was such an ignorant chap as I am."

"Give me the other scull, Gilmore," said Distin, just then.

"All right, but hadn't we better go a little higher first? The stream runs very hard just here."

Distin uttered a sound similar to that made by a turkey-cock before he begins to gobble—a sound that may be represented by the word *Phut*, and they preserved their relative places.

"What are those leaves shaped like spears?" said Macey, giving Vane a peculiar look.

"Arrowheads."

"There, I do know what those are!" cried Macey, quickly as a shoal of good-sized fish darted of from a gravelly shallow into deep water.

"Well, what are they?"

"Roach and dace."

"Neither," said Vane, laughing heartily.

"Well, I—oh, but they are."

"No."

"What then?"

"Chub."

"How do you know?"

"By the black edge round their tails."

"I say!" cried Macey; "how do you know all these precious things so readily?"

"Walks with uncle," replied Vane. "I don't know much but he seems to know everything."

"Why I thought he couldn't know anything but about salts and senna, and bleeding, and people's tongues when they put 'em out."

"Here, Macey and he had better row now," cried Distin, suddenly. "Let's have a rest, Gilmore."

The exchange of position was soon made, and Macey said, as he rolled up his sleeves over his thin arms, which were in peculiar contrast to his round plump face:—

"Now then: let's show old pepper-pot what rowing is."

"No: pull steadily, and don't show off," said Vane quietly. "We want to look at the things on the banks."

"Oh, all right," cried Macey resignedly; and the sculls dipped together in a quiet, steady, splashless pull, the two lads feathering well, and, with scarcely any exertion, sending the boat along at a fair pace, while Vane, with a naturalist's eye, noted the different plants on the banks, the birds building in the water-growth—reed sparrows, and bearded tits, and pointing out the moor-hens, coots, and an occasional duck.

All at once, as they cut into a patch of the great dark flat leaves of the yellow water-lily, there was a tremendous swirl in the river just beyond the bows of the boat—one which sent the leaves heaving and falling for some distance ahead.

"Come now, that was a pike," cried Macey, as he looked at Distin lolling back nonchalantly, with his eyes half-closed.

"Yes; that was a pike, and a big one too," said Vane. "Let's see, opposite those three pollard willows in the big horseshoe bend. We'll come and have a try for him, Aleck, one of these days."

It was a pleasant row, Macey and Vane keeping the oars for a couple of hours, right on, past another mill, and among the stumps which showed where the old bridge and the side-road once spanned the deeps—a bridge which had gradually decayed away and had never been replaced, as the traffic was so small and there was a good shallow ford a quarter of a mile farther on.

The country was beautifully picturesque up here, and the latter part of their row was by a lovely grove of beeches which grew on a chalk ridge—almost a cliff—at whose foot the clear river ran babbling along.

Here, all of a sudden, Macey threw up the blade of his oar, and at a pull or two from Vane, the boat's keel grated on the pebbly sand.

"What's that for?" cried Gilmore, who had been half asleep as he sat right back in the stern, with his hands holding the sides.

"Time to go back," said Macey. "Want my corn."

"He means his thistle," said Distin, rousing himself to utter a sarcastic remark.

"Thistle, if you like," said Macey, good-humouredly. "Donkey enjoys his thistle as much as a horse does his corn, or you did chewing sugar-cane among your father's niggers."

It was an unlucky speech, and like a spark to gunpowder.

Distin sprang up and made for Macey, with his fists doubled, but Vane interposed.

"No," he said; "no fighting in a boat, please. Gilmore and I don't want a ducking, if you do."

There was another change in the Creole on the instant. The fierce angry look gave place to a sneering smile, and he spoke in a husky whisper.

"Oh, I see," he said, gazing at Vane the while, with half-shut eyes. "You prompted him to say that."

Vane did not condescend to answer, but Macey cried promptly,—

"That he didn't. Made it all up out of my own head."

"A miserable insult," muttered Distin.

"But he had nothing to do with it, Distie," said Macey; "all my own; and if you wish for satisfaction—swords or pistols at six sharp, with coffee, I'm your man."

Distin took no heed of him, but stood watching Vane, his dark half-shut eyes flashing as they gazed into the lad's calm wide-open grey orbs.

"I say," continued Macey, "if you wish for the satisfaction of a gentleman—"

"Satisfaction—gentleman!" raged out Distin, as he turned suddenly upon Macey. "Silence, buffoon!"

"The buffoon is silent," said Macey, sinking calmly down into his place; "but don't you two fight, please, till after we've got back and had some food. I say, Gil, is there no place up here where we can buy some tuck?"

"No," replied Gilmore; and then, "Sit down, Vane. Come, Distie, what is the good of kicking up such a row about nothing. You really are too bad, you know. Let's, you and I, row back."

"Keep your advice till it is asked for," said Distin contemptuously. "You, Macey, go back yonder into the stern. Perhaps Mr Vane Lee will condescend to take another seat."

"Oh, certainly," said Vane quietly, though there was a peculiar sensation of tingling in his veins, and a hot feeling about the throat. The peculiar human or animal nature was effervescing within him, and though he hardly realised it himself, he wanted to fight horribly, and there was that mastering him in those moments which would have made it a keen joy to have stood ashore there on the grass beneath the chalk cliff and pummelled Distin till he could not see to get back to the boat.

But he did not so much as double his fist, though he knew that Macey and Gilmore were both watching him narrowly and thinking, he felt sure, that, if Distin struck him, he would not return the blow.

As the three lads took their seats, Distin, with a lordly contempt and arrogance of manner, removed his jacket, and deliberately doubled it up to place it forward. Then slowly rolling up his sleeves he took the sculls, seated himself and began to back-water but without effect, for the boat was too firmly aground forward.

"You'll never get her off that way," cried Macey the irrepressible. "Now lads, all together, make her roll."

"Sit still, sir!" thundered Distin—at least he meant to thunder, but it was only a hoarse squeak.

"Yes, sir; certainly, sir," cried Macey; and then, in an undertone to his companions, "Shall we not sterrike for ferreedom? Are we all—er—serlaves!"

Then he laughed, and slapped his leg, for Distin drew in one scull, rose, and began to use the other to thrust the boat off.

"I say, you know," cried Macey, as Gilmore held up the boat-hook to Distin, but it was ignored, "I don't mean to pay my whack if you break that scull."

"Do you wish me to break yours?" retorted Distin, so fiercely that his words came with a regular snarl.

"Oh, murder! he's gone mad," said Macey, in a loud whisper; and screwing up his face into a grimace which he intended to represent horrible dread, but more resembled the effects produced by a pin or thorn, he crouched down right away in the stern of the boat, but kept up a continuous rocking which helped Distin's efforts to get her off into deep water. When the latter seated himself, turned the head, and began to row back, that is to say, he dipped the sculls lightly from time to time, so as to keep the boat straight, the stream being strong enough to carry them steadily down without an effort on the rower's part.

Macey being right in the stern, Vane and Gilmore sat side by side, making a comment now and then about something they passed, while Distin was of course alone, watching them all from time to time through his half-closed eyes, as if suspicious that their words might be relating to him.

Then a gloomy silence fell, which lasted till Macey burst out in ecstatic tones:

"Oh, I am enjoying of myself!"

Then, after a pause:

"Never had such a glorious day before."

Another silence, broken by Macey once more, saying in a deferential way:—

"If your excellency feels exhausted by this unwonted exertion, your servant will gladly take an oar."

Distin ceased rowing, and, balancing the oars a-feather, he said coldly:—

"If you don't stop that chattering, my good fellow, I'll either pitch you overboard, or set you ashore to walk home."

"Thankye," cried Macey, cheerfully; "but I'll take the dry, please."

Distin's teeth grated together as he sat and scowled at his fellow-pupil, muttering, "Chattering ape;" but he made no effort to put his threats into execution, and kept rowing on, twisting his neck round from time to time, to see which way they were going; Vane and Gilmore went on talking in a low tone; and Macey talked to himself.

"He has made me feel vicious," he said. "I'm a chattering ape, am I? He'll pitch me overboard, will he? I'd call him a beast, only it would be so rude. He'd pitch me overboard, would he? Well, I could swim if he did, and that's more than he could do."

Macey looked before him at Vane and Gilmore, to see that the former had turned to the side and was thoughtfully dipping his hand in the water, as if paddling.

"Halloo, Weathercock!" he cried. "I know what you're thinking about."

"Not you," cried Vane merrily, as he looked back.

"I do. You were thinking you could invent a machine to send the boat along far better than old West Indies is doing it now."

Vane stared at him.

"Well," he said, hesitatingly, "I was not thinking about Distin's rowing, but I was trying to hit out some way of propelling a boat without steam."

"Knew it! I knew it! Here, I shan't read for the bar; I shall study up for a head boss conjurer, thought-reader, and clairvoyant."

"For goodness' sake, Gilmore, lean back, and stuff your handkerchief in that chattering pie's mouth. You had better; it will save me from pitching him into the river."

Then deep silence fell on the little party, and Macey's eyes sparkled.

"Yes, he has made me vicious now," he said to himself; and, as he sat back, he saw something which sent a thought through his brain which made him hug his knees. "Let me see," he mused: "Vane can swim and dive like an otter, and Gil is better in the water than I am. All right, my boy; you shall pitch me in."

Then aloud:

"Keep her straight, Distie. Don't send her nose into the willows."

The rower looked sharply round, and pulled his right scull. Then, a little further on, Macey shouted:—

"Too much port—pull your right."

Distin resented this with an angry look; but Macey kept on in the most unruffled way, and, by degrees, as the rower found that it saved him from a great deal of unpleasant screwing round and neck-twisting, he began to obey the commands, and pulled a little harder, so that they travelled more swiftly down the winding stream.

"Port!" shouted Macey. "Port it is! Straight on!"

Then, after a minute,—

"Starboard! More starboard! Straight on!"

Again: "Pull your right—not too much. Both hands;" and Distin calmly and indifferently followed the orders, till it had just occurred to him that the others might as well row now, when Macey shouted again:—

"Right—a little more right; now, both together. That's the way;" and, as again Distin obeyed, Macey shut his eyes, and drew up his knees. To give a final impetus to the light craft, Distin leaned forward, threw back the blades of the sculls, dipped, and took hold of the water, and then was jerked backwards as the boat struck with a crash on one of the old piles of the ancient bridge, ran up over it a little way, swung round, and directly after capsized, and began to float down stream, leaving its human freight struggling in deep water.

Chapter Six.

Distin is Incredulous.

"Oh, murder!" shouted Macey, as he rose to the surface, and struck out after the boat, which he reached, and held on by the keel.

Gilmore swam after him, and was soon alongside, while Vane made for the bank, climbed out, stood up dripping, and roaring with laughter.

"Hi! Gil!—Aleck, bring her ashore," he cried.

"All right!" came back; but almost simultaneously Vane shouted again, in a tone full of horror:—

"Here, both of you—Distin—where's Distin?"

He ran along the bank as he spoke, gazing down into the river, but without seeing a sign of that which he sought.

Macey's heart sank within him, as, for the first time, the real significance of that which he had done in carefully guiding the rower on to the old rotten pile came home. A cold chill ran through him, and, for the moment, he clung, speechless and helpless, to the drifting boat.

But Vane soon changed all that.

"Here, you!" he yelled, "get that boat ashore, turn her over, and come to me—"

As he spoke, he ran to and fro upon the bank for a few moments, but, seeing nothing, he paused opposite a deep-looking place, and plunged in, to begin swimming about, raising his head at every stroke, and searching about him, but searching in vain, for their companion, who, as far as he knew, had not risen again to the surface.

Meanwhile, Gilmore and Macey tried their best to get the boat ashore, and, after struggling for a few minutes in the shallow close under the bank, they managed to right her, but not without leaving a good deal of water in the bottom. Still she floated as they climbed in and thrust her off, but only for Gilmore to utter a groan of dismay as he grasped the helplessness of their situation.

"No oars—no oars!" he cried; and, standing up in the stern, he plunged into the water again, to swim toward where he could see Vane's head.

"What have I done—what have I done!" muttered Macey, wildly. "Oh, poor chap, if he should be drowned!"

For a moment he hesitated about following Gilmore, but, as he swept the water with his eyes, he caught sight of something floating, and, sitting down, he used one hand as a paddle, trying to get the boat toward the middle of the river to intercept the floating object, which he had seen to be one of the oars.

Vane heard the loud splash, and saw that Gilmore was swimming to his help, then he kept on, looking to right and left in search of their companion; but everywhere there was the eddying water gliding along, and bearing him with it.

For a time he had breasted the current, trying to get toward the deeps where the bridge had stood, but he could make no way, and, concluding from this that Distin would have floated down too, he kept on his weary, useless search till Gilmore swam up abreast.

"Haven't seen him?" panted the latter, hoarsely. "Shall we go lower?"

"No," cried Vane; "there must be an eddy along there. Let's go up again."

They swam ashore, climbed out on to the bank, and, watching the surface as they ran, they made for the spot where the well-paved road had crossed the bridge.

Here they stood in silence for a few moments, and Gilmore was about to plunge in again, but Vane stopped him.

"No, no," he cried, breathing heavily the while; "that's of no use. Wait till we see him rise—if he is here," he added with a groan.

The sun shone brightly on the calm, clear water which here looked black and deep, and after scanning it for some time Vane said quickly—

"Look! There, just beyond that black stump."

"No; there is nothing there but a deep hole."

"Yes, but the water goes round and round there, Gil; that must be the place."

He was about to plunge in, but it was Gilmore's turn to arrest him.

"No, no; it would be no use."

"Yes; I'll dive down."

"But there are old posts and big stones, I daren't let you go."

"Ah!" shouted Vane wildly; "look—look!"

He shook himself free and plunged in as Gilmore caught sight of something close up to the old piece of blackened oak upon which Macey had so cleverly steered the boat. It was only a glimpse of something floating, and then it was gone; and he followed Vane, who was swimming out to the old post. This he reached before Gilmore was half-way, swam round for a few moments, and then paddled like a dog, rose as high as he could, turned over and dived down into the deep black hole.

In a few moments he was up again to take a long breath and dive once more.

This time he was down longer, and Gilmore held on by the slimy post, gazing about with staring eyes, and prepared himself to dive down after his friend, when all at once, Vane's white face appeared, and one arm was thrust forth to give a vigorous blow upon the surface.

"Got him," he cried in a half-choked voice, "Gil, help!"

Gilmore made for him directly, and as he reached his companion's side the back of Distin's head came to the surface, and Gilmore seized him by his long black hair.

Their efforts had taken them out of the eddy into the swift stream once more, and they began floating down; Vane so confused and weak from his efforts that he could do nothing but swim feebly, while his companion made some effort to keep Distin's face above water and direct him toward the side.

An easy enough task at another time, for it only meant a swim of some fifty yards, but with the inert body of Distin, and Vane so utterly helpless that he could barely keep himself afloat, Gilmore had hard work, and, swim his best, he could scarcely gain a yard toward the shore. Very soon he found that he was exhausting himself by his efforts and that it would be far better to go down the stream, and trust to getting ashore far lower down, though, at the same time, a chilly feeling of despair began to dull his energies, and it seemed hopeless to think of getting his comrade ashore alive.

All the same, though, forced as the words sounded, he told Vane hoarsely that it was all right, and that they would soon get to the side.

Vane only answered with a look—a heavy, weary, despairing look—which told how thoroughly he could weigh his friend's remark, as he held on firmly by Distin and struck out slowly and heavily with the arm at liberty.

There was no doubt about Vane's determination. If he had loosed his hold of Distin, with two arms free he could have saved himself with comparative ease, but that thought never entered his head, as they floated down the river, right in the middle now, and with the trees apparently gliding by them and the verdure and water-growth gradually growing confused and dim. To Vane all now seemed dreamlike and strange. He was in no trouble—there was no sense of dread, and the despair of a few minutes before was blunted, as with his body lower in the water, which kept rising now above his lips, he slowly struggled on.

All at once Gilmore shouted wildly,—

"Vane—we can't do it. Let's swim ashore."

Vane turned his eyes slowly toward him, as if he hardly comprehended his words.

"What can I do?" panted Gilmore, who, on his side, was gradually growing more rapid and laboured in the strokes he made; but Vane made no sign, and the three floated down stream, each minute more helpless; and it was now rapidly becoming a certainty that, if Gilmore wished to save his life, he must quit his hold of Distin, and strive his best to reach the bank.

"It seems so cowardly," he groaned; and he looked wildly round for help, but there was none. Then there seemed to be just one chance: the shore looked to be just in front of them, for the river turned here sharply round, forming a loop, and there was a possibility of their being swept right on to the bank.

Vain hope! The stream swept round to their right, bearing them toward the other shore, against which it impinged, and then shot off with increased speed away for the other side; and, though they were carried almost within grasping distance of a tree whose boughs hung down to kiss the swift waters, the nearest was just beyond Gilmore's reach, as he raised his hand, which fell back with a splash, as they were borne right out, now toward the middle once more, and round the bend.

"I can't help it. Must let go," thought Gilmore. "I'm done." Then aloud:

"Vane, old chap! let go. Let's swim ashore;" and then he shuddered, for Vane's eyes had a dull, half-glazed stare, and his lips, nostrils,—the greater part of his face, sank below the stream. "Oh, help!" groaned Gilmore; "he has gone:" and, loosing his hold of Distin, he made a snatch at Vane, who was slowly sinking, the current turning him face downward, and rolling him slowly over.

But Gilmore made a desperate snatch, and caught him by the sleeve as Vane rose again with his head thrown back and one arm rising above the water, clutching frantically at vacancy.

The weight of that arm was sufficient to send him beneath the surface again, and Gilmore's desperate struggle to keep him afloat resulted in his going under in turn, losing his presence of mind, and beginning to struggle wildly as he, too, strove to catch at something to keep himself up.

Another few moments and all would have been over, but the clutch did not prove to be at vacancy. Far from it. A hand was thrust into his, and as he was drawn up, a familiar voice shouted in his singing ears, where the water had been thundering the moment before:

"Catch hold of the side," was shouted; and his fingers involuntarily closed on the gunwale of the boat, while Macey reached out and seized Vane by the collar, drew him to the boat, or the boat to him, and guided the drowning lad's cramped hand to the gunwale too.

" Macey reached out and seized Vane by the collar."

"Now!" he shouted; "can you hold on?"

There was no answer from either, and Macey hesitated for a few moments, but, seeing how desperate a grip both now had, he seized one of the recovered sculls, thrust it out over the rowlock, and pulled and paddled first at the side, then over the stern till, by help of the current, he guided the boat with its clinging freight into shallow water where he leaped overboard, seized Gilmore, and dragged him right up the sandy shallow to where his head lay clear. He then went back and seized Vane in turn, after literally unhooking his cramped fingers from the side, and dragged him through the shallow water a few yards, before he realised that his fellow-pupil's other hand was fixed, with what for the moment looked to be a death-grip, in Distin's clothes.

This task was more difficult, but by the time he had dragged Vane alongside of Gilmore, the latter was slowly struggling up to his feet; and in a confused, staggering way he lent a hand to get Vane's head well clear of the water on to the warm dry pebbles, and then between them they dragged Distin right out beyond the pebbles on to the grass.

"One moment," cried Macey, and he dashed into the water again just in time to catch hold of the boat, which was slowly floating away. Then wading back he got hold of the chain, and twisted it round a little blackthorn bush on the bank.

"I'm better now," gasped Gilmore. And then, "Oh, Aleck, Aleck, they're both dead!"

"They aren't," shouted Macey fiercely. "Look! Old Weathercock's moving his eyes, but I'm afraid of poor old Colonist. Here, hi, Vane, old man! You ain't dead, are you? Catch hold, Gil, like this, under his arm. Now, together off!"

They seized Vane, and, raising his head and shoulders, dragged him up on to the grass, near where Distin lay, apparently past all help, and a groan escaped from Gilmore's lips, as, rapidly regaining his strength and energy, he dropped on his knees beside him.

"It's all right," shouted Macey, excitedly, when a whisper would have done. "Weathercock's beginning to revive again. Hooray, old Vane! You'll do. We must go to Distie."

Vane could not speak, but he made a sign, which they interpreted to mean, go; and the next moment they were on their knees by Distin's side, trying what seemed to be the hopeless task of reviving him. For the lad's face looked ghastly in the extreme; and, though Macey felt his breast and throat, there was not the faintest pulsation perceptible.

But they lost no time; and Gilmore, who was minute by minute growing stronger, joined in his companion's efforts at resuscitation from a few rather hazy recollections of a paper he had once read respecting the efforts to be made with the apparently drowned.

Everything was against them. They had no hot flannels or water-bottles to apply to the subject's feet, no blankets in which to wrap him, nothing but sunshine, as Macey began. After doubling up a couple of wet jackets into a cushion and putting them under Distin's back, he placed himself kneeling behind the poor fellow's head, seized his arms, pressed them hard against his sides, and then drew them out to their full stretch, so as to try and produce respiration by alternately compressing and expanding the chest.

He kept on till he grew so tired that his motions grew slow; and then he gave place to Gilmore, who carried on the process eagerly, while Macey went to see how Vane progressed, finding him able to speak now in a whisper.

"How is Distin?" he whispered.

"Bad," said Macey, laconically.

"Not dead!" cried Vane, frantically.

"Not yet," was the reply; "but I wouldn't give much for the poor fellow's chance. Oh, Vane, old chap, do come round, and help. You are so clever, and know such lots of things. I shall never be happy again if he dies."

For answer to this appeal Vane sat up, but turned so giddy that he lay back again.

"I'll come and try as soon as I can," he said, feebly. "All the strength has gone out of me."

"Let me help you," cried Macey; and he drew Vane into a sitting position, but had to leave him and relieve Gilmore, whose arms were failing fast.

Macey took his place, and began with renewed vigour at what seemed to be a perfectly hopeless task, while Gilmore went to Vane.

"It's no good," muttered Macey, whose heart was full of remorse; and a terrible feeling of despair came over him. "It's of no use, but I will try and try till I drop. Oh, if I could only bring him to, I'd never say an unkind word to him again!"

He threw himself into his task, working Distin's thin arms up and down with all his might, listening intently the while for some faint suggestion of breathing, but all in vain; the arms he held were cold and dank, and the face upon which he looked down, seeing it in reverse, was horribly ghastly and grotesque.

"I don't like him," continued Macey, to himself, as he toiled away; "I never did like him, and I never shall, but I think I'd sooner it was me lying here than him. And me the cause of it all."

"Poor old Distie!" he went on. "I suppose he couldn't help his temper. It was his nature, and he came from a foreign country. How could I be such a fool? Nearly drowned us all."

He bent over Distin at every pressure of the arms, close to the poor fellow's side; and, as he hung over him, the great tears gathered in his eyes, and, in a choking voice, he muttered aloud:—

"I didn't mean it, old chap. It was only to give you a ducking for being so disagreeable; indeed, indeed, I wish it had been me."

"Oh, I say," cried a voice at his ear; "don't take on like that, old fellow. We'll bring him round yet. Vane's getting all right fast."

"I can't help it, Gil, old chap," said Macey, in a husky whisper; "it is so horrible to see him like this."

"But I tell you we shall bring him round. You're tired, and out of heart. Let me take another turn."

"No, I'm not tired yet," said Macey, recovering himself, and speaking more steadily. "I'll keep on. You feel his heart again."

He accommodated his movements to his companion's, and Gilmore kept his hand on Distin's breast, but he withdrew it again without a word; and, as Macey saw the despair and the hopeless look on the lad's face, his own heart sank lower, and his arms felt as if all the power had gone.

But, with a jerk, he recommenced working Distin's arms up and down with the regular pumping motion, till he could do no more, and he again made way for Gilmore.

He was turning to Vane, but felt a touch on his shoulder, and, looking round, it was to gaze in the lad's grave face.

"How is he?"

"Oh, bad as bad can be. Do, pray, try and save him, Vane. We mustn't let him die."

Vane breathed hard, and went to Distin's side, kneeling down to feel his throat, and looking more serious as he rose.

"Let me try now," he whispered, but Gilmore shook his head.

"You're too weak," he said. "Wait a bit."

Vane waited, and at last they were glad to let him take his turn, when the toil drove off the terrible chill from which he was suffering, and he worked at the artificial respiration plan, growing stronger every minute.

Again he resumed the task in his turn, and then again, after quite an hour of incessant effort had been persisted in; while now the feeling was becoming stronger in all their breasts that they had tried in vain, for there was no more chance.

"If we could have had him in a bed, we might have done some good," said Gilmore, sadly. "Vane, old fellow, I'm afraid you must give it up."

But, instead of ceasing his efforts, the lad tried the harder, and, in a tone of intense excitement, he panted:—

"Look!"

"At what?" cried Macey, eagerly; and then, going down on his knees, he thrust in his hand beneath the lad's shirt.

"Yes! you can feel it. Keep on, Vane, keep on."

"What!" shouted Gilmore; and then he gave a joyful cry, for there was a trembling about one of Distin's eyelids, and a quarter of an hour later they saw him open his eyes, and begin to stare wonderingly round.

It was only for a few moments, and then they closed again, as if the spark of the fire of life that had been trembling had died out because there had been a slight cessation of the efforts to produce it.

But there was no farther relaxation. All, in turn, worked hard, full of excitement at the fruit borne by their efforts; and, at last, while Vane was striving his best, the patient's eyes were opened, gazed round once more, blankly and wonderingly, till they rested upon Vane's face, when memory reasserted itself, and an unpleasant frown darkened the Creole's countenance.

"Don't," he cried, angrily, in a curiously weak, harsh voice, quite different from his usual tones; and he dragged himself away, and tried to rise, but sank back.

Vane quitted his place, and made way for Macey, whose turn it would have been to continue their efforts, but Distin gave himself a jerk, and fixed his eyes on Gilmore, who raised him by passing one hand beneath his shoulders.

"Better?"

"Better? What do you mean? I haven't— Ah! How was it the boat upset?"

There was no reply, and Distin spoke again, in a singularly irritable way.

"I said, how was it the boat upset? Did someone run into us?"

"You rowed right upon one of the old posts," replied Gilmore, and Distin gazed at him fixedly, while Macey shrank back a little, and then looked furtively from Vane to Gilmore, and back again at Distin, who fixed his eyes upon him searchingly, but did not speak for some time.

"Here," he said at last; "give me your hand. I can't sit here in these wet things."

"Can you stand?" said Gilmore, eagerly.

"Of course I can stand. Why shouldn't I? Because I'm wet? Oh!"

He clapped his hands to his head, and bowed down a little.

"Are you in pain?" asked Gilmore, with solicitude.

"Of course I am," snarled Distin; "any fool could see that. I must have struck my head, I suppose."

"He doesn't suspect me," thought Macey, with a long-drawn breath full of relief.

"Here, I'll try again," continued Distin. "Where's the boat? I want to get back, and change these wet things. Oh! my head aches as if it would split!"

Gilmore offered his hand again, and, forgetting everything in his desire to help one in pain and distress, Vane ranged up on the other side, and was about to take Distin's arm.

But the lad shrank from him fiercely.

"I can manage," he said. "I don't want to be hauled and pulled about like a child. Now, Gil, steady. Let's get into the boat. I want to lie down in the stern."

"Wait a minute or two; she's half full of water," cried Macey, who was longing to do something helpful. "Come on, Vane."

The latter went to his help, and they drew the boat closer in.

"Oh, I say," whispered the lad, "isn't old Dis in a temper?"

"Yes; I've heard that people who have been nearly drowned are terribly irritable when they come to," replied Vane, in the same tone. "Never mind, we've saved his life."

"You did," said Macey.

"Nonsense; we all did."

"No; we two didn't dive down in the black pool, and fetch him up. Oh, I say, Vane, what a day! If this is coming out for pleasure I'll stop at home next time. Now then, together."

They pulled together, and by degrees lightened the boat of more and more water, till they were able to get it quite ashore, and drain out the last drops over the side. Then launching again, and replacing the oars, Macey gave his head a rub.

"We shall have to buy the miller a new boat-hook," he said. "I suppose the iron on the end of the pole was so heavy that it took the thing down. I never saw it again. Pretty hunt I had for the sculls. I got one, but was ever so long before I could find the other."

"You only just got to us in time," said Vane, with a sigh; and he looked painfully in his companion's eyes.

"Oh, I say, don't look at a fellow like that," said Macey. "I am sorry—I am, indeed."

Vane was silent, but still looked at his fellow-pupil steadily.

"Don't ever split upon me, old chap," continued Macey; "and I'll own it all to you. I thought it would only be a bit of a lark to give him a ducking, for he had been—and no mistake—too disagreeable for us to put up with it any longer."

"Then you did keep on telling him which hand to pull and steered him on to the pile?"

Macey was silent.

"If you did, own to it like a man, Aleck."

"Yes, I will—to you, Vane. I did, for I thought it would be such a game to see him overboard, and I felt it would only be a wetting for us. I never thought of it turning out as it did."

He ceased speaking, and Vane stood gazing straight before him for a few moments.

"No," he said, at last, "you couldn't have thought that it would turn out like it did."

"No, 'pon my word, I didn't."

"And we might have had to go back and tell Syme that one of his pupils was dead. Oh, Aleck, if it had been so!"

"Yes, but don't you turn upon me, Vane. I didn't mean it. You know I didn't mean it; and I'll never try such a trick as that again."

"Ready there?" cried Gilmore.

"Yes; all right," shouted Macey. Then, in a whisper, "Don't tell Distie. He'd never forgive me. Here they come."

For, sallow, and with his teeth chattering, Distin came toward them, leaning on Gilmore's arm; but, as he reached the boat, he drew himself up, and looked fixedly in Vane's face.

"You needn't try to plot any more," he said, "for I shall be aware of you next time."

"Plot?" stammered Vane, who was completely taken aback. "I don't know what you mean."

"Of course not," said Distin, bitterly. "You are such a genius—so clever. You wouldn't set that idiot Macey to tell me which hand to pull, so as to overset the boat. But I'll be even with you yet."

"I wouldn't, I swear," cried Vane, sharply.

"Oh, no; not likely. You are too straightforward and generous. But I'm not blind: I can see; and if punishment can follow for your cowardly trick, you shall have it. Come, Gil, you and I will row back together. It will warm us, and we can be on our guard against treachery this time."

He stepped into the boat, staggered, and would have fallen overboard, had not Vane caught his arm; but, as soon as he had recovered his balance, he shook himself free resentfully and seated himself on the forward thwart.

"Jump in," said Gilmore, in a low voice.

"Yes, jump in, Mr Vane Lee, and be good enough to go right to the stern. You did not succeed in drowning me this time; and, mind this, if you try any tricks on our way back, I'll give you the oar across the head. You cowardly, treacherous bit of scum!"

"No, he isn't," said Macey, boldly, "and you're all out of it, clever as you are. It was not Vane's doing, the running on the pile, but mine. I did it to take some of the conceit and bullying out of you, so you may say and do what you like."

"Oh, yes, I knew you did it," sneered Distin; "but there are not brains enough in your head to originate such a dastardly trick. That was Vane Lee's doing, and he'll hear of it another time, as sure as my name's Distin."

"I tell you it was my own doing entirely," cried Macey, flushing up; "and I'll tell you something else. I'm glad I did it—so there. For you deserved it, and you deserve another for being such a cad."

"What do you mean?" cried Distin, threateningly. "What I say, you ungrateful, un-English humbug. You were drowning; you couldn't be found, and you wouldn't have been here now, if it hadn't been for old Weathercock diving down and fetching you up, and then, half-dead himself, working so hard to help save your life."

"I don't believe it," snarled Distin.

"Don't," said Macey, as he thrust the boat from the side, throwing himself forward at the same time, so that he rode out on his chest, and then wriggled in, to seat himself close by Vane, while Gilmore and Distin began to row hard, so as to get some warmth into their chilled bodies.

They went on in silence for some time, and then Macey leaped up.

"Now, Vane," he cried; "it's our turn."

"Sit down," roared Distin.

"Don't, Aleck," said Vane, firmly. "You are quite right. We want to warm ourselves too. Come, Gil, and take my place."

"Sit down!" roared Distin again; but Gilmore exchanged places with Vane, and Macey stepped forward, and took hold of Distin's oar.

"Now then, give it up," he said; and, utterly cowed by the firmness of the two lads, Distin stepped over the thwart by Vane, and went and seated himself by Gilmore.

"Ready?" cried Macey.

"Yes."

"You pull as hard as you can, and let's send these shivers out of us. You call out, Gil, and steer us, for we don't want to have to look round."

They bent their backs to their work, and sent the boat flying through the water, Gilmore shouting a hint from time to time, with the result that they came in sight of the mill much sooner than they had expected, and Gilmore looked out anxiously, hoping to get the boat moored unseen, so that they could hurry off and get to the rectory by the fields, so that their drenched condition should not be noticed.

But, just as they approached the big willows, a window in the mill was thrown open, the loud clacking and the roar of the machinery reached their ears, and there was the great, full face of the miller grinning down at them.

"Why, hallo!" he shouted; "what game's this? Been fishing?"

"No," said Vane, quietly; "we—"

But, before he could finish, the miller roared:—

"Oh, I see, you've been bathing; and, as you had no towels, you kept your clothes on. I say, hang it all, my lads, didst ta capsize the boat?"

"No," said Vane, quietly, as he leaped ashore with the chain; "we had a misfortune, and ran on one of those big stumps up the river."

"Hey? What, up yonder by old brigg?"

"Yes."

"Hang it all, lads, come into the cottage, and I'll send on to fetch your dry clothes. Hey, but it's a bad job. Mustn't let you catch cold. Here, hi! Mrs Lasby. Kettle hot?"

"Yes, Mester," came from the cottage.

"Then set to, and make the young gents a whole jorum of good hot tea."

The miller hurried the little party into the cottage, where the kitchen-fire was heaped up with brushwood and logs, about which the boys stood, and steamed, drinking plenteously of hot tea the while, till the messenger returned with their dry clothes, and, after the change had been made, their host counselled a sharp run home, to keep up the circulation, undertaking to send the wet things back himself.

Chapter Seven.

Mr Bruff's Present.

That boating trip formed a topic of conversation in the study morning after morning when the rector was not present—a peculiar form of conversation when Distin was there—which was not regularly, for the accident on the river served as an excuse for several long stays in bed—but a free and unfettered form when he was not present. For Macey soon freed Vane from any feeling of an irksome nature by insisting to Gilmore how he had been to blame.

Gilmore looked very serious at first, but laughed directly after.

"I really thought it was an accident," he said; "and I felt the more convinced that it was on hearing poor old hot-headed Distie accuse you, Vane, because, of course, I knew you would not do such a thing; and I thought Macey blamed himself to save you."

"Thought me a better sort of fellow than I am, then," said Macey.

"Much," replied Gilmore, quietly. "You couldn't see old Weathercock trying to drown all his friends."

"I didn't," cried Macey, indignantly. "I only wanted to give Distie a cooling down."

"And nicely you did it," cried Gilmore.

"There, don't talk any more about it," cried Vane, who was busy sketching upon some exercise paper. "It's all over, and doesn't bear thinking about."

"What's he doing?" cried Macey, reaching across the table, and making a snatch at the paper, which Vane tried hurriedly to withdraw, but only saved a corner, while Macey waved his portion in triumph.

"Hoo-rah!" he cried. "It's a plan for a new patent steamboat, and I shall make one, and gain a fortune, while poor old Vane will be left out in the cold."

"Let's look," said Gilmore.

"No, no. It's too bad," cried Vane, making a fresh dash at the paper.

"Shan't have it, sir! Sit down," cried Macey. "How dare you, sir! Look, Gil! It is a boat to go by steam, with a whipper-whopper out at the stern to send her along."

"I wish you wouldn't be so stupid, Aleck. Give me the paper."

"Shan't."

"I don't want to get up and make a struggle for it."

"I should think not, sir. Sit still. Oh, I say, Gil, look. Here it all is. It's not steam. It's a fellow with long arms and queer elbows turns a wheel."

"Get out!" cried Vane, laughing; "those are shafts and cranks."

"Of course they are. No one would think it, though, would they, Gil? I say, isn't he a genius at drawing?"

"Look here, Aleck, if you don't be quiet with your chaff I'll ink your nose."

"Wonderful, isn't he?" continued Macey. "I say, how many hundred miles an hour a boat like that will go!"

"Oh, I say, do drop it," cried Vane, good-humouredly.

"I know," cried Macey; "this is what you were thinking about that day we had Rounds' boat."

"Well, yes," said Vane, quietly. "I couldn't help thinking how slow and laborious rowing seemed to be, and how little change has been made in all these years that are passed. You see," he continued, warming to his subject, "there is so much waste of manual labour. It took two of us to move that boat and not very fast either."

"And only one sitting quite still to upset it," said Gilmore quietly.

Macey started, as if he had been stung.

"There's a coward," he cried. "I thought you weren't going to say any more about it."

"Slipped out all at once, Aleck," said Gilmore.

"But you were quite right," said Vane. "Two fellows toiling hard, and just one idea from another's brain proved far stronger."

"Now you begin," groaned Macey. "Oh, I say, don't! I wouldn't have old Distie know for anything. You chaps are mean."

"Go on, Vane," cried Gilmore.

"There's nothing more to go on about, for I haven't worked out the idea thoroughly."

"I know," cried Macey, with a mischievous twinkle in his eyes.

"I thought," continued Vane dreamily, "that one might contrive a little paddle or screw—"

"And work it with hot-water pipes," cried Macey.

It was Vane's turn to wince now; and he made a pretence of throwing a book at Macey, who ducked down below the table, and then slowly raised his eyes to the level as Vane went on.

"Then you could work that paddle by means of cranks."

"Only want one—old Weathercock. Best crank I know," cried Macey.

"Will you be quiet," cried Gilmore. "Go on, Vane."

"That is nearly all," said the latter, thoughtfully, and looking straight before him, as if he could see the motive-power he mentally designed.

"But how are you going to get the thing to work?"

"Kitchen-boiler," cried Macey.

Gilmore made "an offer" at him with his fist, but Macey dodged again.

"Oh, one might move it by working a lever with one's hands."

"Then you might just as well row," said Gilmore.

"Well, then, by treadles, with one's feet."

"Oh—oh—oh!" roared Macey. "Don't! don't! Who's going to be put on the tread-mill when he wants to have a ride in a boat? Why, I—"

"Pst! Syme!" whispered Gilmore, as a step was heard. Then the door opened, and Distin came in, looking languid and indifferent.

"Morning," cried Gilmore. "Better?"

Distin gave him a short nod, paid no heed to the others, and went to his place to take up a book, yawning loudly as he did so. Then he opened the book slowly.

"Look!" cried Macey, with a mock aspect of serious interest.

"Eh? What at?" said Vane.

"The book," cried Macey; and then he yawned tremendously. "Oh, dear! I've got it now."

Vane stared.

"Don't you see? You, being a scientific chap, ought to have noticed it directly. Example of the contagious nature of a yawn."

Oddly enough, Gilmore yawned slightly just at the moment, and, putting his hand to his mouth, said to himself, "Oh, dear me!"

"There!" cried Macey, triumphantly, "that theory's safe. Distie comes in, sits down, yawns; then the book yawns, I yawn, Gilmore yawns. You might, could, would, or should yawn, only you don't, and—"

"Good-morning, gentlemen. I'm a bit late, I fear. Had a little walk after breakfast, and ran against Doctor Lee, who took me in to see his greenhouse. He tells me you are going to heat it by hot-water. Why, Vane, you are quite a genius."

Macey reached out a leg to kick Vane under the table, but it was Distin's shin which received the toe of the lad's boot, just as Gilmore moved suddenly.

Distin uttered a sharp ejaculation, and looked fiercely across at Gilmore.

"What did you do that for?" he cried.

"What?"

"Kick me under the table."

"I did not."

"Yes, you—"

"Gentlemen, gentlemen," cried the rector reprovingly, "this is not a small boarding-school, and you are not school-boys. I was speaking."

"I beg your pardon, sir," cried Gilmore.

Distin was silent, and Macey, who was scarlet in the face; glanced across at Vane, and seemed as if he were going to choke with suppressed laughter, while Vane fidgeted about in his seat.

The rector frowned, coughed, changed his position, smiled, and went on, going back a little to pick up his words where he had left off.

"Quite a genius, Vane—yes, I repeat it, quite a genius."

"Oh, no, sir; it will be easy enough."

"After once doing, Vane," said the rector, "but the first invention—the contriving—is, I beg to say, hard. However, I am intensely gratified to see that you are putting your little—little—little—what shall I call them?"

"Dodges, sir," suggested Macey, deferentially.

"No, Mr Macey, that is too commonplace—too low a term for the purpose, and we will, if you please, say schemes."

"Yes, sir," said Macey, seriously—"schemes."

"Schemes to so useful a purpose," continued the rector; "and I shall ask you to superintend the fitting up of my conservatory upon similar principles."

"Really, sir, I—" began Vane; but the rector smiled and raised a protesting hand.

"Don't refuse me, Vane," he said. "Of course I shall beg that you do not attempt any of the manual labour—merely superintend; but I shall exact one thing, if you consent to do it for me. That is, if the one at the manor succeeds."

"Of course I will do it, if you wish, sir," said Vane.

"I felt sure you would. I said so to your uncle, and your aunt said she was certain you would," continued the rector; "but, as I was saying, I shall exact one thing: as my cook is a very particular woman, and would look startled if I even proposed to go into the kitchen—"

He paused, and Vane, who was in misery, glanced at Macey—to see that he was thoroughly enjoying it all, while Distin's countenance expressed the most sovereign contempt.

"I say, Vane Lee," said the rector again, as if he expected an answer, "I shall exact one thing."

"Yes, sir. What?"

"That the rule of the queen of the kitchen be respected; but—ah, let me see, Mr Distin, I think we were to take up the introductory remarks made on the differential calculus."

And the morning's study at the rectory went on.

"Best bit of fun I've had for a long time," cried Macey, as he strolled out with Vane when the readings were at an end.

"Yes, at my expense," cried Vane sharply. "My leg hurts still with that kick."

"Oh, that's nothing," cried Macey; "I kicked old Distie twice as hard by mistake, and he's wild with Gilmore because he thinks it's he."

Vane gripped him by the collar.

"No, no, don't. I apologise," cried Macey. "Don't be a coward."

"You deserve a good kicking," cried Vane, loosing his grasp.

"Yes, I know I do, but be magnanimous in your might, oh man of genius."

"Look here," cried Vane, grinding his teeth, "if you call me a genius again, I will kick you, and hard too."

"But I must. My mawmaw said I was always to speak the truth, sir."

"Yes, and I'll make you speak the truth, too. Such nonsense! Genius! Just because one can use a few tools, and scheme a little. It's absurd."

"All right. I will not call you a genius any more. But I say, old chap, shall you try and make a boat go by machinery?"

"I should like to," said Vane, who became dreamy and thoughtful directly. "But I have no boat."

"Old Rounds would lend you his. There was a jolly miller lived down by the Greythorpe river," sang Macey.

"Nonsense! He wouldn't lend me his boat to cut about."

"Sell it you."

Vane shook his head. "Cost too much."

"Then, why cut it? You ought to be able to make a machine that would fit into a boat with screws, or be stuck like a box under the thwarts."

"Yes, so I might. I didn't think of that," cried Vane, eagerly. "I'll try it."

"There," said Macey, "that comes of having a clever chap at your elbow like yours most obediently. Halves!"

"Eh?"

"I say, halves! I invented part of the machine, and I want to share. But when are you going to begin old Syme's conservatory?"

"Oh, dear!" sighed Vane. "I'd forgotten that. Come along. Let's try and think out the paddles as you propose. I fancy one might get something like a fish's tail to propel a boat."

"What, by just waggling?"

"It seems to me to be possible."

"Come on, and let's do it then," cried Macey, starting to trot along the road. "I want to get the taste of Distin out of my mouth.—I say—"

"Well?"

"Don't I wish his mother wanted him so badly that he was obliged to go back to the West Indies at once.—Hallo! Going to the wood?"

"Yes, I don't mean to be beaten over those fungi we had the other day," cried Vane; and to prove that he did not, he inveigled Macey into accompanying him into the woods that afternoon, to collect another basketful—his companion assisting by nutting overhead, while Vane busied himself among the moss at the roots of the hazel stubs.

"Going to have those for supper?" said Macey, as they were returning.

Vane shook his head. "I suppose I mustn't take these home to-day after all."

"Look here, come on with me to the rectory, and give 'em to Mr Syme."

"Pooh!—Why, he laughed at them."

"But you can tell him you had some for dinner at the Little Manor. I won't say anything."

"I've a good mind to, for I've read that they are delicious if properly cooked," cried Vane. "No, I don't like to. But I should like to give them to someone, for I don't care to see them wasted."

"Do bring them to the rectory, and I'll coax Distie on into eating some. He will not know they are yours; and, if they upset him, he will not be of so much consequence as any one else."

But Vane shook his head as they walked thoughtfully back.

"I know," he cried, all at once; "I'll give them to Mrs Bruff."

"But would she cook them?"

"Let's go and see. What time is it?"

"Half-past four," said Macey.

"Plenty of time before he gets home from work."

Vane started off at such a rate that Macey had to cry out for respite as they struck out of the wood, and reached a lane where, to their surprise, they came plump upon the gipsies camped by the roadside, with a good fire burning, and their miserable horse cropping the grass in peace.

The first objects their eyes lit upon were the women who were busily cooking; and Vane advanced and offered his basket of vegetable treasures, but they all laughed and shook their heads, and the oldest woman of the party grunted out the word "poison."

Vane advanced and offered his basket.

"There," said Macey, as they went along the lane, "you hear. They ought to know whether those are good or no. If they were nice, do you think the gipsies would let them rot in the woods."

"But, you see, they don't know," said Vane quietly, and then he gripped his companion's arm. "What's that?" he whispered.

"Some one talking in the wood."

"Poaching perhaps," said Vane, as he peered in amongst the trees.

Just then the voice ceased, and there was a rustling in amongst the bushes at the edge of the wood, as if somebody was forcing his way through, and resulting in one of the gipsy lads they had before seen, leaping out into the narrow deep lane, followed by the other.

The lads seemed to be so astonished at the encounter that they stood staring at Vane and Macey for a few moments, then looked at each other, and then, as if moved by the same impulse, they turned and rushed back into the wood, and were hidden from sight directly.

"What's the matter with them?" said Vane. "They must have been at some mischief."

"Mad, I think," said Macey. "All gipsies are half mad, or they wouldn't go about, leading such a miserable life as they do. Song says a gipsy's life is a merry life. Oh, is it? Nice life in wet, cold weather. They don't look very merry, then."

"Never mind: it's nothing to do with us. Come along."

Half-an-hour's walking brought them into the open fields, and as they stood at the end of the lane in the shade of an oak tree, Macey said suddenly:

"I say, there's old Distie yonder. Where has he been? Bet twopence it was to see the gipsies and get his fortune told."

"For a walk as far as here, perhaps, and now he is going back."

Macey said it "seemed rum," and they turned off then to reach Bruff's cottage, close to the little town.

"I don't see anything rum in it," Vane said, quietly.

"Don't you? Well, I do. Gilmore was stopping back to keep him company, wasn't he? Well, where is Gilmore? And why is Distie cutting along so—at such a rate?"

Vane did not reply, and Macey turned to look at him wonderingly.

"Here! Hi! What's the matter?"

Vane started.

"Matter?" he said, "nothing."

"What were you thinking about? Inventing something?"

"Oh, no," said Vane, confusedly. "Well, I was thinking about something I was making."

"Thought so. Well, I am glad I'm not such a Hobby-Bob sort of a fellow as you are. Syme says you're a bit of a genius, ever since you made his study clock go; but you're the worst bowler, batter, and fielder I know; you're not worth twopence at football; and if one plays at anything else with you—spins a top, or flies a kite, or anything of that kind—you're never satisfied without wanting to make the kite carry up a load, or making one top spin on the top of another, and—"

"Take me altogether, I'm the most cranky, disagreeable fellow you ever knew, eh?" said Vane, interrupting.

"Show me anyone who says so, and I'll punch his head," cried Macey, eagerly.

"There he goes. No; he's out of sight now."

"What, old Distie? Pooh! he's nobody, only a creole, and don't count."

The gardener's cottage stood back from the road; its porch covered with roses, and the little garden quite a blaze of autumn flowers; and as they reached it, Vane paused for a moment to admire them.

"Hallo!" cried Macey, "going to improve 'em?"

"They don't want it," said Vane, quietly. "I was thinking that you always see better flowers in cottage gardens than anywhere else."

At that moment the gardener's wife came to the door, smiling at her visitors, and Vane recollected the object of his visit.

"I've brought you these, Mrs Bruff," he said.

"Toadstools, sir?" said the woman, opening her eyes widely.

"No; don't call them by that name," cried Macey, merrily; "they're philogustators."

"Kind of potaters, sir?" said the woman, innocently. "Are they for Eben to grow?"

"No, for you to cook for his tea. Don't say anything, but stew them with a little water and butter, pepper and salt."

"Oh, thank you, sir," cried the woman. "Are they good?"

"Delicious, if you cook them well."

"Indeed I will, sir. Thank you so much."

She took the basket, and wanted to pay for the present with some flowers, but the lads would only take a rosebud each, and went their way, to separate at the turning leading to the rectory gate.

Chapter Eight.

A Professional Visit.

"Not going up to the rectory?" said the Doctor, next morning.

"No, uncle," said Vane, looking up from a book he was reading. "Joseph came with a note, before breakfast, to say that the rector was going over to Lincoln to-day, and that he hoped I would do a little private study at home."

"Then don't, my dear," said Aunt Hannah. "You read and study too much. Get the others to go out with you for some excursion."

Vane looked at her in a troubled way.

"He was going to excursion into the workshop. Eh, boy?" said the doctor.

"Yes, uncle, I did mean to."

"No, no, no, my dear; get some fresh air while it's fine. Yes, Eliza."

"If you please, ma'am, cook says may she speak to you."

"Yes; send her in," was the reply; and directly after Martha appeared, giving the last touches to secure the clean apron she had put on between kitchen and breakfast-room.

"Cook's cross," said Vane to himself, as his aunt looked up with—

"Well, cook?"

"Sorry to trouble you, ma'am, but I want to know what I'm to do about my vegetables this morning."

"Cook them," said Vane to himself, and then he repeated the words aloud, and added, "not like you did my poor chanterelles."

"Hush, Vane, my dear," said Aunt Hannah, as the cook turned upon him fiercely. "I do not understand what you mean, Martha."

"I mean, ma'am," said the cook, jerkily, but keeping her eyes fixed upon Vane, "that Bruff sent word as he's too ill to come this morning; and I can't be expected to go down gardens, digging potatoes and cutting cauliflowers for dinner. It isn't my place."

"No, no, certainly not, Martha," said Aunt Hannah. "Dear me! I am sorry Bruff is so ill. He was quite well yesterday."

"But I want the vegetables now, ma'am."

"And you shall have them, Martha," said the doctor, rising, bowing, and opening the door for the cook to pass out, which she did, looking wondering and abashed at her master, as if not understanding what he meant.

"Dear me!" continued the doctor, rubbing one ear, and apostrophising his nephew, "what a strange world this is. Now, by and by, Vane, that woman will leave here to marry and exist upon some working man's income, and never trouble herself for a moment about whether it's her place to go down the garden 'to cut a cabbage to make an apple-pie,' as the poet said—or somebody else; but be only too glad to feel that there is a cabbage in the garden to cut, and a potato to dig. Vane, my boy, will you come and hold the basket?"

"No, uncle; I'll soon dig a few, and cut the cauliflower," said Vane, hastily; and he hurried toward the door.

"I'll go with you, my boy," said the doctor; and he went out with his nephew, who was in a state of wondering doubt, respecting the gardener's illness. For suppose that chanterelles were, after all, not good to eat, and he had poisoned the man!

"Come along, Vane. We can find a basket and fork in the tool-house."

The doctor took down his straw hat, and led the way down the garden, looking very happy and contented, but extremely unlike the Savile Row physician, whom patients were eager to consult only a few years before.

Then the tool-house was reached, and he shouldered a four-pronged fork, and Vane took the basket; the row of red kidney potatoes was selected, and the doctor began to dig and turn up a root of fine, well-ripened tubers.

"Work that is the most ancient under the sun, Vane, my boy," said the old gentleman, smiling. "Pick them up."

But Vane did not stir. He stood, basket in hand, thinking; and the more he thought the more uneasy he grew.

"Ready? Pick them up!" cried the doctor. "What are you thinking about, eh?"

Vane gave a jump.

"I beg your pardon, uncle, I was thinking."

"I know that. What about?"

"Bruff being ill."

"Hum! Yes," said the doctor, lifting the fork to remove a potato which he had accidentally impaled. "I think I know what's the matter with Master Bruff."

"So do I, uncle. Will you come on and see him, as soon as we have got enough vegetables?"

"Physician's fee is rather high for visiting a patient, my boy; and Bruff only earns a pound a week. What very fine potatoes!"

"You will come on, won't you, uncle? I'm sure I know what's the matter with him."

"Do you?" said the doctor, turning up another fine root of potatoes. "Without seeing him?"

"Yes, uncle;" and he related what he had done on the previous afternoon.

"Indeed," said the doctor, growing interested. "But you ought to know a chanterelle if you saw one. Are you sure what you gave Mrs Bruff were right?"

"Quite, uncle; I am certain."

"Dear me! But they are reckoned to be perfectly wholesome food. I don't understand it. There, pick up the potatoes, and let's cut the cauliflowers. I'll go and see what's wrong."

Five minutes after the basket was handed in to Martha; and then the doctor washed his hands, changed his hat, and signified to Aunt Hannah where they were going.

"That's right, my dear, I thought you would," said the old lady, beaming. "Going too, Vane, my dear?"

"Yes, aunt."

"That's right. I hope you will find him better."

Vane hoped so, too, in his heart, as he walked with his uncle to the gardener's cottage, conjuring up all kinds of suffering, and wondering whether the man had been ill all the night; and, to make matters worse, a deep groan came from the open bedroom window as they approached.

Vane looked at his uncle in horror.

"Good sign, my boy," said the doctor cheerfully. "Not very bad, or he would not have made that noise. Well, Mrs Bruff," he continued, as the woman appeared to meet them at the door, "so Ebenezer is unwell?"

"Oh, yes, sir, dreadful. He was took badly about two o'clock, and he has been so queer ever since."

"Dear me," said the doctor. "Do you know what has caused it?"

"Yes, sir," said the woman, beginning to sob; "he says it's those nasty toadstools Master Vane brought, and gave me to cook for his tea. Ah, Master Vane, you shouldn't have played us such a trick."

Vane looked appealingly at his uncle, who gave him a reassuring nod.

"You cooked them then?" said the doctor.

"Oh, yes, sir, and we had them for tea, and the nasty things were so nice that we never thought there could be anything wrong."

"What time do you say your husband was taken ill?"

"About two o'clock, sir."

"And what time were you taken ill?"

"Me, sir?" said the woman staring. "I haven't been ill."

"Ah! You did not eat any of the—er—toadstools then?"

"Yes, sir, I did, as many as Ebenezer."

"Humph! What time did your husband come home last night?"

"I don't know, sir, I was asleep. But I tell you it was about two when he woke me up, and said he was so bad."

"Take me upstairs," said the doctor shortly; and he followed the woman up to her husband's room, leaving Vane alone with a sinking heart, and wishing that he had not ventured to give the chanterelles to the gardener's wife.

He could not sit down but walked about, listening to the steps and murmur of voices overhead, meaning to give up all experiments in edible fungi for the future, and ready to jump as he heard the doctor's heavy step again crossing the room, and then descending the stairs, followed by Bruff's wife.

"Do you think him very bad, sir?" she faltered.

"Oh, yes," was the cheerful reply; "he has about as splitting a headache as a poor wretch could have."

"But he will not die, sir?"

"No, Mrs Bruff," said the doctor. "Not just yet; but you may tell him, by-and-by, when you get him downstairs, feeling penitent and miserable, that, if he does not leave off going to the Chequers, he'll have to leave off coming to the Little Manor."

"Why, sir, you don't think that?" faltered the woman.

"No, I do not think, because I am quite sure, Mrs Bruff. He was not hurt by your cookery, but by what he took afterward. You understand?"

"Oh, sir!"

"Come along, Vane. Good-morning, Mrs Bruff," said the doctor, loud enough for his voice to be heard upstairs.

"I am only too glad to come and help when any one is ill; but I don't like coming upon a fool's errand."

The doctor walked out into the road, looking very stern and leaving the gardener's wife in tears, but he turned to Vane with a smile before they had gone far.

"Then you don't think it was the fungi, uncle?" said the lad, eagerly.

"Yes, I do, boy, the produce of something connected with yeast fungi; not your chanterelles."

Vane felt as if a load had been lifted off his conscience.

"Very tiresome, too," said the doctor, "for I wanted to have a chat with Bruff to-day about that greenhouse flue. He says it is quite useless, for the smoke and sulphur get out into the house and kill the plants. Now then, sir, you are such a genius at inventing, why can't you contrive the way to heat the greenhouse without causing me so much expense in the way of fuel, eh? I mean the idea you talked about before. I told Mr Syme it was to be done."

Vane was not ready with an answer to that question, and he set himself to think it out, just as they encountered the gipsy vans again, and the two lads driving the lame pony, at the sight of which the doctor frowned, and muttered something about the police, while the lads favoured Vane with a peculiar look.

Chapter Nine.

How to Heat the Greenhouse.

"Vane, my boy, you are like my old friend Deering," said the doctor one morning.

"Am I, uncle?" said the lad. "I'll have a good look at him if ever I see him."

The doctor laughed.

"I mean he is one of those men who are always trying to invent something fresh; he is a perfect boon to the patent agents."

Vane looked puzzled.

"You don't understand the allusion?"

"No, uncle, I suppose it's something to do with my being fond of—"

"Riding hobbies," said the doctor.

"Oh, I don't want to ride hobbies, uncle," said Vane, in rather an ill-used tone. "I only like to be doing things that seem as if they would be useful."

"And quite right, too, my dear," said Aunt Hannah, "only I do wish you wouldn't make quite such a mess as you do sometimes."

"Yes, it's quite right, mess or no mess," said the doctor pleasantly. "I'm glad to see you busy over something or another, even if it does not always answer. Better than wasting your time or getting into mischief."

"But they always would answer, uncle," said Vane, rubbing one ear in a vexed fashion—"that is, if I could get them quite right."

"Ah, yes, if you could get them quite right. Well, what about the greenhouse? You know I was telling the parson the other day about your plans about the kitchen-boiler and hot-water."

Vane looked for a moment as if he had received too severe a check to care to renew the subject on which he had been talking; but his uncle looked so pleasant and tolerant of his plans that the boy fired up.

"Well, it was like this, uncle: you say it is a great nuisance for any one to have to go out and see to the fire on wet, cold, dark nights."

"So it is, boy. Any one will grant that."

"Yes, uncle, and that's what I want to prevent."

"Well, how?"

"Stop a moment," said Vane. "I've been thinking about this a good deal more since you said you must send for the bricklayer."

"Well, well," said the doctor, "let's hear."

"I expect you'll laugh at me," said Vane; "but I've been trying somehow to get to the bottom of it all."

"Of course; that's the right way," said the doctor; and Aunt Hannah gave an approving nod.

"Well," said Vane; "it seems to me that one fire ought to do all the work."

"So it does, my boy," said the doctor; "but it's a devouring sort of monster and eats up a great deal of coal."

"But I mean one fire ought to do for both the kitchen and the greenhouse, too."

"What, would you have Martha's grate in among the flowers, and let her roast and fry there? That wouldn't do."

"No, no, uncle. Let the greenhouse be heated with hot-water pipes."

"Well?"

"And connect them, as I said before, with the kitchen-boiler."

"As I told Syme," said the doctor.

"No, no, no," cried Aunt Hannah, very decisively. "I'm quite sure that wouldn't do; and I'm certain that Martha would not approve of it."

"Humph!" ejaculated the doctor. "I'm afraid our Martha does not approve of doing anything but what she likes. But that would not do, boy. I told Syme so, but he was hot over it—boiler-hot."

"Well, then, let it be by means of a small boiler fitted somewhere at the side of the kitchen range, uncle; then the one fire will do everything; and, with the exception of a little cost at first, the greenhouse will always afterwards be heated for nothing."

"Come, I like that idea," said the doctor, rubbing his nose. "There's something in that, eh, my dear? Sounds well."

"Yes," said Aunt Hannah, "it sounds very well, but so do all Vane's plans; and, though I like to encourage him so long as he does not make too much mess, I must say that they seldom do anything else but sound."

"Oh, aunt!"

"Well, it's quite true, my dear, and you know it. I could name a dozen things."

"No, no, don't name 'em, aunt," said Vane hurriedly. "I know I have made some mistakes; but then everyone does who tries to invent."

"Then why not let things be as they are, my dear. I'm sure the old corkscrew was better to take out corks than the thing you made."

"It would have been beautiful, aunt," cried Vane, "if—"

"It hadn't broken so many bottles," said the doctor with a humorous look in his eyes. "It wouldn't have mattered if it had been aunt's cowslip wine, but it always chose my best port and sherry."

"And then there was that churn thing," continued Aunt Hannah.

"Oh, come, aunt, that was a success."

"What, a thing that sent all the cream flying out over Martha when she turned the handle! No, my dear, no."

"But you will not see, aunt, that it was because the thing was not properly made."

"Of course I do, my dear," said Aunt Hannah. "That's what I say."

"No, no, aunt, I mean made by a regular manufacturer, with tight lids. That was only a home-made one for an experiment."

"Yes, I know it was, my dear; and I recollect what a rage Martha was in with the thing. I believe that if I had insisted upon her going on using that thing, she would have left."

"I wish you wouldn't keep on calling it a thing, aunt," said Vane, in an ill-used tone; "it was a patent churn."

"Never mind, boy," said the doctor, "yours is the fate of all inventors. People want a deal of persuading to use new contrivances; they always prefer to stick to the old ones."

"Well, my dear, and very reasonably, too," said Aunt Hannah. "You know I like to encourage Vane, but I cannot help thinking sometimes that he is too fond of useless schemes."

"Not useless, aunt."

"Well, then, schemes; and that it would be better if he kept more to his Latin and Greek and mathematics with Mr Syme, and joining the other pupils in their sports."

"Oh, he works hard enough at his studies," said the doctor.

"I'm very glad to hear you say so, my dear," said Aunt Hannah; "and as to the rather unkind remark you made about the churn—"

"No, no, my dear, don't misunderstand me. I meant that people generally prefer to keep to the old-fashioned ways of doing things."

"But, my dear," retorted Aunt Hannah, who had been put out that morning by rebellious acts on the part of Martha, "you are as bad as anyone. See how you threw away Vane's pen-holder that he invented, and in quite a passion, too. I did think there was something in that, for it is very tiresome to have to keep on dipping your pen in the ink when you have a long letter to write."

"Oh, aunty, don't bring up that," said Vane, reproachfully.

But it was too late.

"Hang the thing!" cried the doctor, with a look of annoyance and perplexity on his countenance; "that was enough to put anyone out of temper. The idea was right enough, drawing the holder up full like a syringe, but then you couldn't use it for fear of pressing it by accident, and squirting the ink all over your paper, or on to your clothes. 'Member my new shepherd's-plaid trousers, Vane?"

"Yes, uncle; it was very unfortunate. You didn't quite know how to manage the holder. It wanted studying."

"Studying, boy! Who's going to learn to study a pen-holder. Goose-quill's good enough for me. They don't want study."

Vane rubbed his ear, and looked furtively from one to the other, as Aunt Hannah rose, and put away her work.

"No, my dear," she said, rather decisively; "I'm quite sure that Martha would never approve of anyone meddling with her kitchen-boiler."

She left the room, and Vane sat staring at his uncle, who returned his gaze with droll perplexity in his eyes.

"Aunt doesn't take to it, boy," said the doctor.

"No, uncle, and I had worked it out so thoroughly on paper," cried Vane. "I'm sure it would have been a great success. You see you couldn't do it anywhere, but you could here, because our greenhouse is all against the kitchen wall. You know how well that rose grows because it feels the heat from the fireplace through the bricks?"

"Got your plans—sketches—papers?" said the doctor.

"Yes, uncle," cried the boy, eagerly, taking some sheets of note-paper from his breast. "You can see it all here. This is where the pipe would come out of the top of the boiler, and run all round three sides of the house, and go back again and into the boiler, down at the bottom."

"And would that be enough to heat the greenhouse?"

"Plenty, uncle. I've worked it all out, and got a circular from London, and I can tell you exactly all it will cost—except the bricklayers' work, and that can't be much."

"Can't it?" cried the doctor, laughing. "Let me tell you it just can be a very great deal. I know it of old. There's a game some people are very fond of playing at, Vane. It's called bricks and mortar. Don't you ever play at it much; it costs a good deal of money."

"Oh, but this couldn't cost above a pound or two."

"Humph! No. Not so much as building a new flue, of course. But, look here: how about cold, frosty nights? The kitchen-fire goes out when Martha is off to bed."

"It does now, uncle," said the lad; "but it mustn't when we want to heat the hot-water pipes."

"But that would mean keeping up the fire all night."

"Well, you would do that if you had a stove and flue, uncle."

"Humph, yes."

"And, in this case, the fire on cold winters' nights would be indoors, and help to warm the house."

"So it would," said the doctor, who went on examining the papers very thoughtfully.

"The pipes would be nicer and neater, too, than the brick flue, uncle."

"True, boy," said the doctor, still examining the plans very attentively. "But, look here. Are you pretty sure that this hot-water would run all along the pipes?"

"Quite, uncle, and I did so hope you would let me do it, if only to show old Bruff that he does not know everything."

"But you don't expect me to put my hand in my pocket and pay pounds on purpose to gratify your vanity, boy—not really?" said the doctor.

"No, uncle," cried Vane; "it's only because I want to succeed."

"Ah, well, I'll think it over," said the doctor; and with that promise the boy had to rest satisfied.

Chapter Ten.

Vane's Workshop.

But Vane went at once to the kitchen with the intention of making some business-like measurements of the opening about the range, and to see where a boiler could best be placed. A glance within was sufficient. Martha was busy about the very spot; and Vane turned back, making up his mind to defer his visit till midnight, when the place would be solitary, and the fire out.

There was the greenhouse, though; and, fetching a rule, he went in there, and began measuring the walls once more, to arrive at the exact length of piping required, when he became conscious of a shadow cast from the open door; and, looking up, there stood Bruff, with a grin upon his face—a look so provocative that Vane turned upon him fiercely.

"Well, what are you laughing at?" he cried.

"You, Mester."

"Why?"

"I was thinking as you ought to hev been a bricklayer or carpenter, sir, instead of a scollard, and going up to rectory. Measuring for that there noo-fangle notion of yours?"

"Yes, I am," cried Vane; "and what then?"

"Oh, nowt, sir, nowt, only it wean't do. Only throwing away money."

"How do you know, Bruff?"

"How do I know, sir? Why, arn't I been a gardener ever since I was born amost, seeing as my father and granfa' was gardeners afore me.

You tak' my advice, sir, as one as knows. There's only two ways o' heating places, and one's wi' a proper fireplace an' a flue, and t'other's varmentin wi' hot manner."

Vane's Workshop.

"Varmentin with hot manner, as you call it. Why, don't they heat the vineries at Tremby Court with hot-water?"

"I've heered you say so, sir, but I niver see it. Tak' my advice, sir, and don't you meddle with things as you don't understand. Remember them taters?"

"Oh, yes, I remember the potatoes, Bruff; and I daresay, if the truth was known, you cut all the eyes out, instead of leaving the strongest, as I told you."

"I don't want no one to teach me my trade," said the man, sulkily; and he shuffled away, leaving Vane wondering why he took so much trouble, only to meet with rebuffs from nearly everyone.

"I might just as well be fishing, or playing cricket, or lying on my back in the sun, like old Distin does. Nobody seems to understand me."

He was standing just inside the door, moodily tapping the side-post with the rule, when he was startled by a step on the gravel, and, looking up sharply, he found himself face to face with a little, keen, dark, well-dressed man, who had entered the gate, seen him standing in the greenhouse, and walked across the lawn, whose mossy grass had silenced his footsteps till he reached the path.

"Morning," he said. "Doctor at home?"

"Yes," replied Vane, looking at the stranger searchingly, and wondering whether he was a visitor whom his uncle would be glad to see.

The stranger was looking searchingly at him, and he spoke at once:—

"You are the nephew, I suppose?"

Vane looked at him wonderingly.

"Yes, I thought so. Father and mother dead, and the doctor bringing you up. Lucky fellow! Here, what does this mean?" and he pointed to the rule.

"I was measuring," said Vane, colouring.

"Ah! Thought you were to be a clergyman or a doctor. Going to be a carpenter?"

"No," replied Vane sharply, and feeling full of resentment at being questioned so by a stranger. "I was measuring the walls."

"What for?" said the stranger, stepping into the greenhouse and making the lad draw back.

"Well, if you must know, sir—"

"No, I see. Old flue worn-out;—measuring for a new one."

Vane shook his head, and, in spite of himself, began to speak out freely, the stranger seeming to draw him.

"No; I was thinking of hot-water pipes."

"Good! Modern and better. Always go in for improvements. Use large ones."

"Do you understand heating with hot-water, sir?"

"A little," said the stranger, smiling. "Where are you going to make your furnace?"

"I wasn't going to make one."

"Going to do it with cold hot-water then?" said the stranger, smiling again.

"No, of course not. The kitchen-fireplace is through there," said Vane, pointing with his rule, "and I want to put a boiler in, so that the one fire will answer both purposes."

"Good! Excellent!" said the stranger sharply. "Your own idea?"

"Yes, sir."

"Do it, then, as soon as you can—before the winter. Now take me in to your uncle."

Vane looked at him again, and now with quite a friendly feeling for the man who could sympathise with his plans.

He led the stranger to the front door, and was about to ask him his name, when the doctor came out of his little study.

"Ah, Deering," he said quietly, "how are you? Who'd have thought of seeing you."

"Not you, I suppose," said the visitor quietly. "I was at Lincoln on business, and thought I would come round your way as I went back to town."

"Glad to see you, man: come in. Vane, lad, find your aunt, and tell her Mr Deering is here."

"Can't see that I'm much like him," said Vane to himself, as he went in search of his aunt, and saw her coming downstairs.

"Here's Mr Deering, aunt," he said, "and uncle wants you."

"Oh, dear me!" cried Aunt Hannah, looking troubled, and beginning to arrange her collar and cuffs.

"Why did uncle say that I was like Mr Deering, aunt?" whispered Vane. "I'm not a bit. He's dark and I'm fair."

"He meant like him in his ways, my dear: always dreaming about new inventions, and making fortunes out of nothing. I do hope your uncle will not listen to any of his wild ideas."

This description of the visitor excited Vane's curiosity. One who approved of his plans respecting the heating of the greenhouse was worthy of respect, and Vane was in no way dissatisfied to hear that Mr Deering was quite ready to accept the doctor's hospitality for a day or two.

That afternoon, as Aunt Hannah did not show the least disposition to leave the doctor and his guest alone, the latter rose and looked at Vane.

"I should like a walk," he said. "Suppose you take me round the garden, squire."

Vane followed him out eagerly; and as soon as they were in the garden, the visitor said quickly:—

"Got a workshop?"

Vane flushed a little.

"Only a bit of a shed," he said. "It was meant to be a cow-house, but uncle lets me have it to amuse myself in."

"Show it to me," said the visitor.

"Wouldn't you rather come round the grounds to have a look at uncle's fruit?" said Vane hurriedly.

"No. Why do you want to keep me out of your den?"

"Well, it's so untidy."

"Workshops generally are. Some other reason."

"I have such a lot of failures," said Vane hurriedly.

"Blunders and mistakes, I suppose, in things you have tried to make?"

"Yes."

"Show me."

Vane would far rather have led their visitor in another direction, but there was a masterful decided way about him that was not to be denied, and the lad led him into the large shed which had been floored with boards and lined, so as to turn it into quite a respectable workshop, in which were, beside a great heavy deal table in the centre, a carpenter's bench, and a turning lathe, while nails were knocked in everywhere, shelves ran from end to end, and the place presented to the eye about as strange a confusion of odds and ends as could have been seen out of a museum.

Vane looked at the visitor as he threw open the door, expecting to hear a derisive burst of laughter, but he stepped in quietly enough, and began to take up and handle the various objects which took his attention, making remarks the while.

"You should not leave your tools lying about like this: the edges get dulled, and sometimes they grow rusty. Haven't you a tool-chest?"

"There is uncle's old one," said Vane.

"Exactly. Then, why don't you keep them in the drawers?—Humph! Galvanic battery!"

"Yes; it was uncle's."

"And he gives it to you to play with, eh?"

Vane coloured again.

"I was trying to perform some experiments with it."

"Oh, I see. Well, it's a very good one; take care of it. Little chemistry, too, eh?"

"Yes: uncle shows me sometimes how to perform experiments."

"But he does not show you how to be neat and orderly."

"Oh, this is only a place to amuse oneself in!" said Vane.

"Exactly, but you can get ten times the amusement out of a shop where everything is in its place and there's a place for everything. Now, suppose I wanted to perform some simple experiment, say, to show what convection is, with water, retort and spirit lamp?"

"Convection?" said Vane, thoughtfully, as if he were searching in his mind for the meaning of a word he had forgotten.

"Yes," said the visitor, smiling. "Surely you know what convection is."

"I've forgotten," said Vane, shaking his head. "I knew once."

"Then you have not forgotten. You've got it somewhere packed away. Head's untidy, perhaps, as your laboratory."

"I know," cried Vane—"convection: it has to do with water expanding and rising when it is hot and descending when it is cold."

"Of course it has," said the visitor, laughing, "why you were lecturing me just now on the art of heating greenhouses by hot-water circulating through pipes; well, what makes it circulate?"

"The heat."

"Of course, by the law of convection."

Vane rubbed one ear.

"You had not thought of that?"

"No."

"Ah, well, you will not forget it again. But, as I was saying—suppose I wanted to try and perform a simple experiment to prove, on a small scale, that the pipes you are designing would heat. I cannot see the things I want, and I'll be bound to say you have them somewhere here."

"Oh, yes: I've got them all somewhere."

"Exactly. Take my advice, then, and be a little orderly. I don't mean be a slave to order. You understand?"

"Oh, yes," said Vane, annoyed, but at the same time pleased, for he felt that the visitor's remarks were just.

"Humph! You have rather an inventive turn then, eh?"

"Oh, no," cried Vane, disclaiming so grand a term, "I only try to make a few things here sometimes on wet days."

"Pretty often, seemingly," said the visitor, peering here and there. "Silk-winding, collecting. What's this? Trying to make a steam engine?"

"No, not exactly an engine; but I thought that perhaps I might make a little machine that would turn a wheel."

"And supply you with motive-power. Well, I will tell you at once that it would not."

"Why not?" said Vane, with a little more confidence, as he grew used to his companion's abrupt ways.

"Because you have gone the wrong way to work, groping along in the dark. I'll be bound to say," he continued, as he stood turning over the rough, clumsy contrivance upon which he had seized—a bit of mechanism which had cost the boy a good many of his shillings, and the blacksmith much time in filing and fitting in an extremely rough way—"that Newcomen and Watt and the other worthies of the steam engine's early days hit upon exactly the same ideas. It is curious how men in different places, when trying to contrive some special thing, all start working in the same groove."

"Then you think that is all stupid and waste of time, sir?"

"I did not say so. By no means. The bit of mechanism is of no use—never can be, but it shows me that you have the kind of brain that ought to fit you for an engineer, and the time you have spent over this has all been education. It will teach you one big lesson, my lad. When you try to invent anything again, no matter how simple, don't begin at the very beginning, but seek out what has already been done, and begin where others have left off—making use of what is good in their work as a foundation for yours."

"Yes, I see now," said Vane. "I shall not forget that."

Their visitor laughed.

"Then you will be a very exceptional fellow, Vane Lee. But, there, I hope you will not forget. Humph!" he continued, looking round, "You have a capital lot of material here: machinery and toys. No, I will not call them toys, because these playthings are often the parents of very useful machines. What's that—balloon?"

"An attempt at one," replied Vane.

"Oh, then, you have been trying to solve the flying problem."

"Yes," cried Vane excitedly; "have you?"

"Yes, I have had my season of thought over it, my lad; and I cannot help thinking that it will some day be mastered or discovered by accident."

Vane's lips parted, and he rested his elbows on the workbench, placed his chin in his hands, and gazed excitedly in his companion's face.

"And how do you think it will be done?"

"Ah, that's a difficult question to answer, boy. There is the problem to solve. All I say is, that if we have mastered the water and can contrive a machine that will swim like a fish—"

"But we have not," said Vane.

"Indeed! Then what do you call an Atlantic liner, with the propeller in its tail?"

"But that swims on the top of the water."

"Of course it does, because the people on board require air to breathe. Otherwise it could be made to swim beneath the water as a fish does, and at twenty miles an hour."

"Yes: I did not think of that."

"Well, as we have conquered the water to that extent, I do not see why we should not master the air."

"We can rise in balloons."

"Yes, but the balloon is clumsy and unmanageable. It will not do."

"What then, sir?"

"That's it, my boy, what then? It is easy to contrive a piece of mechanism with fans that will rise in the air, but when tried on a large scale, to be of any real service, I'm afraid it would fail."

"Then why not something to fly like a bird or a bat?" said Vane eagerly.

"No; the power required to move the great flapping wings would be too weighty for it; and, besides, I always feel that there is a something in a bird or bat which enables it to make itself, bulk for bulk, the same weight as the atmosphere."

"But that seems impossible," said Vane.

"Seems, but it may not be so. Fifty years ago the man would have been laughed at who talked about sending a message to Australia and getting the answer back the same day, but we do not think much of it now. We would have thought of the Arabian Nights, and magicians, if a man had spoken to some one miles away, then listened to his tiny whisper answering back; but these telephonic communications are getting to be common business matters now.

Why, Vane, when I was a little boy photography or light-writing was only being thought of: now people buy accurate likenesses of celebrities at a penny a piece on barrows in London streets."

Vane nodded.

"To go back to the flying," continued his companion, "I have thought and dreamed over it a great deal, but without result. I am satisfied, though, of one thing, and it is this, that some birds possess the power of gliding about in the air merely by the exercise of their will. I have watched great gulls floating along after a steamer at sea, by merely keeping their wings extended. At times they would give a slight flap or two, but not enough to affect their progress—it has appeared to me more to preserve their balance. And, again, in one of the great Alpine passes, I have watched the Swiss eagle—the Lammergeyer—rise from low down and begin sailing round and round, hardly beating with his wings, but always rising higher and higher in a vast spiral, till he was above the mountain-tops which walled in the sides of the valley. Then I have seen him sail right away. There is something more in nature connected with flight, which we have not yet discovered. I will not say that we never shall, for science is making mighty strides. There," he added, merrily, "end of the lecture. Let's go out in the open air."

Vane sighed.

"I came from London, my boy, where all the air seems to be second-hand. Out here on this slope of the wolds, the breeze gives one life and strength. Take me for a walk, out in the woods, say, it will do me good, and make me forget the worries and cares of life."

"Are you inventing something?"

Mr Deering gave the lad a sharp look, and nodded his head.

"May I ask what, sir?"

"No, my boy, you may not," said Mr Deering, sadly. "Perhaps I am going straightway on the road to disappointment and failure; but I must go on now. Some day you will hear. Now take me where I can breathe. Oh, you happy young dog!" he cried merrily. "What a thing it is to be a boy!"

"Is it?" said Vane, quietly.

"Yes, it is. And you, sir, think to yourself, like the blind young mole you are, what a great thing it is to be a man. There, come out into the open air, and let's look at nature; I get very weary sometimes of art."

Vane looked wonderingly at his new friend and did not feel so warmly toward him as he had a short time before, but this passed off when they were in the garden, where he admired the doctor's fruit, waxed eloquent over the apples and pears, and ate one of the former with as much enjoyment as a boy.

He was as merry as could be, too, and full of remarks as the doctor's Jersey cow and French poultry were inspected, but at his best in the woods amongst the gnarled old oaks and great beeches, seeming never disposed to tire.

That night Mr Deering had a very long consultation with the doctor; and Vane noted that his aunt looked very serious indeed, but she said nothing till after breakfast the next morning, when their visitor had left them for town, and evidently in the highest spirits.

"Let that boy go on with his whims, doctor," he said aloud, in Vane's hearing. "He had better waste a little money in cranks and eccentrics than in toffee and hard-bake. Good-bye."

And he was gone as suddenly, so it seemed to Vane, as he had come.

It was then that Vane heard his aunt say:

"Well, my dear, I hope it is for the best. It will be a very serious thing for us if it should go wrong."

"Very," said the doctor drily; and Vane wondered what it might be.

Chapter Eleven.

Oiling the Clock.

The plan of the town of Mavis Greythorpe was very simple, being one long street with houses on either side, placed just as the builders pleased. Churchwarden Rounds' long thatched place stood many yards back, which was convenient, for he liked to grow roses that his neighbours could see and admire. Crumps the cowkeeper's, too, stood some distance back, but that was handy, for there was room for the cowshed and the dairy close to the path. Dredge, the butcher, had his open shop, too—a separate building from the house at the back—close to the path, where customers could see the mortal remains of one sheep a week, sometimes two, and in the cold weather a pig, and a half or third of a "beast," otherwise a small bullock, the other portions being retained by neighbouring butchers at towns miles away, where the animal had been slain. But at fair time and Christmas, Butcher, or, as he pronounced it, Buttcher Dredge, to use his own words, "killed hissen" and a whole bullock was on exhibition in his open shop.

The houses named give a fair idea of the way in which architecture was arranged for in Mavis; every man who raised a house planted it where it seemed good in his own eyes; and as in most cases wayfarers stepped down out of the main street into the front rooms, the popular way of building seemed to have been that the builder dug a hole and then put a house in it.

Among those houses which were flush with the main street was that of Michael Chakes, clerk and sexton, who was also the principal shoemaker of Mavis, and his place of business was a low, open-windowed room with bench and seat, where, when not officially engaged, he sat at work, surrounded by the implements and products of his trade, every now and then opening his mouth and making a noise after repeating a couple of lines, under the impression that he was singing. Upon that point opinions differed.

Vane Lee wanted a piece of leather, and as there was nothing at home that he could cut up, saving one of the doctor's Wellington boots, which were nearly new, he put on his cap, thrust his hands in his pockets, and set off for the town street, as eagerly as if his success in life depended upon his obtaining that piece of leather instanter.

The place was perfectly empty as he reached the south end, the shops looked nearly the same, save that at Grader the baker's there were four covered glasses, containing some tasteless looking biscuits full of holes; a great many flies, hungry and eager to get out, walking in all directions over the panes; and on the lowest shelf Grader's big tom-cat, enjoying a good sleep in the sun.

Vane did not want any of those biscuits, but just then he caught sight of Distin crossing the churchyard, and to avoid him he popped in at the baker's, to be saluted by a buzz from the flies, and a slow movement on the part of the cat who rose, raised his back into a high arch, yawned and stretched, and then walked on to the counter, and rubbed his head against Vane's buttons, as the latter thrust his hands into his pocket for a coin, and tapped on the counter loudly once, then twice, then the third time, but there was no response, for the simple reason that Mrs Grader had gone to talk to a neighbour, and John Grader, having risen at three to bake his bread, and having delivered it after breakfast, was taking a nap.

"Oh, what a sleepy lot they are here!" muttered Vane, as he went to the door which, as there was no sign of Distin now, and he did not want any biscuits, he passed, and hurried along the street to where Michael Chakes sat in his open window, tapping away slowly at the heavy sole of a big boot which he was ornamenting with rows of hob-nails.

Vane stepped in at once, and the sexton looked up, nodded, and went on nailing again.

"Oughtn't to put the nails so close, Mike."

"Nay, that's the way to put in nails, Mester Vane!" said the sexton.

"I want a nice strong bit of leather."

"But if they were open they'd keep a man from slipping in wet and frost."

"Don't want to keep man from slipping, want to make 'em weer."

"Oh, all right; have it your own way. Here, I want a nice strong new bit of leather, about six inches long."

"What for?"

"Never you mind what for, get up and sell me a bit."

"Nay, I can't leave my work to get no leather to-day, Mester. Soon as I've putt in these here four nails, I'm gooing over to belfry."

"What for? Some one dead?"

"Nay, not they. Folk weant die a bit now, Mester Vane. I dunno whether it's Parson Syme's sarmints or what, but seems to me as if they think it's whole dooty a man to live to hundred and then not die."

"Nonsense, cut me my bit of leather, and let me go."

"Nay, sir, I can't stop to coot no leather to-day. I tellee I'm gooin' to church."

"But what for?"

"Clock's stopped."

"Eh! Has it?" cried Vane eagerly. "What's the matter with it?"

"I d'know sir. Somethin' wrong in its inside, I spect. I'm gooing to see."

"Forgotten to wind it up, Mike."

"Nay, that I arn't, sir. Wound her up tight enew."

"Then that's it. Wound up too tight, perhaps."

"Nay, she's been wound up just the same as I've wound her these five-and-twenty year, just as father used to. She's wrong inside."

"Goes stiff. Wants a little oil. Bring some in a bottle with a feather and I'll soon put it right."

The sexton pointed with his hammer to the chimney-piece where a small phial bottle was standing, and Vane took it up at once, and began turning a white fowl's feather round to stir up the oil.

"You mean to come, then?" said the sexton.

"Of course. I'm fond of machinery," cried Vane.

"Ay, you be," said the sexton, tapping away at the nails, "and you'd like to tak' that owd clock all to pieces, I know."

"I should," cried Vane with his eyes sparkling. "Shall I?"

"What?" cried the sexton, with his hammer raised. "Why, you'd never get it put together again."

"Tchah! that I could. I would somehow," added the lad. "Ay somehow; but what's the good o' that! Suppose she wouldn't goo when you'd putt her together somehow. What then?"

"Why, she won't go now," cried Vane, "so what harm would it do?"

"Well, I don't know about that," said the sexton, driving in the last nail, and pausing to admire the iron-decorated sole.

"Now, then, cut my piece of leather," cried Vane.

"Nay, I can't stop to coot no pieces o' leather," said the sexton. "Church clock's more consekens than all the bits o' leather in a tanner's yard. I'm gooing over yonder now."

"Oh, very well," said Vane, as the man rose, untied his leathern apron, and put on a very ancient coat, "it will do when we come back."

"Mean to go wi' me, then?"

"Of course I do."

The sexton chuckled, took his hat from behind the door, and stepped out on to the cobble-stone pathway, after taking the oil bottle and a bunch of big keys from a nail.

The street looked as deserted as if the place were uninhabited, and not a soul was passed as they went up to the church gate at the west end of the ancient edifice, which had stood with its great square stone fortified tower, dominating from a knoll the tiny town for five hundred years—ever since the days when it was built to act as a stronghold to which the Mavis Greythorpites could flee if assaulted by enemies, and shoot arrows from the narrow windows and hurl stones from the battlements. Or, if these were not sufficient, and the enemy proved to be very enterprising indeed, so much so as to try and batter in the hugely-thick iron-studded belfry-door, why there were those pleasant openings called by architects machicolations, just over the entrance, from which ladlesful of newly molten lead could be scattered upon their heads.

Michael Chakes knew the bunch of keys by heart, but he always went through the same ceremony—that of examining them all four, and blowing in the tubes, as if they were panpipes, keeping the one he wanted to the last.

"Oh, do make haste, Mike," cried the boy. "You are so slow."

"Slow and sewer's my motter, Mester Vane," grunted the sexton, as he slowly inserted the key. "Don't you hurry no man's beast; you may hev an ass of your own some day."

"If I do I'll make him go faster than you do. I say, though, Mike, do you think it's true about those old bits of leather?"

As he spoke, Vane pointed to a couple of scraps of black-looking, curl-edged hide, fastened with broad headed nails to the belfry-door.

"True!" cried the sexton, turning his grim, lined, and not over-clean face to gaze in the frank-looking handsome countenance beside him. "True! Think o' that now, and you going up to rectory every day, to do your larning along with the other young gents, to Mester Syme. Well, that beats all."

"What's that got to do with it?" cried Vane, as the sexton ceased from turning the key in the door, and laid one hand on the scraps of hide.

"Got to do wi' it, lad? Well I am! And to call them leather."

"Well, so they are leather," said Vane. "And do you mean to say, standing theer with the turn-stones all around you as you think anything bout t'owd church arn't true?"

"No, but I don't think it's true about those bits of leather."

"Leather, indeed!" cried the sexton. "I'm surprised at you, Mester Vane—that I am. Them arn't leather but all that's left o' the skins o' the Swedums and Danes as they took off 'em and nailed up on church door to keep off the rest o' the robbin', murderin' and firin' wretches as come up river in their ships and then walked the rest o' the way across the mash?"

"Oh, but it might be a bit of horse skin."

"Nay, nay, don't you go backslidin' and thinking such a thing as that, mester. Why, theer was a party o' larned gentlemen come one day all t'way fro' Lincoln, and looked at it through little tallerscope things, and me standing close by all the time to see as they didn't steal nowt, for them sort's terruble folk for knocking bits off wi' hammers as they carries in their pockets and spreadin' bits o' calico over t' brasses, and rubbin' 'em wi' heel balls same as I uses for edges of soles; and first one and then another of 'em says—'Human.' That's what they says. Ay, lad, that's true enough, and been here to this day."

"Ah, well, open the door, Mike, and let's go in. I don't believe people would have been such wretches as to skin a man, even if he was a Dane, and then nail the skin up there. But if they did, it wouldn't have lasted."

The sexton shook his head very solemnly and turned the great key, the rusty lock-bolt shooting back reluctantly, and the door turning slowly on its hinges, which gave forth a dismal creak.

"Here, let's give them a drop of oil," cried Vane; but the sexton held the bottle behind him.

"Nay, nay," he said; "they're all right enew. Let 'em be, lad."

"How silent it seems without the old clock ticking," said Vane, looking up at the groined roof where, in place of bosses to ornament the handsome old ceiling of the belfry, there were circular holes intended to pour more lead and arrows upon besiegers, in case they made their way through the door, farther progress being through a narrow lancet archway and up an extremely small stone spiral staircase toward which Vane stepped, but the sexton checked him.

"Nay, Mester, I go first," he said.

"Look sharp then."

But the only thing sharp about the sexton were his awls and cutting knives, and he took an unconscionably long time to ascend to the floor above them where an opening in the staircase admitted them to a square chamber, lighted by four narrow lancet windows, and into which hung down from the ceiling, and through as many holes, eight ropes, portions of which were covered with worsted to soften them to the ringers' hands.

Vane made a rush for the rope of the tenor bell, but the sexton uttered a cry of horror.

"Nay, nay, lad," he said, as soon as he got his breath, "don't pull: 'twould make 'em think there's a fire."

"Oh, all right," said Vane, leaving the rope.

"Nay, promise as you weant touch 'em, or I weant go no further."

"I promise," cried Vane merrily. "Now, then, up you go to the clock."

The sexton looked relieved, and went to a broad cupboard at one side of the chamber, opened it, and there before them was the great pendulum of the old clock hanging straight down, and upon its being started swinging, it did so, but with no answering *tic-tac*.

"Where are the weights, Mike?" cried Vane, thrusting in his head, and looking up. "Oh, I see them."

"Ay, you can see 'em, lad, wound right up. There, let's go and see."

The sexton led the way up to the next floor, but here they were stopped by a door, which was slowly opened after he had played his tune upon the key pipes.

"Oh I say, Mike, what a horrible old bore you are," cried the boy, impatiently.

"Then thou shouldstna hev coom, lad," said the sexton as they stood now in a chamber through which the bell ropes passed and away up through eight more holes in the next ceiling, while right in the middle stood the skeleton works of the great clock, with all its wheels and escapements open to the boy's eager gaze, as he noted everything, from the portion which went out horizontally through the wall to turn the hands on the clock's face, to the part where the pendulum hung, and on either side the two great weights which set the machine in motion, and ruled the striking of the hours.

The clock was screwed down to a frame-work of oaken beams, and looked, in spite of its great age and accumulation of dust, in the best of condition, and, to the sexton's horror, Vane forgot all about the eight big bells overhead, and the roof of the tower, from which there was a magnificent view over the wolds, and stripped off his jacket.

"What are you going to do, lad?" cried the sexton.

"See what's the matter. Why the clock won't go."

"Nay, nay, thou must na touch it, lad. Why, it's more than my plaace is worth to let anny one else touch that theer clock."

"Oh, nonsense! Here, give me the oil."

Vane snatched the bottle, and while the sexton looked on, trembling at the sacrilege, as it seemed to him, the lad busily oiled every bearing that he could reach, and used the oil so liberally that at last there was not a drop left, and he ceased his task with a sigh.

"There, Mike, she'll go now," he cried. "Can't say I've done any harm."

"Nay, I wean't say that you hev, mester, for I've been standing ready to stop you if you did."

Vane laughed.

"Now, then, start the pendulum," he said; "and then put the hands right."

He went to the side to start the swinging regulator himself but the sexton again stopped him.

"Nay," he said; "that's my job, lad;" and very slowly and cautiously he set the bob in motion.

"There, I told you so," cried Vane; "only wanted a drop of oil."

For the pendulum swung *tic—tac—tic—tac* with beautiful regularity. Then, as they listened it went *tic—tic*. Then *tic* two or three times over, and there was no more sound.

"Didn't start it hard enough, Mike," cried Vane; and this time, to the sexton's horror, he gave the pendulum a good swing, the regular *tic—tac* followed, grew feeble, stopped, and there was an outburst as if of uncanny laughter from overhead, so real that it was hard to think that it was only a flock of jackdaws just settled on the battlements of the tower.

"Oh, come, I'm not going to be beaten like this," cried Vane, "I know I can put the old clock right."

"Nay, nay, not you," said the sexton firmly.

"But I took our kitchen clock to pieces, and put it together again; and now it goes splendidly—only it doesn't strike right."

"Mebbe," said the sexton, "but this arn't a kitchen clock. Nay, Master Vane, the man 'll hev to come fro Lincun to doctor she."

"But let me just—"

"Nay, nay, you don't touch her again."

The man was so firm that Vane had to give way and descend, forgetting all about the piece of leather he wanted, and parting from the sexton at the door as the key was turned, and then walking back home, to go at once to his workshop and sit down to think.

There was plenty for him to do—any number of mechanical contrivances to go on with, notably the one intended to move a boat without oars, sails, or steam, but they were not church clocks, and for the time being nothing interested him but the old clock whose hands were pointing absurdly as to the correct time.

All at once a thought struck Vane, and he jumped up, thrust a pair of pliers, a little screw-wrench and a pair of pincers into his pockets and went out again.

Chapter Twelve.

Those Two Wheels.

As Vane walked along the road the tools in his pocket rattled, and they set him thinking about Mr Deering, and how serious he had made his uncle look for a few days. Then about all their visitor had said about flying, and that set him wondering whether it would be possible to contrive something which might easily be tested.

"I could go up on to the leads of the tower, step off and float down into the churchyard."

Vane suddenly burst out laughing.

"Why, if I had said that yonder," he thought, "old Macey would tell me that it would be just in the right place, for I should be sure to break my neck."

Then he began thinking about Bruff the gardener, for he passed his cottage; and about his coming to work the next day after being ill, and never saying another word about the chanterelles.

Directly after his thoughts turned in another direction, for he came upon the two gipsy lads, seated under the hedge, with their legs in the ditch, proof positive that the people of their tribe were somewhere not very far away.

The lads stared at him very hard, and Vane stared back at them, thinking what a curious life it seemed—for two big strong boys to be always hanging about, doing nothing but drive a few miserable worn-out horses from fair to fair.

Just as he was abreast of the lads, one whispered something to the other, but what it was Vane could not understand, for it sounded mere gibberish.

Then the other replied, without moving his head, and Vane passed on.

"I don't believe it's a regular language they talk," he said to himself. "Only a lot of slang words they've made up. What do they call it? Rum—Rum—Romany, that is it. Well, it doesn't sound Roman-like to me."

About a hundred yards on he looked back, to see that the two gipsy lads were in eager converse, and one was gesticulating so fiercely, that it looked like quarrelling.

But Vane had something else to think about, and he went on, holding the tools inside his pockets, to keep them from clicking together as he turned up toward the rectory, just catching sight of the gipsy lads again, now out in the road and slouching along toward the town.

"Wonder whether Mr Symes is at home again," thought Vane, but he did not expect that he would be, as it was his hour for being from the rectory, perhaps having a drive, so that he felt pretty easy about him. But he kept a sharp look-out for Gilmore and the others.

"Hardly likely for them to be in," he thought; and then he felt annoyed with himself because his visit seemed furtive and deceptive.

As a rule, he walked up to the front of the house, feeling quite at home, and as if he were one of its inmates, whereas now there was the feeling upon him that he had no business to go upon his present mission, and that the first person he met would ask him what right he had to come sneaking up there with tools in his pockets.

For a moment he thought he would go back, but he mastered that, and went on, only to hesitate once more, feeling sure that he had heard faintly the rector's peculiar clearing of his voice—"Hah-errum!"

His active brain immediately raised up the portly figure of his tutor before him, raising his eyebrows, and questioning him about why he was there; but these thoughts were chased away directly after, as he came to an opening in the trees, through which he could look right away to where the river went winding along through the meadows, edged with pollard willows, and there, quite half-a-mile away, he could see a solitary figure standing close to the stream.

"That's old Macey," muttered Vane, "fishing for perch in his favourite hole."

Feeling pretty certain that the others would not be far away, he stood peering about till he caught sight of another figure away to his right.

"Gilmore surely," he muttered; and then his eyes wandered again till they lighted upon a figure seated at the foot of a tree close by the one he had settled to be Gilmore.

"Old Distie," said Vane, with a laugh. "What an idle fellow he is. Never happy unless he is sitting or lying down somewhere. I suppose it's from coming out of a hot country, where people do lie about a great deal."

"That's all right," he thought, "they will not bother me, and I needn't mind, for it's pretty good proof that the rector is out."

Feeling fresh confidence at this, but, at the same time, horribly annoyed with himself because of the shrinking feeling which troubled him, he went straight up the path to the porch and rang.

Joseph, the rector's footman, came hurrying into the hall, pulling down the sides of his coat, and looked surprised and injured on seeing that it was only one of "Master's pupils."

"I only wanted the keys of the church, Joe," said Vane, carelessly.

"There they hang, sir," replied the man, pointing to a niche in the porch.

"Yes, I know, but I didn't like to take them without speaking," said Vane; and the next minute he was on his way to the churchyard through the rectory garden, hugging the duplicate keys in his pocket, and satisfied that he could reach the belfry-door without being seen by the sexton.

It was easy enough to get there unseen. Whether he could open the door unheard was another thing.

There was no examining each key in turn, and no whistling in the pipes, but the right one chosen at once and thrust in.

"*Tah*!" came from overhead loudly; and Vane started back, when quite a chorus arose, and the flock of jackdaws flew away, as if rejoicing at mocking one who was bent upon a clandestine visit to the church.

"How stupid!" muttered Vane; but he gave a sharp glance round to see if he were observed before turning the key, and throwing open the door.

"Why didn't he let me oil it?" he muttered, for the noise seemed to be twice as loud now, and after dragging out the key the noise was louder still, he thought, as he thrust to the door, and locked it on the inside.

Then, as he withdrew the key again, he hesitated and stood listening.

Everything look strange and dim, and he felt half disposed to draw back, but laughing to himself at his want of firmness, he ran up the winding stairs again, as fast as the worn stones would let him, passed the ringers' chamber, and went on up to the locked door, which creaked dismally, as he threw it open. The next moment he was by the clock.

But he did not pause here. Drawing back into the winding staircase he ascended to where the bells hung, and had a good look at the one with the hammer by it—that on which the clock struck the hours—

noted how green it was with verdigris, and then hurried down to the clock-chamber, took out his tools, pulled off his jacket and set to work.

For there was this peculiarity about the doctor's nephew—that he gave the whole of his mind and energies to any mechanical task which took his fancy, and, consequently, there was neither mind nor energy left to bestow upon collateral circumstances.

Another boy would have had a thought for the consequences of what he was attempting—whether it was right for him to meddle, whether the rector would approve. Vane had not even the vestige of a thought on such matters. He could only see wheels and pinions taken out after the removal of certain screws, cleaned, oiled, put back, and the old clock pointing correctly to the time of day and, striking decently and in order, as a church clock should.

Pincers, pliers and screw-driver were laid on the floor and the screw-wrench was applied here and there, after which a cloth or rag was required to wipe the different wheels, and pivots; but unfortunately nothing of the kind was at hand, so a clean pocket-handkerchief was utilised, not to its advantage—and the work went on.

Vane's face was a study as he used his penknife to scrape and pare off hardened oil, which clogged the various bearings; and as some pieces of the clock, iron or brass, was restored to its proper condition of brightness, the lad smiled and looked triumphant.

Time went on, though that clock stood still, and all at once, as he set down a wheel and began wishing that he had some one to help him remove the weights, it suddenly dawned upon him that it was getting towards sunset, that he had forgotten all about his dinner, and that if he wanted any tea, he must rapidly replace the wheels he had taken out, and screw the frame-work back which he had removed.

He had been working at the striking part of the clock, and he set to at once building up again, shaking his head the while at the parts he had not cleaned, having been unable to remove them on account of the line coiled round a drum and attached to a striking weight.

"A clockmaker would have had that weight off first thing, I suppose," he said to himself, as he toiled away. "I'll get Aleck to come and help me to-morrow and do it properly, while I'm about it."

"It's easy enough," he said half-aloud at the end of an hour. "I believe I could make a clock in time if I tried. There you are," he muttered as he turned the final screw that he had removed. "Hullo, what a mess I'm in!"

He looked at his black and oily hands, and began thinking of soap and soda with hot-water as he rose from his knees after gathering up his tools, and then he stopped staring before him at a ledge beneath the back of the clock face.

"Why, I forgot them," he said, taking from where they lay a couple of small cogged wheels which he had cleaned very carefully, and put on one side early in his task.

"Where do they belong to?" he muttered, as he looked from them to the clock and back again.

There seemed to be nothing missing: every part fitted together, but it was plain enough that these two wheels had been left out, and that to find out where they belonged and put them back meant a serious task gone over again.

"Well, you two will have to wait," said the boy at last. "It doesn't so much matter as I'm going to take the clock to pieces again, but all the same, I don't like missing them."

He hesitated for a few moments, as to what he should do with the wheels, and ended by reaching in and laying them just beneath the works on one of the squared pieces of oak to which the clock was screwed.

Ten minutes later he was at the rectory porch, where he hung up the keys just inside the hall, and then trotted home with his hands in his pockets to hide their colour.

He was obliged to show them in the kitchen though, where he went to beg a jug of hot-water and some soda.

"Why, where have you been, sir?" cried Martha; "and the dinner kept waiting a whole hour, and orders from your aunt to broil chicken for your tea, as if there wasn't enough to do, and some soda? I haven't got any."

"But you've got some, cookie," said Vane.

"Not a bit, if you speak to me in that disrespectful way, sir. My name's Martha, if you please. Well, there's a bit, but how a young gentleman can go on as you do making his hands like a sweep's I don't know, and if I was your aunt I'd—"

Vane did not hear what, for he had hurried away with the hot-water and soda, the odour of the kitchen having had a maddening effect upon him, and set him thinking ravenously of the dinner he had missed and the grilled chicken to come.

But there was no reproof for him when, clean and decent once more, he sought the dining-room. Aunt Hannah shook her head, but smiled as she made the tea, and kissed him as he went to her side.

"Why, Vane, my dear, you must be starving," she whispered. But his uncle was deep in thought over some horticultural problem and did not seem to have missed him. He roused up, though, over the evening meal, while Vane was trying to hide his nails, which in spite of all his efforts looked exceedingly black and like a smith's.

It was the appetising odour of the grilled chicken that roused the doctor most, for after sipping his tea and partaking of one piece of toast he gave a very loud sniff and began to look round the table.

Vane's plate and the dish before him at once took his attention.

"Meat tea?" he said smiling pleasantly. "Dear me! and I was under the impression that we had had dinner just as usual. Come, Vane, my boy, don't be greedy. Remember your aunt; and I'll take a little of that. It smells very good."

"But, my dear, you had your dinner, and Vane was not there," cried Aunt Hannah.

"Oh! bless my heart, yes," said the doctor. "Really I had quite forgotten all about it."

"Hold your plate, uncle," cried Vane.

"Oh, no, thank you, my boy. It was all a mistake, I was thinking about the greenhouse, my dear, you know that the old flue is worn-out, and really something must be done to heat it."

"Oh, never mind that," said Aunt Hannah, but Vane pricked up his ears.

"But I must mind it, my dear," said the doctor. "It does not matter now, but the cold weather will come, and it would be a pity to have the choice plants destroyed."

"I think it is not worth the trouble," said Aunt Hannah. "See how tiresome it is for someone to be obliged to come to see to that fire late on cold winter nights."

"There can be no pleasure enjoyed, my dear, without some trouble," said the doctor. "It is tiresome, I know, all that stoking and poking when the glass is below freezing point, and once more, I say I wish there could be some contrivance for heating the greenhouse without farther trouble."

Vane pricked up his ears again, and for a few moments his uncle's words seemed about to take root; but those wheels rolled into his mind directly after, and he was wondering where they could belong to, and how it was that he had not missed them when he put the others back.

Then the grilled chicken interfered with his power of thinking, and the greenhouse quite passed away.

The evenings at the Little Manor House were very quiet, as a rule. The doctor sat and thought, or read medical or horticultural papers; Aunt Hannah sat and knitted or embroidered and kept looking up to nod at Vane in an encouraging way as he was busy over his classics or mathematics, getting ready for reading with the rector next day; and the big cat blinked at the fire from the hearthrug.

But, on this particular night, Vane hurried through the paper he had to prepare for the next day, and fetched out of the book-cases two or three works which gave a little information on horology, and he was soon deep in toothed-wheels, crown-wheels, pinions, ratchets, pallets, escapements, free, detached, anchor, and half-dead. Then he read on about racks, and snails; weights, pendulums, bobs, and compensations.

Reading all this was not only interesting, but gave the idea that taking a clock to pieces and putting it together again was remarkably easy; but there was no explanation about those missing wheels.

Bedtime at last, and Vane had another scrub with the nail-brush at his hands before lying down.

It was a lovely night, nearly full-moon, and the room looked so light after the candle was out that Vane gave it the credit of keeping him awake. For, try how he would, he could not get to sleep. Now he was on his right side, but the pillow grew hot and had to be turned; now on his left, with the pillow turned back. Too many clothes, and the counterpane stripped back. Not enough: his uncle always said that warmth was conducive to sleep, and the counterpane pulled up. But no sleep.

"Oh, how wakeful I do feel!" muttered the boy impatiently, as he tossed from side to side. "Is it the chicken?"

No; it was not the chicken, but the church clock, and those two wheels, which kept on going round and round in his mind without cessation. He tried to think of something else: his studies, Greek, Latin, the mathematical problems upon which he was engaged; but, no: ratchets and pinions, toothed-wheels, free and detached, pendulums and weights, had it all their own way, and at last he jumped out of bed, opened the window and stood there, looking out, and cooling his heated, weary head for a time.

"Now I can sleep," he said to himself, triumphantly, as he returned to his bed; but he was wrong, and a quarter of an hour after he was at the washstand, pouring himself out a glass of water, which he drank.

That did have some effect, for at last he dropped off into a fitful unrefreshing sleep, to be mentally borne at once into the chamber of the big stone tower, with the clockwork tumbled about in heaps all round him; and he vainly trying to catch the toothed-wheels, which kept running round and round, while the clock began to strike.

Vane started up in bed, for the dream seemed real—the clock was striking.

No: that was not a clock striking, but one of the bells, tolling rapidly in the middle of the night.

For a moment the lad thought he was asleep, but the next he had sprung out of bed and run to the window to thrust out his head and listen.

It was unmistakable: the big bell was going as he had never heard it before—not being rung, but as if someone had hold of the clapper and were beating it against the side—*Dang, dang, dang, dang*—stroke following stroke rapidly; and, half-confused by the sleep from which he had been awakened, Vane was trying to make out what it meant, when faintly, but plainly heard on the still night air, came that most startling of cries—

"Fire! Fire! Fire!"

The Alarm of Fire.

Chapter Thirteen.

A Disturbed Night.

Just as Vane shivered at the cry, and ran to hurry on some clothes, there was the shape of the door clearly made out in lines of light, and directly after a sharp tapping.

"Vane, my boy, asleep?"

"No, uncle; dressing."

"You heard the bell, then. I'm afraid it means fire."

"Yes, fire, fire! I heard them calling."

"I can't see anything, can you?"

"No, uncle, but I shall be dressed directly, and will go and find out where it is?"

"O hey! Master Vane!" came from the outside. "Fire!"

It was the gardener's voice, and the lad ran to the window.

"Yes, I heard. Where is it?"

"Don't know yet, sir. Think it's the rectory."

"Oh, dear! oh, dear!" came from Vane's door. "Hi, Vane, lad, I'll dress as quickly as I can. You run on and see if you can help. Whatever you do, try and save the rector's books."

Vane grunted and went on dressing, finding everything wrong in the dark, and taking twice as long as usual to get into his clothes.

As he dressed, he kept on going to the window to look out, but not to obtain any information, for the gardener had run back at a steady trot, his steps sounding clearly on the hard road, while the bell kept up its incessant clamour, the blows of the clapper following one another rapidly as ever, and with the greatest of regularity. But thrust his head out as far as he would, there was no glare visible, as there had been the year before when the haystack was either set on fire or ignited spontaneously from being built up too wet. Then the whole of the western sky was illumined by the flames, and patches of burning hay rose in great flakes high in air, and were swept away by the breeze.

"Dressed, uncle. Going down," cried Vane, as he walked into the passage.

"Shan't be five minutes, my boy."

"Take care, Vane, dear," came in smothered and suggestive tones. "Don't go too near the fire."

"All right, aunt," shouted the boy, as he ran downstairs, and, catching up his cap, unfastened the front door, stepped out, ran down the path, darted out from the gate, and began to run toward where the alarm bell was being rung.

It was no great distance, but, in spite of his speed, it seemed to be long that night; and, as Vane ran, looking eagerly the while for the glow from the fire, he came to the conclusion that the brilliancy of the moon was sufficient to render it invisible, and that perhaps the blaze was yet only small.

"Hi! Who's that?" cried a voice, whose owner was invisible in the shadow cast by a clump of trees.

"I—Vane Lee. Is the rectory on fire, Distin?"

"I've just come out of it, and didn't see any flames," said the youth contemptuously.

"Here, hi! Distie!" came from the side-road leading to the rectory grounds. "Wait for us. Who's that? Oh, you, Vane. What's the matter?"

"I don't know," replied Vane. "I jumped out of bed when I heard the alarm bell."

"So did we, and here's Aleck got his trousers on wrong way first."

"I haven't," shouted Macey; "but that's my hat you've got."

As he spoke, he snatched the hat Gilmore was wearing, and tossed the one he held toward his companion.

"Are you fellows coming?" said Distin, coldly.

"Of course we are," cried Macey. "Come on, lads; let's go and help them get out the town squirt."

They started for the main street at a trot, and Vane panted out:—

"I'll lay a wager that the engine's locked up, and that they can't find the keys."

"And when they do, the old pump won't move," cried Gilmore.

"And the hose will be all burst," cried Macey.

"I thought we were going to help," said Distin, coldly. "If you fellows chatter so, you'll have no breath left."

By this time they were among the houses, nearly everyone of which showed a light at the upper window.

"Here's Bruff," cried Vane, running up to a group of men, four of whom were carrying poles with iron hooks at the end—implements bearing a striking family resemblance to the pole drags said to be "kept in constant readiness," by wharves, bridges, and docks.

"What have you got there, gardener?" shouted Gilmore.

"Hooks, sir, to tear off the burning thack."

"But where is the burning thatch?" cried Vane.

"I dunno, sir," said the gardener. "I arn't even smelt fire yet."

"Have they got the engine out?"

"No, sir. They arn't got the keys yet. Well, did you make him hear?" continued Bruff, as half-a-dozen men came trotting down the street.

"Nay, we can't wacken him nohow."

"What, Chakes?" cried Vane.

"Ay; we've been after the keys."

"But he must be up at the church," said Vane. "It's he who is ringing the bell."

"Nay, he arn't theer," chorused several. "We went theer first, and doors is locked."

By this time there was quite a little crowd in the street, whose components were, for the most part, asking each other where the fire was; and, to add to the confusion, several had brought their dogs, some of which barked at the incessant ringing of the big bell, while three took part in a quarrel, possibly induced by ill-temper consequent upon their having been roused from their beds.

"Then he must have locked himself in," cried Vane.

"Not he," said Distin. "Go and knock him up; he's asleep still."

"Well," said Bruff, with a chuckle, as he stood his hook pole on end, "owd Mike Chakes can sleep a bit, I know; but if he can do it through all this ting dang, he bets me."

"Come and see," cried Vane, making for the church-tower.

"No; come and rout him out of bed," cried Distin.

Just then a portly figure approached, and the rector's smooth, quick voice was heard asking:—

"Where is the fire, my men?"

"That's what we can't none on us mak' out, Parson," said a voice. "Hey! Here's Mester Rounds; he's chutch-waarden; he'll know."

"Nay, I don't know," cried the owner of the name; "I've on'y just got out o' bed. Who's that pullin' the big bell at that rate?"

"We think it's saxton," cried a voice.

"Yes, of course. He has locked himself in."

"Silence!" cried the rector; and, as the buzz of voices ceased, he continued, "Has anyone noticed a fire?"

"Nay, nay, nay," came from all directions.

"But at a distance—at either of the farms?"

"Nay, they're all right, parson," said the churchwarden. "We could see if they was alight. Hi! theer! How'd hard!" he roared, with both hands to his mouth. "Don't pull the bell down."

For the clangour continued at the same rate,—*Dang, dang dang, dang*.

"Owd Mikey Chakes has gone mad, I think," said a voice.

"Follow me to the church," said the rector; and, leading the way with his pupils, the rector marched the little crowd up the street, amidst a buzz of voices, many of which came from bedroom windows, now all wide-open, and with the occupants of the chambers gazing out, and shouting questions to neighbours where the fire might be.

A few moments' pause was made at the sexton's door, but all was silent there, and no response came to repeated knocks.

"He must be at the church, of course," said the rector; and in a few minutes all were gathered at the west door, which was tried, and, as before said, found to be fastened.

"Call, somebody with a loud voice."

"We did come and shout, sir, and kicked at the door."

"Call again," said the rector. "The bell makes so much clamour the ringer cannot hear. Hah! he has stopped."

For, as he spoke, the strokes on the bell grew slower, and suddenly ceased.

A shout was raised, a curious cry, composed of "Mike"—"Chakes!"—"Shunk" and other familiar appellations.

"Hush, hush!" cried the rector. "One of you—Mr Rounds, will you have the goodness to summon the sexton."

"Hey! hey! Sax'on!" shouted the miller in a voice of thunder; and he supplemented his summons by kicking loudly at the door.

"Excuse me, Mr Rounds," said the rector; "the call will suffice."

"But it don't suffice, Parson," said the bluff churchwarden. "Hi, Chakes, man, coom down an' open doooor!"

"Straange and queer," said the butcher. "Theer arn't nobody, or they'd say summat."

There was another shout.

"Plaace arn't harnted, is it?" said a voice from the little crowd.

"Will somebody have the goodness to go for my set of the church keys," said the rector with dignity. "You? Thank you, Mr Macey. You know where they hang."

Macey went off at a quick pace; and, to fill up the time, the rector knocked with the top of his stick.

By this time the doctor had joined the group.

"It seems very strange," he said. "The sexton must have gone up himself, nobody else had keys."

"And there appears to be nothing to cause him to raise an alarm," said the rector. "Surely the man has not been walking in his sleep."

"Tchah!" cried the churchwarden; "not he, sir. Wean't hardly walk a dozen steps, even when he's awake. Why, hallo! what now?"

"Here he is! Here he is!" came excitedly from the crowd, as the sexton walked deliberately up with a lantern in one hand, a bunch of keys in the other.

"Mr Chakes," said the rector sternly, "what is the meaning of this?"

"Dunno, sir. I come to see," replied the sexton. "I thowt I heerd bell tolling, and I got up and as there seems to be some'at the matter I comed."

"Then, you did not go into the belfry to ring the alarm," cried the doctor.

"Nay, I ben abed and asleep till the noise wackened me."

"It is very strange," said the rector. "Ah, here is Mr Macey. Have the goodness to open the door; and, Mr Rounds, will you keep watch over the windows to see if any one escapes. This must be some trick."

As the door was opened the rector turned to his pupils.

"Surely, young gentlemen," he said in a whisper, "you have not been guilty of any prank."

They all indignantly disclaimed participation, and the rector led the way into the great silent tower, where he paused.

"I'm afraid I must leave the search to younger men," he said. "That winding staircase will be too much for me."

Previously all had hung back out of respect to the rector, but at this a rush was made for the belfry, the rectory pupils leading, and quite a crowd filling the chamber where the ropes hung perfectly still.

"Nobody here, sir," shouted Distin, down the staircase.

"Dear me!" exclaimed the rector; who was standing at the foot, almost alone, save that he had the companionship of the doctor and that they were in close proximity to the churchwarden and the watchers outside the door.

"Go up higher. Perhaps he is hiding by the clock or among the bells."

This necessitated Chakes going up first, and unlocking the clock-chamber door, while others went higher to see if any one was hidden among the bells or on the roof.

"I know'd there couldn't be no one in here," said Chakes solemnly, as he held up his lantern, and peered about, and round the works of the clock.

"How did you know?" said Distin suspiciously.

"That's how," replied the sexton, holding up his keys. "No one couldn't get oop here, wi'out my key or parson's."

This was received with a solemn murmur, and after communications had been sent to and fro between the rector and Distin, up and down the spiral staircase, which made an excellent speaking-tube, the rector called to everyone to come back.

He was obeyed, Chakes desiring the pupils to stay with him while he did the locking up; and as he saw a look exchanged between Macey and Gilmore, he raised his keys to his lips, and blew down the pipes.

"Here, hallo!" cried Gilmore, "where's the show and the big drum? He's going to give us Punch and Judy."

"Nay, sir, nay, I always blows the doost out. You thought I wanted you to stay because— Nay, I arn't scarred. On'y thought I might want someone to howd lantern."

He locked the clock-chamber door, and they descended to the belfry, where several of the people were standing, three having hold of the ropes.

"Nay, nay, you mustn't pull they," shouted Chakes. "Bell's been ringing 'nuff to-night. Latt 'em be."

"Why, we never looked in those big cupboards," cried Macey suddenly, pointing to the doors behind which the weights hung, and the pendulum, when the clock was going, swung to and fro.

"Nay, there's nowt," said the sexton, opening and throwing back the door to show the motionless ropes and pendulum.

Vane had moved close up with the others, and he stood there in silence as the doors were closed again, and then they descended to join the group below, the churchwarden now coming to the broad arched door.

"Well?" he cried; "caught 'em?"

"There's no one there," came chorused back.

"Then we must all hev dreamed we heard bell swing," said the churchwarden. "Let's all goo back to bed."

"It is very mysterious," said the rector.

"Very strange," said the doctor. "The ringing was of so unusual a character, too."

"Owd place is harnted," said a deep voice from the crowd, the speaker having covered his mouth with his hand, so as to disguise his voice.

"Shame!" said the rector sternly. "I did not think I had a parishioner who could give utterance to such absurd sentiments."

"Then what made bell ring?" cried another voice.

"I do not know yet," said the rector, gravely; "but there must have been some good and sufficient reason."

"Perhaps one of the bells was left sticking up," said Macey—a remark which evoked a roar of laughter.

"It is nearly two o'clock, my good friends," said the rector, quietly; "and we are doing no good discussing this little puzzle. Leave it till daylight, and let us all return home to our beds. Chakes, have the goodness to lock the door. Good-night, gentlemen. Doctor, you are coming my way; young gentlemen, please."

He marched off with the doctor, followed by his four pupils, till Distin increased his pace a little, and contrived to get so near that the doctor half turned and hesitated for Distin to come level.

"Perhaps you can explain it, my young friend," he said; and Distin joined in the conversation.

Meanwhile Gilmore and Macey were talking volubly, while Vane seemed to be listening.

"It's all gammon about haunting and ghosts and goblins," said Gilmore. "Chaps who wrote story-books invented all that kind of stuff, same as they did about knights in full armour throwing their arms round beautiful young ladies, and bounding on to their chargers and galloping off."

"Oh, come, that's true enough," said Macey.

"What!" cried Gilmore, "do you mean to tell me that you believe a fellow dressed in an ironmonger's shop, and with a big pot on his head, and a girl on his arm, could leap on a horse?"

"Yes, if he was excited," cried Macey.

"He couldn't do it, without the girl."

"But they did do it."

"No, they didn't. It's impossible. If you want the truth, read some of the proper accounts about the armour they used to wear. Why, it was so heavy that—"

"Yes, it was heavy," said Macey, musingly.

"Yes, so heavy, that when they galloped at each other with big clothes-prop things, and one of 'em was knocked off his horse, and lay flat on the ground, he couldn't get up again without his squires to help him."

"You never read that."

"Well, no, but Vane Lee did. He told me all about it. I suppose, then, you're ready to believe that the church-tower's haunted?"

"I don't say that," said Macey, "but it does seem very strange."

"Oh, yes, of course it does," said Gilmore mockingly. "Depend upon it there was a tiny chap with a cloth cap, ending in a point sitting up on the timbers among the bells with a big hammer in his hands, and he was pounding away at the bell till he saw us coming, and then off he went, hammer and all."

"I didn't say I believed that," said Macey; "but I do say it's very strange."

"Well, good-night, Syme," said the doctor, who had halted at the turning leading up to the rectory front door. "It is very curious, but I can't help thinking that it was all a prank played by some of the town lads to annoy the sexton. Well, Vane, my boy, ready for bed once more?"

Vane started out of a musing fit and said good-night to his tutor and fellow-pupils to walk back with his uncle.

"I can't puzzle it out, Vane. I can't puzzle it out," the doctor said, and the nephew shivered, for fear that the old gentleman should turn upon him suddenly and say, "Can you?"

But no such question was asked, for the doctor began to talk about different little mysteries which he had met with in his career, all of which had had matter-of-fact explanations that came in time, and then they reached the house, to find a light in the breakfast-room, where Aunt Hannah was dressed, and had prepared some coffee for them.

"Oh, I have been so anxious," she cried. "Whose place is burned?"

"No one's," said the doctor, cheerily; and then he related their experience.

"I'm very thankful it's no worse," said Aunt Hannah. "Some scamps of boys must have had a string tied to the bell, I suppose."

Poor old lady, she seemed to think of the great tenor bell in the old tower as if it were something which could easily be swung by hand.

They did not sit long; and, ill at ease, and asking himself whether he was going to turn into a disingenuous cowardly cur, Vane gladly sought his chamber once more to sit down on the edge of his bed, and ponder over his day's experience.

"It must have been through leaving out those two wheels," he muttered, "that made something go off, and start the weight running down as fast as it could. I must speak about it first thing to-morrow morning, or the people will think the place is full of ghosts. Yes, I'll tell uncle in the morning and he can do what he likes."

On coming to this resolve Vane undressed and slipped into bed once more, laid his head on the pillow, and composed himself to sleep; but no sleep came, and with his face burning he glided out of bed again, put on a few things, and then stole out of his bedroom into the passage, where he stood hesitating for a few minutes.

"No," he muttered as he drew a deep breath, "I will not be such a coward;" and, creeping along the passage, he tapped softly on the next bedroom door.

"Eh? Yes. Someone ill?" cried the doctor. "Down directly."

"No, no, uncle, don't get up," cried Vane hoarsely. "I only wanted to tell you something."

"Tell me something? Well, what is it?"

"I wanted to say that I had been trying to clean the church clock this afternoon, and I left out two of the wheels."

"What!" roared the doctor. "Hang it all, boy, I think nature must have left out two of your wheels."

Chapter Fourteen.

Macey in Difficulties.

"Well, no," said the doctor emphatically, after hearing Vane's confession at breakfast next morning. "No harm was done, so I think we will make it a private affair between us, Vane, for the rector would look upon it as high treason if he knew."

"I'll go and tell him if you say I am to, uncle."

"Then I do not say you are to, boy. By the way, do your school-fellows—I beg their pardons—your fellow-pupils know?"

"I have only told you and aunt, sir."

"Ah, well, let it rest with us, and I daresay the clockmaker will have his own theory about how the two wheels happened to be missing from the works of the clock. Only don't you go meddling with things which do not belong to your department in future or you may get into very serious trouble indeed."

The doctor gave his nephew a short sharp nod which meant dismissal, and Vane went off into the conservatory to think about his improvement of the heating apparatus.

But the excitement of the previous night and the short rest he had had interfered with his powers of thought, and the greenhouse was soon left for the laboratory, and that place for the rectory, toward which Vane moved with a peculiarly guilty feeling.

He wished now that the doctor had given him leave to speak out, for then he felt that he could have gone more comfortably to the study, instead of taking his seat imagining that the rector suspected him, or that he had been told that his pupil had been seen going into the church-tower with Chakes, and afterwards alone.

"He can't help knowing," Vane said to himself, as he neared the grounds; "and I shall have to confess after all."

But he did not, for on reaching the rectory Joseph met him with the announcement that master was so unwell that he had decided not to get up.

"Then there will be no study this morning, Joseph?"

"No, sir, not a bit, and the young gents have gone off—rabbiting, I think."

"Which way?"

"Sowner's woods, sir. I think if you was to look sharp you'd ketch 'em up."

Vane felt quite disposed to "look sharp," and overtake the others, one reason being that he hoped to find Distin more disposed to become friendly again, for he argued it was so stupid for them, working together at the same table, to be separated and to carry on a kind of feud.

It was about a couple of miles to Sowner's wood, and with the intention of taking all the short cuts, and getting there in less than half an hour, Vane hurried on, feeling the soft sweet breeze upon his cheeks and revelling in the joy of being young, well and hearty. The drowsy sensations he had felt at breakfast were rapidly passing off, and his spirits rose as he now hoped that there would be no trouble about his escapade with the clock, as he had done the right thing in explaining matters to the doctor.

It was a glorious morning, with the country round looking lovely in the warm mellow light of early autumn, and, gaze which way he would, some scene of beauty met his eye.

His course was along the main road for some distance, after which he would have to turn down one of the many narrow lanes of that part of the country—lanes which only led from one farm to another, and for the most part nearly impassable in winter from the scarcity of hard material for repairing the deep furrows made by the waggon-wheels.

But these lanes were none the less beautiful with their narrow borders of grass in the place of paths, each cut across at intervals, to act as a drain to the road, though it was seldom that they did their duty and freed the place from the pools left by the rain.

The old Romans, when they made roads, generally drew them straight. The Lincolnshire farmers made them by zigzagging along the edge of a man's land, so that there was no cause for surprise to Vane when after going along some distance beneath the overhanging oak trees he came suddenly upon his old friends the gipsies once more, with the miserable horses grazing, the van and cart drawn up close to the hedge, and the women cooking at their wood fire as of old.

They saluted him with a quiet nod, and as Vane went on, he was cognisant of the fact that they were watching him; but he would not look back till he had gone some distance. When he did the little camp was out of sight, but the two gipsy lads were standing behind as if following him. As soon as they saw that they were observed, they became deeply intent upon the blackberries and haws upon the hedges, picking away with great eagerness, but following again as Vane went on.

"I suppose they think I'm going rabbiting or fishing, and hope to get a job," thought Vane. "Well, they'll be disappointed, but they must find it out for themselves."

He was getting hot now, for the sun came down ardently, and there was no wind down in the deeply-cut lane, but he did not check his pace for he was nearing Sowner's woods now, and eager to find out the object which had brought his three fellow-pupils there.

"What are they after?" he said. "Distin wouldn't stoop to go blackberrying or nutting. He doesn't care for botany. Rabbiting! I'll be bound to say they've got a gun and are going to have a day at them.

"Well, I don't mind," he concluded after a pause, "but I don't believe old Distin would ever hit a rabbit if he tried, and—"

He stopped short, for, on turning a corner where the lane formed two sides of a square field, he saw that the two great hulking lads were slouching along after him still, and had lessened the distance between them considerably.

Vane's musings had been cut short off and turned into another track.

"Well," he said, "perhaps they may have a chance to hunt out wounded rabbits, or find dead ones, and so earn sixpence a piece."

Then, as he hurried on, taking off his hat now to wipe his steaming brow, he began to wonder who had given the pupils leave for a day's rabbit-shooting, and came to the conclusion at last that Churchwarden Rounds, who had some land out in this direction had obtained permission for them.

"Don't matter," he said; "perhaps they're not after rabbits after all."

Soon after the lane turned in another direction and, as he passed round the corner, thinking of what short cuts any one might make who did not mind forcing his way through or leaping hedges, he once more glanced back at the gipsy lads, and found that he was only being followed by one.

"The other has given it up as a bad job," he said to himself, and then, "How much farther is it? and what a wild-goose chase I am coming. They may have gone in quite another direction, for Joseph couldn't be sure."

Just then, though, an idea occurred to him— That he would easily find out where they were when they fired.

"I wonder whose gun they have borrowed?" For, knowing that they owned none, he began to run over in his mind who would be the most ready to lend a gun in the expectation of getting half a crown for its use.

"Why, he has a stick."

"Gurner's got one, because he goes after the wild geese in the winter," thought Vane; "and Bruff has that big flint-lock with the pan lined with silver. He'd lend it to anybody for a shilling and be glad of it.—Well, look at that! Why he must have made a regular short cut so as to get there. Why did he do that?"

This thought was evoked by Vane suddenly catching sight of the second gipsy lad turned into the first. In other words, the one whom he supposed to have gone back, had gone on, and Vane found himself in that narrow lane with high banks and hedges on either side and with one of these great lawless lads in front, and the other behind.

For the first time it now occurred to Vane that the place was very lonely, and that the nearest farm was quite a mile away, right beyond Sowner wood, whose trees now came in view, running up the slope of a great chalk down.

"Whatever do they mean?" thought Vane, for the gipsy lad in front had suddenly stopped, turned round, and was coming toward him.

"Why, he has a stick," said Vane to himself, and looking sharply round he saw that the other one also carried a stick.

For a moment a feeling of dread ran through him, but it passed off on the instant, and he laughed at himself for a coward.

"Pooh!" he said, "they want to beat for rabbits and that's why they have got their sticks."

In spite of himself Vane Lee wondered why the lads had not been seen to carry sticks before; then, laughing to himself as he credited them with having had them tucked up somewhere under their clothes, he walked on boldly.

"What nonsense!" he thought; "is it likely that those two fellows would be going to attack me!"

But all the same their movements were very suggestive, for there was a furtive, peculiar action on the part of the one in front, who was evidently uneasy, and kept on looking behind him and to right and left, as if in search of danger or a way of escape, and in both a peculiar hesitancy that struck Vane at once.

Under the circumstances, he too, had hard work to keep from looking about for a way of escape, should the lads mean mischief: but he did not, for fear that they should think him cowardly, and walked steadily on, with the result that the boy in front stopped short and then began slowly to retreat.

"They are up to some game," thought Vane with his heart beginning to beat hard, and a curious feeling of excitement running through him as he thought of his chances against two strong lads armed with sticks if they did dare to attack him. But again he cast aside the thought as being too absurd, and strode boldly on.

"These are not the days for footpads and highwaymen," he said to himself, and just then the lad in front gave vent to a peculiar whistle, made a rush up the bank on his left, looked sharply round, ducked down, whistled again, and disappeared.

"I'd give something to know what game they call this," said Vane to himself, as he watched the spot where the lad had disappeared; and then he turned sharply round to question the one who was following him, but, to his astonishment, he found that the lane behind him was vacant.

Vane paused for a few moments and then made a dash forward till he reached the trampled grass and ferns where the first boy had scrambled up the bank, climbed to the top, and stood looking round for him. But he was gone, and there was not much chance for anyone not gifted with the tracking power of an Indian to follow the fugitive through the rough tangle of scrub oak, ferns, brambles and gorse which spread away right to the borders of the wood.

Just as he was standing on the highest part of the bank looking sharply round, he heard a shout. Then—

"Weathercock, ahoy! Coo-ee!"

He looked in the direction, fully expecting to see Macey, whose voice he recognised, but for some minutes he was invisible. Then he saw the tall ferns moving, and directly after he caught sight of his fellow-pupil's round face, and then of his arms waving, as he literally waded through the thick growth.

Vane gave an answering shout, and went to meet him, trying the while to arrive at a settlement of the gipsy lads' conduct, and feeling bound to come to the conclusion that they had meant mischief; but heard Macey coming, perhaps the others, for he argued that they could not be very far away.

Vane laughed to himself, as he advanced slowly, for he knew the part he was in well enough, and it amused him as he fought his way on, to think of the struggles Macey, a London boy, was having to get through the tangle of briar and furze. For he had often spent an hour in the place with the doctor, collecting buckthorn and coral-moss, curious lichens, sphagnum, and the round, and long-leaved sundews, or butterwort: for all these plants abounded here, with the bramble and bracken. There were plenty of other bog plants, too, in the little pools and patches of water, while the dry, gravelly and sandy mounds here and there were well known to him as the habitat of the long-legged parasol mushrooms, whose edible qualities the doctor had taught him in their walks.

"Poor old Macey!" he said, as he leaped over or parted the great thorny strands of the brambles laden with their luscious fruit which grew here in abundance, and then he stopped short and laughed, for a yell came from his fellow-pupil, who had also stopped.

"Come on," cried Vane.

"Can't! I'm caught by ten million thorns. Oh, I say, do come and help a fellow out."

Vane backed a little way, and selecting an easier path, soon reached the spot where Macey was standing with his head and shoulders only visible.

"Why didn't you pick your way?" he cried.

"Couldn't," said Macey dolefully; "the thorns wouldn't let me. I say, do come."

"All right," said Vane, confidently, but the task was none too easy, for Macey had floundered into the densest patch of thorny growth anywhere near, and the slightest movement meant a sharp prick from blackberry, rose, or furze.

"Whatever made you try to cross this bit?" said Vane, who had taken out his knife to divide some of the strands.

"I was trying to find the lane. Haven't seen one about anywhere, have you?"

"Why, of course I have," said Vane, laughing at his friend's doleful plight. "It's close by."

"I began to think somebody had taken it away. Oh! Ah! I say—do mind; you're tearing my flesh."

"But I must cut you out. Now then, lift that leg and put your foot on this bramble."

"It's all very fine to talk, but I shall be in rags when I do get out."

"That's better: now the other. There, now, put your hand on my shoulder and give a jump."

"I daren't."

"Nonsense—why?"

"I should leave half my toggery behind."

"You wouldn't: come along. Take my hands."

Macey took hold of his companion's hands, there was a bit of a struggle, and he stood bemoaning his injuries; which consisted of pricks and scratches, and a number of thorns buried deeply beneath his clothes.

"Nice place this is," he said dolefully.

"Lovely place for botanists," said Vane, merrily.

"Then I'm thankful I'm not a botanist."

"Where are the others?" asked Vane.

"I don't know. Distin wanted to lie down in the shade as soon as we reached the edge of the wood, and Gil wouldn't leave him, out of civility."

"Then you didn't come rabbit-shooting?"

"Rabbit-grandmothering! We only came for a walk, and of course I didn't want to sit down and listen to Distin run down England and puff the West Indies, so I wandered off into the wood and lost myself."

"What, there too?"

"Yes, and spent my time thinking about you."

"What! Because you wanted me to act as guide?"

"No, I didn't: it was because I got into a part where the oak trees and fir trees were open, and there was plenty of grass. And there I kept on finding no end of toadstools such as you delight in devouring."

"Ah!" exclaimed Vane eagerly. "Where was it?"

"Oh, you couldn't find the place again. I couldn't, but there were such big ones; and what do you think I said?"

"How should I know?" said Vane, trampling down the brambles, so as to make the way easier for his companion.

"I said I wish the nasty pig was here, and he could feast for a month."

"Thank you," said Vane. "I don't care. I can only pity ignorant people. But whereabouts did you leave Gil and Distin?"

"I don't know, I tell you. Under an oak tree."

"Yes, but which?"

"Oh, somewhere. I had a pretty job to find my way out, and I didn't till I had picked out a great beech tree to sleep in to-night, and began thinking of collecting acorns for food."

"Why didn't you shout?"

"I did, till I was so hoarse I got down to a whisper. Oh, I say, why did you let that bit of furze fly back?"

"Couldn't help it."

"I'm getting sick of Greythorpe. No police to ask your way, no gas lamps, no cabs."

"None at all. It's a glorious place, isn't it, Aleck?"

"Well, I suppose it is when you know your way, and are not being pricked with thorns."

"Ah, you're getting better," cried Vane. "What shall we do—go back alone, or try and find them?"

"Go back, of course. I'm not going through all that again to-day to find old Distin, and hear him sneer about you. He's always going on. Says Syme has no business to have you at the rectory to mix with gentlemen."

"Oh, he says that, does he?"

"Yes, and I told him you were more of a gentleman than he was, and he gave me a back-handed crack over the mouth."

"And what did you do—hit him back?"

"Not with my fist. With my tongue. Called him a nigger. That hits him hardest, for he's always fancying people think there's black blood in his veins, though, of course, there isn't, and it wouldn't matter if there were, if he was a good fellow. Let's get on. Where's the lane?"

"Just down there," said Vane; and they reached it directly after, but there were no signs of the gipsies, and Vane said nothing about them then, feeling that he must have been mistaken about their intentions, which could only have been to beg.

Chapter Fifteen.

Two Busy Days.

It is curious to study the different things which please boys.

Anything less likely to form a fortnight's amusement for a lad than the iron-pipes, crooks, bends, elbows, syphons and boiler delivered by waggon from the nearest railway, it would be hard to conceive. But to Vane they were a source of endless delight, and it thoroughly puzzled him to find Bruff, the gardener, muttering and grumbling about their weight.

"It arn't gardener's work, sir, that's why I grumbled," said the man. "My work's flowers and vegetables and sech. I arn't used to such jobs as that."

"Why, what difference does it make?" cried Vane.

"A deal, sir. Don't seem respectful to a man whose dooty's flowers and vegetables and sech, to set him hauling and heaving a lot o' iron-pipes just got down for your pranks."

"Well, of all the ungrateful, grumbling fellows!" cried Vane. "Isn't it to save you from coming up here on cold, frosty nights to stoke the fire?"

"Nay, bud it wean't," said Bruff, with a grin. "Look here, Mester Vane, I've sin too many of your contraptions not to know better. You're going to have the greenhouse pulled all to pieces, and the wall half knocked down to try your bits o' tricks, and less than a month they'll all have to be pulled out again, and a plain, good, old English flue 'll have to be put up as ought to be done now."

"You're a stubborn old stick-in-the-way, Bruff. Why, if you could have done as you liked, there would never have been any railway down here. Mind! don't break that. Cast-iron's brittle."

"Brittle! It's everything as is bad, sir. But you're right, theere. Niver a bit o' railway would I hev hed. Coach and waggon was good enew for my feyther, and it was good enew for me."

"Come along," said Vane; "let's get all in their places, as they'll be in the greenhouse."

"Ay, we'll get 'em in, I suppose," grumbled the gardener, "bud you mark my words, Mester Vane; them water pipes 'll nivver get hot, and, when they do, they'll send out a nasty, pysonous steam as'll kill ivery plahnt in the greenhouse. Now, you see?"

"Grumble away," said Vane; and Bruff did grumble. He found fault at being taken away from his work to help in Master Vane's whims, murmured at having to help move the boiler, and sat down afterwards, declaring that he had hurt his back, and could do no more that day; whereupon Vane, who was much concerned, was about to fetch the doctor, but Bruff suddenly felt a little better, and gradually came round.

Matters had gone as far as this when voices were heard in the avenue, and Gilmore and Macey made their appearance.

Vane's first movement was to run and get his jacket to put on; but he stopped himself, and stood fast.

"I don't mind their seeing me," he muttered. But he did, and winced as the joking began, Gilmore taking a high tone, and asking Vane for an estimate for fitting up a vinery for him.

Gilmore and Macey both saw that their jokes gave annoyance; and, to turn them off, offered to help, Macey immediately taking off his coat, hanging it over the greenhouse door, and seizing the end of a pipe to move it where it was not wanted.

"Don't be jealous, Bruff," he cried, as he saw the gardener stare. "I'll leave a little bit of work for you to do."

Bruff grinned and scratched his head.

"Oh, if it comes to that, Mester Macey," he said, "you come here any time, and I'll give you some sensible work to do, diggin' or sweeping."

"I say," whispered Vane, the next minute, when he had contrived to get Macey alone, "what made you take off your coat?"

"So as to help."

"No, it wasn't, or not alone for that. You were thinking about what Distin said about my not being fit to associate with gentlemen."

Macey flushed a little, like a girl.

"Nonsense!" he said.

"Now, confess. The truth!"

"Oh, I don't know. Well, perhaps. Here, come along, or we shan't get done to-day."

They did not get done that day; in fact they had hardly begun when it was time to leave off; and though there was plenty of fun and joking and banging together of pieces of iron-pipe and noise which brought out the doctor to see, and Aunt Hannah in a state of nervousness to make sure that nobody was hurt, Vane did not enjoy his work, for he could not help glancing at his dirty hands, and asking himself whether Distin was not right. And at these times his fellow-pupil's fastidiously clean hands and unruffled, prim and dandified aspect came before him, making him feel resolved to be more particular as to the character of the hobbies he rode.

At parting, when Gilmore and Macey were taking leave after a visit to Vane's room and a plenteous application of soap and nail-brushes, in spite of their declaration that they had had a jolly day, their leader—their foreman of the works, as Gilmore called him—had quite made up his mind that he would let the bricklayer and blacksmith finish the job. In consequence of his resolve, he was up by six o'clock next morning when the men came, meaning to superintend, but he soon lapsed, and was as busy as either of them.

Vane fully expected a severe encounter with Martha apropos of her kitchen-fire being left unlit, and the litter of brick and mortar rubbish made by the bricklayer; but to his surprise the cook did not come into the kitchen, and during breakfast Vane asked why this was.

"Aunt's diplomancy," said the doctor, merrily.

"No, no, my dear. Your uncle's," cried Aunt Hannah.

"Ah, well, halves," cried the doctor. "Martha wanted a holiday to visit her friends, and she started last night for two days. Can you get the boiler set and all right for Mrs Bruff to clean up before Martha comes back?"

"You must, my dear, really," cried Aunt Hannah. "You must."

"Oh, very well, aunt, if the bricklayer will only work well, it shall be done."

"Thank you, my dear, for really I should not dare to meet Martha if everything were not ready; and pray, pray, my dear, see that nothing is done to interfere with her kitchen-fire."

The doctor laughed. Vane promised, and forgetful entirely of appearances he deputed his uncle to go to the rectory and excuse him for two days, and worked like a slave. The result was that not only was the boiler set in the wall behind the kitchen-fire, and all put perfectly straight before the next night, but the iron-pipes, elbows, and syphons were joined together with their india-rubber rings, and supported on brick piers, the smith having screwed in a couple of taps for turning off the communication in hot weather, and the fitting of the boiler; and pipes through the little iron cistern at the highest point completing the work.

"Ought by rights, sir, to stand for a few days for the mortar to set," said the bricklayer on leaving; and this opinion being conveyed to Aunt Hannah, she undertook that Martha, should make shift in the back kitchen for a day or two—just as they had during her absence.

"She will not like it, my dear," said Aunt Hannah, "but as there is no muddle to clean up, and all looks right, I don't mind making her do that."

"Real tyrant of the household, Vane," said the doctor. "Don't you ever start housekeeping and have a cook."

Everything had been finished in such excellent time, consequent upon certain bribery and corruption in the shape of half-crowns, that early in the evening, Vane, free from all workmanlike traces, was able to point triumphantly to the neat appearance of the job, and explain the working of the supply cistern, and of the stop-cocks between the boiler and the pipes to his aunt and uncle.

"I thought there ought only to be one tap," said Vane; "but they both declared that there ought to be one to each pipe, so as to stop the circulation; and as it only cost a few shillings more I didn't stop the smith from putting it in."

"Humph!" said the doctor as Vane turned first one and then the other tap on and off, "seems to work nice and easy."

"And it does look very much neater than all those bricks," said Aunt Hannah. "But I must say one thing, my dear, though I don't like to damp your project, it does smell very nasty indeed."

"Oh, aunt, dear," cried Vane merrily; "that's nothing: only the Brunswick black with which they have painted the pipes. That smell will all go off when it's hard and dry. That wants to dry slowly, too, so you'll be sure and tell Martha about not lighting the fire."

"Oh, yes, my dear, I'll see to that."

"Then now I shall go up to the rectory and tell them I'm coming to lessons in the morning, and—" he hesitated—"I think I shall give up doing rough jobs for the future."

"Indeed," said the doctor with a humorous twinkle in his eye; "wouldn't you like to take the church clock to pieces, and clean it and set it going again?"

Vane turned sharply on his uncle with an appealing look.

"Now really, my dear, you shouldn't," cried Aunt Hannah. "Don't, don't, pray, set the boy thinking about doing any more such dirty work."

"Dirty work? quite an artist's job. I only mentioned it because Mr Syme told me that a man would be over from Lincoln to-morrow to see to the clock. Quite time it was done."

Vane hurried off to escape his uncle's banter, and was soon after in the lane leading up to the rectory, where, as luck had it, he saw Distin walking slowly on in front, and, acting on the impulse of the moment, he ran after him.

"Evening," he cried.

Distin turned his head slowly, and looked him coldly in the face.

"I beg your pardon," he drawled, "were you speaking to me?"

"Oh, hang it, Distie, yes," cried Vane. "What's the good of us two being out. Shake hands. I'm sorry if I said anything to offend you and hope you'll forgive me if there is anything to forgive."

Distin stared at him haughtily.

"Really," he said in rather a drawling manner, "I am at a loss to understand what you mean by addressing me like this, sir."

"Oh, I say, Distie, don't take that queer tone to a fellow," cried Vane, who could not help feeling nettled. "Here, shake hands—there's a good fellow."

He held out his own once more for the other to take, but Distin ignored it, and half turning away he said:—

"Have the goodness to address me next time when I have spoken to you. I came down here to read with Mr Syme, and I shall go on doing so, but I presume it is open to me to choose whom I please for my associates, and I shall select gentlemen."

"Well," said Vane, shortly, "my father was a gentleman; and do you mean to insinuate that my uncle and aunt are not a gentleman and lady?"

"I refuse to discuss matters with every working-class sort of boy I am forced to encounter," said Distin, haughtily. "Have the goodness to keep yourself to yourself, and to associate with people of your own class. Good-evening."

"Have the goodness to associate with people of your own class!" said Vane, unconsciously repeating his fellow-pupil's words. "I don't like fighting, but, oh, how he did make my fingers itch to give him one good solid punch in the head."

Vane stood looking at the retiring figure thoroughly nettled now.

"Ugh!" he exclaimed, "what a nasty mean temper to have. It isn't manly. It's like a spiteful boarding-school girl. Well, I'm not going down on my knees to him. I can get on without Distin if he can get on without me. But it is so petty and mean to go on about one liking to do a bit of mechanical work. One can read classics and stick to one's mathematics all the same, and if I can't write a better paper than he can it's a queer thing."

Vane turned to go back to the Little Manor, for, in spite of his defiant, careless way of treating Distin's words, he could not help feeling too much stung to care about continuing his journey to the rectory, for the feeling would come to the front that his fellow-pupil had some excuse for what he had said.

"I suppose I did look like a blacksmith's or bricklayer's boy to-day," he said to himself. "But if I did, what business is it of his? There's nothing disgraceful in it, or uncle would soon stop me. And, besides, Gilmore and Macey don't seem to mind, and their families are far higher than Distin's. There: I don't care. I was going to give up all kind of work that dirties one's hands, but now I will not, just out of spite. Dirty work, indeed! I'll swear I never looked half so dirty over my carpentering and turning and scheming as I've seen him look after a game at football on a wet day."

But all the same, the evening at the Little Manor seemed to be a very dull one; and when, quite late, the carrier's cart stopped at the gate, and cook got down, Vane felt no interest in knowing what she would say about the alterations in her kitchen, nor in knowing whether Aunt Hannah had spoken to her about not lighting the kitchen-fire.

But he revived a little after his supper, and was eager to take a candle and go out of the hall-door and along the gravel-path, shading the light, on his way to the greenhouse, where he had a good quiet inspection of his work, and was delighted to find that the india-rubber joints hardly leaked in the least, and no more than would be cured by the swelling of the caoutchouc, as soon as the pipes were made hot, and the rings began to fit more tightly, by filling up the uneven places in the rough iron.

Everything looked delightfully fresh and perfect; the pipes glistened of an ebon blackness; the two brass taps shone new and smooth; and the various plants and flowers exhaled their scent and began to master that of the Brunswick black.

Soon after satisfying himself that all was right, he made his way up to his bedroom, so thoroughly tired out by the bodily exertion of the two past days that he dropped off at once into a heavy, dreamless sleep, which was brought to an end about eight o'clock the next morning by a sensation of his having been seized by a pair of giant hands and thrown suddenly and heavily upon the bedroom floor.

Chapter Sixteen.

A Lesson on Steam.

Half-stunned, confused, and wondering, Vane Lee awoke to the fact that he really was lying upon the carpet at the side of his bed, and for a few moments, he felt that he must have fallen out; but, in an indistinct fashion, he began to realise that he had heard a tremendous noise in his sleep, and started so violently that he had rather thrown himself than fallen out of bed, while to prove to him that there was something terribly wrong, there were loud shrieks from the lower part of the house, and from the passage came his uncle's voice.

"Vane, my lad, quick! jump up!"

"It's an earthquake," panted Vane, as he hurried on his clothes, listening the while with fear and trembling, to the screams which still rose at intervals from below.

"That's Eliza's voice," he thought, and directly after as he waited, full of excitement, for the next shock, and the crumbling down of the house, "That's cook."

Almost at the same moment a peculiar odour came creeping in beneath and round the door; and Vane, as he forced a reluctant button through the corresponding hole with fumbling fingers took a long sniff.

"'Tisn't an earthquake," he thought; "that's gunpowder!"

The next moment, after trying to think of what gunpowder there was on the premises, and unable to recall any, he was for attributing the explosion, for such he felt it to be, to some of the chemicals in the laboratory.

That idea he quickly dismissed, for the screams were from the kitchen, and he was coming round to the earthquake theory again, when a thought flashed through his brain, and he cried aloud in triumph, just as the doctor threw open his door:—

"It is gunpowder."

"Smells like it, boy," cried the doctor, excitedly, "but I had none. Had you?"

"No, uncle," cried Vane, as a fresh burst of screaming, arose; "but it's cook. She has been blowing up the copper hole to make the fire draw."

"Come along! That's it!" cried the doctor. "Stupid woman! I hope she is not much burned."

This all took place as they were hurrying down into the hall, where the odour was stifling now: that dank, offensive, hydrogenous smell which is pretty familiar to most people, and as they hurried on to the kitchen from which the cries for help came more faintly now, they entered upon a dimly-seen chaos of bricks, mortar, broken crockery, and upset kitchen furniture.

"A pound of powder at least," cried the doctor, who then began to sneeze violently, the place being full of steam, and dust caused by the ceiling having been pretty well stripped of plaster. "Here, cook—Eliza—where are you?"

"Oh, master, master, master!"

"Help!—help!—help!"

Two wild appeals for aid from the back kitchen, where the copper was set, and into which uncle and nephew hurried, expecting to find the two maids half buried in *débris*. But, to the surprise of both, that office was quite unharmed, and cook was seated in a big Windsor chair, sobbing hysterically, while Eliza was on the floor, screaming faintly with her apron held over her face.

"How could you be so foolish!—how much powder?—where did you get it?—where are you hurt?" rattled out the doctor breathlessly.

"Anything the matter, cook?" said Bruff, coming to the door.

"Matter? Yes," cried the doctor, growing cool again. "Here, help me lift Eliza into a chair."

"No, no, don't touch me; I shall fall to pieces," sobbed the maid wildly.

"Nonsense! Here, let me see where you are hurt," continued the doctor, as Eliza was lifted carefully.

"Oh, Master Vane—oh, Master Vane! Is it the end of the world?" groaned cook, as the lad took one of her hands, and asked her where she was injured.

"No, no," cried Vane. "Tell me where you are harmed."

"I don't know—I don't know—I don't know," moaned the trembling woman, beginning in a very high tone and ending very low. "It's all over—It's all over now."

"Give her water," said the doctor. "She's hysterical. Here, cook," he cried sternly, "how came you to bring powder into the house?"

"I don't know—I don't know—I don't know," moaned the trembling woman. "Oh, master, give me something. Don't let me die just yet."

"Die! nonsense!" cried the doctor. "Be quiet, Eliza. Hang it, women, I can't do anything if you cry out like this. Wherever are you hurt? You, Eliza, speak."

His firm way had its effect; and as Bruff and Vane stood looking on, the maid faltered:—

"I was a-doing the breakfast-room, sir, when it went off; and, soon as I heered cook scream, I tried to get to her, but had to go round by the back."

"Did you know she was going to blow up the copper hole with gunpowder?"

"No, sir. Last time I see her, she was lighting the kitchen-fire."

"What!" yelled Vane.

"Yes, sir," cried cook, sitting up suddenly, and speaking indignantly: "and I won't stop another day in a house where such games is allowed. I'd got a good fire by half-past six, and was busy in the back kitchen when it went off. Me get powder to blow up copper holes? I scorn the very idee of it, sir. It's that master Vane put powder among the coals to play me a trick."

"I didn't," cried Vane.

"Don't say that, sir," interposed Bruff, "why, I see the greenhouse chockfull o' smoke as I come by."

Vane had turned quite cold, and was staring at his uncle, while his uncle with his face full of chagrin and perplexity was staring at him.

"You've done it this time, my boy," said the doctor, sadly.

"Is anybody killed?—is anybody killed?" cried Aunt Hannah from the hall. "I can't come through the kitchen. My dear Vane! oh, do speak."

"No one hurt," shouted the doctor. "Come, Vane."

"Scarcely a thing in the place had escaped damage."

He led the way through the shattered kitchen, which was a perfect wreck; but before he could reach the hall, Vane had passed him.

"Aunt! Aunt!" he cried; "did you tell cook not to light the kitchen-fire?"

"Oh, dear me!" cried Aunt Hannah; "what a head I have. I meant to, but I quite forgot."

There was silence in the hall for a few moments, only broken by a sob or two from the back kitchen. Then Aunt Hannah spoke again.

"Oh, I am so sorry, my dear. But is anybody very badly hurt?"

"Yes," said the doctor, dryly. "Vane is—very."

"My dear, my dear! Where?" cried Aunt Hannah, catching the lad by the arm.

"Only in his *amour propre*" said the doctor, and Vane ran out of the hall and through the front door to get round to the greenhouse, but as he opened the door of the glass building the doctor overtook him, and they entered in silence, each looking round eagerly for the mischief done.

Here it was not serious: some panes of glass were broken, and two or three pipes nearest to the wall were blown out of their places; but there was the cause of all mischief, the two taps in the small tubes which connected the flow and return pipes were turned off, with the consequence, that there was no escape for the steam, and the closed boiler had of course exploded as soon as sufficient steam had generated, with the consequences seen.

"Pretty engineer you are, sir," cried the doctor, "to have both those stop-cocks turned."

"There ought not to have been a second one, uncle," said Vane dolefully. "I let them get the better of me yesterday, and put in the second. If it had not been for that, one pipe would have been always open, and there could have been no explosion."

"Humph! I see," said the doctor.

"But I ought to have left them turned on, and I should have done so, only I did not think that there was going to be any fire this morning."

"Here, come back, and let's see the extent of the mischief in the kitchen. That piece of new wall is blown out, you see."

He pointed to the loose bricks and mortar thrust out into quite a bow; and then they walked sadly back into the house, where cook's voice could be heard scolding volubly, mingled with Aunt Hannah's milder tones, though the latter could hardly be heard as they entered the devastated kitchen, from which the smoke and dust had now pretty well disappeared, making the damage plain to see. And very plain it was: the new boiler stood in front of the grate, with a hole ripped in one side, the wrought iron being forced out by the power of the steam, just as if it had been composed of paper; the kitchen range was broken, and the crockery on the dresser exactly opposite to the fireplace looked as if it had been swept from the shelves and smashed upon the floor. Chairs were overturned; the table was lying upon its side; tins, coppers, graters, spoons and ladles were here, there, and everywhere. The clock had stopped, and the culinary implements that ornamented the kitchen chimney-piece had evidently flown up to the ceiling. In short, scarcely a thing in the place had escaped some damage, while dust and fragments of plaster covered every object, and the only witness of the explosion, the cat, which had somehow been sheltered and escaped unhurt, was standing on the top of the cupboard, with its eyes glowering and its tail standing straight up, feathered out like a plume.

"Oh, my dear, my dear, what a scene!" cried Aunt Hannah, piteously. "Vane must never perform any more experiments here."

She had just come to the back kitchen-door, and was looking in.

"Oh, Aunt! Aunt!" cried Vane.

"All very well to blame the poor boy," said the doctor with mock severity. "It was your doing entirely."

"Mine, Thomas!" faltered Aunt Hannah.

"Of course it was. You were told not to have the kitchen-fire lit."

"Yes—yes," wailed Aunt Hannah; "and I forgot it."

"It was not only that, Aunt, dear," said Vane, going to her side, and taking her hand. "It was my unlucky experiment was the principal cause."

"Not another day, Eliza," came from the back kitchen. "No, no, not if they went down on their bended knees and begged me to stop."

"What, amongst all this broken crockery?" cried the doctor. "Hold your tongue, you stupid woman, and send Bruff to ask his wife to come and help clear up all this mess."

Cook, invisible in the back, uttered a defiant snort.

"Ah!" shouted the doctor. "Am I master here. See to a fire there at once, and I should like one of those delicious omelettes for my breakfast, cook. Let's have breakfast as soon as you can. There, no more words. Let's be very thankful that you were neither of you badly scalded. You heard what I said, Bruff?"

"Yes, sir, of course."

"Then go and fetch your wife directly. Cook will give you some breakfast here."

Bruff scurried off, and Eliza entered the kitchen, wiping her eyes.

"Bit of a fright for you, eh, my girl?" said the doctor, taking her hand, and feeling her pulse. "Well done! Brave little woman. You are as calm as can be again. You're not going to run away at a moment's notice."

"Oh, no, sir," cried Eliza eagerly.

"Nor cook neither," said the doctor aloud. "She's too fond of us to go when we are in such a state as this."

There was a sniff now from the back kitchen and the doctor gave Vane a humorous look, as much as to say, "I can manage cook better than your aunt."

"There, my dear," he said, "it's of no use for you to cry over spilt milk. Better milk the cow again and be more careful. See what is broken by and by, and then come to me for a cheque. Vane, my boy, send a letter up at once for another boiler."

"But surely, dear—" began Aunt Hannah.

"I am not about to have the boiler set there again? Indeed I am. Vane is not going to be beaten because we have had an accident through trusting others to do what we ought to have done for ourselves. There, come and let's finish dressing; and cook!"

"Yes, sir," came very mildly from the back kitchen, in company with the crackling of freshly-lit wood.

"You'll hurry the breakfast all you can."

"Yes, sir."

"Don't feel any the worse now, do you?"

"No, sir, only a little ketchy about the throat."

"Oh, I'll prescribe for that."

"Thank you, sir, but it will be better directly," said cook hastily.

"After you've taken my dose, make yourself a good strong cup of tea. Come along, my dear. Now, Vane, your face wants washing horribly, my boy. Hannah, my dear, you understand now the tremendous force of steam."

"Yes, my dear," said Aunt Hannah, sorrowfully. "I do indeed."

"And if ever in the future you see anyone sitting upon the safety valve to get up speed, don't hesitate for a moment, go and knock him off."

"My dear Thomas," said Aunt Hannah, dolefully, "this is no subject for mirth."

"Eh? Isn't it? I think it is. Why, some of us might have been scalded to death, and we have all escaped. Don't you call that a cause for rejoicing? What do you say, Vane?"

"I say, sir, that I shall never forgive myself," replied the lad sadly.

"Not your place, Weathercock, but mine, and your aunt's. I'll forgive you freely, and as for your aunt, she can't help it because she was partly to blame."

Chapter Seventeen.

Anxieties.

"Hallo, boiler-burster," cried Gilmore, next time they met, while Macey ran into a corner of the study to turn his face to the wall and keep on exploding with laughter, "when are you going to do our conservatory up here?"

"Oh, I say, don't chaff me," cried Vane, "I have felt so vexed about it all."

"Distie has been quite ill ever since with delight at your misfortune. It has turned him regularly bilious."

"Said it was a pity you weren't blown up, too," cried Macey.

"Bah! don't tell ugly tales," said Gilmore.

"I wish I could feel that he did not," thought Vane, who had a weakness for being good friends with everybody he knew.

He had to encounter plenty of joking about the explosion, and for some time after, Bruff used to annoy him by turning away when they met, and shaking his shoulders as if convulsed with mirth, but after a sharp encounter with Vane, when he had ventured to say he knew how it would be, he kept silence, and later on he was very silent indeed.

For the new boiler came down, and was set without any objection being made by cook, who was for some time, however, very reluctant to go near the thing for fear it should go off; but familiarity bred contempt, and she grew used to it as it did not go off, and to Bruff's great disgust it acted splendidly, heating the greenhouse in a way beyond praise, and with scarcely any trouble, and an enormous saving of fuel.

Vane was so busy over the hot-water apparatus, and had so much to think about with regard to the damages in connection with the explosion, that he had forgotten all about the adventure in the lane just prior to meeting Macey, till one day, when out botanising with the doctor, they came through that very lane again, and in their sheltered corner, there were the gipsies, looking as if they had never stirred for weeks. There, too, were the women cooking by the fire, and the horses and ponies grazing on the strips of grass by the roadside.

But closer examination would have proved that the horses which drew cart and van were different, and several of the drove of loose ones had been sold or changed away.

There, too, were the boys whose duty it was to mind the horses slouching about the lane, and their dark eyes glistened as the doctor and Vane came along.

"Dear me!" said the doctor suddenly.

"What, uncle?"

"I thought I saw someone hurry away through the furze bushes as we came up, as if to avoid being seen. Your friend Macey I think."

"Couldn't have been, uncle, or he would have stopped."

"I was mistaken perhaps.—A singular people these, so wedded to their restless life. I should like to trace them back and find out their origin. It would be a curious experience to stay with them for a year or two," continued the doctor, after a long silence, "and so find out exactly how they live. I'm afraid that they do a little stealing at times when opportunity serves. Fruit, poultry, vegetables, any little thing they can snap up easily. Then, too, they have a great knowledge of herbs and wild vegetables, with which, no doubt, they supplement their scanty fare. Like to join them for a bit, Vane?"

"Oh, no," said the boy laughing. "I don't think I should care for that. Too fond of a comfortable bed, uncle, and a chair and table for my meals."

"If report says true, their meals are not bad," continued the doctor. "Their women are most clever at marketing and contrive to buy very cheaply of the butchers, and they are admirable cooks. They do not starve themselves."

"Think there's any truth about the way they cook fowls or pheasants, uncle?"

"What, covering them all over with clay, and then baking them in the hot embers of a wood fire? Not a doubt about it, boy. They serve squirrels and hedgehogs in the same way, even a goose at times. When they think it is done, the clay is burned into earthenware. Then a deft blow with a stick or stone cracks the burnt clay and the bird or animal is turned out hot and juicy, the feathers or bristles remaining in the clay."

"Don't think I could manage hedgehog or squirrel, uncle."

"I should not select them for diet. They are both carnivorous, and the squirrel, in addition, has its peculiar odorous gland like the pole-cat tribe."

"But a squirrel isn't carnivorous, uncle," said Vane, "he eats nuts and fruit."

"And young birds, too, sometimes, my boy. Flesh-eating things are not particularly in favour for one's diet. Even the American backwoodsman who was forced to live on crows did not seem very favourably impressed. You remember?"

"No, uncle; it's new to me."

"He was so short of food, winter-game being scarce, that he had to shoot and eat crows. Someone asked him afterwards whether they were nice, and he replied that he 'didn't kinder hanker arter 'em.'"

"Well, I don't 'kinder hanker arter' squirrel," said Vane, merrily, "and I don't 'kinder hanker arter' being a gipsy king ha—ha—as the old song says. You'll have to make me an engineer, uncle."

"Steam engineer, boy?" said the doctor, smiling.

"Oh, anything, as long as one has to be contriving something new. Couldn't apprentice me to an inventor, could you?"

"To Mr Deering, for instance?"

Vane shook his head.

"I don't know," he said, dubiously. "I liked— You don't mind my speaking out, uncle?"

"No, boy, speak out," said the doctor, looking at him curiously.

"I was going to say that I liked Mr Deering for some things. He was so quick and clever, but—"

"You didn't like him for other things?"

Vane nodded, and the doctor looked care-worn and uneasy; his voice sounded a little husky, too, as he said sharply:—

"Oh, he is a very straightforward, honourable man. We were at school together, and I could trust Deering to any extent. But he has been very unfortunate in many ways, and I'm afraid has wasted a great deal of his life over unfruitful experiments with the result that he is still poor."

"But anyone must have some failures, uncle. All schemes cannot be successful."

"True, but there is such a large proportion of disappointment that I should say an inventor is an unhappy man."

"Not if he makes one great hit," cried Vane warmly. "Oh, I should like to invent something that would do a vast deal of good, and set everyone talking about it. Why, it would mean a great fortune."

"And when you had made your great fortune, what then?"

"Well, I should be a rich man, and I could make you and aunt happy."

"I don't know that, Vane," said the doctor, laying his hand upon the lad's shoulder. "I saved a pleasant little competence out of my hard professional life, and it has been enough to keep us in this pleasant place, and bring up and educate you. I am quite convinced that if I had ten times as much I should be no happier, and really, my boy, I don't think I should like to see you a rich man."

"Uncle!"

"I mean it, Vane. There, dabble in your little schemes for a bit, and you shall either go to college or to some big civil engineer as a pupil, but you must recollect the great poet's words."

"What are they, uncle?" said Vane, in a disappointed tone.

> "'There is a divinity that shapes our ends,
> Rough-hew them how we may.'

"Now let's have a little more botany. What's that?"

"Orange peziza," said Vane, pouncing upon a little fungus cup; and this led the doctor into a dissertation on the beauty of these plants, especially of those which required a powerful magnifying glass to see their structure.

Farther on they entered a patch of fir-wood where a little search rewarded them with two or three dozen specimens of the orange milk mushroom, a kind so agreeable to the palate that the botanists have dubbed it delicious.

"Easy enough to tell, Vane," said the doctor, as he carefully removed every scrap of dirt and grass from the root end of the stem, and carefully laid the neatly-shaped dingy-green round-table shaped fungi in his basket upon some moss. "It is not every edible fungus that proves its safety by invariably growing among fir trees and displaying this thick rich red juice like melted vermilion sealing-wax."

"And when we get them home, Martha will declare that they are rank poison," said Vane.

"And all because from childhood she has been taught that toadstools are poison. Some are, of course, boy, so are some wild fruits, but it would be rather a deprivation for us if we were to decline to eat every kind of fruit but one."

"I should think it would," cried Vane, "or two."

"And yet, that is what people have for long years done in England. Folks abroad are wiser. There, it's time we went back."

Vane was very silent on his homeward way, for the doctor had damped him considerably, and the bright career which he had pictured for himself as an inventor was beginning to be shrouded in clouds.

"Civil engineer means a man who surveys and measures land for roads and railways, and makes bridges," said Vane to himself. "I don't think I should like that. Rather go to a balloon manufactory and—"

He stopped to think of the subject which the word balloon brought up, and at last said to himself:

"Oh, if I could only invent the way how to fly."

"The boy has too much gas in his head," the doctor said to himself, as they reached home; "and he must be checked, but somehow he has spoiled my walk."

He threw himself into an easy chair after placing his basket on the table, and into which Aunt Hannah peeped as Vane went up to his room.

"Botanical specimens, my dear," she said.

"Yes, for the cook," said the doctor dreamily.

"Oh, my dear, you should not bring them home. You know how Martha dislikes trying experiments. My dear, what is the matter?"

"Oh, nothing—nothing, only Vane was talking to me, and it set me thinking whether I have done right in trusting Deering as I have."

Aunt Hannah looked as troubled as the doctor now, and sighed and shook her head.

"No," cried the doctor firmly, "I will not doubt him. He is a gentleman, and as honest as the day."

"Yes," said Aunt Hannah quietly, "but the most honourable people are not exempt from misfortune."

"My dear Hannah," cried the doctor, "don't talk like that. Why it would ruin Vane's prospects if anything went wrong."

"And ours too," said Aunt Hannah sadly, just as Vane was still thinking of balloons.

Chapter Eighteen.

A Tell-Tale Shadow.

"What's going on here?" said Vane to himself, as he was walking up the town, and then, the colour rose to his cheeks, and he looked sharply round to see if he was observed.

But Greythorpe town street was as empty as usual. There was Grader's cat in the window, a dog asleep on a step, and a few chickens picking about in front of the carrier's, while the only sounds were the clink, clink of the blacksmith's hammer upon his anvil, and the brisk tapping made by Chakes, as he neatly executed repairs upon a pair of shoes.

A guilty conscience needs no accuser, and, if it had not been for that furtive visit to the clock, Vane would not have looked round to see if he was observed before hurrying up to the church, and entering the tower, for the open door suggested to him what was going on.

He mounted the spiral staircase, and, on reaching the clock-chamber, its door being also open, Vane found himself looking at the back of a bald-headed man in his shirt-sleeves, standing with an oily rag in his hand, surrounded by wheels and other portions of the great clock.

Vane stopped short, and there was a good deal of colour in his face still, as he watched the man till he turned.

"Come to put the clock right, Mr Gramp?" he said.

"How do, sir; how do? Yes, I've come over, and not before it was wanted. Clocks is like human beings, sir, and gets out of order sometimes. Mr Syme sent word days ago, but I was too busy to come sooner."

"Ah!" said Vane, for the man was looking at him curiously.

"I hear she went a bit hard the other night, and set all the bells a-ringing."

"Watch and clock making 's a hart."

"No, only one," said Vane, quickly.

"And no wonder, when folks gets a-meddling with what they don't understand. Do you know, sir—no, you'll never believe it—watch and clock making's a hart?"

"A difficult art, too," said Vane, rather nervously.

"Eggs—actly, sir, and yet, here's your shoemaker—bah! your cobbler, just because the church clock wants cleaning, just on the strength of his having to wind it up, thinks he can do it without sending for me. No, you couldn't believe it, sir, but, as true as my name's Gramp, he did; and what does he do? Takes a couple of wheels out, and leaves 'em tucked underneath. But, as sure as his name's Chakes, I'm going straight up to the rectory as soon as I'm done, and if I don't—"

"No, no, don't," cried Vane, excitedly, for the turn matters had taken was startling. "It was not Chakes, Mr Gramp; it was I."

"You, Mr Lee, sir? You?" cried the man, aghast with wonder. "Whatever put it into your head to try and do such a thing as that? Mischief?"

"No, no, it was not that; the clock wouldn't go, and I came up here all alone, and it did seem so tempting that I began to clean a wheel or two, and then I wanted to do a little more, and a little more, and I got the clock pretty well all to pieces; and then—somehow—well, two of the wheels were left out."

The clockmaker burst into a hearty fit of laughter.

"I should think they were left out," he cried. "Then I must use your name instead of Chakes, eh?"

"No, no, Mr Gramp; pray don't do that; the rector doesn't know. I only told my uncle, and I wasn't thinking about you when I tried to set it going."

"But, you see, sir, it was such a thing to do—to meddle with a big church clock. If it had been an old Dutch with wooden works and sausage weights, or a brass American, I shouldn't have said a word; but my church clock, as I've tended for years! really, sir, you know it's too bad a deal."

"Yes, Mr Gramp, it was too bad; a great piece of—of—assumption."

"Assumption, sir; yes, sir, that's the very word. Well, really, I hardly know what to say."

"Say nothing, Mr Gramp."

"You did tell the doctor, sir?"

"Yes, I told uncle."

"Hum! I'm going to call at the Little Manor to see the doctor about the tall eight-day. Perhaps I'd better consult him."

"Well, yes, speak to uncle if you like, but go by what he says."

The clockmaker nodded, and went on with his work, and from looking on, Vane came to helping, and so an hour passed away, when it suddenly occurred to him that Aunt Hannah had said something about a message she wanted him to take, so he had unwillingly to leave the clock-chamber.

"Good-day, sir, good-day. I shall see you this evening."

"Yes, of course," said Vane; and then, as he hurried down the stairs, it seemed as if there was to be quite a vexatious re-opening of the case.

"I do wish I had not touched the old thing," muttered Vane, as he went back. "I couldn't offer him half-a-crown to hold his tongue. Clockmaker's too big."

But he did not see the clockmaker again that day, for, as he entered the little drawing-room—

"My dear," cried Aunt Hannah, "I was wishing that you would come. I want you to go over to Lenby for me, and take this packet—a bottle, mind, for Mrs Merry. It's a liniment your uncle has made up for her rheumatism."

"Mrs Merry, aunt?"

"Yes, my dear, at the far end of the village; she's quite a martyr to her complaint, and I got your uncle to call and see her last time you were out for a drive. Have the pony if you like."

"Yes, take her, boy," said the doctor. "She is getting too fat with good living. No; I forgot she was to be taken to the blacksmith's to be shod this afternoon."

"All right, uncle, I'll walk over," cried Vane, "I shall enjoy it."

"Well, it will not do you any harm. Go across the rough land at the edge of the forest. You may find a few ferns worth bringing for the greenhouse. And pray try for a few fungi."

Vane nodded, thrust the packet in his breast, and, taking trowel and basket, he started for his three-miles cross-country walk to Lenby, a tiny village, famous for its spire, which was invisible till it was nearly reached, the place lying in a nook in the wold hills, which, in that particular part, were clothed with high beeches of ancient growth.

The late autumn afternoon was glorious, and the little town was soon left behind, the lane followed for a time, but no gipsy van or cart visible, though there was the trace of the last fire. Being deep down in the cutting-like hollow, Vane could not see over the bank, where a donkey was grazing amongst the furze, while, completely hidden in a hollow, there was one of those sleeping tents, formed by planting two rows of willow sticks a few feet apart and then bending over the tops, tying them together, and spreading a tilt over all.

This was invisible to the boy and so were the heads of the two stout gipsy lads, who peered down at him from a little farther on, and then drew softly away to shelter themselves among the bushes and ferns till they were beyond hearing. When, stooping low, they ran off towards the wood, but in a stealthy furtive manner as if they were trying to stalk some wild animal and cut it off farther on, where the place was most solitary and wild.

In happy ignorance of the interest taken in his proceedings, Vane trudged along till it seemed to him that it was time to climb up out of the lane by the steep sand bank, and this he did, but paused half-way without a scientific or inventive idea in his head, ready to prove himself as boyish as anyone of his years, for he had come upon a magnificent patch of brambles sending up in the hot autumn sunshine cone after cone of the blackest of blackberries such as made him drive his toes into the loose sand to get a better foothold, and long for a suitable basket, the one he carried being a mere leather bag.

"Aunt would like a lot of these," he thought, and resisting the temptation to have a feast he left them on the chance of finding them next day when he could come provided with a basket. For blackberries found as much favour with Aunt Hannah as the doctor's choicest plums or apples.

A little higher, though, Vane paused again to stain his fingers and lips with the luscious fruit, which, thanks to the American example, people have just found to be worthy of cultivation in their gardens.

"'Licious," said Vane, with a smack of the lips, and then, mounting to the top of the bank he stood for a few moments gazing at the glorious prospect, all beautiful cultivation on his right, all wild grass, fern, and forest on his left.

This last took most of his attention, as he mapped out his course by the nearest way to the great clump of beeches which towered above the oaks, and then at once strode onward, finding an easy way where a stranger would soon have found himself stuck fast, hedged in by thorns.

"I'll come back by the road," thought Vane. "After all it's better and less tiring."

But with the beeches well in view, he made light of the difficulties of the little trodden district, which seemed to be quite a sanctuary for the partridges, three coveys rising, as he went on, with a tremendous rush and whirr of wing, to fly swiftly for a distance, and then glide on up and down, rising at clumps of furze, and clearing them, to descend into hollows and rise again apparently, after the first rush, without beat of wing.

"It's very curious, that flying," said Vane to himself, as he stood sheltering his eyes to watch the last covey till it passed out of sight—"ten of them, and they went along just as if they had nothing to do but will themselves over the ground. It must be a fine thing to fly. Find it out some day," he said; and he hurried on again to reach the spot where a little rill made a demarcation between the sand and bog he had traversed, and the chalk which rose now in a sharp slope on the other side.

He drew back a little way, took a run and leaped right across the cress-bordered clear water, alighting on hard chalk pebbles, and causing a wild splashing and rustling as a pair of moor-hens rose from amongst the cress, their hollow wings beating hard, their long green legs and attenuated toes hanging apparently nerveless beneath them, and giving a slight glimpse of their coral-coloured beak, and crests and a full view of the pure white and black of their short barred tail ere they disappeared amongst the bulrushes which studded one side of the winding stream.

Vane watched them for a moment or two, and shook his head.

"Partridges beat them hollow. Wonder whether I can find uncle any truffles."

He made for the shade of the beeches, passing at once on to a crackling carpet of old beech-mast and half rotten leaves, while all around him the great trees sent up their wonderfully clean, even-lined trunks, and boughs laden with dark green leaves, and the bronzy brown-red cases of the tiny triangular nuts, the former ready now to gape and drop their sweet contents where those of the past year had fallen before.

"Pity beech-nuts are so small," he said, as he stood looking up in the midst of a glade where the tall branches of a dozen regularly planted trees curved over to meet those of another dozen, and touching in the centre, shutting out the light, and forming a natural cathedral nave, such as might very well have suggested a building to the first gothic architect for working the design in stone.

"Ought to be plenty here," said Vane to himself after drinking his fill of the glorious scene with its side aisles and verdant chapels all around; and stooping down at the foot of one tree, he began with the little trowel which he had taken from his pocket to scrape away the black coating of decayed leaves, and then dig here and there for the curious tubers likely to be found in such a place, but without result.

"Hope uncle hasn't bought a turkey to stuff with truffles," he said with a laugh, as he tried another place; "the basket does not promise to be very heavy."

He had no better luck here, and he tried another, in each case carefully scratching away the dead leaves to bare the soft leaf-mould, and then dig carefully.

"Want a truffle dog, or a pig," he muttered; and then he pounced upon a tuber about twice as large as a walnut, thrusting it proudly into his basket.

"Where one is, there are sure to be others," he said; and he resumed his efforts, finding another and another, all in the same spot.

"Why, I shall get a basketful," he thought, and he began to dwell pleasantly upon the satisfaction the sight of his successful foray would give the doctor, who had a special penchant for truffles, and had often talked about what expensive delicacies they were for those who dwelt in London.

Encouraged then by his success, he went on scraping and grubbing away eagerly with more or less success, while the task grew more mechanical, and after feeling that his bottle was safe in his breast-pocket, he began to think that it was time to leave off, and go on his mission; but directly after, as he was rubbing the clean leaf-mould from off a tuber, his thoughts turned to Distin, and the undoubted enmity he displayed.

"If it was not such a strong term," he said to himself, "I should be ready to say he hates me, and would do me any ill-turn he could."

He had hardly thought this, and was placing his truffle in the basket, when a faint noise toward the edge of the wood where the sun poured in, casting dark shadows from the tree-trunks, made him look sharply in that direction.

For a few moments he saw nothing, and he was about to credit a rabbit with the sound, when it suddenly struck him that one of the shadows cast on the ground not far distant had moved slightly, and as he fixed his eyes upon it intently, he saw that it was not a shadow cast by a tree, unless it was one that had a double trunk for some distance up and then these joined. The next moment he was convinced:—for it was the shadow of a human being hiding behind a good-sized beech, probably in profound ignorance that his presence was clearly shown to the person from whom he was trying to hide.

Chapter Nineteen.

Vane is Missing.

Aunt Hannah had been very busy devoting herself according to her custom in watching attentively while Eliza bustled about, spreading the cloth for high tea—a favourite meal at the Little Manor. She had kept on sending messages to Martha in the kitchen till that lady had snorted and confided to Eliza, "that if missus sent her any more of them aggrawating orders she would burn the chicken to a cinder."

For Aunt Hannah's great idea in life was to make those about her comfortable and happy; and as Vane would return from his long walk tired and hungry, she had ordered roast chicken for tea with the sausages Mrs Rounds had sent as a present after the pig-killing.

That was all very well. Martha said "yes, mum," pleasantly and was going to do her best; but unfortunately, Aunt Hannah made a remark which sent the cook back to her kitchen, looking furious.

"As if I ever did forget to put whole peppers in the bread sauce," she cried to Eliza with the addition of a snort, and from that minute there were noises in the kitchen. The oven door was banged to loudly; saucepans smote the burning coals with their bottoms heavily; coals were shovelled on till the kitchen became as hot as Martha's temper, and the plates put down to heat must have had their edges chipped, so hardly were they rattled together.

But in the little drawing-room Aunt Hannah sat as happy and placid as could be till it was drawing toward the time for Vane's return, when she took her keys from her basket, and went to the store-room for a pot of last year's quince marmalade and carried it into the dining-room.

"Master Vane is so fond of this preserve, Eliza," she said. "Oh, and, by the way, ask Martha to send in the open jam tart. I dare say he would like some of that."

"I did tell Martha so, ma'am."

"That was very thoughtful of you, Eliza."

"But she nearly snapped my head off, ma'am."

"Dear, dear, dear, I do wish that Martha would not be so easily put out."

Aunt Hannah gave a glance over the table, and placing a fresh bunch of flowers in a vase in the centre, and a tiny bowl of ornamental leaves, such as the doctor admired, by his corner of the table, smiled with satisfaction to see how attractive everything looked. Then she went back to her work in the drawing-room, but only to pop up again and go to the window, open it, and look out at where the doctor was busy with his penknife and some slips of bass, cutting away the old bindings and re-tying some choice newly-grafted pears which had begun to swell and ask for more room to develop.

"It's getting very nearly tea-time, my dear," she cried. "Bruff went half an hour ago."

"Yes, quarter of an hour before his time," said the doctor. "That's a curious old silver watch of his, always fast, but he believes in it more than he does in mine."

"But it is time to come in and wash your hands, love."

"No. Another quarter of an hour," said the doctor. "Vane come back?"

"No, dear, not yet. But he must be here soon."

"I will not keep his lordship waiting," said the doctor, quietly going on with his tying; and Aunt Hannah toddled back to look at the drawing-room mantel-clock.

"Dear me, yes," she said; "it is nearly a quarter to six." Punctually to his time, the doctor's step was heard in the little hall, where he hung up his hat before going upstairs to change his coat and boots and wash his hands. Then descending.

"Time that boy was back, isn't it?" he said going behind Aunt Hannah, who was looking out of the window at a corner which afforded a glimpse of the road.

"Oh, my dear, how you startled me!" cried Aunt Hannah.

"Can't help it, my dear. I always was an ugly man."

"My dear, for shame! yes, it's quite time he was back. I am growing quite uneasy."

"Been run over perhaps by the train."

"Oh, my dear!" cried Aunt Hannah in horrified tones. "But how could he be? The railway is not near where he has gone."

"Of course it isn't. There, come and sit down and don't be such an old fidget about that boy. You are spoiling him."

"That I am sure I am not, my dear."

"But you are—making a regular Molly of him. He'll be back soon. I believe if you had your own way you would lead him about by a string."

"Now that is nonsense, my dear," cried Aunt Hannah. "How can I help being anxious about him when he is late?"

"Make more fuss about him than if he was our own child."

Aunt Hannah made no reply, but sat down working and listening intently for the expected step, but it did not come, and at last she heaved a sigh.

"Yes, he is late," said the doctor, looking at his watch. "Not going anywhere else for you, was he?"

"Oh, no, my dear; he was coming straight back."

"Humph!" ejaculated the doctor; "thoughtless young dog! I want my tea."

"He can't be long now," said Aunt Hannah.

"Humph! Can't be. That boy's always wool-gathering instead of thinking of his duties."

Aunt Hannah's brow wrinkled and she looked five years older as she rose softly to go to the window, and look out.

"That will not bring him here a bit sooner, Hannah," said the doctor drily. "I dare say he has gone in at the rectory, and Syme has asked him to stay."

"Oh, no, my dear, I don't think he would do that, knowing that we should be waiting."

"Never did, I suppose," said the doctor.

Aunt Hannah was silent. She could not deny the impeachment, and she sat there with her work in her lap, thinking about how late it was; how hungry the doctor would be, and how cross it would make him, for he always grew irritable when kept waiting for his meals.

Then she began to think about going and making the tea, and about the chicken, which would be done to death, and the doctor did not like chickens dry.

Just then there was a diversion.

Eliza came to the door.

"If you please 'm, cook says shall she send up the chicken? It's half-past six."

Aunt Hannah looked at the doctor, and the doctor looked at his watch.

"Wait a minute," he said; and then: "No, I'll give him another quarter of an hour."

"What a tantrum Martha will be in," muttered Eliza, as she left the room.

"Oh, that poor chicken!" thought Aunt Hannah, and then aloud:—

"I hope Vane has not met with any accident."

"Pshaw! What accident could he meet with in walking to the village with a bottle of liniment and back, unless—"

"Yes?" cried Aunt Hannah, excitedly; "unless what, my dear?"

"He has opened the bottle and sat down by the roadside to drink it all."

"Oh, my dear, surely you don't think that Vane would be so foolish."

"I don't know," cried the doctor, "perhaps so. He is always experimentalising over something."

"But," cried Aunt Hannah, with a horrified look, "it was liniment for outward application only!"

"Exactly: that's what I mean," said the doctor. "He has not been content without trying the experiment of how it would act rubbed on inside instead of out."

"Then that poor boy may be lying somewhere by the roadside in the agonies of death—poisoned," cried Aunt Hannah in horror; but the doctor burst out into a roar of laughter.

"Oh, it's too bad, my dear," cried Aunt Hannah, tearfully. "You are laughing at me and just, too, when I am so anxious about Vane."

"I'm not: a young rascal. He has met those sweet youths from the rectory, and they are off somewhere, or else stopping there."

The doctor rose and rang the bell.

"Are you going to send up to see, my dear?"

"No, I am not," said the doctor, rather tartly. "I am going to—"

Eliza entered the room.

"We'll have tea directly, Eliza," said the doctor; and Aunt Hannah hurried into the dining-room to measure out so many caddy spoonfuls into the hot silver pot, and pour in the first portion of boiling water, but listening for the expected footstep all the time.

That meal did not go off well, for, in spite of the doctor's assumed indifference, he was also anxious about his nephew. Aunt Hannah could not touch anything, and the doctor's appetite was very little better; but he set this down to the chicken being, as he said, dried to nothing, and the sausages being like horn—exaggerations, both—for, in spite of Martha's threats, she was too proud of her skill in cooking to send up anything overdone.

The open jam tart was untouched, and the opening of that pot of last year's quince marmalade proved to have been unnecessary; for, though Aunt Hannah paused again and again with her cup half-way to her lips, it was not Vane's step that she heard; and, as eight o'clock came, she could hardly keep back her tears.

"Don't be angry with him."

All at once the doctor rose and went into the hall, followed by Aunt Hannah, who looked at him wistfully as he put on a light overcoat, and took hat and stick.

"I'll walk to the rectory," he said, "and bring him back."

Aunt Hannah laid her hand upon his arm, as he reached the door.

"Don't be angry with him, my dear," she whispered.

"Why not? Is that boy to do just as he pleases here? I'll give him a good sound thrashing, that's what I'll do with him."

Aunt Hannah took away the doctor's walking stick, which he had made whish through the air and knock down one of Vane's hats.

"There, I'll do it with my fist," cried the doctor. "You cannot amputate that."

"My dear!" whispered Aunt Hannah, handing back the stick.

"All right, I will not hit him, but I'll give him a most tremendous tongue thrashing, as they call it here."

"No, no; there is some reason for his being late."

"Very well," cried the doctor. "I shall soon see."

The door closed after him, and Aunt Hannah began to pace the drawing-room, full of forebodings.

"I am sure there is something very wrong," she said, "or Vane would not have behaved like this."

She broke down here, and had what she called "a good cry." But it did not seem to relieve her, and she recommenced her walking once more.

At every sound she made for the door, believing it was Vane come back, and, truth to tell, thinking very little of the doctor, but every time she hurried to the door and window she was fain to confess it was fancy, and resumed her weary agitated walk up and down the room.

At last, though, there was the click of the swing-gate, and she hurried to the porch where she was standing as the doctor came up.

"Yes, dear," she cried, before he reached the door. "Has he had his tea?"

The doctor was silent, and came into the hall where Aunt Hannah caught his arm.

"There is something wrong?" she cried.

"No, no, don't be agitated, my dear," said the doctor gently. "It may be nothing."

"Then he is there—hurt?"

"No, no. They have not seen him."

"He has not been with the pupils?"

"No."

"Oh, my dear, my dear, what does it mean?" cried Aunt Hannah.

"It is impossible to say," said the doctor, "but we must be cool. Vane is not a boy to run away."

"Oh, no."

"So I have sent Bruff over to ask what time he got to Lenby, and what time he left, and, if possible, to find out which way he returned. Bruff may meet him. We don't know what may have kept him. Nothing serious, of course."

But the doctor's words did not carry conviction; and, as if sympathising with his wife, he took and pressed her hand.

"Come, come," he whispered, "try and be firm. We have no reason for thinking that there is anything wrong."

"No," said Aunt Hannah, with a brave effort to keep down her emotion.—"Yes, Eliza, what is it?"

There had been a low whispering in the hall, followed by Eliza tapping at the door and coming in.

"I beg pardon, ma'am," said the maid, hastily, "but cook and me's that anxious we hoped you wouldn't mind my asking about Master Vane."

A curious sound came from the passage, something between a sigh and a sob.

"There is nothing to tell you," said the doctor, "till Bruff comes back. Mr Vane has been detained; that's all."

"Thank you, sir," said Eliza. "It was only that we felt we should like to know."

In spite of the trouble she was in there was room for a glow of satisfaction in Aunt Hannah's mind on finding how great an interest was felt by the servants; and she set herself to wait as patiently as she could for news.

"It will not be so very long, will it dear?" she whispered, for she could not trust herself to speak aloud.

"It must be two hours," said the doctor gravely. "It is a long way. I am sorry I did not make Bruff drive, but I thought it would take so long to get the pony ready that I started him at once;" and then ready to reprove his wife for her anxiety and eagerness to go to door or window from time to time, the doctor showed himself to be just as excited, and at the end of the first hour, he strode out into the hall.

Aunt Hannah followed him.

"I can't stand it any longer, my dear," he cried. "I don't believe I care a pin about the young dog, for I am sure he is playing us some prank, but I must go and meet Bruff."

"Yes, do, do," cried Aunt Hannah, hurriedly getting the doctor's hat and stick. "But couldn't I go, too?"

The doctor bent down, and kissed her.

"No, no, my dear, you would only hinder me," he said, tenderly, and to avoid seeing her pained and working face he hurried out and took the road for Lenby, striking off to the left, after passing the church.

But after walking sharply along the dark lane, for about a couple of miles, it suddenly occurred to the doctor that the chances were, that Bruff, who knew his way well, would take the short cuts, by the fields, and, after hesitating for a few minutes, he turned and hurried back.

"A fool's errand," he muttered. "I ought to have known better."

As matters turned out, he had done wisely in returning, and the walk had occupied his mind, for, as he came within hearing of the Little Manor again, he fancied that a sound in front was the click of the swing-gate.

It was: for he reached the door just as Eliza was on her way to the drawing-room to announce that Bruff had come back.

"Bring him here," said the doctor, who had entered. "No: stop: I'll come and speak to him in the kitchen."

But Aunt Hannah grasped his hand.

"No, no," she whispered firmly now. "I must know the worst."

"Send Bruff in," said the doctor, sternly, and the next minute the gardener was heard rubbing his boots on the mat, and came into the hall, followed by the other servants.

"Well, Bruff," said the doctor, in a short, stern way, "you have not found him?"

"No, sir, arn't seen or heard nowt."

"But he had been and left the medicine?"

"Nay, sir, not he. Nobody had seen nowt of him. He hadn't been there."

Aunt Hannah uttered a faint gasp.

"But didn't you ask at either of the cottages as you passed?" asked the doctor sharply.

"Cottages, sir? Why, there arn't none. I cut acrost the fields wherever I could, and the only plaace nigh is Candell's farm—that's quarter of a mile down a lane."

"Yes, yes, of course," said the doctor. "I had forgotten. Then you have brought no news at all?"

"Well, yes, sir; a bit as you may say."

"Well, what is it, man? Don't keep us in suspense."

"Seems like news to say as he arn't been nowheres near Lenby."

"Can you form any idea of where he is likely to have gone?"

Bruff looked in his hat and pulled the lining out a little way, and peered under that as if expecting to find some information there, but ended by shaking his head and looking in a puzzled fashion at the doctor.

"Come with me," said the latter, and turning to Aunt Hannah, he whispered: "Go and wait patiently, my dear. I don't suppose there is anything serious the matter. I daresay there is a simple explanation of the absence if we could find it; but I feel bound to try and find him, if I can, to-night."

"But how long will you be?"

"One hour," said the doctor, glancing at his watch. "If I am not back then you will have a message from me in that time, so that you will be kept acquainted with all I know."

"Please, sir, couldn't we come and help?" said cook eagerly. "Me and 'Liza's good walkers."

"Thank you," said the doctor; "the best help you can render is to sit up and wait, ready to attend to your mistress."

He turned to Aunt Hannah who could not trust herself to speak, but pressed his hand as he passed out into the dark night, followed by Bruff.

"The rectory," he said briefly; and walked there rapidly to ring and startle Joseph, who was just thinking of giving his final look round before going to bed.

"Some one badly, sir?" he said, as he admitted the doctor and gardener, jumping at the conclusion that his master was wanted at a sick person's bedside.

"No. Have you seen Mr Vane since he left after lessons this morning?"

"No, sir."

"Where is the rector?"

"In his study, sir."

"And the young gentlemen?"

"Just gone up to bed, sir."

"Show me into the study."

Joseph obeyed, and the rector, who was seated with a big book before him, which he was not reading, jumped up in a startled way.

"Vane Lee?" he cried.

"Yes: I'm very anxious about Vane. He was sent over to Lenby, this afternoon and has not returned. I want to ask Macey and Gilmore if they know anything of his whereabouts."

"But some one came long ago. They have not seen him since luncheon."

"Tut—tut—tut!" ejaculated the doctor.

"Not been back then?"

The doctor shook his head, and the rector suggested that he had stayed at Lenby and half a dozen other things which could be answered at once.

"Would you mind sending for the lads to come down?"

"Certainly not. Of course," cried the rector; and he rang and sent up a message.

"I don't suppose they are in bed," he said. "They always have a good long gossip; and, as long as they are down in good time I don't like to be too strict. But, my dear Lee. You don't think there is anything serious?"

"I don't know what to think, Syme," cried the doctor, agitatedly.

"Is it an escapade—has he run off?"

"My dear sir, you know him almost as well as I do. Is he the sort of boy to play such a prank?"

"Vane Missing."

"I should say, no. But, stop, you have had some quarrel. You have been reproving him."

"No—no—no," cried the doctor. "Nothing of the kind. If there had been I should have felt more easy."

"But, what can have happened? A walk to Lenby and back by a boy who knows every inch of the way."

"That is the problem," said the doctor. "Ah, here is someone."

For there was a tap at the door, and Macey entered, to look wonderingly from one to the other.

"Aleck, my boy," said the doctor, "Vane is missing. Can you suggest anything to help us? Do you know of any project that he had on hand or of any place he was likely to have gone to on his way to Lenby?"

"No," said Macey, quickly.

"Take time, my dear boy, and think," said the rector.

"But I can't think, sir, of anything," cried Macey. "No. Unless—"

"Yes," cried the doctor; "unless what?"

"He was going to Lenby, you say."

"Yes."

"Well, mightn't he have stopped there?"

"No, no, my boy," cried the doctor, in disappointed tones, as Gilmore came in, and directly after Distin, both looking wonderingly round. "We sent there."

"Then I don't know," said Macey, anxiously. "He might have gone over the bit of moor though."

"Yes," said the doctor; "he could have gone that way."

"Well, sir, mightn't he have been caught among the brambles, or lost his way?"

"No, my boy, absurd!"

"I once did, sir, and he came and helped me out."

"Oh, no," cried the doctor; "impossible."

"But there are some very awkward pieces of bog and peat and water-holes, sir," said Gilmore; and as he said this Distin drew a deep breath, and took a step back from the shaded lamp.

The rector also drew a deep breath, and looked anxiously at the doctor, who stood with his brow contracted for a few moments, and then shook his head.

"He was too clever and active for that," he cried. "No, Gilmore, that is not the solution. He is not likely to have come upon poachers? There are a great many pheasants about there?"

"No poachers would be about in the afternoon," said the rector. "My dear Lee, I do not like to suggest so terrible a thing, but I must say, I think it is our duty to get all the help we can, and search the place armed with lanterns."

The doctor looked at him wildly.

"Of course we'll help. What do you say?"

"Yes," said the doctor hoarsely. "Let us search."

The rector rang the bell, and Joseph answered directly.

"Wait a moment," cried the doctor. "Mr Distin, you have not spoken yet. Tell me: what is your opinion. Do you think Vane can have come to harm in the moor strip yonder?"

Distin shrank back as he was addressed, and looked round wildly, from one to the other.

"I—I?" he faltered.

"Yes, you—my dear boy," said the rector, sharply. "Answer at once, and do, pray, try to master that nervousness."

Distin passed his tongue over his lips, and his voice sounded very husky as he said, almost inaudibly at first, but gathering force as he went on:—

"I don't know. I have not seen him since this morning."

"We know that," said the doctor; "but should you think it likely, that he has met with an accident, or can you suggest anywhere likely for him to have gone?"

"No, sir, no," said Distin, firmly now. "I can't think of anywhere, nor should I think he is likely to have sunk in either of the bog holes, though he is very fond of trying to get plants of all kinds when he is out."

"Yes, yes," said the doctor, hoarsely. "I taught him;" and as he spoke Distin gave a furtive look all round the room, to see that nearly everyone was watching him closely.

"We must hope for the best, Lee," said the doctor, firmly. "Joseph, take Doctor Lee's man with you, go down the town street and spread the alarm. We want men with lanterns as quickly as possible. That place must be searched."

The two men started at once, and the rector, after an apology, began to put on his boots once more.

"I promised to go or send word to the Manor," said the doctor, "but I feel as if I had not the heart to go."

"To tell Mrs Lee, sir?" said Distin, quickly.

"Yes, to say that we are all going to search for Vane," said the doctor, "but not what we suspect."

"I understand," said Distin, quickly; and, as if glad to escape, he hurried out of the room, and directly after they heard the closing of the outer door, and his steps on the gravel as he ran.

Chapter Twenty.

No News.

"Distin seems curiously agitated and disturbed," said the doctor.

"Yes: he is a nervous, finely-strung youth," replied the rector. "The result of his birth in a tropical country. It was startling, too, his being fetched down from bed to hear such news."

"Of course—of course," said the doctor; and preparations having been rapidly made by the rector, who mustered three lanterns, one being an old bull's-eye, they all started.

"Better go down as far as the church, first, and collect our forces. Then we'll make a start for the moor. But who shall we have for guide?"

"Perhaps I know the place best," said the doctor; and they started in silence, passing down the gravel drive, out at the gate, and then along the dark lane with the lights dancing fitfully amongst the trees and bushes on either side, and casting curiously weird shadows behind.

As they reached the road, Macey, who carried one lantern, held it high above his head and shouted.

"Hush—hush!" cried the doctor, for the lad's voice jarred upon him in the silence.

"Distin's coming, sir," said Macey.

There was an answering hail, and then the *pat-pat* of steps, as Distin trotted after and joined them.

By the time the church was reached, there was plenty of proof of Vane's popularity, for lanterns were dancing here and there, and lights could be seen coming from right up the street, while a loud eager buzz of voices reached their ears. Ten minutes after the doctor found himself surrounded by a band of about forty of the townsfolk, everyone of whom had some kind of lantern and a stick or pole, and all eager to go in search of the missing lad.

Rounds the miller was one of the foremost, and carried the biggest lantern, and made the most noise. Chakes the sexton, was there, too, with his lantern—a dim, yellow-looking affair, whose sides were of horn sheets, with here and there fancy devices punched in the tin to supply air to the burning candle within.

Crumps, from the dairy, Graders the baker, and John Wrench the carpenter, all were there, and it seemed a wonder to Macey where all the lanterns had come from. But it was no wonder, for Greythorpe was an ill-lit place, where candles and oil-lamps took the place of gas even in the little shops, and there were plenty of people who needed the use of a stable-light.

There were two policemen stationed in Greythorpe, but they were off on their nightly rounds, and it was not until the weird little procession of light-bearers had gone half a mile from the town that there was a challenge from under a dark hedge, and two figures stepped out into the road.

"Eh? Master Vane Lee lost?" said one of the figures, the lights proclaiming them to be the policemen, who had just met at one of their appointed stations; "then we'd better jyne you."

This added two more lanterns to the bearers of light, but for a long time they were not opened, but kept as a reserved force—ready if wanted.

At last, in almost utter silence, the moor was reached, the men were spread out, and the search began. But it was ended after an hour's struggling among the bushes, and an extrication of Chakes, and Wrench the carpenter, from deep bog holes into which they had suddenly stepped, and, on being drawn out, sent home.

Then Rounds spoke out in his loud, bluff way.

"Can't be done, doctor, by this light. It's risking the lives of good men and true. I want to find young Mester, and I'll try as if he was a son of my own, but we can't draw this mash to-night."

There was a dead silence at this, and then the rector spoke out.

"I'm afraid he is right, Lee. I would gladly do everything possible, but this place really seems impassable by night."

The doctor was silent, and the rector spoke again:

"What do you say, constable?"

"As it can't be done, sir, with all respect to you as the head of the parish."

"Seems to me like getting up an inquess, sir," said Dredge the butcher, "with ooz all dodging about here with our lights, like so many will-o'-the-wispies."

"Ay, I was gooin' to say as theered be job for owd Chakes here 'fore morning if he gets ower his ducking."

"I'm afraid you are right," said the doctor, sadly. "If I were sure that my nephew was somewhere here on the moor, I should say keep on at all hazards, but it is too dangerous a business by lantern light."

"Let's give a good shout," cried the miller; "p'r'aps the poor lad may hear it. Now, then, all together: one, two three, and *Ahoy*!"

The cry rang far out over the moor, and was faintly answered, so plainly that Macey uttered a cry of joy.

"Come on," he cried; "there he is."

"Nay, lad," said the miller; "that was on'y the echo."

"No, no," said Macey; "it was an answer."

"It did sound like it," said the rector; and the doctor remained in doubt.

"You listen," said the miller; and, putting his hands on either side of his mouth, he gave utterance to a stentorian roar.

"Vane, ho!"

There was a pause, and a "ho!" came back.

"All right?" roared the miller.

"Right!" came back.

"Good-night!" shouted the miller again.

"Night!"

"There, you see. Only an echo," said the miller. "Wish it wasn't. Why, if it had been his voice, lads, we'd soon ha' hed him home."

"Yes, it's an echo, Aleck," said Gilmore, sadly.

"But we could stop, and go on searching, sir," cried Macey. "It's such a pity to give up."

"Only till daybreak, my lad," said the doctor, sadly. "We can do no good here, and the risk is too great."

Gilmore uttered a low sigh, and Macey a groan, as, after a little more hesitation, it was decided to go back to the town, and wait till the first dawn, when the search could be resumed.

"And, look here, my lads," cried the miller; "all of you as can had better bring bill-hooks and sickles, for it's bad going through these brambles, even by day."

"And you, constables," said the rector; "you are on duty along the roads. You will keep a sharp look-out."

"Of course, sir, and we'll communicate with the other men we meet from Lenby and Riby, and Dunthorpe. We shall find him, sir, never fear."

The procession of lanterns was recommenced, but in the other direction now, and in utter despondency the doctor followed, keeping with the rector and his pupils, all trying in turn to suggest some solution of the mystery, but only for it to close in more darkly round them, in spite of all.

The police then left them at the spot where they had been encountered, and promised great things, in which nobody felt any faith; and at last, disheartened and weary, the churchyard was reached, and the men dismissed, all promising to be ready to go on at dawn. Then there was a good deal of opening of lanterns, the blowing out of candle and lamp, the closing of doors, and an unpleasant, fatty smell, which gradually dispersed as all the men departed but the miller.

"Hope, gentlemen," he said, in his big voice, "you don't think I hung back from helping you."

"No, no, Rounds," said the doctor, sadly; "you are not the sort of man to fail us in a pinch."

"Thankye, doctor," said the bluff fellow, holding out his hand. "Same to you. I aren't forgot the way you come and doctored my missus when she was so bad, and you not a reg'lar doctor, but out o' practice. But nivver you fear; we'll find the lad. I shan't go to bed, but get back and light a pipe. I can think best then; and mebbe I'll think out wheer the young gent's gone."

"Thank you, Rounds," said the doctor. "Perhaps we had all better go and try and think it out, for Heaven grant that it may not be so bad as we fear."

"Amen to that!" cried the miller, "as clerk's not here. And say, parson, I'll goo and get key of owd Chakes, and, at the first streak o' daylight, I'll goo to belfry, and pull the rope o' the ting-tang to rouse people oop. You'll know what it means."

He went off; and the rest of the party, preceded by Joseph Bruff having sought his cottage, walked slowly back, all troubled by the same feeling, omitting Distin, that they had done wrong in giving up so easily, but at the same time feeling bound to confess that they could have done no good by continuing the search.

As they reached the end of the rectory lane and the doctor said "good-night," the rector urged him to come up to the rectory and lie down on a couch till morning, but Doctor Lee shook his head.

"No," he said, "it is quite time I was back. There is someone sorrowing there more deeply than we can comprehend. Till daybreak, Syme. Good-night."

Macey stood listening to the doctor's retiring footsteps and then ran after him.

"Hi! Macey!" cried Gilmore.

"Mr Macey, where are you going?" cried the rector.

But the boy heard neither of them as he ran on till the doctor heard the footsteps and stopped.

"Yes," he said, "what is it?"

"Only me—Aleck Macey, sir."

"Yes, my lad? Have you brought a message from Mr Syme?"

"No, sir; I only wanted—I only thought—I—I—Doctor Lee, please let me come and wait with you till it's time to start."

Macey began falteringly, but his last words came out with a rush.

"Why not go back to bed, my lad, and get some rest—some sleep?"

"Rest?—sleep? Who is going to sleep when, for all we know, poor old Vane's lying helpless somewhere out on the moor. Let me come and stop with you."

For answer the doctor laid his hand upon Macey's shoulder, and they reached the Little Manor swing-gate and passed up the avenue without a word.

There were lights burning in two of the front windows, and long before they reached the front door in the porch, it was opened, and a warm glow of light shone out upon the advancing figures. It threw up, too, the figure of Aunt Hannah, who, as soon as she realised the fact that there were two figures approaching, ran out and before the doctor could enlighten her as to the truth, she flung her arms round Macey's neck, and hugged him to her breast, sobbing wildly.

"Oh, my dear, my dear, where have you been—where have you been?"

As she spoke, she buried her face upon the lad's shoulder, while Macey looked up speechlessly at the doctor, and he, choked with emotion as he was, could not for some moments find a word to utter.

Still, clinging to him in the darkness Aunt Hannah now took tightly hold of the boy's arm, as if fearing he might again escape from her, and drawing him up toward the door from which the light shone now, showing Eliza and Martha both waiting, she suddenly grasped the truth, and uttered a low wail of agony.

"Not found?" she cried. "Oh, how could you let me, how could you! It was too cruel, indeed, indeed!"

Aunt Hannah's sobs broke out loudly now; and, unable to bear more, Macey glided away, and did not stop running after passing the gate till he reached the rectory door.

Chapter Twenty One.

In the Early Morning.

Churchwarden Rounds kept his word, for at the first break of day his vigorous arms sent the ting-tang ringing in a very different way to that adopted by old Chakes for the last few minutes before service commenced on Sunday morning and afternoon. And he did not ring in vain, for though the search was given up in the night the objections were very genuine. Everyone was eager to help so respected a neighbour as the doctor, and to a man the searchers surrounded him as he walked up to the church; even Wrench the carpenter, and Chakes the sexton putting in an appearance in a different suit to that worn over-night and apparently none the worse for the cold plunge into peaty water they had had.

The rector was not present, and the little expedition was about to start, when Macey came running up to say that Mr Syme was close behind.

This decided the doctor to pause for a few minutes, and while it was still twilight the rector with Gilmore and Distin came up, the former apologising for being so late.

"I'm afraid that I fell asleep in my chair, Lee," he whispered. "I'm very sorry."

"There is no need to say anything," said the doctor sadly. "It is hardly daybreak even now."

Gilmore looked haggard, and his face on one side was marked by the leather of the chair in which he had been asleep. Macey looked red-eyed too, but Distin was perfectly calm and as neat as if he had been to bed as usual to enjoy an uninterrupted night's rest.

When the start was made, it having been decided to follow the same course as over-night, hardly a word was said, for in addition to the depression caused by the object in view, the morning felt chilly, and everything looked grim and strange in the mist.

The rector and doctor led the way with the churchwarden, then followed the rector's three pupils, and after them the servants and townspeople in silence.

Macey was the first of the rectory trio to speak, and he harked back to the idea that Vane must be caught in the brambles just as he had been when trying to make a short cut, but Gilmore scouted the notion at once.

"Impossible!" he said, "Vane wouldn't be so stupid. If he is lost on the moor it is because he slipped into one of those black bog holes, got tangled in the water-weeds and couldn't get out."

"Ugh!" exclaimed Macey with a shudder. "Oh, I say: don't talk like that. It's too horrid. You don't think so, do you, Distie? Why it has made you as white as wax to hear him talk like that."

Distin shivered as if he were cold, and he forced a smile as he said hastily:—

"No: of course I don't. It's absurd."

"What is?" said Gilmore.

"Your talking like this. It isn't likely. I think it's a great piece of nonsense, this searching the country."

"Why, what would you do?" cried Macey.

"I—I—I don't know," cried Distin, who was taken aback. "Yes, I do. I should drive over to the station to see if he took a ticket for London, or Sheffield, or Birmingham, or somewhere. It's just like him. He has gone to buy screws, or something, to make a whim-wham to wind up the sun."

"No, he hasn't," said Macey sturdily; "he wouldn't go and upset the people at home like that; he's too fond of them."

"Pish!" ejaculated Distin contemptuously.

"Distie's sour because he is up so early, Gil," continued Macey. "Don't you believe it. Vane's too good a chap to go off like that."

"Bah! he is always changing about. Why, you two fellows call him Weathercock."

"Well!" cried Gilmore; "it isn't because we don't like him."

"No," said Macey, "only in good-humoured fun, because he turns about so. I wish," he added dolefully, "he would turn round here now."

"You don't think as the young master's really drownded, do you?" said a voice behind, and Macey turned sharply, to find that Bruff had been listening to every word.

"No, I don't," he cried angrily; "and I'll punch anybody's head who says he is. I believe old Distie wishes he was."

"You're a donkey," cried Distin, turning scarlet.

"Then keep away from my heels—I might kick. It makes me want to with everybody going along as cool as can be, as if on purpose, to fish the best chap I ever knew out of some black hole among the bushes."

"Best chap!" said Distin, contemptuously.

"Yes: best chap," retorted Macey, whose temper was soured by the cold and sleeplessness of the past night.

Further words were stopped by the churchwarden's climbing up the sandy bank of the deep lane, and stopping half-way to the top to stretch out his hand to the rector whom he helped till he was amongst the furze, when he turned to help the doctor, who was, however, active enough to mount by himself.

The rest of the party were soon up in a group, and then there was a pause and the churchwarden spoke.

"If neither of you gentlemen, has settled what to do," he said, "it seems to me the best thing is to make a line of our-sens along top of the bank here, and then go steady right along towards Lenby—say twenty yards apart."

The doctor said that no better plan could be adopted, but added:—

"I should advise that whenever a pool is reached the man who comes to it should shout. Then all the line must stop while I come to the pool and examine it."

"But we've got no drags or hooks, mester," whispered the churchwarden, and the doctor shuddered.

"No," he said hastily, "but I think there would certainly be some marks of struggling at the edge—broken twigs, grass, or herbage torn away."

"Look at Distie," whispered Gilmore.

"Was looking," replied Macey who was gazing fixedly at his fellow-pupil's wild eyes and hollow cheeks. "Hasn't pitched, or shoved him in, has he?"

"Hush! Don't talk like that," whispered Gilmore again; and just then the object of their conversation looked up sharply, as if conscious that he was being canvassed, and gazed suspiciously from one to the other.

Meanwhile the miller who had uncovered so as to wipe his brow, threw his staring red cotton handkerchief sharply back into the crown of his hat and knocked it firmly into its place.

"Why, of course," he said: "That's being a scientific gentleman. I might have thought of that, but I didn't."

Without further delay half the party spread out toward the wood which formed one side of the moor, while the other half spread back toward the town; and as soon as all were in place the doctor, who was in the centre, with Rounds the miller on his right, and the rector on his left, gave the word. The churchwarden shouted and waved his hat and with the soft grey dawn gradually growing brighter, and a speck or two of orange appearing high up in the east, the line went slowly onward towards Lenby, pausing from time to time for pools to be examined and for the more luckless of the party to struggle out of awkward places.

The rector's three pupils were on the right—the end nearest the town, Distin being the last in the line and in spite of Macey's anticipations, he struggled on as well as the best man there.

Patches of mist like fleecy clouds, fallen during the night, lay here and there; and every now and then one who looked along the line could see companions walk right into these fogs and disappear for minutes at a time to suddenly step out again on to land that was quite clear.

Hardly a word was spoken, the toil was sufficient to keep every one silent. For five minutes after a start had been made every one was drenched with dew to the waist, and as Macey afterwards said if they had forded the river they could not have been more wet.

Every now and then birds were startled by someone, to rise with a loud *whirr* if they were partridges, with a rapid beating of pinions and frightened quacking if wild-fowl; and for a few moments, more than once, both Macey and Gilmore forgot the serious nature of their mission in interest in the various objects they encountered.

For these were not few.

Before they had gone a quarter of a mile there was a leap and a rush, and unable to contain himself, Bruff, who was next on Macey's left suddenly shouted "*loo—loo—loo—loo*."

"See him, Mester Macey!" he cried. "Oh, if we'd had a greyhound."

But they had no long-legged hound to dart off after the longer-eared animal; and the hare started from its form in some dry tussock grass, went off with its soft fur streaked to its sides with the heavy dew, and was soon out of reach.

Then a great grey flapped-wing heron rose from a tiny mere and sailed heavily away.

That pool had to be searched as far as its margin was concerned; and as it was plainly evident that birds only had visited it lately, the line moved on again just as the red disk of the sun appeared above the mist, and in one minute the grim grey misty moor was transformed into a vast jewelled plain spangled with myriads upon myriads of tiny gems, glittering in all the colours of the prism, and sending a flash of hopeful feeling into the boys' breasts.

"Oh!" cried Macey; "isn't it lovely! I am glad I came."

"Yes," said Gilmore; and then correcting himself. "Who can feel glad on a morning like this!"

"I can," said Macey, "for it all makes me feel now that we are stupid to think anything wrong can have happened to poor old Weathercock. He's all right somewhere."

Something akin to Macey's feeling of light-heartedness had evidently flashed into the hearts of all in the line, for men began to shout to one another as they hurried on with more elasticity of tread; they made lighter of their difficulties, and no longer felt a chill of horror whenever Rounds summoned all to a halt, while the doctor passed along the line to examine some cotton-rush dotted margin about a pool.

Working well now, the line pressed on steadily in the direction of Lenby, and a couple of miles must have been gone over when a halt was called, and after a short discussion in the centre, the churchwarden came panting along the line giving orders as he went till he reached the end where the three pupils were.

"Now, lads," he cried, "we're going to sweep round now, like the soldiers do—here by this patch of bushes. You, Mr Distin, will march right on, keeping your distance as before, and go the gainest way for the wood yonder, where you'll find the little stream. Then you'll keep back along that and we shall sweep that side of the moor till we get to the lane again."

"But we shall miss ever so much in the middle," cried Gilmore.

"Ay, so we shall, lad, but we'll goo up along theer afterwards, and back'ards, and forwards till we've been all over."

"But, I say," cried Macey, "you don't think we shall find him here, do you?"

"Nay, I don't, lad; but the doctor has a sort of idee that we may, and I'm not the man to baulk him. He might be here, you see."

"Yes," said Macey; "he might. There: all right, we'll go on when you give the word."

"Forrard, then, my lads; there it is, and I wish we may find him. Nay, I don't," he said, correcting himself, "for, poor lad he'd be in a bad case to have fallen down here for the night. Theer's something about it I can't understand, and if I were you, Mr Distin, sir, I'd joost chuck an eye now and then over the stream towards the edge of the wood."

Distin nodded and the line was swung round, so as to advance for some distance toward the wood which began suddenly just beyond the stream. There another shout, and the waving of the miller's hat, altered the direction again, and with Distin close by the flowing water, the line was marched back toward the lane with plenty of repetitions of their outward progress but it was at a slower rate, for the tangle was often far more dense.

And somehow, perhaps from the brilliancy of the morning, and the delicious nature of the pure soft air, the lads' spirits grew higher, and they had to work hard to keep their attention to the object they had in view, for nature seemed to be laying endless traps for them, especially for Macey, who certainly felt Vane's disappearance most at heart, but was continually forgetting him on coming face to face with something fresh. Now it was an adder coiled up in the warm sunshine on a little dry bare clump among some dead furze. It was evidently watching him but making no effort to get out of his way.

He had a stick, and it would have been easy to kill the little reptile, but somehow he had not the heart to strike at him, and he walked on quickly to overtake the line which had gone on advancing while he lagged behind.

Ten minutes later he nearly stepped upon a rabbit which bounded away, as he raised his stick to hurl it after the plump-looking little animal like a boomerang.

But he did not throw, and the rabbit escaped. He did not relax his efforts, but swept the tangle of bushes and brambles from right to left and back to the right, always eagerly trying to find something, if only a footprint to act as a clue that he might follow, but there was no sign.

All at once in a sandy spot amongst some furze bushes he stopped again, with a grim smile on his lip.

"Very evident that he hasn't been here," he muttered, as he looked at some scattered specimens of a fungus that would have delighted Vane, and been carried off as prizes. They were tall-stemmed, symmetrically formed fungi, with rather ragged brown and white tops, which looked as if in trying to get them open into parasol shape the moorland fairies had regularly torn up the outer skin of the tops with their little fingers; those unopened though showed the torn up marks as well, as they stood there shaped like an egg stuck upon a short thin stick.

"Come on!" shouted Gilmore. "Found anything?"

Macey shook his head, and hurried once more onward to keep the line, to hear soon afterwards *scape, scape,* uttered shrilly by a snipe which darted off in zigzag flight.

"Oh, how poor old Vane would have liked to be here on such a morning!" thought Macey, and a peculiar moisture, which he hastily dashed away, gathered in his eyes and excused as follows:—

"Catching cold," he said, quickly. "No wonder with one's feet and legs so wet, why, I'm soaking right up to the waist. Hallo! what bird's that?"

For a big-headed, thick-beaked bird flew out of a furze bush, showing a good deal of white in its wings.

"Chaffinch, I s'pose. No; can't be. Too big. Oh, I do wish poor old Vane was here: he knows everything of that kind. Where can he be? Where can he be?"

It was hot work that toiling through the bushes, but no one murmured or showed signs of slackening as he struggled along. There were halts innumerable, and the doctor could be seen hurrying here and hurrying there along the straggling line till at last a longer pause than usual was made at some pool, and heads were turned toward those who seemed to be making a more careful examination than usual; while, to relieve the tedium of the halt, Distin suddenly went splashing through the shallow stream on to the pebbly margin on the other side.

"Shan't you get very wet?" shouted Gilmore.

"Can't get wetter than I am," was shouted back then. "I say it's ten times better walking here. Look out! Moor-hens!"

"And wild ducks," cried Gilmore, as a pair of pointed-winged mallards flew up with a wonderfully graceful flight.

But the birds passed away unnoticed, for just then Distin uttered a cry which brought Macey tearing over the furze and brambles following Gilmore, who was already at the edge of the stream, and just then the signal was given by the miller to go on.

Chapter Twenty Two.

Vane is Taken at a Disadvantage.

Vane felt for the moment quite startled, the place being so silent and solitary, but the idea of danger seemed to him absurd, and he stood watching the shadow till all doubt of its being human ceased, for an arm was raised and then lowered as if a signal was being made.

"What can it mean?" he thought. And then:—"I'll soon see."

Just as he had made up his mind to walk forward, there was a slight movement and a sharp crack as of a twig of dead wood breaking under the pressure of a foot, and he who caused the sound, feeling that his presence must be known, stepped out from behind the tree.

"Why, I fancied it was Distie," said Vane to himself with a feeling of relief that he would have found it hard to explain, for it was one of the gipsy lads approaching him in a slow, furtive way.

"Thought they were gone long enough ago," he said to himself; and then speaking: "Hi! you, sir; come here!—Make him try and dig some up. Wonder they don't hunt for truffles themselves," he added. "Don't think they are wholesome, perhaps."

The lad came slowly toward him, but apparently with great unwillingness.

"Come on," cried Vane, "and I'll give you a penny. Hallo! Here's the other one!"

For the second lad came slouching along beneath the trees.

"Here, you two," cried Vane, waving his trowel; "come along and dig up some of these. That's right. You've got sticks. You can do it with the points."

The second boy had come into sight from among the trees to Vane's left, and advanced cautiously now, as if doubtful of the honesty of his intentions.

"That's right," cried Vane. "Come along, both of you, and I'll give you twopence a piece. Do you hear? I shan't hurt you."

But they did not hasten their paces, advancing very cautiously, stick in hand, first one and then the other, glancing round as if for a way of escape, as it seemed.

"Why, they're as shy as rabbits," thought Vane, laughing to himself. "It's leading such a wild life, I suppose. Here," he cried to the first lad, who was now within a yard of him, while the other was close behind; "see these? I want some of them. Come on, and I'll show you how to find them. Why, what did you do that for?"

Vane gave a bound forward, wincing with pain, for he had suddenly received a heavy blow on the back from the short cudgel the boy behind him bore, and as he turned fiercely upon him, thrusting the trowel into his basket and doubling his fist to return the blow, the first boy struck him heavily across the shoulder with his stick.

If the gipsy lads imagined that the blows would cow Vane, and make him an easy victim for the thrashing they had evidently set themselves to administer, they were sadly mistaken. For uttering a cry of rage as the second blow sent a pang through him, Vane dashed down his basket and trowel, spun round and rushed at his second assailant, but only to receive a severe blow across one wrist while another came again from behind.

"You cowards!" roared Vane; "put down those sticks, or come in front."

The lads did neither, and finding in spite of his rage the necessity for caution, Vane sprang to a tree, making it a comrade to defend his back, and then struck out wildly at his assailants.

So far his efforts were in vain. Sticks reach farther than fists, and his hands both received stinging blows, one on his right, numbing it for the moment and making him pause to wonder what such an unheard-of attack could mean.

Thoughts fly quickly at all times, but with the greatest swiftness in emergencies, and as Vane now stood at bay he could see that these two lads had been watching him for some time past, and that the attack had only been delayed for want of opportunity.

"I always knew that gipsies could steal," he thought, "but only in a little petty, pilfering way. This is highway robbery, and if I give them all I've got they will let me go."

Then he considered what he had in his pockets—about seven shillings, including the half-pence—and a nearly new pocket-knife. He was just coming to the conclusion that he might just as well part with this little bit of portable property and escape farther punishment, when one of the boys made a feint at his head and brought his stick down with a sounding crack, just above his left knee, while the other struck him on the shoulder.

Vane's blood was up now, and forgetting all about compromising, he dashed at one of his assailants, hitting out furiously, getting several blows home, in spite of the stick, and the next minute would have torn it from the young scoundrel's grasp if the other had not attacked him so furiously behind that he had to turn and defend himself there.

This gave the boy he was beating time to recover himself, and once more Vane was attacked behind and had to turn again.

All this was repeated several times, Vane getting far the worst of the encounter, for the gipsy lads were as active as cats and wonderfully skilful at dealing blows; but all the same they did not escape punishment, as their faces showed, Vane in his desperation ignoring the sticks and charging home with pretty good effect again and again.

The fight with the gipsies.

"It's no good; I shall be beaten," he thought as he now protected himself as well as he could by the shelter afforded by the tree he had chosen, though poor protection it was, for first one and then the other boy would dart in feinting with his stick and playing into the other's hand and giving him an opportunity to deliver a blow. "I shall have to give in, and the young savages will almost kill me."

And all this time he was flinching, dodging and shrinking here and there, and growing so much exhausted that his breath came thick and fast.

"Oh, if I only had a stick!" he panted, as he avoided a blow on one side to receive one on the other; and this made him rush savagely at one of the lads; but he had to draw back, smarting from a sharp blow across the left arm, right above the elbow, and one which half numbed the member.

But though he cast longing eyes round, there was no sticks save those carried by the boys, who, with flashing eyes, kept on darting in and aiming wherever they could get a chance. There was one fact, however, which Vane noticed, and which gave him a trifle of hope just when he was most despairing: his adversaries never once struck at his head, contenting themselves by belabouring his arms, back and legs, which promised to be rendered quite useless if the fight went on.

And all the time neither of the gipsy lads spoke a word, but kept on leaping about him, making short runs, and avoiding his blows in a way that was rapidly wearing him out.

Should he turn and run? No, he thought; they would run over the ground more swiftly than he, and perhaps get him down.

Then he thought of crying for help, but refrained, for he felt how distant they were from everyone, and that if he cried aloud he would only be expending his breath.

And lastly, the idea came again that he had better offer the lads all he had about him. But hardly had the thought crossed his brain, than a more vicious blow than usual drove it away, and he rushed from the shelter of the tree-trunk at the boy who delivered that blow. In trying to avoid Vane's fist, he caught his heel, staggered back, and in an instant his stick was wrested from his hand, whistled through the air, and came down with a sounding crack, while what one not looking on might have taken to be an echo of the blow sounded among the trees.

But it was not an echo, only the real thing, the second boy having rushed to his brother's help, and struck at Vane's shoulder, bringing him fiercely round to attack in turn, stick-armed now, and on equal terms. For Vane's blow had fallen on the first boy's head, and he went down half-stunned and bleeding, to turn over and then begin rapidly crawling away on hands and knees.

Vane saw this, and he forgot that he was weak, that his arms were numbed and tingling, and that his legs trembled under him. If victory was not within his grasp, he could take some vengeance for his sufferings; and the next minute the beechen glade was ringing with the rattle of stick against stick, as in a state of blind fury now, blow succeeded blow, many not being fended off by the gipsy lad's stick, but reaching him in a perfect hail on head, shoulders, arms, everywhere. They flew about his head like a firework, making him see sparks in a most startling way till Vane put all his remaining strength into a tremendous blow which took effect upon a horizontal bough; the stick snapped in two close to his hand, and he stood defenceless once more, but the victor after all, for the second boy was running blindly in and out among the trees, and the first was quite out of sight.

As he grasped the position, Vane uttered a hoarse shout and started in pursuit, but staggered, reeled, tried to save himself, and came down, heavily upon something hard, from which he moved with great rapidity and picked up to look at in dismay.

It was the trowel.

A faint, rustling sound amongst the leaves overhead roused Vane to the fact that he must have been sitting there some time in a giddy, half-conscious state, and, looking up, he could see the bright eyes of a squirrel fixed upon him, while its wavy bushy tail was twitching, and the little animal sounded as if it were scolding him for being there; otherwise all was still, and, in spite of his sufferings, it seemed very comical to Vane that the pretty little creature should be abusing him, evidently looking upon him as a thief come poaching upon the winter supply of beech-nuts.

Then the giddy feeling grew more oppressive, the trees began to slowly sail round him, and there appeared to be several squirrels and several branches all whisking their bushy tails and uttering that peculiar sound of theirs—*chop, chop, chop,*—as if they had learned it from the noise made by the woodman in felling trees.

What happened then Vane did not know, for when he unclosed his eyes again, it was to gaze at the level rays of the ruddy sun which streamed in amongst the leaves and twigs of the beeches, making them glorious to behold.

For a few minutes he lay there unable to comprehend anything but the fact that his head was amongst the rough, woody beech-mast, and that one hand grasped the trowel while the other was full of dead leaves; but as his memory began to work more clearly and he tried to move, the sharp pains which shot through him chased all the mental mists away and he sprang up into a sitting posture unable to resist uttering a groan of pain as he looked round to see if either of the gipsy boys was in sight.

Chapter Twenty Three.

Where Vane Spent the Night.

The squirrel and the squirrel only. There was not even a sound now. Vane could see the basket he had brought and the two pieces of the strong ash stick which he had broken over the fight with the second boy. The ground was trampled and the leaves kicked up, but no enemy was near, and he naturally began to investigate his damages.

"They haven't killed me—not quite," he said, half-aloud, as he winced in passing his hand over his left shoulder and breast; and then his eyes half-closed, a deathly feeling of sickness came over him and he nearly fainted with horror, for at the touch of his hand a severe pain shot through his shoulder, and he could feel that his breast and armpit was soaking wet.

Recovering from the shock of the horrible feeling he took out his handkerchief to act as a bandage, for he felt that he must be bleeding freely from one of the blows, and he knew enough from his uncle's books about injured arteries to make him set his teeth and determine to try and stop that before he attempted to get to his feet and start for home.

His first effort was to unbutton his Norfolk jacket and find the injury which he felt sure must be a cut across the shoulder, but at the first touch of his hand he winced again, and the sick feeling came back with a faint sensation of horror, for there was a horrible grating sound which told of crushed bone and two edges grinding one upon the other.

Again he mastered his weakness and boldly thrust his hand into his breast, withdrew it, and burst out into a wild hysterical laugh as he gave a casual glance at his hand before passing it cautiously into his left breast-pocket and bringing out, bit by bit, the fragments of the bottle of preparation which the doctor had dispensed, and that it had been his mission to deliver that afternoon. For in the heat of the struggle, a blow of one of the sticks had crushed the bottle, saturating his breast and side with the medicament, and suggesting to his excited brain a horrible bleeding wound and broken bones.

"Oh, dear!" he groaned; and he laughed again, "how easy it is to deceive oneself;" and he busied himself, as he spoke, in picking out the remains of the bottle, and finally turned his pocket inside out and shook it clear.

"Don't smell very nice," he said with a sigh; "but I hope it's good for bruises. Well, it's of no use for me to go on now, so I may as well get back."

He was kneeling now and feeling his arms and shoulders again, and then he cautiously touched his face and head. But there was no pain, no trace of injury in that direction, and he began softly passing his hands up and down his arms, and over his shoulders, wincing with agony at every touch, and feeling that he must get on at once if he meant to reach home, for a terrible stiffness was creeping over him, and when at last he rose to his feet, he had to support himself by the nearest tree, for his legs were bruised from hip to ankle, and refused to support his weight.

"It is of no good," he said at last, after several efforts to go on, all of which brought on a sensation of faintness. "I can't walk; what shall I do?"

He took a step or two, so as to be quite clear of the broken bottle, and then slowly lowered himself down upon the thick bed of beech-mast and leaves, when the change to a recumbent position eased some of his sufferings, and enabled him to think more clearly. And one of the results of this was a feeling of certainty that it would be impossible for him to walk home.

Then he glanced round, wondering whether his assailants had gone right away or were only watching prior to coming back to finish their work.

"I don't know what it means," he said, dolefully. "I can't see why they should attack me like this. I never did them any harm. It must be for the sake of money, and they'll come back when I'm asleep."

Vane ground his teeth, partly from rage, partly from pain, as he thrust his hand into his pocket, took out all the money he had, and then after looking carefully round, he raised the trowel, scraped away the leaves, dug a little hole and put in the coins, then covered them up again, spreading the leaves as naturally as possible, and mentally making marks on certain trees so as to remember the spot.

At the same time he was haunted by the feeling that his every act was being watched, and that the coins would be found.

"Never mind," he muttered, "they must find them," and he lay back once more to think about getting home, and whether he could manage the task after a rest, but he grew more and more certain that he could not, for minute by minute he grew cooler, and in consequence his joints and muscles stiffened, so that at last he felt as if he dared not stir.

He lay quite still for a while, half-stunned mentally by his position, and glad to feel that he was not called upon to act in any way for the time being, all of which feeling was of course the result of the tremendous exertion through which he had passed, and the physical weakness and shock caused by the blows.

It was a soft, deliciously warm evening, and it was restful to lie there, gazing through the trees at the glowing west, which was by slow degrees paling. The time had gone rapidly by during the last two hours or so, and it suddenly occurred to him in a dull, hazy way that the evening meal, a kind of high tea, would be about ready now at the little manor; that Aunt Hannah would be getting up from her work to look out of the window and see if he was coming; and that after his afternoon in the garden, the doctor would have been up to his bedroom and just come down ready to take his seat at the snug, comfortable board.

"And they are waiting for me," thought Vane.

The idea seemed more to amuse than trouble him in his half-stupefied state, for everything was unreal and dreamy. He could not fully realise that he was lying there battered and bruised, but found himself thinking as of some one else in whose troubles he took an interest.

It was a curious condition of mind to be in, and, if asked, he could not have explained why he felt no anxiety nor wonder whether, after waiting tea for a long time, the doctor would send to meet him, and later on despatch a messenger to the village, where no news would be forthcoming. Perhaps his uncle and aunt would be anxious and would send people in search of him, and if these people were sent they would come along the deep lane and over the moorland piece, thinking that perhaps he would have gone that way for a short cut.

Perhaps. It all seemed to be perhaps, in a dull, misty way, and it was much more pleasant to lie listening to the partridges calling out on the moor—that curiously harsh cry, answered by others at a distance, and watch the sky growing gradually grey, and the clouds in the west change from gold to crimson, then to purple, and then turn inky black, while now from somewhere not far away he heard the flapping of wings and a hoarse, crocketing sound which puzzled him for the moment, but as it was repeated here and there, he knew it was the pheasants which haunted that part of the forest, flying up to their roosts for the night, to be safe from prowling animals—four-legged, or biped who walked the woods by night armed with guns.

For it did not matter; nothing mattered now. He was tired; and then all was blank.

Sleep or stupor, one or the other. Vane had been insensible for hours when he woke up with a start to find that lie was aching and that his head burned. He was puzzled for a few minutes before he could grasp his position. Then all he had passed through came, and he lay wondering whether any search had been made.

But still that did not trouble him. He wanted to lie still and listen to the sounds in the wood, and to watch the bright points of light just out through the narrow opening where he had seen the broad red face of the sun dip down, lower and lower out of sight. The intense darkness, too, beneath the beeches was pleasant and restful, and though there were no partridges calling now, there were plenty of sounds to lie and listen to, and wonder what they could be.

At another time he would have felt startled to find himself alone out there in the darkness, but in his strangely dulled state now every feeling of alarm was absent, and a sensation akin to curiosity filled his brain. Even the two gipsy lads were forgotten. He had once fancied that they might return, but he had had reasoning power enough left to argue that they would have come upon him long enough before, and to feel that he must have beaten them completely,—frightened them away.

And as he lay he awoke to the fact that all was not still in that black darkness, for there was a world of active, busy life at work. Now there came, like a whispering undertone, a faint clicking noise as the leaves moved. There were tiny feet passing over him; beetles of some kind that shunned the light; wood-lice and pill millipedes, hurrying here and there in search of food; and though Vane could not see them he knew that they were there.

Again there was the soft rustling movement of a leaf, and then of another a short distance away on the other side of his head. And Vane smiled as he lay there on his back staring up at the overhanging boughs through which now and then he could catch sight of a fine bright ray.

For he knew that sound well enough. It was made by great earth worms which reached out of their holes in the cool, moist darkness, feeling about for a soft leaf which they could seize with their round looking mouths, hold tightly, and draw back after them into the hole from which their tails had not stirred.

Vane lay listening to this till he was tired, and then waited for some other sound of the night.

It was not long in coming—a low, soft, booming buzz of some beetle, which sailed here and there, now close by, now so distant that its hum was almost inaudible, but soon came nearer again till it was right over his head, when there was a dull flip, then a tap on the dry beech-mast.

"Cockchafer," said Vane softly, and he knew that it had blundered up against some twig and fallen to earth, where, though he could not see it, he knew that it was lying upon its back sprawling about with its awkward-looking legs, vainly trying to get on to them again and start upon another flight.

Once more there was silence, broken only by a faint, fine hum of a gnat, and the curious wet crackling or rustling sound which rose from the leaves.

Then Vane smiled, for in the distance there was a resonant, "Hoi, hoi," such as might have been made by people come in search of him. But he knew better, as the shout rose up, and nearer and nearer still at intervals, for it was an owl sailing along on its soft, silent pinions, the cry being probably to startle a bird from its roost or some unfortunate young bird or mouse into betraying its whereabouts, so that a feathered leg might suddenly be darted down to seize, with four keen claws all pointing to one centre, and holding with such a powerful grip that escape was impossible.

The owl passed through the dark shadowy aisles, and its cry was heard farther and farther away till it died out; but there was no sense of loneliness in the beech-wood. There was always something astir.

Now it was a light tripping sound of feet over the dead leaves, the steps striking loudly on the listener's ear. Then they ceased, as if the animal which made the sounds were cautious and listening for danger. Again trip, trip, trip, plainly heard and coming nearer, and from half-a-dozen quarters now the same tripping sounds, followed by pause after pause, and then the continuation as if the animals were coming from a distance to meet at some central spot.

Rap!

A quick, sharp blow of a foot on the ground, followed by a wild, tearing rush of rabbits among the trees, off and away to their burrows, not one stopping till its cotton-wool-like tail had followed its owner into some sandy hole.

Another pause with the soft petillation of endless life amongst the dead leaves, and then from outside the forest, down by the sphagnum margined pools, where the cotton-rushes grew and the frogs led a cool, soft splashing life, there came a deep-toned bellowing roar, rising and falling with a curious ventriloquial effect as if some large animal had lost its way, become bogged, and in its agony was calling upon its owner for rescue.

No large quadruped, only a brown-ruffed, long necked, sharp-billed bittern, the now rare marsh bird which used to haunt the watery solitudes with the heron, but save here and there driven away by drainage and the naturalist's gun.

And as Vane lay and listened, wondering whether the bird uttered its strange, bellowing song from down by a pool, or as it sailed round and round, and higher and higher, over the boggy mere, he recalled the stories Chakes had told him of the days when "bootherboomps weer as plentiful in the mash as wild ducks in winter." And then he tried to fit the bird's weird bellowing roar with the local rustic name—"boomp boomp—boother boomp!" but it turned out a failure, and he lay listening to the bird's cry till it grew fainter and less hoarse. Then fainter still, and at last all was silent, for Vane had sunk once more into a half-insensible state, it could hardly be called sleep, from which he was roused by the singing of birds and the dull, chattering wheezing chorus kept up by a great flock of starlings, high up in the beech tops.

The feverish feeling which had kept him from being cold had now passed off, and he lay there chilled to the bone, aching terribly and half-puzzled at finding himself in so strange a place. But by degrees he recalled everything, and feeling that unless he made some effort to crawl out of the beech-wood he might lie there for many hours, perhaps days, he tried to turn over so as to get upon his knees and then rise to his feet.

He was not long in finding that the latter was an impossibility, for at the slightest movement the pain was intense, and he lay still once more.

But it was terribly cold; he was horribly thirsty, and fifty yards away the beech trees ended and the sun was shining hotly on the chalky bank, while just below there was clear water ready for scooping up with his hand to moisten his cracked lips. In addition, there were blackberries or, if not, dew-berries which he might reach. Only a poor apology for breakfast, but delicious now if he could only get some between his lips.

He tried again, then again, each time the pain turning him sick; but there was a great anxiety upon him now. His thoughts were no longer dull and strained in a selfish stupor; he was awake, fully awake, and in mental as well as bodily agony. For his thoughts were upon those at the little manor, and he knew that they must have passed a sleepless night on his account, and he knew, too, that in all probability his uncle had been out with others searching for him, certain that some evil must have befallen or he would have returned.

It was a terrible wrench, and he felt as if his muscles were being torn; but with teeth set, he struggled till he was upon hands and knees, and then made his first attempt to crawl, if only for a foot or two.

At last, after shrinking again and again, he made the effort, and the start made, he persevered, though all the time there was a singing in his ears, the dead leaves and blackened beech-mast seemed to heave and fall like the surface of the sea, and a racking agony tortured his limbs. But he kept on foot by foot, yard by yard, with many halts and a terrible drag upon his mental powers before he could force himself to recommence. How long that little journey of fifty or sixty yards took he could not tell; all he knew was that he must get out of the forest and into the sunshine, where he might be seen by those who came in search of him; and there was water there—the pure clear water which would be so grateful to his parched lips and dry, husky throat.

"Poor old chap," said Macey.

The feeling of chill was soon gone, for his efforts produced a burning pain in every muscle, but in a dim way he knew that he was getting nearer the edge, for it was lighter, and a faint splashing sound and the beating of wings told of wild-fowl close at hand in that clear water.

On then again so slowly, but foot by foot, till the last of the huge pillar-like trunks which had seemed to bar his way was passed, and he slipped down a chalky bank to lie within sight of the water but unable to reach it, utterly spent, when he heard a familiar voice give the Australian call— "Coo-ee!" and he tried to raise a hand but it fell back.

Directly after a voice cried:

"Hi! Here he is!"

The voice was Distin's, and as he heard it Vane fainted dead away.

Chapter Twenty Four.

The Law Asks Questions.

Seeing the rush made by Gilmore and Macey, Bruff hesitated for a few moments, and then turned and shouted to Joseph, the next man.

"They've fun suthin," and ran after them.

Joseph turned and shouted to Wrench, the carpenter.

"They've got him," and followed Bruff.

Wrench shouted to Chakes and ran after Joseph, and in this House-that-Jack-built fashion the news ran along the line to the doctor and rector, and right to the end, with the result that all came hurrying along in single-file, minute by minute increasing the size of the group about where Vane lay quite insensible now.

"Poor old chap," cried Macey, dropping on his knees by his friend's side, Gilmore kneeling on the other, and both feeling his hands and face, which were dank and cold, while Distin stood looking down grimly but without offering to stir.

"Don't say he's dead, sir," panted Bruff.

"No, no, he's not dead," cried Macey. "Fetch some water; no, run for the doctor."

"He's coming, sir," cried Joseph, shading his eyes to look along the line. "He won't be long. Hi—hi—yi! Found, found, found!" roared the man, and his cry was taken up now and once more the news flew along the line, making all redouble their exertions, even the rector, who had not done such a thing for many years, dropping into the old football pace of his youth, with his fists up and trotting along after the doctor.

But the progress was very slow. It was a case of the more haste the worst speed, for a bee-line through ancient gorse bushes and brambles is not perfection as a course for middle-aged and elderly men not accustomed to go beyond a walk. Every one in his excitement caught the infection, and began to run, but the mishaps were many. Chakes, whose usual pace was one mile seven furlongs per hour, more or less, tripped and went down; and as nobody stopped to help him, three men passed him before he had struggled up and began to look about for his hat. The next to go down was Rounds, the miller, who, after rushing several tangles like an excited rhinoceros, came to grief over an extra tough bramble strand, and went down with a roar.

"Are you hurt, Mr Rounds?" panted the doctor.

"Hurt!" cried the churchwarden, "I should think I am, sir. Five hundred million o' thorns in me. But don't you wait. You go on, and see to that boy," he continued, as he drew himself into a sitting position. "Dessay he wants you more than I do."

"Then I will go on, Mr Rounds; forgive me for leaving you."

"All right, sir, and you too, parson; goo on, niver mind me."

The rector seemed disposed to stay, for he was breathless, but he trotted on, and was close to the doctor, as he reached the group on the other side of the stream.

"Not dead?" panted the doctor.

"Oh no, sir," cried Macey, "but he's very bad; seems to have tumbled about among the trees a great deal. Look at his face."

The doctor knelt down after making the men stand back.

"Must have fallen heavily," he said, as he began his examination. "Head cut, great swelling, bruise across his face, and eye nearly closed. This is no fall, Mr Syme. Good heavens! look at his hand and wrist. The poor fellow has been horribly beaten with sticks, I should say."

"But tell me," panted the rector; "he is not—"

"No, no, not dead; insensible, but breathing."

"Found him, gentlemen?" said a voice; and as the rector looked up, it was to see the two police constables on their way to join them.

"Yes, yes," cried the rector; "but, tell me, was there any firing in the night—any poachers about?"

"No, sir; haven't seen or heard of any lately; we keep too sharp a look-out. Why, the young gent has got it severely. Some one's been knocking of him about."

"Don't stop to talk," cried the doctor. "I must have him home directly."

"Here, how is he?" cried a bluff voice; and Rounds now came up, dabbing his scratched and bleeding face with his handkerchief.

"Bad, bad, Rounds," said the doctor.

"Bad? Ay, he is. But, halloo, who is been doing this?"

He looked around at his fellow-townsmen, and then at Vane's fellow-pupils so fiercely that Gilmore said quickly:

"Not I, Mr Rounds."

"Silence!" cried the doctor angrily. "It is of vital importance that my nephew should be carried home at once."

"Oh, we'll manage that, sir," said one of the constables as he slipped off his greatcoat and spread it on the ground. "Now, if we lift him and lay him upon that, and half-a-dozen take hold of the sides and try to keep step, we can get him along."

"Yes, that's right," cried the doctor, superintending the lifting, which drew a faint groan from Vane. "Poor lad!" he said; "but I'm glad to hear that. Now then, better keep along this side of the stream till we can cut across to the lane. Here, I want a good runner."

"I'll go," said Gilmore quickly.

"Yes, you," said the doctor, "go and tell my wife to have Vane's bed ready. Say we have found him hurt, but not very badly."

"Why not take him to the rectory?" said Mr Syme. "It is nearer."

"Thank you, but I'll have him at home," said the doctor.

"One moment, gentlemen," said the first constable, book in hand. "I want to know exactly where he was found."

"Here, man, here," cried the doctor. "Now then, lift him carefully, and keep step. If I say stop, lower him directly."

"Yes, sir; go on," said the constable. "We must have a look round before we come away. P'r'aps you'd stop along with us, Mr Churchwarden, sir, and maybe one of you young gents would stay," he continued, addressing Distin.

"Me—me stay!" said the lad starting, and flushing to his brow.

"Yes, sir. Young gents' eyes are sharp and see things sometimes."

"Yes, Distin, my dear boy," said the rector, "stop with them. You are going to search?"

"Yes, sir. That young gent couldn't have got into that state all by himself, and we want to find out who did it."

The man glanced sharply at Distin again as he spoke, and the young Creole avoided his eye with the result that the constable made a note in his book with a pencil which seemed to require wetting before it would mark.

"I think," said the rector, "it is my duty to stay here, as this matter is assuming a serious aspect."

"Thank ye, sir; I should be glad if you would," said the constable. "It do begin to look serious."

"Joseph, run on after Dr Lee, and tell him why I am staying. Say that he is to use the carriage at once if he wishes to send for help or nurse. I shall not be very long."

Joseph ran off at a sharp trot after the departing group, and the constable went slowly forward after carefully examining the ground where Vane had been found.

"Keep back, everybody, please. Plenty of footprints here," he said, "but all over, I'm afraid. Hah! Look here, sir," he continued, pointing down at the loose sand and pebbles; "he crawled along here on his hands and knees."

Distin looked sallow and troubled now, and kept on darting furtive looks at those about, several of the men having stopped back to see what the constable might find.

"Don't see no steps but his," said the constable, who seemed to be keenly observant for so rustic-looking a man. "Hah, that's where he come down, regularly slipped, you see."

He pointed to the shelving bank of chalk, on the top of which the beeches began, and over which their long, lithe branches drooped.

"Steady, please. I'll go on here by myself with you two gents. You see as no one else follows till I give leave."

The second constable nodded, and the bank was climbed, the rector telling Distin to hold out a hand to help him—a hand that was very wet and cold, feeling something like the tail of a codfish.

Here the constable had no difficulty in finding Vane's track over the dead leaves and beech-mast for some distance, and then he uttered an ejaculation as he pounced upon a broken stick, one of the pieces being stained with blood.

"It's getting warm," he said. "Oh, yes, don't come forward, gentlemen. Here we are: ground's all trampled and kicked up, and what's this here? Little trowel and a basket and—"

He turned over the contents of the basket with a puzzled expression.

"Aren't taters," he said, holding the basket to the rector.

"No, my man, they are truffles."

"Oh, yes, sir, I can see they're trifles."

"Truffles, my man, troofles," said the rector. "The poor fellow must have been digging them up."

"But no one wouldn't interfere with him for digging up that stuff, sir. I mean keepers or the like. And there's been two of 'em here, simminly. Oh, yes, look at the footmarks, only they don't tell no tales. I like marks in soft mud, where you can tell the size, and what nails was in the boots. Stuff like this shows nothing. Halloo, again."

"Found something else?" cried the rector excitedly.

"Bits o' broken glass, sir,—glass bottle. There's a lot of bits scattered about."

The constable searched about the grass of the beech grove where the struggle had taken place, but not being gifted with the extraordinary eyes and skill of an American Indian, he failed to find the track of

Vane's assailants going and coming, and he was about to give up when the rector pointed to a couple of places amongst the dead leaves which looked as if two hands had torn up some of the dead leaves.

"Ay, that's someat," said the constable quickly. "I see, sir, you're quite right. Some one went down here and—Phee-ew!" he whistled as he picked up a leaf. "See that, sir?"

The rector looked, shuddered and turned away, but Distin pressed forward with a curious, half-fascinated aspect, and stared down at the leaf the constable held out, pointing the while to several more like it which lay upon the ground.

"Blood?" said Distin in a hoarse voice.

"Yes, sir, that's it. Either the young gent or some one else had what made that. Don't look nice, do it?"

Distin shuddered, and the constable made another note in his book, moistening his pencil over and over again and glancing thoughtfully at Distin as he wrote in a character that might have been called cryptographic, for it would have defied any one but the writer to have made it out.

"Well, constable," said the rector at last, "what have you discovered?"

"That the young gent was out here, sir, digging up them tater things as he was in the habit of grubbing up—weeds and things. I've seen him before."

"Yes, yes," said the rector. "Well?"

"And then some one come and went at him."

"Some one," said the rector, "I thought you said two."

"So I did, sir, and I thought so at first, but I don't kind o' find marks of more than one, and he broke this stick about Mr Vane, and the wonder to me is as he hasn't killed him. Perhaps he has."

"But what motive? It could not have been the keepers."

"Not they, sir. They liked him."

"Could it be poachers?"

"Can't say, sir. Hardly. What would they want to 'tack a young gent like that for?"

"Have there been any tramps about who might do it for the sake of robbery?"

"Ha'n't been a tramp about here for I don't know how long, sir. We're quite out of them trash. Looks to me more like a bit o' spite."

"Spite?"

"Yes, sir. Young gent got any enemies as you know on?"

The rector laughed and Distin joined in, making the constable scratch his head.

"Oh, no, my man, we have no enemies in my parish. You have not got the right clue this time. Try again."

"I'm going to, sir, but that's all for to-day," said the man, buttoning up his book in his pocket. "I think we'll go back to the town now."

"By all means," said the rector. "Very painful and very strange. Come, Distin."

As he spoke he walked from under the twilight of the great beech-wood out into the sunshine, where about a dozen of the searchers were waiting impatiently in charge of the second constable for a report of what had been done.

As the rector went on, Distin looked keenly round and then bent down over the leaves which bore the ugly stains, and without noticing that the constable had stolen so closely to him, that when he raised his head he found himself gazing full in the man's searching eyes.

"Very horrid, sir, aren't it," he said.

"Yes, yes, horrible," cried Distin, hastily, and he turned sharply round to follow the rector.

At that moment the constable touched him on the shoulder with the broken stick, and Distin started round and in spite of himself shivered at the sight of the pieces.

"Yes," he said hoarsely, as his face now was ghastly. "You want to speak to me?"

"Yes, sir, just a word or two. Would you mind telling me where you was yesterday afternoon—say from four to six o'clock?"

"I—I don't remember," said Distin. "Why do you ask?"

"The law has a right to ask questions, sir, and doesn't always care about answering of them," said the man with a twinkle of the eye. "You say you don't know where you was?"

"No. I am not sure. At the rectory, I think."

"You aren't sure, sir, but at the rectory, you think. Got rather a bad memory, haven't you, sir?"

"No, excellent," cried Distin desperately.

"You says as you was at the rectory yesterday afternoon when this here was done?"

"How do you know it was done in the afternoon," said Distin, quickly.

"Reason one, 'cause the young gent went in the afternoon to Lenby. Reason two, 'cause he was digging them trifles o' taters, and young gents don't go digging them in the dark. That do, sir?"

"Yes. I feel sure now that I was at the rectory," said Distin, firmly.

"Then I must ha' made a mistake, sir—eyes nothing like so good as they was."

"What do you mean," cried Distin, changing colour once more.

"Oh, nothing, sir, nothing, only I made sure as I see you when I was out in my garden picking apples in the big old tree which is half mine, half my mate's. But of course it was my mistake. Thought you was going down the deep lane."

"Oh, no, I remember now," said Distin, carelessly; "I go out so much to think and study, that I often quite forget. Yes, I did go down the lane—of course, and I noticed how many blackberries there were on the banks."

"Ay, there are a lot, sir—a great lot to-year. The bairns gets quite basketsful of 'em."

"Are you coming, Distin?" cried the rector.

"Yes, sir, directly," cried Distin; and then haughtily, "Do you want to ask me any more questions, constable?"

"No, sir, thankye; that will do."

"Then, good-morning."

Distin walked away with his head up, and a nonchalant expression on his countenance, leaving the constable looking after him.

"Want to ask me any more questions, constable," he said, mimicking Distin's manner. "Then good-morning."

He stood frowning for a few minutes, and nodded his head decisively.

"Well," he said, "you're a gentleman, I suppose, and quite a scholard, or you wouldn't be at parson's, but if you aren't about as artful as they make 'em, I'm as thick-headed as a beetle. Poor lad! Only a sort o' foreigner, I suppose. What a blessing it is to be born a solid Englishman. Not as I've got a word again your Irishman and Scotchman, or your Welsh, if it comes to that, but what can you expect of a lad born out in a hot climate that aren't good for nobody but blacks?"

He took a piece of string out of his pocket, and very carefully tied the trowel and pieces of broken stick together as firmly as if they were to be despatched on a long journey. Then he opened the basket, peeped in, and frowned at the truffles, closed it up and went out.

"Any of you as likes can go in now," he said, and shaking his head solemnly as questions began to pour upon him from all sides respecting the stick and basket, he strode off with his colleague in the direction of the town, gaining soon upon the rector, who was too tired and faint to walk fast, for it was not his habit to pass the night out of bed, and take a walk of some hours' duration at early dawn.

Chapter Twenty Five.

Bates is Obstinate.

Gilmore reached the Little Manor to find Aunt Hannah ready to hurry out and meet him, and he shrank from giving his tidings, fearing that it would be a terrible shock.

But he could keep nothing back with those clear, trusting eyes fixed upon him, and he gave his message.

"You would not deceive me, Mr Gilmore?" she said. "You are sure that he is only badly hurt; the doctor—my husband—hasn't sent you on to soften worse news to come?"

"Indeed no," cried Gilmore warmly. "Don't think that. He is very bad. It is not worse."

Aunt Hannah closed her eyes, and he saw her lips move for a few moments. He could not hear the words she spoke, but he took off his hat, and bent his head till she laid her hand upon his arm.

"Thank God!" she said fervently. "I feared the worst. They are coming on, you say?"

"Yes, but it will be quite an hour before they can get here. You will excuse me, Mrs Lee, I want to get back to poor old Vane's side."

"Yes, go," she said cheerfully. "I shall be very busy getting ready for him. The doctor did not say that you were to take anything back?"

"No," said Gilmore; and he hurried away, admiring the poor little lady's fortitude, for he could see that she was suffering keenly, and only too glad to be alone.

As he hurried back to the town he was conscious for the first time that his lower garments were still saturated and patched with dust;

that his hands were torn and bleeding, and that his general aspect was about as disordered as it could possibly be. In fact he felt that he looked as if he had been spending the early morning trying to drag a pond, and that every one who saw him would be ready to jeer.

On the contrary, though he met dozens of people all eager to question him about Vane, no one appeared to take the slightest notice of his clothes, and he could not help learning how popular his friend was among the townsfolk, as he saw their faces assume an aspect of joy and relief.

"I wonder whether they would make so much fuss about me," he said to himself; and, unable to arrive at a self-satisfying conclusion, he began to think what a blank it would have made in their existence at the rectory if Vane had been found dead. From that, as he hurried along, he began to puzzle himself about the meaning of it all, and was as far off from a satisfactory conclusion as when he began, on coming in sight of the little procession with the doctor walking on one side of Vane, and Macey upon the other.

He had not spoken, but lay perfectly unconscious, and there was not the slightest change when, followed by nearly the whole of the inhabitants of Greythorpe, he was borne in at the Little Manor Gate, the crowd remaining out in the road waiting for such crumbs of news as Bruff brought to them from time to time.

There was not much to hear, only that the doctor had carefully examined Vane when he had been placed in bed, and found that his arms and shoulders were horribly beaten and bruised, and that the insensibility still lasted, while Doctor Lee had said something about fever as being a thing to dread.

They were the words of wisdom, for before many hours had passed Vane was delirious and fighting to get out of bed and defend himself against an enemy always attacking him with a stick.

He did not speak, only shrank and cowered and then attacked in turn fiercely, producing once more the whole scene so vividly that the doctor and Aunt Hannah could picture everything save the enemy who had committed the assault.

The next evening, while the rector sat thinking over the bad news he had heard from the Little Manor half-an-hour before, Joseph tapped at the door to announce a visitor, and the rector said that he might be shown in.

Macey was at the Little Manor. Gilmore and Distin were in the grounds when the visitor was seen entering the gate, and the latter looked wildly round, as if seeking for the best way to escape; but mastering himself directly, he stood listening to Gilmore, who exclaimed:

"Hallo! here's Mr PC. Let's go and ask him if he has any news about the brute who nearly killed poor old Vane."

"No," said Distin, hoarsely; "let's wait till he comes out."

"All right," replied Gilmore; and he stood in the gloom beneath the great walnut tree watching the constable go up to the porch, ring, and, after due waiting, enter, his big head, being seen soon after, plainly shown against the study shaded lamp.

"Well, constable," said the rector; "you have news for me?"

"Yes, sir."

"About the assailant of my poor pupil?"

"Yes, sir, and I should have been here before, only it was Magistrates' day, and I had to go over to the town to attend a case."

"Well, what have you found out? Do you know who the person was that assailed Mr Vane Lee?"

"Yes, sir: I'm pretty sure."

"Not some one in this town?"

"Your pupil, sir. Mr. Dustin."

"Yes, sir."

"Surely not. I cannot think that any one would be so cruel."

"Sorry to say it is so, sir, as far as I know; and I'm pretty sure now."

"But who? We have so few black sheep here, I am thankful to say. Not Tompkins?"

"No, sir."

"Jevell?"

"No, sir, some one much nigher home than that, sir, I'm sorry to say."

"Well, speak, and put me out of my suspense."

"Some one here, sir," said the constable, after drawing a long breath.

"What!"

"Fact, sir. Some one as lives here at the rectory."

"In the name of common sense, man," cried the rector, angrily, "whom do you mean—me?"

"No, sir, that would be too bad," said the constable.

"Whom, then?"

"Your pupil, sir, Mr Distin."

Had a good solid Japanese earthquake suddenly shaken down all the walls of the rectory and left the Reverend Morton Syme seated in his easy chair unhurt and surrounded by débris and clouds of dust, he could not have looked more astonished. He stared at the constable, who stood before him, very stiff, much buttoned up and perfectly unmoved, as a man would stand who feels his position unassailable.

Then quietly and calmly taking out his gold-rimmed spring eye-glasses, the rector drew a white pocket-handkerchief from his breast, carefully polished each glass, put them on and stared frowningly at his visitor, who returned the look for a time, and then feeling his position irksome and that it called for a response, he coughed, saluted in military fashion and settled his neck inside his coat collar.

"You seem to be perfectly sober, Bates," said the rector at last.

"Sober, sir?" said the man quickly. "Well, I think so, sir."

"Then, my good man, you must be mad."

The constable smiled.

"Beg pardon, sir. That's just what criminals make a point of saying when you charge 'em. Not as I mean, sir," he added hastily, "that you are a criminal, far from it."

"Thank you, my man, I hope not. But what in the name of common sense has put it into your head that my pupil, Mr Distin, could be guilty of such a terrible deed? Oh, it's absurd—I mean monstrous."

The constable looked at him stolidly, and then said slowly:

"Suckumstarnces, sir, and facks."

"But, really, my good man, I—Stop! You said you had been over to the town and met your chief officer. Surely you have not started this shocking theory there."

"Oh, yes, sir. In dooty bound. I told him my suspicions."

"Well, what did he say?"

The constable hesitated, coughed, and pulled himself tightly together.

"I asked you what your chief officer said, sir."

"Well, sir, if I must speak I must. He said I was a fool."

"Ah, exactly," cried the rector, eagerly. Then, checking himself, he said with a deprecating smile: "No, no, Bates, I do not endorse that, for I have always found you a very respectable, intelligent officer, who has most efficiently done his duty in Greythorpe; and unless it were for your benefit, I should be very sorry to hear of your being removed."

"Thankye, sir; thankye kindly," said the constable.

"But in this case, through excess of zeal, I am afraid you have gone much too far. Mr Lance Distin is a gentleman, a student, and of very excellent family. A young man of excellent attainments, and about as likely to commit such a brutal assault as you speak of, as—as, well, for want of a better simile, Bates, as I am."

The constable shook his head and looked very serious.

"Now, tell me your reasons for making such a charge."

The explanations followed.

"Flimsy in the extreme, Bates," said the rector triumphantly, and as if relieved of a load. "And you show no more common sense than to charge a gentleman with such a crime solely because you happened to see him walking in that direction."

"Said he wasn't out, sir."

"Well, a slip—a piece of forgetfulness. We might either of us have done the same. But tell me, why have you come here?"

"Orders was to investigate, and if I found other facts, sir, to communicate with the chief constable."

"Of course. Now, you see, my good man, that what I say is correct—that through excess of zeal you are ready to charge my pupil—a gentleman entrusted to my charge by his father in the West Indies—a pupil to whom, during his stay in England, I act *in loco parentis*—and over whose career I shall have to watch during his collegiate curriculum—with a crime that must have been committed by some tramp. You understand me?"

"Yes, sir, all except the French and the cricklum, but I daresay all that's right."

The rector smiled.

"Now, are you satisfied that you have made a mistake?"

"No, sir, not a bit of it," said the constable stolidly.

The rector made a deprecating gesture with his hand, rose and rang the bell. Then he returned to his seat, sat back and waited till the bell was answered.

"Have the goodness, Joseph, to ask Mr Distin to step here."

"If I might make so bold, sir," interposed the constable, "I should like you to have 'em all in."

"One of my pupils, Mr Macey, is at the manor."

"Macey? That's the funny one," said the constable. "Perhaps you'd have in them as is at home."

"Ask Mr Gilmore to step in too."

Joseph withdrew, and after a painful silence, steps were heard in the porch.

"By the way, Bates," said the rector, hastily, "have you spread this charge?"

"No, sir; of course not."

"Does not Doctor Lee know?"

"Not yet, sir. Thought it my dooty to come fust to you."

"I thank you, Bates. It was very considerate of you. Hush!"

Distin's voice was heard saying something outside in a loud, laughing way, and the next moment he tapped and entered.

"Joseph said you wished to see me, sir." Then, with an affected start as he saw the constable standing there, "Have you caught them?"

"Be good enough to sit down, Distin. Gilmore, take a chair." Then, after a pause:

"You are here, Gilmore, at the constable's request, but the matter does not affect you. My dear Distin, it does affect you, and I want you to help me convince this zealous but wrong-headed personage that he is labouring under a delusion."

"Certainly, sir," replied Distin, cheerfully. "What is the delusion?"

"In plain, simple English, my dear boy, he believes that you committed that cruel assault upon poor Vane Lee."

"Oh," exclaimed Distin, springing up and gazing excited at the constable, his eyes full of reproach—a look which changed to one of indignation, and with a stamp of the foot like one that might be given by an angry girl, he cried: "How dare he!"

"Ah, yes! How dare he," said the rector. "But pray do not be angry, my dear boy. There is no need. Bates is a very good, quiet, sensible man who comes here in pursuance of what he believes to be his duty, and I am quite convinced that as soon as he realises the fact that he has made a great mistake he will apologise, and there will be an end of it."

The constable did not move a muscle, but stood gazing fixedly at Distin, who uttered a contemptuous laugh.

"Well, Mr Syme," he said, "what am I to do? Pray give me your advice."

"Certainly, and it is my duty to act as your counsel; so pray forgive me for asking you questions which you may deem unnecessary—for I grant that they are as far as I am concerned, but they are to satisfy this man."

"Pray ask me anything you like, sir," cried Distin with a half-contemptuous laugh.

"Then tell me this, on your honour as a gentleman: did you assault Vane Lee?"

"No!" cried Distin.

"Did you meet him in the wood the day before yesterday?"

"No."

"Did you encounter him anywhere near there, quarrel with and strike him?"

"No, no, no," cried Distin, "and I swear—"

"There is no need to swear, Mr Distin. You are on your honour, sir," said the rector.

"Well, sir, on my honour I did not see Vane Lee from the time he left this study the day before yesterday till I found him lying below the chalk-bank by that stream."

"Thank you, Distin. I am much obliged for your frank disclaimer," said the rector, gravely. "As I intimated to you all this was not necessary to convince me, but to clear away the scales from this man's eyes. Now, Bates," he continued, turning rather sternly to the constable, "are you satisfied?"

"No, sir," said the man bluntly, "not a bit."

"Why, you insolent—"

"Silence, Mr Distin," said the rector firmly.

"But, really, sir, this man's—"

"I said silence, Mr Distin. Pray contain yourself. Recollect what you are. I will say anything more that I consider necessary."

He cleared his throat, sat back for a few moments, and then turned to the constable.

"Now, my good fellow, you have heard Mr Distin's indignant repudiation of this charge, and you are obstinately determined all the same."

"Don't know about obstinate, sir," replied the constable, "I am only doing my duty, sir."

"What you conceive to be your duty, Bates. But you are wrong, my man, quite wrong. You are upon the wrong scent. Now I beg of you try to look at this in a sensible light and make a fresh start to run down the offender. You see you have made a mistake. Own to it frankly, and I am sure that Mr Distin will be quite ready to look over what has been said."

Just then there was a tap at the door.

"May I come in, sir?"

"Yes, come in, my dear boy. You have just arrived from the Manor?"

"Yes, sir," said Macey.

"How is Vane?"

Macey tried to answer, but something seemed to rise in his throat, and when he did force out his words they sounded low and husky.

"Awfully bad, sir. The doctor took me up, but he doesn't know anybody. Keeps going on about fighting."

"Poor lad," said the rector, with a sigh. "But, look here, Macey, you must hear this. The constable here—Bates—has come to announce to me his belief that the assault was committed by your fellow-pupil."

"Distin?" cried Macey, sharply, and as he turned to him the Creole's jaw dropped.

"Yes, but it is of course a mistake, and has been disproved. I was pointing out to Bates here the folly of an obstinate persistence in such an idea, when you entered." Then turning once more to the constable, "Come, my man, you see now that you are in the wrong."

"No, sir," said the constable, "I didn't see it before, but I feel surer now that I'm right."

"What?"

"That young gent thinks so too."

"Mr Macey? Absurd!"

"See how he jumped to it directly, sir."

"Nonsense, man! Nonsense," cried the rector. "Here, Macey, my dear boy, I suppose, as a man of peace, I must strive to convince this wrong-headed personage. Tell him that he is half mad."

"For thinking Distin did it, sir?" replied Macey, slowly.

"Exactly—yes."

"It wouldn't be quite fair, sir, because I'm afraid I thought so, too."

The constable gave his leg a slap.

"You—you dare to think that," cried Distin.

"Hush! hush! hush!" said the rector, firmly. "Macey, my dear boy, what cause have you for thinking such a thing."

"Distin hates him."

The constable drew a long breath, and he had hard work to preserve his equanimity in good official style.

"My dear Macey," cried the rector reproachfully, "surely you are not going, on account of a few boyish disagreements, to think that your fellow-pupil would make such a murderous attack. Come, you don't surely believe that?"

"No," said Macey slowly, "I don't now: I can't believe that he would be such a wretch."

"There!" cried the rector, triumphantly. "Now, constable, there is no more to say, except that I beg you will not expose me and mine to painful trouble, and yourself to ridicule by going on with this baseless charge."

"Can't say, sir, I'm sure," replied the constable. "I want to do my dooty, and I want to show respect to you, Mr Syme, sir, as has always been a good, kind gentleman to me; but we're taught as no friendly or personal feelings is to stand in the way when we want to catch criminals. So, with all doo respect to you, I can't make no promises."

"I shall not ask you, my man," replied the rector; "what I do say is go home and think it over. In a day or two I hope and trust that my pupil Vane Lee will be well enough to enlighten us as to who were his assailants."

"I hope so, sir. But suppose he dies?"

"Heaven forbid! my man. There, do as I say: go back and think over this meeting seriously, and believe me I shall be very glad to see you come to me to-morrow and say frankly, from man to man—I have been in the wrong. Don't shrink from doing so. It is an honour to anyone to avow that he was under a misapprehension."

"Thankye, sir, and good-night," said the constable, as the rector rang for Joseph to show him out; and the next minute all sat listening to his departing steps on the gravel, followed by the *click click click click* of the swing-gate.

The rector looked round as if he were about to speak, but he altered his mind, and the three pupils left the room, Distin going up to his chamber without a word, while attracted by the darkness Gilmore and Macey strolled out through the open porch into the grounds.

"Suppose he dies?" said Macey, almost unconsciously repeating the constable's words.

"Oh, I say, don't talk like that," cried Gilmore. "It isn't likely, and you shouldn't have turned against poor old Distie as you did."

"I couldn't help it," said Macey, sadly. "You'd have thought the same if the doctor had let you go up to see poor old Weathercock. It was horrid. His face is dreadful, and his arms are black and blue from the wrist to the shoulder."

"But Dis declared that he hadn't seen him," cried Gilmore.

"I hope he hadn't, for it's too horrid to think a fellow you mix with could be such a wretch."

Gilmore turned sharply round to his companion, but it was too dark to see his face. There was something, however, in his tone of voice which struck him as being peculiar. It did not sound confident of Distin's innocence. There was a want of conviction in his words too, and this set Gilmore thinking as to the possibility of Distin having in a fit of rage and dislike quarrelled with and then beaten Vane till the stick was broken and his victim senseless.

The idea grew rapidly as he stood there beside Macey in the darkness, and he recalled scores of little incidents all displaying Distin's dislike of his fellow-pupil; and as Gilmore thought on, a conscious feeling of horror, almost terror, crept over him till his common sense began to react and argue the matter out so triumphantly that in a voice full of elation he suddenly and involuntarily exclaimed:

"It's absurd! He couldn't."

"What's absurd? Who couldn't," cried Macey, starting from a reverie.

"Did I say that aloud?" said Gilmore, wonderingly.

"Why, you shouted it."

"I was thinking about whether it was possible that the constable was right."

"That's queer," said Macey; "I was thinking just the same."

"And that Distie had done it?"

"Yes."

"Well, don't you see that it is impossible?"

"No, I wish I could," said Macey sadly; "can you?"

"Why, of course. Vane's as strong as Distie, isn't he?"

"Yes, quite."

"And he can use his fists."

"I should rather think he can. I put on the gloves with him one day and he sent me flying. But what has that got to do with it?"

"Everything. Do you think Distie could have pitched into Vane with a stick and not got something back?"

"Why, of course he couldn't."

"Well, there you are, then. He hasn't got a scratch."

"Hist! What's that," said Macey, softly.

"Sounded like a window squeaking."

"Come away," whispered Macey taking his companion by the arm, and leading him over the turf before he stopped some distance now from the house.

"What is it?" said Gilmore then.

"That noise; it was old Distie at his window. I could just make him out. He had been listening to what we said."

"Listeners never hear—" began Gilmore.

"Any good of themselves," said Macey, finishing the old saying.

"Well, I don't mind."

"More don't I."

And the two lads went in.

Chapter Twenty Six.

Sympathy.

Those were sad and weary hours at the Little Manor, and when Vane's delirium was at its height and he was talking most rapidly, Doctor Lee for almost the first time in his life felt doubtful of his own knowledge and ability to treat his patient. He was troubled with a nervous depression, which tempted him to send for help, and he turned to white-faced, red-eyed Aunt Hannah.

"I'm afraid I'm not treating him correctly," he whispered. "I think I will send Bruff over to the station to telegraph for help."

But Aunt Hannah shook her head.

"If you cannot cure him, dear," she said firmly, "no one can. No, do not send."

"But he is so very bad," whispered the doctor; "and when this fever passes off he will be as weak as a babe."

"Then we must nurse him back to strength," said Aunt Hannah. "No, dear, don't send. It is not a case of doubt. You know exactly what is the matter, and of course how to treat him for the best."

The doctor was silenced and stood at the foot of the bed, while Aunt Hannah laid her cool, soft hand upon the sufferer's burning brow.

Neither aunt nor uncle troubled to think much about the causes of the boy's injuries; their thoughts were directed to the nursing and trying to allay the feverish symptoms, for the doctor was compelled to own that his nephew's condition was grave, the injuries being bad enough alone without the exposure to the long hours of a misty night just on the margin of a moor.

It was not alone in the chamber that sympathetic conversation went on, for work was almost at a standstill in house and garden. For the three servants talked together, as they found out how much Vane had had to do with their daily life, and what a blank his absence on a bed of sickness had caused.

"Oh, dear!" sighed Martha, "poor, poor fellow!"

The tears were rolling down her cheeks, and to keep up an ample supply of those signs of sorrow she took a very long sip of warm tea, for the pot had been kept going almost incessantly since Vane had been borne up to his bed.

"Yes, it is.—Oh, dear," sighed Eliza. "Poor dear! Only to think of it and him only as you may say yesterday alive and well."

"Ay, and so it is, and so it always will be," said Bruff, who was standing by the kitchen-door turning some ale round and round in the bottom of a mug.

"Ah!" sighed Martha.

"Ah, indeed!" sighed Eliza.

"And me so ready to make a fuss about the poor dear because he'd made a litter sometimes with his ingenuous proceedings."

"And me too," sighed Eliza, "and ready to bite my very tongue off now for saying the things I did."

"Yes, as Mr Syme says, we're a many of us in black darkness," muttered Bruff. "Why, that there hot-water apparatus is a boon and a blessin' to men, as the song says."

"About the pens?" added Eliza.

"You can most see the things grow."

"Ah," sighed Martha.

"He weer as reight as reight. It was all them turning off the scape-yokes."

"And Missus forgetting to tell Martha about not lighting the fire."

"And if he'd only get well again," sobbed Martha, wiping her eyes, "the biler might be busted once a week, and not a word would I say."

"No," sighed Bruff giving his ale another twist round and slowly pouring it down his throat. "There's a rose tree in the garden as he budded hisself, though I always pretended it was one of my doing, and sorry I am now."

"Ah," sighed Martha, "we all repents when it's too late."

Pop!

A cinder flew out of the fire on to the strip of carpet lying across the hearth, and a pungent odour of burning wool arose. But Bruff stooped down and using his hardened fingers as tongs, picked up the cinder and tossed it inside the fender.

Martha started as the cinder flew out and looked aghast at Eliza, her ruddy face growing mottled, while the housemaid's cheeks were waxen as the maids gave themselves up to the silly superstition that, like many more, does not die hard but absolutely refuses to die at all.

"Oh, my poor dear!" cried Martha, sobbing aloud, while Eliza buried her face in her apron, and the reason thereof suddenly began to dawn upon Bruff, who turned to the fireplace again, stooped down and carefully picked up the exploded bubble of coke and gas, turned it over two or three times, and then by a happy inspiration giving it a shake and producing a tiny tinkling noise.

Bruff's face expanded into a grin.

"Why, it aren't," he cried holding out the cinder; "it's a puss o' money."

"No, no," sighed Martha, "that isn't the one."

"That it is," cried Bruff, sturdily. "I'm sure on it. Look 'Liza."

The apron was slowly drawn away from the girl's white face and she fixed her eyes on the hollow cinder, but full of doubt.

"It is. Hark!" cried Bruff, and he shook the cinder close to Eliza's ear. "Can't you hear?"

"It does tinkle," she said. "But are you sure that's the one?"

"Of course I am, and it's a sign as he'll get well again, and be rich and happy."

"No, no; that isn't the one, that isn't the one," sobbed Martha.

"Tell you it is," cried Bruff so fiercely that the cook doubtingly took the piece of cinder, shook it, and by degrees a smile spread over her countenance and she rose and put the scrap on the chimney-piece between two bright brass candlesticks.

"For luck," she said; and this time she wiped her eyes dry and examined a saucepan of beef tea which she had stewed down. "In case it's wanted," she said confidentially, though there was not the slightest likelihood thereof for some time to come.

"Well," said Bruff at last, "I suppose I had better go out to work."

But he only looked out of the kitchen window at the garden and shook his head.

"Don't seem to hev no 'art in it," he said, looking from one to the other, as if this were quite a new condition for him to be in. "Seems to miss him so, and look wheer you will theer's a something as puts you in mind of him. Well, all I says is this, and both of you may hear it, only let him get well and he may do any mortal thing in my garden, and I won't complain."

Bruff took up his mug, looked inside it, and set it down again with a frown.

"My missus is coming up to see if she can do owt for you 's afternoon."

"Ah!" sighed cook, "you never know what neighbours is till you're in trouble, 'Liza."

"No."

"Go up, soft like, and ask missus if I may send her a cup o' tea."

"No," said Eliza, decisively; "pour one out and I'll take it up. And I say, dear, you know what a one master is for it; why don't you send him up the little covered basin o' beef tea. There, I'll go and put a napkin over a tray."

Perhaps it was due to being called "dear," perhaps to the fact there was an outlet for the strong beef tea she had so carefully prepared; at any rate Martha smiled and went to the cupboard for the pepper, and then to the salt-box, to season the beef tea according to her taste.

Five minutes later the tray was borne up with the herbaceous and the flesh tea, and in addition some freshly-made crisp brown toast.

The refreshments were most welcome, for both the doctor and Aunt Hannah were exhausted and faint, and as soon as they were alone again, and Eliza gone down with the last bulletin, Aunt Hannah shed a few tears.

"So sympathetic and thoughtful of the servants, dear," she said.

The doctor nodded, and then as he dipped the dry toast in the beef tea he thought to himself that Vane had somehow managed to make himself a friend everywhere.

But an enemy, too, he thought directly after, and he set himself to try and think out who it could be—an occupation stopped by messengers from the rectory, Gilmore, Distin and Macey having arrived to ask how the patient was getting on. While on their way back, they met Bates, the constable, looking very solemn as he saluted them and went on, thinking a great deal, but waiting until Vane recovered his senses before proceeding to act.

Chapter Twenty Seven.

Vane Recollects.

"Hah, that's better," said the doctor one fine morning, "feel stronger, don't you?"

"Oh yes, uncle," said Vane rather faintly, "only my head feels weak and strange, and as if I couldn't think."

"Then don't try," said the doctor, and for another day or two Vane was kept quiet.

But all the time there was a curious mental effervescence going on as the lad lay in bed, the object of every one's care; and until he could clearly understand why he was there, there was a constant strain and worry connected with his thoughts.

"Give him time," the doctor used to say to Aunt Hannah, "and have confidence in his medical man. When nature has strengthened him enough his mind will be quite clear."

"But are you sure, dear?" said Aunt Hannah piteously; "it would be so sad if the poor fellow did not quite recover his memory."

"Humph!" ejaculated the doctor, "this comes of having some one you know by heart for medical attendant. You wouldn't have asked Doctor White or Doctor Black such a question as that."

"It is only from anxiety, my dear," said Aunt Hannah; "I have perfect confidence in you. It is wonderful how he is improved."

Just then two visitors arrived in the shape of Gilmore and Macey.

They had come to make inquiries on account of the rector, they said; and on hearing the doctor's report, Macey put in a petition on his own account.

"Let you go up and sit with him a bit?" said the doctor. "Well, I hardly know what to say. He knows us now; but will you promise to be very quiet?"

"Oh, of course, sir," cried Macey.

"I can't let two go up," said the doctor.

Macey looked at Gilmore.

"I'll give way if you'll promise to let me have first turn next time."

"Agreed," said Macey; and Gilmore went off back to give the doctor's report to the rector, while Macey was led upstairs gently by Aunt Hannah, and after again promising to be very quiet, let into Vane's room, and the door closed behind him.

Vane was lying, gazing drowsily at the window, but the closing of the door made him turn his eyes toward the new comer, when his face lit up directly.

"What, Aleck!" he said faintly.

"What, old Weathercock!" cried Macey, running to the bed. "Oh, I say, old chap, it does one good to see you better, I say you're going to be quite well now, aren't you?"

"Yes, I am better. But have they caught them?"

"Eh? Caught what?"

"Those two young scoundrels of gipsies," said Vane quickly. Then, as he realised what he had said, he threw his arms out over the sheet. "Why, that's what I've been trying to think of for days, and now it's come. Have they caught them?"

"What for?" said Macey, wonderingly.

"For knocking me about as they did. They ought to be punished; I've been very ill, haven't I?"

"Awful," said Macey, quickly. "But, I say, was it those two chaps?"

Vane looked at him half wonderingly.

"Yes, of course," he said. "I remember it all now. It's just as if a cloud had gone away from the back of my head, and I could see clearly right back now."

"Why did they do it?" cried Macey, speaking out, but feeling dubious, for Vane's manner was rather strange, and he might still be wandering.

"I don't know," said Vane; "I was getting truffles for uncle when they came along, and it was fists against sticks. They won, I suppose."

"Well, rather so I think," said Macey, edging toward the door.

"Don't go, old chap. You've only just come."

"No, but you're talking too much, and you're to be kept quiet."

"Well, I'm lying quiet. But, tell me, have they caught those two fellows for knocking me about last night?"

"No, not yet; and I must go now, old fellow."

"But tell me this: What did Syme say this morning because I didn't come?"

"Oh, nothing much; he was tackling me. I got it horribly for being so stupid."

"Not you. But tell him I shall be back in the morning."

"All right. Good-bye."

They shook hands, and Macey hurried down to the doctor and Mrs Lee.

"Here, he's ever so much better and worse, too, sir," cried Macey.

The doctor started up in alarm.

"Oh, no, sir; he's quiet enough, but he thinks it was only last night when he was knocked about."

"Convalescents are often rather hazy about their chronology," said the doctor.

"But he's clear enough in one thing, sir; he says it was the two gipsy lads who set upon him with sticks."

"Ah!" cried the doctor.

"And I came down to ask you if these two fellows ought not to be caught."

"Yes, yes, of course," cried the doctor. "But first of all we must be sure whether he is quite clear in his head. This may be an illusion."

"Well, sir, it may be," replied Macey, "but if I'd had such a knocking about as poor Vane, I shouldn't make any mistake about it as soon as I could begin to think."

"Stay here," said the doctor. "I'll go up and see him."

He went up and all doubt about his nephew's clearness of memory was at an end, for Vane began at once.

"I've been lying here some time, haven't I, uncle?"

"Yes, my boy; a long while."

"I was very stupid just now when Macey was here. It seemed to me that it was only last night that I was in the wood getting truffles, when those two gipsy lads attacked me, but, of course, I've been very ill since."

"Yes, my boy, very."

"The young scoundrels! There was the basket and trowel, I remember."

"Yes, my boy, they brought them home."

"That's right. It was your little bright trowel, and—oh, of course I remember that now. I was taking the bottle of liniment, and one of the lad's sticks struck me on the breast, where I had the bottle in my pocket, and shivered it."

"Struck you with his stick?"

"Yes. I made as hard a fight of it as I could, but they were too much for me."

"Don't think about it any more now, but try and have a nap," said the doctor quietly. "I want to go down."

Vane sighed.

"What's the matter, boy, fresh pain?"

"No, I was thinking what a trouble I am to you, uncle."

"Trouble, boy? Why, it's quite a treat," said the doctor, laughing. "I was quite out of practice, and I'm in your debt for giving me a little work."

"Don't thank me, uncle," said Vane with a smile, though it was only the shadow of his usual hearty laugh. "I wouldn't have given you the job if I could have helped it."

The doctor nodded, patted the boy's shoulder and went down, for Vane in his weakness willingly settled himself off to sleep, his eyes being half-closed as the doctor shut the door.

"Well, sir," cried Macey, eagerly, as the doctor entered the drawing-room, "he's all right in the head again, isn't he?"

"I don't think there's a doubt of it, my lad," said the doctor. "You are going close by, will you ask the policeman to come down?"

"Yes; I'll tell him," cried Macey, eagerly.

"No, no, leave me to tell him. I would rather," said the doctor, "because I must speak with some reserve. It is not nice to arrest innocent people."

"But I may tell Mr Syme and Gilmore?"

"Oh, yes, you can tell what you know," replied the doctor; and, satisfied with this concession, Macey rushed off.

As he reached the lane leading to the rectory, habit led him up it a few yards. Then recollecting himself, he was turning back when he caught sight of Distin and Gilmore coming toward him, and he waited till they came up.

"It's all right," he cried. "Vane knows all about it now, and he told me and the doctor who it is that he has to thank for the knocking about."

"What! he knows?" cried Distin, eagerly; and Gilmore caught his companion's arm.

"Yes," he cried, catching Distin's arm in turn, "come on with me."

"Where to?" said Distin, starting.

"To the police—to old Bates."

"Want me, gents?"

Distin gave Macey a curious look, and then walked on beside him, Macey repeating all he knew as they went along toward Bates' cottage, where they found the constable looking singularly unofficial, for he was in his shirt-sleeves weeding his garden.

"Want me, gents?" he said with alacrity as he rose and looked from one to the other, his eyes resting longest upon Distin, as if he had some doubt about him that he could not clear up.

"We don't, but the doctor does," cried Macey. "I've just come from there."

"Phee-ew!" whistled the constable. "They been at his fowls again? No; they'd have known in the morning. Why—no—yes—you don't mean to say as Mr Vane's come round enough to say who knocked him about?"

"The doctor told me to tell you he wanted you to step down to see him," said Macey coolly; "so look sharp."

The constable ran to the pump to wash his hands, and five minutes after he was on the way to the Little Manor.

"I'm wrong," he muttered as he went along—"ever so wrong. Somehow you can't be cock-sure about anything. I could ha' sweered as that yallow-faced poople had a finger in it, for it looked as straight as straight; but theer, it's hard work to see very far. Now, let's hear what the doctor's got to say."

Chapter Twenty Eight.

Rowing Superseded.

"That there Mr Distin 'll have his knife into me for what I said about him. Oh, dear me, what a blunder I did make!"

"Yes, wrong as wrong," said Constable Bates, as he came away from the Little Manor, "and me niver to think o' they two lungeing looking young dogs. Why, of course it was they. I can see it clear now, as clear—a child could see it. Well, I'll soon run them down."

Easier said than done, for the two gipsy lads seemed to have dropped quite out of sight, and in spite of the help afforded by members of the constabulary all round the county the two furtive, weasel-like young scamps could not be heard of. They and their gang had apparently migrated to some distant county, and the matter was almost forgotten.

"It doesn't matter," Vane said, as he grew better. "I don't want to punish the scamps, I want to finish my boat;" and as soon as he grew strong he devoted all his spare time to the new patent water-walker as Macey dubbed it, and at which Distin now and then delivered a covert sneer.

For this scheme was the outcome of the unfortunate ride on the river that day when Vane sat dreaming in the boat and watching the laborious work of those who wielded the oars and tried to think out a means of sending a boat gliding through the water almost without effort.

He had thought over what had already been done as far as he knew, and pondered over paddle-wheels and screws with the mighty engines which set them in motion, but his aquatic mechanism must need neither fire nor steam. It must be something simple, easily applicable to a small boat, and either depend upon a man's arm or foot, as in the treadle of a lathe, or else be a something that he could wind up like old Chakes did the big clock, with a great winch key, and then go as long as he liked.

It took so much thinking, and he was so silent indoors, that Aunt Hannah told the doctor in confidence one night that she was sure poor Vane was sickening for something, and she was afraid that it was measles.

"Yes," said the doctor with a laugh, "sort of mental measles. You'll see he will break out directly with a rash—"

"Oh, my dear," cried Aunt Hannah, "then hadn't he better be kept in a warm bed?"

"Hannah, my beloved wife," said the doctor, solemnly, "is it not time you learned to wait till your ill-used husband has finished his speech before you interrupt him? I was saying break out directly with a rash desire to spend more money upon a whim-wham to wind up the sun."

"Ah, now you are joking," said Aunt Hannah. "Then you do not think he is going to be ill again?"

"Not a bit."

It all came out in a day or two, and after listening patiently to the whole scheme—

"Well," said the doctor, "try, only you are not to go beyond five pounds for expenses."

"Then you believe in it, uncle," cried Vane, excitedly.

"I am not going to commit myself, boy," said the doctor. "Try, and if you succeed you may ride us up and down the river as often as you like."

Vane went off at once to begin.

"Five pounds, my dear," said Aunt Hannah, shaking her head, "and you do not believe in it. Will it not be money wasted."

"Not more so than five pounds spent in education," replied the doctor, stoutly. "The boy has a turn for mechanics, so let him go on. He'll fail, but he will have learned a great deal about ics, while he has been amusing himself for months."

"About Hicks?" said Aunt Hannah, innocently, "is he some engineer?"

"Who said *Hicks*?" cried the doctor, "I said ics—statics, and dynamics and hydraulics, and the rest of their nature's forces."

"Oh," said Aunt Hannah, "I understand," which can only be looked upon as a very innocent fib.

Meanwhile Vane had hurried down to the mill, for five pounds does not go very far in mechanism, and there would be none to spare for the purchase of a boat.

"Hallo, squire," roared the miller, who saw him as he approached the little bridge, "you're too late."

"What for—going out?"

"Going out? What, with all this water on hand. Nay, lad, mak' your hay while the sun shines. Deal o' grinding to do a day like this."

"Then why did you say I was too late?" said Vane.

"For the eels running. They weer coming down fast enew last night. Got the eel trap half full. Come and look."

He led the way down through a flap in the floor to where, in a cellar-like place close to the big splashing mill wheel, there was a tub half full of the slimy creatures, anything but a pleasant-looking sight, and Vane said so.

"Reight, my lad," said the miller, "but you wait till a basketful goes up to the Little Manor and your Martha has ornamented 'em with eggs and crumbs and browned 'em and sent 'em up on a white napkin, with good parsley. Won't be an unpleasant sight then, eh? Come down to fish?"

"No," said Vane, hesitating now.

"Oh, then, you want the boat?"

"Yes, it was about the boat."

"Well, lad, there she is chained to the post. You're welcome, only don't get upset again and come back here like drowned rats."

"I don't want to row," said Vane. "I—er—that is—oh, look here, Mr Rounds," he cried desperately, "you can only say no. I am inventing a plan for moving boats through the water without labour."

"Well, use the oars; they aren't labour."

"But I mean something simpler or easier."

"Nay, theer aren't no easier way unless you tak a canoe and paddle."

"But I'm going to invent an easier way, and I want you to lend me the boat for an experiment."

"What!" roared the miller, "you want to coot my boat to pieces for some new fad o' yourn. Nay, lad, it aren't likely."

"But I don't want to cut it up."

"Say, coot, lad, coot; don't chop your words short; sounds as if you were calling puss wi' your cat."

"Well, then I don't want to coot up the boat, only to fit my machine in when it's ready, and propel the boat that way."

"Oh, I see," said the miller, scratching his big head. "You don't want to coot her aboot."

"No, not at all; I won't even injure the paint."

"Hum, well, I don't know what to say, lad. You wouldn't knock her aboot?"

"No; only bring my machine and fit it somewhere in the stern."

"Sort o' windmill thing?"

"Oh, no."

"Oh, I see, more like my water-mill paddles, eh?"

"Well, I don't quite know yet," said Vane.

"What, aren't it ready?"

"No; I haven't begun."

"Oh. Mebbe it never will be."

"Oh, yes, I shall finish it," said Vane.

"Hey, what a lad thou art for scheming things; I wish you'd mak' me a thing to grind corn wi'out weering all the face off the stones, so as they weant bite."

"Perhaps I will some day."

"Ay, there'd be some sense in that, lad. Well, thou alway was a lad o' thy word when I lent you the boat, so you may have her when you like; bood I'll lay a wager you don't get a machine done as'll row the boat wi' me aboard."

"We'll see," cried Vane, excitedly.

"Ay, we will," said the miller. "Bood, say, lad, what a one thou art for scheming! I say I heered some un say that it was one o' thy tricks that night when church clock kep' on striking nine hundred and nineteen to the dozen."

"Well, Mr Round—"

"I know'd: thou'd been winding her oop wi' the kitchen poker, or some game o' that sort, eh?"

"No, I only tried to clean the clock a little, and set it going again."

"Ay, and left all ta wheels out. Haw—haw—haw!"

The miller's laugh almost made the mill boards rattle.

"I say, don't talk about it, Mr Round," cried Vane; "and, really, I only forgot two."

The miller roared again.

"On'y left out two! Hark at him! Why, ivery wheel has some'at to do wi' works. Theer, I weant laugh at thee, lad, only don't fetch us all oot o' bed another night, thinking the whole plaace is being bont aboot our ears. Theer tak' the boat when you like; you're welcome enew."

Vane went off in high glee, and that day he had long interviews with Wrench the carpenter, and the blacksmith, who promised to work out his ideas as soon as he gave them models or measurements, both declaring that they had some splendid "stooff" ready to "wuck off," and Vane went back to his own place and gave every spare moment to his idea.

That propeller took exactly two months to make, for the workmen always made the parts entrusted to them either too short or too long, and in fact just as a cobbler would make a boot that ought to have been the work of a skilful veteran.

"It's going to be a rum thing," said Macey, who helped a great deal by strolling down from the rectory, sitting on a box, and drumming his heels on the side, while he made disparaging remarks, and said that the whole affair was sure to fail.

The doctor came in too, and nodded as the different parts were explained; but as the contrivance was worked out, Vane found that he had to greatly modify his original ideas; all the same though, he brought so much perseverance to bear that the blacksmith's objections were always overridden, and Wrench the carpenter's growls suppressed.

One of the greatest difficulties encountered was the making the machine so self-contained that it could be placed right in the stern of the boat without any need for nails or stays.

But Vane had a scheme for every difficulty, and at last the day came when the new propeller was set up in the little workshop, and Distin, brought by curiosity, accompanied Gilmore and Macey to the induction.

Vane was nervous enough, but proud, as he took his fellow-pupils into the place, and there, in the middle, fixed upon a rough, heavy bench, stood the machine.

"Why, you never got that made for five pounds?" cried Gilmore.

"N–no," said Vane, wincing a little, "I'm afraid it will cost nearly fifteen. I had to make some alterations."

"Looks a rum set-out," continued Gilmore, and Distin stood and smiled. "Oh, I say, while I remember," cried Gilmore, "there was a little girl wanted you this morning, Dis. Said she had a message for you."

"Oh, yes, I saw her," said Distin, nonchalantly. "Begging—I saw her."

"She'll always be following you," said Macey. "Why, that makes four times she has been after you, Dis."

"Oh, well, poor thing, what can one do," said Distin, hurriedly; "some mother or sister very ill, I believe. But I say, Vane," he continued, as if eager to change the conversation, "where is this thing to go?"

"In the stern of the boat."

"Stern? Why, it will fill the boat, and there will not be room for anything else."

"Oh, but the future ones will be made all of iron, and not take up half the space."

Gilmore touched a lever and moved a crank.

"Don't, don't," yelled Macey, running to the door, "it will go off."

There was a roar of laughter, in which all joined, and Vane explained the machine a little more, and above all that this was only a tentative idea and just to see if the mechanism would answer its purpose.

"But, I say," cried Gilmore, "it looks like a wooden lathe made to turn water."

"Or a mangle," said Distin, with a sneer of contempt.

"Wrong, both of you," cried Macey, getting toward the door, so as to be able to escape if Vane tried to get at him. "I'll tell you what it's like—a knife-grinder's barrow gone mad."

"All right," said Vane, "laugh away. Wait till you see how it works."

"When are you going to try it?" said Gilmore.

"To-morrow afternoon. Mr Round's going to send a cart for it and four of his men to get it down."

"We will be there," said Macey with a scowl such as would be assumed by the wicked man in a melodrama, and then the workshop was locked up.

Chapter Twenty Nine.

Trying an Experiment.

"Pray, pray, be careful, Vane, my dear," cried Aunt Hannah, the next afternoon, when the new propeller had been carefully lifted on to the miller's cart, and the inventor rushed in to say good-bye and ask the doctor and his aunt to come down for the trial, which would take place in two hours' time exactly.

Then he followed the cart, but only to be overtaken by the rector's other three pupils, Macey announcing that Mr Syme was going to follow shortly.

Vane did not feel grateful, and he would have rather had the trial all alone, but he was too eager and excited to mind much, and soon after the boat was drawn up to the side of the staging, at the end of the dam, the ponderous affair lifted from the cart, and the miller came out to form one of the group of onlookers.

"Why, hey, Vane Lee, my lad, she's too big enew. She'll sink the boat."

"Oh, no," cried Vane. "It looks heavier than it is."

"Won't be much room for me," said the miller, with a chuckle.

"You mustn't come," cried Vane in alarm. "Only Macey and I are going in the boat. We work the pedals and hand cranks. This is only an experiment to see if it will go."

"Hey bood she'll goo reight enew," said the miller, seriously, "if I get in. Reight to the bottom, and the mill 'll be to let."

The Experiment.

There was a roar of laughter at this, and Macey whispered:—

"I say, Weathercock, if they're going to chaff like this I shall cut off."

"No, no, don't be a coward," whispered back Vane; "it's only their fun. It don't hurt."

"Oh, doesn't it. I feel as if gnats were stinging me."

"That theer boat 'll never carry her, my lad," said the miller.

"It will, I tell you," cried Vane, firmly.

"Aw reight. In wi' her then, and when she's at the bottom you can come and fish for her. It's straange and deep down there."

"Now then, ready?" cried Vane after a due amount of preparation.

An affirmative answer was given; the frame-work with its cranks was carefully lifted on to the platform and lowered into the boat's stern, which it fitted exactly, and Vane stepped in, and by the help of a screw-hammer fitted some iron braces round the boat, screwed them up tightly. The machine was fairly fixed in its place and looked extremely top-heavy, and with Vane in the stern as well, sent the boat's gunwale down within four inches of the surface and the bows up correspondingly high.

By this time the rector and the Little Manor people had arrived, while quite a little crowd from the town had gathered to stand on the edge of the dam and for the most part grin.

"There," said Vane as he stood up covered with perspiration from his efforts. "That's about right. In a boat made on purpose the machine would be fitted on the bottom and be quite out of the way."

"Couldn't be, lad," said the miller. "But goo on, I want to see her move."

"Wish there was another boat here, Gil," said Distin. "You and I would race them."

"Let them talk," said Vane, to encourage Macey, who looked very solemn, and as he spoke he carefully examined the two very small paddles which dropped over each side, so arranged that they should, when worked by the cranks and hand levers, churn up the water horizontally instead of vertically like an ordinary paddle wheel.

There were a good many other little things to do, such as driving in a few wedges between the frame-work and side of the boat, to get all firmer, but Vane had come provided with everything necessary, and when he could no longer delay the start, which he had put off as long as possible, and when it seemed as if Macey would be missing if they stopped much longer, the lad rose up with his face very much flushed and spoke out frankly and well, explaining that it was quite possible that his rough machine would not work smoothly at first, but that if the principle was right he would soon have a better boat and machine.

Hereupon Gilmore cried, "Hooray!" and there was a hearty cheer, accompanied by a loud tapping of the rector's walking stick, on the wooden gangway.

"Now, Vane, lad, we're getting impatient," cried the doctor, who was nearly as anxious as his nephew. "Off with you!"

"Well said, doctor," cried the miller; "less o' the clapper, my lads, and more of the spinning wheels and stones."

"Ready, Macey?" whispered Vane.

"No," was whispered back.

"Why?"

"I'm in such an awful stew."

"Get out. It's all right. Now then. You know. Come down and sit in your place steadily."

Macey stepped down into the boat, which gave a lurch, and went very near the water, as far as the gunwale was concerned.

"Hi theer; howd hard," cried the miller; "he's too heavy. Coom out, lad, and I'll tak thy place."

There was another roar of laughter at this.

"Oh, I say, Mr Round, don't chaff us or we can't do it," whispered Vane to the jolly-looking great twenty-stone fellow.

"Aw reight, lad. I'll be serious enew now. Off you go! Shall I give you a shove?"

"No," said Vane. "I want to prove the boat myself. Now, Macey, you sit still till I've worked her round even, and then when I say off, you keep on stroke for stroke with me."

"All right," cried Macey, and Vane began to work his crank and paddle on the boat's starboard side with the result that they began to move and curve round. Then, applying more force and working hard, he gave himself too much swing in working his lever, with the result that his side rose a little. In the midst of the cheering that had commenced the little horizontal paddle came up level with the surface, spun round at a great rate, and sent a tremendous shower of spray all over those on the gangway, Distin getting the worst share, and in his effort to escape it nearly going off into the dam.

"You did that on purpose," he roared furiously, his voice rising above the shout of laughter.

"Oh, I've had enough of this," said Macey. "Let me get out."

"No, no, sit still. It's all right," whispered Vane. Then, aloud, "I didn't, Dis, it was an accident. All right, Aleck, keep the boat level. Now we're straight for the river. Work away."

Macey tugged at his lever and pushed with his feet; his paddle now revolved, and though the boat swayed dangerously, and Aunt Hannah was in agony lest it should upset, the paddles kept below the surface, and cheer after cheer arose.

For the two lads, in spite of the clumsiness and stiffness of the mechanism, were sending the boat steadily right out of the dam and into the river, where they ran it slowly for some four hundred yards before they thought it time to turn, and all the while with a troop of lads and men cheering with all their might.

"Sit steady; don't sway," said Vane, "she's rather top-heavy."

"I just will," responded Macey. "She'd be over in a moment. But, I say, isn't it hard work?"

"The machinery's too stiff," said Vane.

"My arms are," said Macey, "and I don't seem to have any legs."

"Never mind."

"But I do."

"Stop now," said Vane, and the boat glided on a little way and then the stream checked her entirely, right in the middle.

"That's the best yet," said Macey, with a sigh of relief.

But there was no rest for him.

"Now," cried Vane, "we're going back."

"Can't work 'em backwards."

"No, no, forward," said Vane. "I'll work backwards. Work away."

Macey obeyed, and a fresh burst of cheers arose as, in obedience to the reverse paddling, the boat turned as if on a pivot. Then as soon as it was straight for the mill, Vane reversed again, and accompanied by their sympathisers on the bank and working as hard as they could, the two engineers sent the boat slowly along, right back into the pool, and by judicious management on Vane's part, alongside of the wooden staging which acted as a bridge to the mill on its little island.

Here plenty more cheers saluted the navigators.

"Bravo! bravo!" cried the rector.

"Well done, Vane," cried the doctor.

"Viva," shouted Distin, with a sneering look at Vane, who winced as if it had been a physical stab, and he did not feel the happier for knowing that the cheers were for nothing, since he did not want Macey's words to tell him that his machine was a failure from the amount of labour required.

"Why, I could have taken the boat there and back home myself with a pair of sculls, and nearly as fast again," whispered the boy.

It was quite correct, and Vane felt anything but happy, as he stepped on to the top of the camp-shed, where the others were.

"Can't wark it by mysen," said the miller. "Won't join me, I suppose, doctor?"

"Any one else, not you," said the doctor, merrily.

"Come," said the rector, "another trial. Gilmore, Distin, you have a turn."

"All right, sir," cried Gilmore, getting into the boat; "come on, Dis."

"Oh, I don't know," said the young creole.

"He's afraid," said Macey, mischievously, and just loud enough for Distin to hear.

The latter darted a furious look at him, and then turned to Gilmore.

"Oh, very well," he said in a careless drawl. "I don't mind having a try."

"It'll take some of the fat conceit out of him, Weathercock," said Macey, wiping his streaming brow. "Oh, I say, I am hot."

Gilmore had taken off his jacket and vest before getting into the boat. Distin kept his on, and stepped down, while Vane held the boat's side from where he kneeled on the well-worn planks.

"Take off your things, man," said Gilmore, as Distin sat down.

"Work the levers steadily, Gil," said Vane.

"All right, old fellow."

"I dare say we can manage; thank you," said Distin, in a low, sarcastic tone, meant for Vane's ears alone, for, saving the miller, the others were chatting merrily about the success of the trial. "It does not seem to be such a wonderfully difficult piece of performance."

"It isn't," said Vane, frankly. "Only trim the boat well she's top-heavy."

"Thank you once more," said Distin, as he took off jacket and vest, and began to fold them.

"I'll give her head a push off," said Vane, taking up the boat-hook and beginning to thrust the boat's head out so that the fresh engineers could start together.

"Thank you again," said Distin, sarcastically, as the bows went round, and Vane after sending the prow as far as he could, ran and caught the stern, and drew that gently round till the boat was straight for the river and gliding forward.

"Ready, Dis?" said Gil, who had hold of his lever, and foot on the treadle he had to work.

"One moment," said Distin, rising in the boat to place his carefully folded clothes behind him, and it was just as Vane gave the boat a final thrust and sent it gliding.

"Give us a shout, you fellows," cried Gilmore. "Steady Dis!" he roared.

"Hooray!" came from the little crowd.

"Oh, what a lark!" shouted Macey, but Aunt Hannah uttered a shriek.

Vane's thrust had not the slightest thing to do with the mishap, for the boat was already so crank that the leverage of Distin's tall body, as he stood up, was quite enough to make it settle down on one side. As this disturbed his balance, he made a desperate effort to recover himself, placed a foot on the gunwale, and the next moment, in the midst of the cheering, took a header right away into the deep water, while the boat gradually continued its motion till it turned gently over, and floated bottom upwards, leaving Gilmore slowly swimming to the side, where he clung to the camp-shedding laughing, till it seemed as if he would lose his hold.

"Help! help!" cried Aunt Hannah.

"All right, ma'am," said the miller, snatching the boat-hook from Vane.

"Mr Distin! Mr Distin," shrieked Aunt Hannah.

The miller literally danced with delight.

"Up again directly, ma'am," he said, "only a ducking, and the water's beautifully clean. There he is," he continued, as Distin's head suddenly popped up with his wet black hair streaked over his forehead, and catching him deftly by the waistband of his trowsers with the boat-hook, the miller brought the panting youth to the gangway, and helped him out.

"You did that on purpose," cried Distin, furiously; but the miller only laughed the more, and soon after the boat had been drawn to its moorings, and righted, it was chained up, so that it should do no more mischief, the miller said.

That brought the experiment to a conclusion, and when the machine had been taken back dry to the workshop, as it had been proved that it was only labour in a novel way and much increased, Vane broke it up, and the doctor, when the bills were paid, said quietly:

"I think Vane will have a rest now for a bit."

Chapter Thirty.

Money Troubles.

"Going out, Vane?"

"Only to the rectory, uncle; want me?"

"No, my boy, no," said the doctor, sadly. "Er—that is, I do want to have a chat with you, but another time will do."

"Hadn't you better tell me now, uncle," said Vane. "I don't like to go on waiting and thinking that I have a scolding coming, and not know what it's about."

The doctor, who was going out into the garden, smiled as he turned, shook his head, and walked back to his chair.

"You have not been doing anything, Vane, my lad," he said quickly and sadly. "If anyone deserves a scolding it is I; and your aunt persistently refuses to administer it."

"Of course," said Aunt Hannah, looking up from her work, "you meant to do what was right, my dear. I am sorry more on your account than on my own, dear," and she rose and went behind the doctor's chair to place her hands on his shoulder.

He took them both and pressed them together to hold them against his cheek.

"Thank you, my dear," he said, turning his head to look up in her eyes. "I knew it would make no difference in you. For richer or poorer, for better or worse, eh? There, go and sit down, my dear, and let's have a chat with Vane here."

Aunt Hannah bowed her head and went back to her place, but contrived so that she might pass close to Vane and pass her hand through his curly hair.

"Vane, boy," said the doctor sharply and suddenly, "I meant to send you to college for the regular terms."

"Yes, uncle."

"And then let you turn civil engineer."

"Yes, uncle, I knew that," said the lad, wonderingly.

"Well, my boy, times are altered. I may as well be blunt and straightforward with you. I cannot afford to send you to college, and you will have to start now, beginning to earn your own living, instead of five or six years hence."

Vane looked blank and disappointed for a few moments, and then, as he realised that his aunt and uncle were watching the effect of the latter's words keenly, his face lit up.

"All right, uncle," he said; "I felt a bit damped at first, for I don't think I shall like going away from home, but as to the other, the waiting and college first, I shan't mind. I am sorry though that you are in trouble. I'm afraid I've been a great expense to you."

"There, don't be afraid about that any longer, my boy," said the doctor, rising. "Thank you, my lad—thank you. That was very frank and manly of you. There, you need not say anything to your friends at present, and—I'll talk to you another time."

The doctor patted Vane on the shoulder, then wrung his hand and hurried out into the garden.

"Why, auntie, what's the matter?" cried Vane, kneeling down by the old lady's chair, as she softly applied her handkerchief to her eyes.

"It's money, my dear, money," she said, making an effort to be calm. "I did hope that we were going to end our days here in peace, where, after his long, anxious toil in London, everything seems to suit your uncle so, and he is so happy with his botany and fruit and flowers; but Heaven knows what is best, and we shall have to go into quite a small cottage now."

"But I thought uncle was ever so rich, aunt," cried Vane. "Oh, if I'd known I wouldn't have asked him for money as I have for my schemes."

"Oh, my dear, it isn't that," cried Aunt Hannah. "I was always afraid of it, but I did not like to oppose your uncle."

"It? What was it?" cried Vane.

"Perhaps I ought not to tell you, dear, but I don't know. You must know some time. It was that Mr Deering. Your uncle has known him ever since they were boys at school together; and then Mr Deering, who is a great inventor, came down and told your uncle that he had at last found the means of making his fortune over a mechanical discovery, if some one would be security for him. Your uncle did not like to refuse."

"Oh, dear!" muttered Vane.

"You see it was not to supply him with money then, only to be security, so that other people would advance him money and enable him to start his works and pay for his patents."

"Yes, aunt, I understand," cried Vane. "And now—"

"His invention has turned out to be a complete failure, and your poor uncle will have to pay off Mr Deering's liabilities. When that is done, I am afraid we shall be very badly off, my dear."

"That you shan't, auntie," cried Vane, quickly; "I'll work for you both, and I'll make a fortune somehow. I don't see why I shouldn't invent."

"No, no, don't, boy, for goodness' sake," said the doctor, who had heard part of the conversation as he returned. "Let's have good hard work, my lad. Let someone else do the inventing."

"All right, uncle," said Vane, firmly; "I'll give up all my wild ideas now about contriving things, and set to work."

"That's right, boy," said the doctor. "I'm rather sick of hearing inventions named."

"Don't say that, dear," said Aunt Hannah, quietly and firmly; "and I should not like all Vane's aspirations to be damped because Mr Deering has failed. Some inventions succeed: the mistake seems to me to be when people take it for granted that everything must be a success."

"Hear! hear!" cried the doctor, thumping the table. "Here hi! You Vane, why don't you cheer, sir, when our Queen of Sheba speaks such words of wisdom. Your aspirations shall not be stopped, boy. There, no more words about the trouble. It's only the loss of money, and it has done me good. I was growing idle and dyspeptic."

"You were not, dear," said Aunt Hannah, decidedly.

"Oh, yes, I was, my dear, and this has roused me up. There, I don't care a bit for the loss, since you two take it so bravely. And, perhaps after all, in spite of all the lawyers say, matters may not turn out quite so badly. Deering says he shall come down, and I like that: it's honourable and straightforward of him."

"I wish he would not come," said Aunt Hannah, "I wish we had never seen his face."

"No, no! tut, tut," said the doctor.

"I'm sure I shall not be able to speak civilly to him," cried Aunt Hannah.

"You will, dear, and you will make him as welcome as ever. His misfortune is as great as ours—greater, because he has the additional care of feeling that he has pretty well ruined us and poor Vane here."

"Oh, it hasn't ruined me, uncle," cried Vane. "I don't so much mind missing college."

"But, suppose I had some money to leave you, my boy, and it is all gone."

"Oh," cried Vane, merrily, "I'm glad of that. Mr Syme said one day that he always pitied a young man who had expectations from his elders, for, no matter how true-hearted the heir might be, it was always a painful position for him to occupy, that of waiting for prosperity till other people died. It was something like that, uncle, but I haven't given it quite in his words."

"Humph! Syme is a goose," said the doctor, testily. "I'm sure you never wanted me dead, so as to get my money, Vane."

"Why, of course not, uncle. I never thought about money except when I wanted to pay old Wrench or Dance for something he made for me."

"There, I move that this meeting be adjourned," cried the doctor. "One moment, though, before it is carried unanimously. How will Aunt behave to poor Deering, when he comes down."

"Same as she behaves to every one, uncle," cried Vane, laughing.

"There, old lady," said the doctor, "and as for the money, bah! let it take wings and fly away, and—"

The doctor's further speech was checked by Aunt Hannah throwing her arms about his neck and burying her face in his breast, while

Vane made a rush out into the garden and then ran rapidly down the avenue.

"If I'd stopped a minute longer, I should have begun blubbering like a great girl," he muttered. "Why, hanged if my eyes aren't quite wet."

Chapter Thirty One.

History Repeats Itself.

Vane made his way straight to the rectory, with a fixed intention in his mind. The idea had been growing for days: now it was quite ripe, consequent, perhaps, on the state of mind produced by the scene at the manor.

"It will be more frank and manly," he said to himself. "He's different to us and can't help his temper, so I'll look over everything, and say 'what's the good of our being bad friends. Shake hands and forgive me. I'm a rougher, coarser fellow than you are, and I dare say I've often said things that hurt you when I didn't mean it.'"

"Come, he can't get over that," said Vane, half-aloud, and full of eagerness to get Distin alone, he turned up the rectory lane, and came at once upon Gilmore and Macey.

"Hullo, Weathercock," cried the latter, "which way does the wind blow?"

"Due east."

"That's rectory way."

"Yes; is Distie in?"

"No; what do you want with him. He doesn't want you. Come along with us," said Gilmore.

"No, I want to see Distie—which way did he go?"

"Toward the moor," said Macey, with an air of mock mystery. "There's something going on, old chap."

"What do you mean?"

"A little girl came and waited about the gate till we were in the grounds, and then she began to signal and I went to her. But she didn't want me. She said she wanted to give this to that tall gentleman."

"This?" said Vane. "What was this?"

"A piece of stick, with notches cut in it," said Macey.

"You're not chaffing, are you?"

"Not a bit of it. I went and told Distie, and he turned red as a bubby-jock and went down to the gate, took the stick, stuck it in his pocket, and then marched off."

"Why, what does that mean?" cried Vane.

"I don't know," said Macey. "Distie must belong to some mysterious bund or verein, as the Germans call it. Perhaps he's a Rosicrucian, or a member of a mysterious sect, and this was a summons to a meeting."

"Get out," cried Vane.

"Well, are you coming with us? Aleck has had a big tip from home, and wants to spend it."

"Yes; do come, Vane."

"No, not to-day," cried the lad, and he turned off and walked away sharply to avoid being tempted into staying before he had seen Distin, and "had it out," as he termed it.

"Hi! Weathercock!" shouted Macey, "better stop. I've invented something—want your advice."

"Not to be gammoned," shouted back Vane; and he went off at a sharp trot, leaped a stile and went on across the fields, his only aim being to get away from his companions, but as soon as he was out of sight, he hesitated, stopped, and then went sharply off to his left.

"I'll follow Distie," he muttered. "The moor's a good place for a row. He can shout at me there, and get in a passion. Then he'll cool down, and we shall be all right again—and a good job too," he added. "It is so stupid for two fellows studying together to be bad friends."

By making a few short cuts, and getting over and through hedges, Vane managed to take a bee-line for the moor, and upon reaching it, he had a good look round, but there was no sign of Distin.

"He may be lying down somewhere," thought Vane, as he strode on, making his way across the moor in the direction of the wood, but still there was no sign of Distin, even after roaming about for an hour, at times scanning the surface of the long wild steep, at others following the line of drooping trees at the chalk-bank edge, but for the most part forgetting all about the object of his search, as his attention was taken up by the flowers and plants around. There was, too, so much to think about in the scene at home, that afternoon, and as he recalled it all, Vane set his teeth, and asked himself whether the time was not coming when he must set aside boyish things, and begin to think seriously of his future as a man.

He went on and on, so used to the moor that it seemed as if his legs required no guidance, but left his brain at liberty to think of other things than the course he was taking, while he wondered how long it would be before he left Greythorpe, and whether he should have to go to London or some one of the big manufacturing towns.

There was Mr Deering, too, ready to take up a good deal of his thought. And now it seemed cruel that this man should have come amongst them to disturb the current of a serene and peaceful life.

"I think he ought to be told so, too," said Vane to himself; "but I suppose that it ought not to come from me."

He had to pause for a few moments to extricate himself from a tangle of brambles consequent upon his having trusted his legs too much, and, looking up then, he found that he was a very short distance from the edge of the beech-wood, and a second glance showed him that he was very near the spot where he had dug for the truffles, and then encountered the two gipsy lads.

A feeling of desire sprang up at once in him to see the spot again, and, meaning to go in among the trees till he had passed over the ground on his way along the edge of the wood to where he could strike across to the deep lane, he waded over the pebbles of the little stream, dried his boots in the soft, white sand on the other side, and ran lightly up the bank, to step at once in among the leaves and beech-mast.

It was delightfully cool and shady after the hot sunshine of the moor, and he was winding in and out among the great, smooth tree-trunks, looking for the spot where he had had his struggle, when he fancied that he heard the murmur of voices not far away.

"Fancy—or wood pigeons," he said to himself; and, involuntarily imitating the soft, sweet *too roochetty coo roo* of the birds, he went on, but only to be convinced directly after that those were voices which he had heard; and, as he still went on in his course, he knew that, after all, he was going to encounter Distin, for it was undoubtedly his voice, followed by a heavy, dull utterance, like a thick, hoarse whisper.

Vane bore off a little to the left. His curiosity was deeply stirred, for he knew that Distin had received some kind of message, and he had followed him, but it was with the idea of meeting him on his return. For he could not play the eavesdropper; and, feeling that he had inadvertently come upon business that was not his, he increased his pace, only to be arrested by an angry cry, followed by these words, distinctly heard from among the trees:

"No, not another sixpence; so do your worst!"

The voice was Distin's, undoubtedly; and, as no more was said, Vane began to hurry away. He had nothing to do with Distin's money matters, and he was walking fast when there was the rapid beat of feet away to his right, but parallel with the way he was going. Then there was a rush, a shout, a heavy fall, and a half-smothered voice cried "Help!"

That did seem to be Vane's business, and he struck off to the right directly, to bear through a denser part of the wood, and come to an opening, which struck him at once as being the one where he had had his encounter with the gipsy lads. The very next moment, with every nerve tingling, he was running toward where he could see his two enemies kneeling upon someone they had got down; and, though he could not see the face, he knew it was Distin whom they were both thumping with all their might.

"Now will you?" he heard, as he rushed forward toward the group, all of whose constituents were so much excited by their struggle that they did not hear his approach.

"No," shouted Vane, throwing himself upon them, but not so cleverly as he had meant, for his toe caught in a protruding root, and he pitched forward more like a skittle-ball than a boy, knocking over the two gipsy lads, and himself rolling over amongst the beech-mast and dead leaves.

Distin's two assailants were so startled and astonished that they, too, rolled over and over hurriedly several times before they scrambled to their feet, and dived in among the trees.

But Vane was up, too, on the instant.

"Here, Dis!" he shouted; "help me take them."

Distin had risen, too, very pale everywhere in the face but about the nose, which was very ruddy, for reasons connected with a blow, but, as Vane ran on, he did not follow.

" *His two enemies kneeling upon someone.*"—Page 300.

"Do you hear? Come on!" cried Vane, looking back. "Help me, and we can take them both."

But Distin only glanced round for a way of retreat, and, seeing that Vane was alone, the two gipsy lads dodged behind a tree, and cleverly kept it between them as he rushed on, and then sprang out at him, taking him in the rear, and getting a couple of blows home as he turned to defend himself.

"History repeats itself," he muttered, through his set teeth; "but they haven't got any sticks;" and, determined now to make a prisoner of one of them, he attacked fiercely, bringing to bear all the strength and skill he possessed, for there was no sign of shrinking on the part of the two lads, who came at him savagely, as if enraged at his robbing them of their prey.

There were no sticks now, as Vane had said; it was an attack with nature's weapons, but the two gipsy lads had had their tempers whetted in their encounter with Distin, and, after the first fright caused by Vane's sudden attack, they met him furiously.

They were no mean adversaries, so long as spirit nerved them, for they were active and hard as cats, and had had a long experience in giving and taking blows. So that, full of courage and indignation as he was, Vane soon began to find that he was greatly overmatched, and, in the midst of his giving and taking, he looked about anxiously for Distin, but for some time looked in vain.

All at once, though, as he stepped back to avoid a blow he saw Distin peering round the trunk of one of the trees.

"Oh, there you are," he panted, "come on and help me."

Distin did not stir, and one of the gipsy lads burst into a hoarse laugh.

"Not he," cried the lad. "Why, he give us money to leather you before."

Distin made an angry gesture, but checked himself.

"Take that for your miserable lie," cried Vane, and his gift was a stinging blow in the lad's mouth, which made him shrink away, and make room for his brother, who seized the opportunity of Vane's arm and body being extended, to strike him full in the ear, and make him lose his balance.

"'Tarn't a lie," cried this latter. "He did give us three shillin' apiece to leather you."

The lad speaking followed up his words with blows, and Vane was pretty hard set, while a conscious feeling of despair came over him on hearing of Distin's treachery.

But he forced himself not to credit it, and struck out with all his might.

"I don't believe it," he roared, "a gentleman wouldn't do such a thing."

"But he aren't a gent," said the first lad, coming on again, with his lips bleeding. "Promised to pay us well, and he weant."

"Come and show them it's all a lie, Dis," cried Vane, breathlessly. "Come and help me."

But Distin never stirred. He only stood glaring at the scene before him, his lips drawn from his white teeth, and his whole aspect betokening that he was fascinated by the fight.

"Do you hear?" roared Vane at last, hoarsely. "You're never going to be such a coward as to let them serve me as they did before."

Still Distin did not stir, and a burst of rage made the blood flush to Vane's temples, as he ground his teeth and raged out with:

"You miserable, contemptible cur!"

He forgot everything now. All sense of fear—all dread of being beaten by two against one—was gone, and as if he had suddenly become possessed with double his former strength, he watchfully put aside several of the fierce blows struck at him, and dodged others, letting his opponents weary themselves, while he husbanded his strength.

It was hard work, though, to keep from exposing himself in some fit of blind fury, for the lads, by helping each other, kept on administering stinging blows, every one of which made Vane grind his teeth, and long to rush in and close with one or the other of his adversaries.

But he mastered the desire, knowing that it would be fatal to success, for the gipsies were clever wrestlers, and would have the advantage, besides which, one of them could easily close and hold while the other punished him.

"I wouldn't have believed it. I wouldn't have believed it," he kept on muttering as he caught sight of Distin's pallid face again and again, while avoiding the dodges and attempts to close on the part of the gipsies.

At last, feeling that this could not go on, and weakened by his efforts, Vane determined to try, and, by a sudden rush, contrive to render one of his adversaries *hors de combat*, when, to his great delight, they both drew off, either for a few minutes' rest, or to concoct some fresh mode of attack.

Whatever it might be, the respite was welcome to Vane, who took advantage of it to throw off his Norfolk jacket; but watching his adversaries the while, lest they should make a rush while he was comparatively helpless.

But they did not, and tossing the jacket aside he rapidly rolled up his sleeves, and tightened the band of his trousers, feeling refreshed and strengthened by every breath he drew.

"Now," he said to himself as the gipsies whispered together, "let them come on."

But they did not attack, one of them standing ready to make a rush, while the other went to the edge of the wood to reconnoitre.

"It means fighting to the last then," thought Vane, and a shiver ran through him as he recalled his last encounter.

Perhaps it was this, and the inequality of the match which made him turn to where Distin still stood motionless.

"I say, Dis," he cried, appealingly, "I won't believe all they said. We'll be friends, when it's all over, but don't leave me in the lurch like this."

Distin looked at him wildly, but still neither spoke nor stirred, and Vane did not realise that he was asking his fellow-pupil that which he was not likely to give. For the latter was thinking,—

"Even if he will not believe it, others will," and he stared wildly at Vane's bruised and bleeding face with a curious feeling of envy at his prowess.

"Right," shouted the gipsy lad who had been on the look-out, and running smartly forward, he dashed at Vane, followed by his brother, and the fight recommenced.

"If they would only come on fairly, I wouldn't care," thought Vane, as he did his best to combat the guerilla-like warfare his enemies kept up, for he did not realise that wearisome as all their feinting, dodging and dropping to avoid blows, and their clever relief of each other might be, a bold and vigorous closing with them would have been fatal. And, oddly enough, though they had sought to do this at first, during the latter part of the encounter they had kept aloof, though perhaps it was no wonder, for Vane had given some telling blows, such as they did not wish to suffer again.

"I shall have to finish it, somehow," thought Vane, as he felt that he was growing weaker; and throwing all the vigour and skill into his next efforts, he paid no heed whatever to the blows given him by one of the lads, but pressed the other heavily, following him up, and at last, when he felt nearly done, aiming a tremendous left-handed blow at his cheek.

As if to avoid the blow, the lad dropped on his hands and knees, but this time he was a little too late; the blow took effect, and his falling was accelerated so that he rolled over and over, while unable to stop himself, Vane's body followed his fist and he, too, fell with a heavy thud, full on his adversary's chest.

Vane was conscious of both his knees coming heavily upon the lad, and he only saved his face from coming in contact with the ground by throwing up his head.

Then, he sprang up, as, for the first time during the encounter, Distin uttered a warning cry.

It warned Vane, who avoided the second lad's onslaught, and gave him a smart crack on the chest and another on the nose.

This gave him time to glance at his fallen enemy, who did not try to get up.

It was only a momentary glance, and then he was fighting desperately, for the second boy seemed to be maddened by the fate of the first. Casting off all feinting now, he dashed furiously at Vane, giving and receiving blows till the lads closed in a fierce wrestling match, in which Vane's superior strength told, and in another moment or two, he would have thrown his adversary, had not the lad lying unconscious on the dead leaves, lent his brother unexpected aid. For he was right in Vane's way, so that he tripped over him, fell heavily with the second gipsy lad upon his chest, holding him down with his knees and one hand in his collar, while he raised the other, and was about to strike him heavily in the face, when there was a dull sound and he fell over upon his brother, leaving Vane free.

"Thankye, Dis," he panted, as he struggled to his knees; "that crack of yours was just in time," and the rector's two pupils looked each other in the face.

It was only for a moment, though, and then Vane seated himself to recover breath on the uppermost of his fallen foes.

Chapter Thirty Two.

Having it out.

"Now," said Vane, after sitting, panting for a few minutes, "I came out to-day on purpose to find you, and ask you to shake hands. Glad I got here in time to help you. Shake hands, now."

"No," said Distin, slowly; "I can't do that."

"Nonsense! I say these two have got it. Why not?"

"Because," said Distin, with almost a groan, "I'm not fit. My hands are not clean."

"Wash 'em then, or never mind."

"You know what I mean," said Distin. "What they said was true."

Vane stared at him in astonishment.

"Yes, it's quite true," said Distin, bitterly. "I've behaved like a blackguard."

Just at that moment, the top gipsy began to struggle, and Vane gave him a tremendous clout on the ear.

"Lie still or I'll knock your head off," he cried, fiercely.

"You don't mean to say you set these two brutes to knock me about with sticks?"

"Yes, he did," cried the top boy.

"Yes, I did," said Distin, after making an effort as if to swallow something. "I paid them, and they have pestered me for money ever since. They sent to me to-day to come out to them, and I gave them more, but they were not satisfied and were knocking me about when you came."

The lower prisoner now began to complain, and with cause, for his brother was lying across his chest, so that he had the weight of two to bear; but Vane reached down suddenly and placed his fist on the lad's nose, with a heavy grinding motion.

"You dare to move, that's all," he growled, threateningly, and the lad drew a deep breath, and lay still, while Distin went on as if something within him were forcing this confession.

"There," he said, "it's all over now. They've kept out of sight of the police all this time, and sent messages to me from where they were in hiding, and I've had to come and pay them. I've been like a slave to them, and they've degraded me till I've felt as if I couldn't bear it."

"And all for what?" said Vane, angrily. "I never did you any harm."

"I couldn't help it," said Distin. "I hated you, I suppose. I tell you, I've behaved like a blackguard, and I suppose I shall be punished for it, but I'd rather it was so than go on like I have lately."

"Look here," cried Vane, savagely, and he raised himself up a little as if he were riding on horseback, and then nipped his human steed with his knees, and bumped himself down so heavily that both the gipsy lads yelled. "Yes, I meant to hurt you. I say, look here, I know what you both mean. You are going to try and heave me off, and run for it, but don't you try it, my lads, or it will be the worse for you. It's my turn this time, and you don't get away, so be still. Do you hear? Lie still!"

Vane's voice sounded so deep and threatening that the lads lay perfectly quiescent, and Distin went on.

"Better get out your handkerchief," he said, taking out his own, "and we'll tie their hands behind them, and march them to Bates' place."

"You'll help me then?" said Vane.

"Yes."

"Might as well have helped me before, and then I shouldn't have been so knocked about."

Distin shook his head, and began to roll up his pocket-handkerchief to form a cord.

"There's no hurry," said Vane, thoughtfully. "I want a rest."

The lowermost boy uttered a groan, for his imprisonment was painful.

"Better let's get it over," said Distin, advancing and planting a foot on a prisoner who looked as if he were meditating an attempt to escape.

"No hurry," said Vane, quietly, "you haven't been fighting and got pumped out. Besides, it wants thinking about. I don't quite understand it yet. I can't see why you should do what you did. It was so cowardly."

"Don't I know all that," cried Distin, fiercely. "Hasn't it been eating into me? I'm supposed to be a gentleman, and I've acted toward you like a miserable cad, and disgraced myself forever. It's horrible and I want to get it over."

"I don't," said Vane, slowly.

"Can't you see how maddening it is. I've got to go with you to take these beasts—no, I will not call them that, for I tempted them with money to do it all, and they have turned and bitten me."

"Yes: that was being hoist with your own petard, Mr Engineer," cried Vane, merrily.

"Don't laugh at me," cried Distin with a stamp of the foot. "Can't you see how I'm degraded; how bitter a sting it was to see you, whom I tried to injure, come to my help. Isn't it all a judgment on me?"

"Don't know," said Vane looking at him stolidly and then frowning and administering a sounding punch in the ribs to his restive seat, with the effect that there was another yell.

"You make light of it," continued Distin, "for you cannot understand what I feel. I have, I say, to take these brutes up to the police—"

"No, no," cried the two lads, piteously.

"—And then go straight to Syme, and confess everything, and of course he'll expel me. Nice preparation for a college life; and what will they say at home?"

"Yes," said Vane, echoing the other's words; "what will they say at home? You mean over in Trinidad?"

Distin bowed his head, his nervous-looking face working from the anguish he felt, and his lower lip quivering with the mental agony and shame.

"Trinidad's a long way off," said Vane, thoughtfully.

"No place is far off now," cried Distin, passionately. "And if it were ten times as far, what then? Don't I know it? Do you think I can ever forget it all?"

"No," said Vane; "you never will. I suppose it must have made you uncomfortable all along."

"Don't—don't talk about it," cried Distin, piteously. "There, come along, you must be rested now."

"Look here," cried one of the lads, shrilly; "if you tak' us up to Greytrop we'll tell all about it."

Vane gave another bump.

"What's the good of that, stupid," he said. "Mr Distin would tell first."

"Yes," said the young fellow firmly; and as Vane looked at his determined countenance, he felt as if he had never liked him so well before; "I shall tell first. Come what may, Vane Lee, you shan't have it against me that I did not speak out openly. Now, come."

"Not yet," said Vane, stubbornly. "I'm resting."

There was a pause, and one of the gipsy lads began to snivel.

"Oh, pray, good, kind gen'l'man, let us go this time, and we'll never do so any more. Do, please, good gen'l'man, let us go."

"If you don't stop that miserable, pitiful, cowardly howling, you cur," cried Vane so savagely that the lad stared at him with his mouth open, "I'll gag that mouth of yours with moss. Lie still!"

Vane literally yelled this last order at the lad, and the mouth shut with a snap, while its owner stared at him in dismay.

"I only wish I could have you standing up and lying down too," cried Vane, "or that it wasn't cowardly to punch your wretched heads now you are down."

There was another pause, during which the lowermost boy began to groan, but he ceased upon Vane giving a fresh bump.

"I shall be obliged now, Mr Lee," said Distin, quickly, "by your helping to tie those two scoundrels."

"No more a scoundrel than you are," said the lowermost boy fiercely; and Vane gave another bump.

"Don't hurt him," said Distin. "He only spoke the truth. Come, let's turn this one over."

Vane did not stir, but sat staring hard in Distin's face.

"Look here," he said at last; "you mean what you say about the police and Mr Syme?"

"Yes, of course."

"And you understand what will follow?"

Distin bowed as he drew his breath hard through his teeth.

"You will not be able to stop at the rectory even if that busybody Bates doesn't carry it over to the magistrates."

"I know everything," said Distin, firmly, and he drew a long breath now of relief. "I am set upon it, even if I never hold up my head again."

"All right," said Vane in his peculiar, hard, stubborn way. "You've made up your mind; then I've made up mine."

"What do you mean?" said Distin.

"Wait and see," said Vane, shortly.

"But I wish to get it over."

"I know you do. But you're all right. Look at me, I can't see, but expect my face is all puffy; and look at my knuckles. These fellows have got heads like wood."

"I am sorry, very sorry," said Distin, sadly; "but I want to make all the reparation I can."

"Give me that handkerchief," said Vane sharply; and he snatched it from Distin's hand. "No, no, keep back. I'll do what there is to do. They're not fit to touch. Ah, would you!"

The top boy had suddenly thrown up his head in an effort to free himself. But his forehead came in contact with Vane's fist and he dropped back with a groan.

"Hurt, did it!" said Vane, bending down, and whispering a few words. Then aloud, as he rose. "Now, then, get up and let me tie your hands behind you."

The lad rose slowly and painfully.

"Turn round and put your hands behind you," cried Vane.

The lad obeyed, and then as if shot from a bow he leaped over his prostrate brother with a loud whoop and dashed off among the trees.

"No, no, it's of no use," cried Vane as Distin started in pursuit; "you might just as well try to catch a hare. Now you, sir, up with you."

The second lad rose, groaning as if lame and helpless, turning his eyes piteously upon his captor; and then, quick as lightning, he too started off.

"Loo, loo, loo!" shouted Vane, clapping his hands as if cheering on a greyhound. "I say, Distie, how the beggars can run."

A defiant shout answered him, and Vane clapped his hands to his mouth and yelled:

"Po-lice—if you ever come again."

"Yah!" came back from the wood, and Distin cried, angrily:

"You let them go on purpose."

"Of course I did," said Vane. "Here's your handkerchief. You don't suppose I would take them up, and hand them over to the police, and let you lower yourself like you said, do you?"

"Yes—yes," cried Distin, speaking like a hysterical girl. "I will tell everything now; how I was tempted, and how I fell."

"Bother!" cried Vane, gruffly. "That isn't like an English lad should speak. You did me a cowardly, dirty trick, and you confessed to me that you were sorry for it. Do you think I'm such a mean beast that I want to take revenge upon you!"

"But it is my duty—I feel bound—I must speak," cried Distin, in a choking voice.

"Nonsense! It's all over. I'm the person injured, and I say I won't have another word said. I came out this afternoon to ask you to make friends, and to shake hands. There's mine, and let the past be dead."

Vane stood holding out his hand, but it was not taken.

"Do you hear?" he cried. "Shake hands."

"I can't," groaned Distin, with a piteous look. "I told you before mine are not clean."

"Mine are," said Vane, meaning, of course, metaphorically; "and perhaps—no, there is no perhaps—mine will clean yours."

Vane took the young Creole's hand almost by force, and gave it a painful grip, releasing it at last for Distin to turn to the nearest tree, lay his arm upon the trunk, and then lean his forehead against it in silence.

Vane stood looking at him, hesitating as to what he should say or do. Then, with a satisfied nod to himself, he said, cheerily:

"I'm going down to the stream to have a wash. Come on soon."

It was a bit of natural delicacy, and the sensitive lad, born in a tropic land, felt it as he stood there with his brain filled with bitterness and remorse, heaping self-reproaches upon himself, and more miserable than he had ever before been in his life.

"I do believe he's crying," thought Vane, as he hurried out of the woodland shade, and down to the water's edge, where, kneeling down by a little crystal pool, he washed his stained and bleeding hands, and then began to bathe his face and temples.

"Not quite so hot as I was," he muttered; "but, oh, what a mess I'm in! I shan't be fit to show myself, and must stop out till it's dark. What would poor aunt say if she saw me! Frighten her nearly into fits."

He was scooping up the fresh, cool water, and holding it to his bruises, which pained him a good deal, but, in spite of all his sufferings, he burst into a hearty fit of laughter at last, and, as his eyes were closed, he did not notice that a shadow was cast over him, right on to the water.

It was Distin, for he had come quietly down the bank, and was standing just behind him.

"Are you laughing at me?" he said, bitterly.

"Eh? You there?" cried Vane, raising his head. "No, I was grinning at the way those two fellows scuttled off. They made sure they were going to be in the lock-up to-night."

"Where they ought to have been," said Distin.

"Oh, I don't know. They're half-wild sort of fellows—very cunning, and all that sort of thing. I daresay I should have done as they did if I had been a gipsy. But, never mind that now. They'll keep away from Greythorpe for long enough to come."

He began dabbing his face with his handkerchief, and looking merrily at Distin.

"I say," he cried; "I didn't know I could fight like that. Is my face very queer?"

"It is bruised and swollen," said Distin, with an effort. "I'm afraid it will be worse to-morrow."

"So am I, but we can't help it. Never mind, it will be a bit of a holiday for me till the bruises don't show; and I can sit and think out something else. Come and see me sometimes."

"I can't, Vane, I can't," cried Distin, wildly. "Do you think I have no feeling?"

"Too much, I should say," cried Vane. "There, why don't you let it go? Uncle says life isn't long enough for people to quarrel or make enemies. That's all over; and, I say, I feel ever so much more comfortable now. Haven't got such a thing as a tumbler in your pocket, have you?"

Distin looked in the bruised and battered face before him, wondering at the lad's levity, as Vane continued:

"No, I suppose you haven't, and my silver cup is on the sideboard. Never mind: here goes. Just stand close to me, and shout if you see any leeches coming."

As he spoke, he lay down on his chest, reaching over another clear portion of the stream.

"I must drink like a horse," he cried; and, placing his lips to the surface, he took a long draught, rose, wiped his lips, drew a deep breath, and exclaimed, "Hah! That was good."

Then he reeled, caught at the air, and would have fallen, but Distin seized him, and lowered him to the ground, where he lay, looking very ghastly, for a few minutes.

"Only a bit giddy," he said, faintly. "It will soon go off."

"I'll run and fetch help," cried Distin, excitedly.

"Nonsense! What for? I'm getting better. There: that's it."

He sat up, and, with Distin's help, struggled to his feet.

"How stupid of me!" he said, with a faint laugh. "I suppose it was leaning over the water so long. I'm all right now."

He made a brave effort, and the two lads walked toward the lane, but, before they had gone many yards, Vane reeled again.

This time the vertigo was slighter, and, taking Distin's arm, he kept his feet.

"Let's walk on," he said. "I daresay the buzzy noise and singing in my head will soon pass off."

He was right: it did, and they progressed slowly till they reached the lane, where the walking was better, but Vane was still glad to retain Distin's help, and so it happened that, when they were about a mile from the rectory, Gilmore and Macey, who were in search of them, suddenly saw something which made them stare.

"I say," cried Macey; "'tisn't real, is it? Wait till I've rubbed my eyes."

"Why, they've made it up," cried Gilmore. "I say, Aleck, don't say a word."

"Why not?"

"I mean don't chaff them or Dis may go off like powder. You know what he is."

"I won't speak a word, but, I say, it's Weathercock's doing. He has invented some decoction to charm creoles, and henceforth old Dis will be quite tame."

As they drew nearer, Gilmore whispered:

"They've been having it out."

"Yes, and Weathercock has had an awful licking; look at his phiz."

"No," said Gilmore. "Vane has licked; and it's just like him, he hasn't hit Dis in the face once. Don't notice it."

"Not I."

They were within speaking distance now; and Distin's sallow countenance showed two burning red spots in the cheeks.

"Hullo!" cried Vane. "Come to meet us?"

"Yes," said Gilmore; "we began to think you were lost."

"Oh, no," said Vane, carelessly. "Been some distance and the time soon goes. I think I'll turn off here, and get home across the meadows. Good-evening, you two. Good-night, Dis, old chap."

"Good-night," said Distin, huskily, as he took the bruised and slightly bleeding hand held out to him. Then turning away, he walked swiftly on.

"Why, Vane, old boy," whispered Gilmore, "what's going on?"

Vane must have read of Douglas Jerrold's smart reply, for he said, merrily:

"I am; good-night," and he was gone.

"I'm blest!" cried Macey; giving his leg a slap.

"He has gone in back way so as not to be seen," cried Gilmore.

"That's it," cried Macey, excitedly. "Well, of all the old Weathercocks that ever did show which way the wind blew—"

He did not finish that sentence, but repeated his former words—

"I'm blest!"

Chapter Thirty Three.

In Hiding.

Vane meant to slip in by the back after crossing the meadows, but as a matter of course he met Bruff half-way down the garden, later than he had been there for years.

"Why, Master Vane!" he cried, "you been at it again."

"Hush! Don't say anything," cried the lad. But Bruff's exclamation had brought Martha to the kitchen-door; and as she caught sight of Vane's face, she uttered a cry which brought out Eliza, who shrieked and ran to tell Aunt Hannah, who heard the cry, and came round from the front, where, with the doctor, she had been watching for the truant, the doctor being petulant and impatient about his evening meal.

Then the murder was out, and Vane was hurried into the little drawing-room, where Aunt Hannah strove gently to get him upon the couch.

"No, no, no," cried Vane. "Uncle, tell Bruff and those two that they are not to speak about it."

The doctor nodded and gave the order, but muttered, "Only make them talk."

"But what has happened, my dear? Where have you been?"

"Don't bother him," said the doctor, testily. "Here, boy, let's look at your injuries."

"They're nothing, uncle," cried Vane. "Give me some tea, aunt, and I'm as hungry as a hunter. What have you got?"

"Oh, my dear!" cried Aunt Hannah; "how can you, and with a face like that."

"Nothing the matter with him," said the doctor, "only been fighting like a young blackguard."

"Couldn't help it, uncle," said Vane. "You wouldn't have had me lie down and be thrashed without hitting back."

"Oh, my dear!" cried Aunt Hannah, "you shouldn't fight."

"Of course not," said the doctor, sternly. "It is a low, vulgar, contemptible, disgraceful act for one who is the son of a gentleman—to—to— Did you win?"

"Yes, uncle," cried Vane; and he lay back in the easy chair into which he had been forced by Aunt Hannah, and laughed till the tears rolled down his cheeks.

Aunt Hannah seized him and held him.

"Oh, my love," she cried to the doctor, "pray give him something: sal-volatile or brandy: he's hysterical."

"Nonsense!" cried the doctor. "Here—Vane—idiot, you leave off laughing, sir?"

"I can't, uncle," cried Vane, piteously; "and it does hurt so. Oh my! oh my! You should have seen the beggars run."

"Beggars? You've been fighting beggars, Vane!" cried Aunt Hannah. "Oh, my dear! my dear!"

"Will you hold your tongue, Hannah," cried the doctor, sternly. "Here, Vane, who ran? Some tramps?"

"No, uncle: those two gipsy lads."

"What! who attacked you before?"

"Yes, and they tried it again. Aunt, they got the worst of it this time."

"You—you thrashed them?" cried the doctor, excitedly.

"Yes, uncle."

"Alone?"

"Oh, yes: only with someone looking on."

"But you beat them alone; gave them a thorough good er—er—licking, as you call it, sir?"

"Yes, uncle; awful."

"Quite beat them?"

"Knocked them into smithereens; had them both down, one on the other, and sat on the top for half an hour."

The doctor caught Vane's right hand in his left, held it out, and brought his own right down upon it with a sounding spank, gripped it, and shook the bruised member till Vane grinned with pain.

"Oh, my dear!" remonstrated Aunt Hannah, "you are hurting him, and you are encouraging him in a practice that—"

"Makes perfect," cried the doctor, excitedly. "By George! I wish I had been there!"

"My dear!"

"I do, Hannah. It makes me feel quite young again. But come and have your tea, you young dog—you young Roman—you Trojan, you—well done, Alexander. But stop!—those two young scoundrels. Hi! where's Bruff?"

"Stop, uncle," cried Vane, leaping up and seizing the doctor's coat-tails. "What are you going to do?"

"Send Bruff for Bates, and set him on the young scoundrels' track. I shan't rest till I get them in jail."

"No, no, uncle, sit down," said Vane, with a quiver in his voice. "We can't do that."

Then he told them all.

As Vane ended his narrative, with the doctor pacing up and down the room, and Martha fussing because the delicate cutlets she had prepared were growing cold, Aunt Hannah was seated on the carpet by her nephew's chair, holding one of his bruised hands against her cheek, and weeping silently as she whispered, "My own brave boy!"

As she spoke, she reached up to press her lips to his, but Vane shrank away.

"No, no, aunt dear," he said, "I'm not fit to kiss."

"Oh, my own brave, noble boy," she cried; and passing her arms about his neck, she kissed him fondly.

"Who's encouraging the boy in fighting now?" cried the doctor, sharply.

"But, how could he help it, my dear?" said Aunt Hannah.

"Of course; how could he help it." Then changing his manner, he laid his hand upon Vane's shoulder.

"You are quite right, Vane, lad. Let them call you Weathercock if they like, but you do always point to fair weather, my boy, and turn your back on foul. No: there must be no police business. The young scoundrels have had their punishment—the right sort; and Mr Distin has got his in a way such a proud, sensitive fellow will never forget."

"But ought not Vane to have beaten him, too?" said Aunt Hannah, naïvely.

"What!" cried the doctor, in mock horror. "Woman! You are a very glutton at revenge. Three in one afternoon? But to be serious. He was beaten, then, my dear—with forgiveness. Coals of fire upon his enemy's head, and given him a lesson such as may form a turning point in his life. God bless you, my boy! You've done a finer thing to-day than it is in your power yet to grasp. You'll think more deeply of it some day, and— Hannah, my darling, are you going to stand preaching at this poor boy all the evening, when you see he is nearly starved?"

Aunt Hannah laughed and cried together, as she fondled Vane.

"I'll go and fetch you a cup of tea, my dear. Don't move."

The doctor took a step forward, and gave Vane a slap on the back.

"Cup of tea—brought for him. Come along, boy. Aunt would spoil us both if she could, but we're too good stuff, eh? Now, prize-fighter, give your aunt your arm, and I'll put some big black patches on your nose and forehead after tea."

Vane jumped up and held out his arm, but Aunt Hannah looked at him wildly.

"You don't think, dear, that black patches—oh!"

"No, I don't," said the doctor gaily; "but we must have some pleasant little bit of fiction to keep him at home for a few days. Little poorly or—I know. Note to the rectory asking Syme to forgive me, and we'll have the pony-carriage at six in the morning, and go down to Scarboro' for a week, till he is fit to be seen."

"Yes," said Aunt Hannah, eagerly, "the very thing;" and to her great delight, save that his mouth was stiff and sore, Vane ate and drank as if nothing whatever had been the matter. The next morning they started for their long drive, to catch the train.

"Third-class now, my boy," said the doctor, sadly; "economising has begun."

"And I had forgotten it all," thought Vane. "Poor uncle!—poor aunt! I must get better, and go to work."

Chapter Thirty Four.

The Mouse and the Lion.

The stay at Scarboro' was short, for a letter came from Aunt Hannah, announcing that Mr Deering was coming down, and adding rather pathetically that she wished he would not.

The doctor tossed the letter over to Vane, who was looking out of the hotel window, making a plan for sliding bathing machines down an inclined plane; and he had mentally contrived a delightful arrangement when he was pulled up short by the thought that the very next north-east gale would send in breakers, and knock his inclined plane all to pieces.

"For me to read, uncle," he said.

The doctor nodded.

"Then you'll want to go back."

"Yes, and you must stay by yourself."

Vane rose and went to the looking-glass, stared at his lips, made a grimace and returned.

"I say, uncle, do I look so very horrid?" he said.

"That eye's not ornamental, my boy."

"No, but shall you mind very much?"

"I? Not at all."

"Then I shall come back with you."

"Won't be ashamed to be seen?"

"Not I," said Vane; "I don't care, and I should like to be at home when Mr Deering comes."

"Why?"

"He may be able to get me engaged somewhere in town."

"Humph!" ejaculated the doctor. "Want to run away from us then, now we are poor."

"Uncle!" shouted Vane, fiercely indignant; but he saw the grim smile on the old man's countenance, and went close up and took his arm. "You didn't mean that," he continued. "It's because I want to get to work so as to help you and aunt now, instead of being a burden to you."

"Don't want to go, then?"

Vane shook his head sadly. "No, uncle, I've been so happy at home, but of course should have to go some day."

"Ah, well, there is no immediate hurry. We'll wait. I don't think that Mr Deering is quite the man I should like to see you with in your first start in life. I'm afraid, Vane, boy, that he is reckless. Yesterday, I thought him unprincipled too, but he is behaving like a man of honour in coming down to see me, and show me how he went wrong. It's a sad business, but I daresay we shall get used to it after a time."

The journey back was made so that they reached home after dark, Vane laughingly saying that it would screen him a little longer, and almost the first person they encountered was Mr Deering himself.

"Hah, Doctor," he said quietly, "I'm glad you're come back. I only reached here by the last train."

The doctor hesitated a moment, and then shook hands.

"Well, youngster," said the visitor, "I suppose you have not set the Thames on fire yet."

"No," said Vane, indignantly, for their visitor's manner nettled him, "and when I try to, I shall set to work without help."

Deering's eyes flashed angrily.

"Vane!" said Aunt Hannah, reproachfully.

"You forget that Mr Deering is our guest, Vane," said the doctor.

"Yes, uncle, I forgot that."

"Don't reprove him," said Deering. "I deserve it, and I invited the taunt by my manner toward your nephew."

"Dinner's ready," said Aunt Hannah, hastily.

"Or supper," said the doctor, and ten minutes later they were all seated at the meal, talking quietly about Scarboro', its great cliffs and the sea, Mr Deering showing a considerable knowledge of the place. No allusion whatever was made to the cause of their guest's visit till they had adjourned to the drawing-room, Mr Deering having stopped in the hall to take up a square tin box, and another which looked like a case made to contain rolled up plans.

The doctor frowned, and seeing that some business matters were imminent, Aunt Hannah rose to leave the room, and Vane followed her example.

"No, no, my dear Mrs Lee," said Deering, "don't leave us, and there is nothing to be said that the lad ought not to hear. It will be a lesson to him, as he is of a sanguine inventive temperament like myself, not to be too eager to place faith in his inventions."

"Look here, Deering," said the doctor, after clearing his voice, "this has been a terrible misfortune for us, and, I believe, for you too."

"Indeed it has," said Deering, bitterly. "I feel ten years older, and in addition to my great hopes being blasted, I know that in your eyes, and those of your wife, I must seem to have been a thoughtless, designing scoundrel, dishonest to a degree."

"No, no, Mr Deering," said Aunt Hannah, warmly, "nobody ever thought that of you."

"Right," said the doctor, smiling.

"I have wept bitterly over it, and grieved that you should ever have come down here to disturb my poor husband in his peaceful life, where he was resting after a long laborious career. It seemed so cruel—such a terrible stroke of fate."

"Yes, madam, terrible and cruel," said Deering, sadly and humbly.

"There now, say no more about it," said the doctor. "It is of no use to cry over spilt milk."

"No," replied Deering, "but I do reserve to myself the right to make some explanations to you both, whom I have injured so in your worldly prospects."

"Better let it go, Deering. There, man, we forgive you, and the worst we think of you is that you were too sanguine and rash."

"Don't say that," cried Deering, "not till you have heard me out and seen what I want to show you; but God bless you for what you have said. Lee, you and I were boys at school together; we fought for and helped each other, and you know that I have never willingly done a dishonest act."

"Never," said the doctor, reaching out his hand, to which the other clung. "You had proof of my faith in you when I became your bondman."

"Exactly."

"Then, now, let's talk about something else."

"No," said Deering, firmly. "I must show you first that I was not so rash and foolish as you think. Mrs Lee, may I clear this table?"

"Oh, certainly," said Aunt Hannah, rather stiffly. "Vane, my dear, will you move the lamp to the chimney."

Vane lifted it and placed it on the mantelpiece, while Mr Deering moved a book or two and the cloth from the round low table, and then opening a padlock at the end of the long round tin case, he drew out a great roll of plans and spread them on the table, placing books at each corner, to keep them open.

"Here," he said, growing excited, "is my invention. I want you all to look—you, in particular, Vane, for it will interest you from its similarity to a plan you had for heating your conservatory."

Vane's attention was centred at once on the carefully drawn and coloured plans, before which, with growing eagerness, their visitor began to explain, in his usual lucid manner, so that even Aunt Hannah became interested.

The idea was for warming purposes, and certainly, at first sight, complicated, but they soon grasped all the details, and understood how, by the use of a small furnace, water was to be heated, and to circulate by the law of convection, so as to supply warmth all through public buildings, or even in houses where people were ready to dispense with the ruddy glow of fire.

"Yes," said the doctor, after an hour's examination of the drawings; "that all seems to be quite right."

"But the idea is not new," said Vane.

"Exactly. You are quite right," said Deering; "it is only a new adaptation in which I saw fortune, for it could be used in hundreds of ways where hot-water is not applicable now. I saw large works springing up, and an engineering business in which I hoped you, Vane, would share; for with your brains, my boy, I foresaw that you would be invaluable to me, and would be making a great future for yourself. There, now, you see my plans, Lee. Do I seem so mad and reckless to you both? Have I not gone on step by step, and was I not justified in trying to get monetary help to carry out my preparations for what promised so clearly to be a grand success?"

"Well, really, Deering, I can't help saying yes," said the doctor. "It does look right, doesn't it, my dear?"

"Yes," said Aunt Hannah, with a sigh; "it does certainly look right."

"I would not go far till, as I thought, I had tested my plans in every way."

"That was right," said the doctor. "Well, what's the matter—why hasn't it succeeded?"

"Ah, why, indeed?" replied Deering. "Some law of nature, which, in spite of incessant study, I cannot grasp, has been against me."

Vane was poring over the plans, with his forehead full of lines and his mouth pursed up, and, after bringing sheet after sheet to the top, he ended by laying the fullest drawing with all its colourings and references out straight, and, lifting the lamp back upon it in the centre of the table to give a better light; and while his aunt and untie were right and left, Mr Deering was facing him, and he had his back to the fire:

"But you should have made models, and tested it all thoroughly."

"I did, Lee, I did," cried Mr Deering, passionately. "I made model after model, improving one upon the other, till I had reached, as I thought, perfection. They worked admirably, and when I was, as I thought, safe, and had obtained my details, I threw in the capital, for which you were security, started my works, and began making on a large scale. Orders came in, and I saw, as I told you, fortune in my grasp."

"Well, and what then?"

"Failure. That which worked so well on a small scale was useless on a large."

Vane was the only one standing, and leaning his elbows on the great drawing, his chin upon his hands, deeply interested in the pipes, elbows, taps, furnace, and various arrangements.

"But that seems strange," said the doctor. "I should have thought you were right."

"Exactly," said Deering, eagerly. "You would have thought I was right. I felt sure that I was right. I would have staked my life upon it. If I had had a doubt, Lee, believe me I would not have risked that money, and dragged you down as I have."

"I believe you, Deering," said the doctor, more warmly than he had yet spoken; "but, hang it, man, I wouldn't give up. Try again."

"I have tried again, till I feel that if I do more my brain will give way—I shall go mad. No: nature is against me, and I have made a terrible failure."

Aunt Hannah sighed.

"There is nothing for me but to try and recover my shattered health, get my nerves right again, and then start at something else."

"Why not have another try at this?" said the doctor.

"I cannot," said Deering. "I have tried, and had disastrous explosions. In one moment the work of months has been shattered, and now, if I want men to work for me again, they shake their heads, and refuse. It is of no use to fence, Lee. I have staked my all, and almost my life, on that contrivance, and I have failed."

"It can't be a failure," said Vane, suddenly. "It must go."

Deering looked at him pityingly.

"You see," he said to Aunt Hannah, "your nephew is attracted by it, and believes in it."

"Yes," said Aunt Hannah, with a shudder. "Roll up the plans now, my dear," she added, huskily; "it's getting late."

"All right, aunt. Soon," said Vane, quietly; and then, with some show of excitement, "I tell you it must go. Why, it's as simple as simple. Look here, uncle, the water's heated here and runs up there and there, and out and all about, and comes back along those pipes, and gradually gets down to the coil here, and is heated again. Why, if that was properly made by good workmen, it couldn't help answering."

Deering smiled sadly.

"You didn't have one made like that, did you?"

"Yes. Six times over, and of the best material."

"Well?"

"No, my boy, ill. There was a disastrous explosion each time."

Vane looked searchingly in the inventor's face.

"Why, it couldn't explode," cried Vane.

"My dear Vane, pray do not be so stubborn," said Aunt Hannah.

"I don't want to be, aunt, but I've done lots of things of this kind, and I know well enough that if you fill a kettle with water, solder down the lid, and stop up the spout, and then set it on the fire, it will burst, just as our boiler did; but this can't. Look, uncle, here is a place where the steam and air can escape, so that it can't go off."

"But it did, my boy, it did."

"What, made from that plan?"

"No, not from that, but from the one I had down here," said Mr Deering; and he took out his keys, opened the square tin box, and drew out a carefully folded plan, drawn on tracing linen, and finished in the most perfect way.

"There," said the inventor, as Vane lifted the lamp, and this was laid over the plan from which it had been traced; "that was the work-people's reference—it is getting dirty now. You see it was traced from the paper."

"Yes, I see, and the men have followed every tracing mark. Well, I say that the engine or machine, or whatever you call it, could not burst."

The inventor smiled sadly, but said no more, and Vane went on poring over the coloured drawing, with all its reference letters, and sections and shadings, while the doctor began conversing in a low tone.

"Then you really feel that it is hopeless?" he said.

"Quite. My energies are broken. I have not the spirit to run any more risks, even if I could arrange with my creditors," replied Deering, sadly. "Another such month as I have passed, and I should have been in a lunatic asylum."

The doctor looked at him keenly from beneath his brows, and involuntarily stretched out a hand, and took hold of his visitor's wrist.

"Yes," he said, "you are terribly pulled down, Deering."

"Now, Vane, my dear," said Aunt Hannah, softly; "do put away those dreadful plans."

"All right, aunt," said the boy; "just lift up the lamp, will you?"

Aunt Hannah raised the lamp, and Vane drew the soiled tracing linen from beneath, while, as the lamp was heavy, the lady replaced it directly on the spread-out papers.

Vane's face was a study, so puckered up and intent it had grown, as he stood there with the linen folded over so that he could hold it beneath the lamp-shade, and gaze at some detail, which he compared with the drawing on the paper again and again.

"My dear!" whispered Aunt Hannah; "do pray put those things away now; they give me quite a cold shudder."

Vane did not answer, but drew a long breath, and fixed his eyes on one particular spot of the pencilled linen, then referred to the paper beneath the lamp, which he shifted a little, so that the bright circle of light shed by the shade was on one spot from which the tracing had been made.

"Vane," said Aunt Hannah, more loudly, "put them away now."

"Yes," said Deering, starting; "it is quite time. They have done their work, and to-morrow they shall be burned."

"No," yelled Vane, starting up and swinging the linen tracing round his head as he danced about the room. "Hip, hip, hip, hurray, hurray, hurray!"

"Has the boy gone mad?" cried the doctor.

"Vane, my dear child!" cried Aunt Hannah.

"Hip, hip, hip, hurray," roared Vane again, leaping on the couch, and waving the plan so vigorously, that a vase was swept from a bracket and was shivered to atoms.

"Look there, look here!"

"Oh, I didn't mean that," he cried. "But of course it burst."

"What do you mean?" cried Deering, excitedly.

"Look there, look here!" cried Vane, springing down, doubling the linen tracing quickly, so that he could get his left thumb on one particular spot, and then placing his right forefinger on the plan beneath the lamp. "See that?"

"That?" cried Deering, leaning over the table a little, as he sat facing the place lately occupied by Vane. "That?" he said again, excitedly, and then changing his tone, "Oh, nonsense, boy, only a fly-spot in the plan, or a tiny speck of ink."

"Yes, smudged," cried Vane; "but, look here," and he doubled the tracing down on the table; "but they've made it into a little stop-cock here."

"What?" roared Deering.

"And if that wasn't in your machine, of course it blew up same as my waterpipes did in the conservatory, and wrecked the kitch—"

Vane did not finish his sentence, for the inventor sprang up with the edge of the table in his hands, throwing up the top and sending the lamp off on to the floor with a crash, while he fell backward heavily into his chair, as if seized by a fit.

Chapter Thirty Five.

Mrs Lee is Incredulous.

"Help, help," cried Aunt Hannah, excitedly, as the lamp broke on the floor, and there was a flash of flame as the spirit exploded, some having splashed into the fire, and for a few minutes it seemed as if the fate of the Little Manor was sealed.

But Vane only stared for a moment or two aghast at the mischief, and then seized one end of the blazing hearthrug. Mr Deering seized the other, and moved by the same impulse, they shot the lamp into the hearth, turned the rug over, and began trampling upon it to put out the flame.

"Get Mrs Lee out," shouted Deering. "Here, Vane, the table cover; fetch mats."

The fire was still blazing up round the outside of the rug; there was a rush of flame up the chimney from the broken lamp; and the room was filling fast with a dense black evil-smelling smoke.

But Vane worked well as soon as the doctor had half carried out Mrs Lee, and kept running back with door-mats from the hall; and he was on his way with the dining-room hearthrug, when Martha's voice came from kitchen-ward, full of indignation:

"Don't tell me," she said evidently to Eliza, "it's that boy been at his sperriments again, and it didn't ought to be allowed."

Vane did not stop to listen, but bore in the great heavy hearthrug.

"Here, Vane, here," cried the doctor; and the boy helped to spread it over a still blazing patch, and trampled it close just as Aunt Hannah and Eliza appeared with wash-hand jug of water and Martha with a pail.

"No, no," cried the doctor; "no water. The fire is trampled out."

The danger was over, and they all stood panting by the hall-door, which was opened to drive out the horrible black smoke.

"Why, Vane, my boy," cried the doctor, as the lad stood nursing his hands, "not burned?"

"Yes, uncle, a little," said Vane, who looked as if he had commenced training for a chimney-sweep; "just a little. I shan't want any excuse for not going to the rectory for a few days."

"Humph!" muttered the doctor, as Mr Deering hurried into the smoke to fetch out his drawings and plans; "next guest who comes to my house had better not be an inventor." Then aloud: "But what does this mean, Vane, lad, are you right?"

"Right?—yes," cried Deering, reappearing with his blackened plans, which he bore into the dining-room, and then, regardless of his sooty state, he caught the doctor's hands in his and shook them heartily before turning to Aunt Hannah, who was looking despondently at her ruined drawing-room.

"Never mind the damage, Mrs Lee," he cried, as he seized her hands. "It's a trifle. I'll furnish your drawing-room again."

"Oh, Mr Deering," she said, half-tearfully, half in anger, "I do wish you would stop in town."

"Hannah, my dear!" cried the doctor. Then, turning to Deering: "But; look here, has Vane found out what was wrong?"

"Found out?" cried Deering, excitedly; "why, his sharp young eyes detected the one little bit of grit in the wheel that stopped the whole of the works. Lee, my dear old friend, I can look you triumphantly in the face again, and say that your money is not lost, for I can return it, tenfold—Do you hear, Mrs Lee, tenfold, twentyfold, if you like; and as for you—You black-looking young rascal!" he cried, turning and seizing Vane's hand, "if you don't make haste and grow big enough to become my junior partner, why I must take you while you are small."

"Oh, oh!" shouted Vane; "my hands, my hands!"

"And mine too," said Deering, releasing Vane's hands to examine his own. "Yes, I thought I had burned my fingers before, but I really have this time. Doctor, I place myself and my future partner in your hands."

Aunt Hannah forgot her blackened and singed hearthrugs and broken lamp as soon as she realised that there was real pain and suffering on the way, and busily aided the doctor as he bathed and bandaged the rather ugly burns on Vane's and Mr Deering's hands. And at last, the smoke having been driven out, all were seated once more, this time in the dining-room, listening to loud remarks from Martha on the stairs, as she declared that she was sure they would all be burned in their beds, and that she always knew how it would be—remarks which continued till Aunt Hannah went out, and then there was a low buzzing of voices, and all became still.

And now, in spite of his burns, Deering spread out his plans once more, and compared them for a long time in silence, while Vane and the doctor looked on.

"Yes," he said at last, "there can be no mistake. Vane is right. This speck was taken by the man who traced it for a stop-cock, and though this pipe shows so plainly here in the plan, in the engine itself it is right below here, and out of sight. You may say that I ought to have seen such a trifling thing myself; but I did not, for the simple reason that I knew every bit of mechanism by heart that ought to be there; but of this I had no knowledge whatever. Vane, my lad, you've added I don't know how many years to my life, and you'll never do a better day's work as long as you live. I came down here to-day a broken and a wretched man, but I felt that, painful as it would be, I must come and show my old friend that I was not the scoundrel he believed."

The doctor uttered a sound like a low growl, and just then Aunt Hannah came back looking depressed, weary, and only half-convinced, to hear Deering's words.

"There is not a doubt about it now, Mrs Lee," he cried, joyfully. "Vane has saved your little fortune."

"And his inheritance," said the doctor, proudly.

"No," cried Deering, clapping Vane on the shoulder, "he wants no inheritance, but the good education and training you have given him. Speak out, my lad, you mean to carve your own way through life?"

"Oh, I don't know," cried Vane; "you almost take my breath away. I only found out that little mistake in your plans."

"And that was the hole through which your uncle's fortune was running out. Now, then, answer my question, boy. You mean to fight your own way in life?"

"Don't call it fighting," said Vane, raising one throbbing hand. "I've had fighting enough to last me for years."

"Well, then, *carve* your way, boy?"

"Oh, yes, sir, I mean to try. I say, uncle, what time is it?"

"One o'clock, my boy," said the doctor, heartily; "the commencement of another and I hope a brighter day."

Chapter Thirty Six.

"I am Glad."

Trivial as Vane's discovery may seem, it was the result of long months and study of applied science, and certain dearly bought experiences, and though Mr Deering blamed himself for not having noticed the little addition which had thwarted all his plans and brought him to the verge of ruin, he frankly avowed over and over again that he was indebted to his old friend's nephew for his rescue from such a perilous strait.

He was off back to town that same day, and in a week the doctor, who was beginning to shake his head and feel doubtful whether he ought to expect matters to turn out so well, received a letter from the lawyer, to say that there would be no need to call upon him for the money for which he had been security.

"But I do not feel quite safe yet, Vane, my boy," he said, "and I shall not till I really see the great success. Who can feel safe over an affair which depends on the turning on or off of a tap."

But he need not have troubled himself, for he soon had ample surety that he was perfectly safe, and that he need never fear having to leave the Little Manor.

Meanwhile matters went on at the rectory in the same regular course, Mr Syme's pupils working pretty hard, and there being a cessation of the wordy warfare that used to take place with Distin, Macey, and Gilmore, and their encounters, in which Vane joined, bantering and being bantered unmercifully; but Distin was completely changed. The sharp bitterness seemed to have gone out of his nature, and he became quiet and subdued. Vane treated him just the same as of old, but there was no warm display of friendship made, only on Distin's part a steady show of deference and respect till the day came when he was to leave Greythorpe rectory for Cambridge.

It was just at the last; the good-byes had been said, and the fly was waiting to take him to the station, when he asked Vane to walk on with him for a short distance, and bade the fly-man follow slowly.

Vane agreed readily enough, wondering the while what his old fellow-pupil would say, and he wondered still more as they walked on and on in silence.

Then Vane began to talk of the distance to Cambridge; the college life; and of how glad he would be to get there himself; starting topics till, to use his own expression, when describing the scene to his uncle, he felt "in a state of mental vacuum."

A complete silence had fallen upon them at last, when they were a couple of miles on the white chalky road, and the fly-man was wondering when his passenger was going to get in, as Vane looked at his watch.

"I say, Dis, old chap," he said, "you'll have to say good-bye if you mean to catch that train."

"Yes," cried Distin, hoarsely, as he caught his companion's hand. "I had so much I wanted to say to you, about all I have felt during those past months, but I can't say it. Yes," he cried passionately, "I must say this: I always hated you, Vane. I couldn't help it, but you killed the wretched feeling that day in the wood, and ever since I have fought with myself in silence, but so hard."

"Oh, I say," cried Vane; "there, there, don't say any more. I've forgotten all that."

"I must," cried Distin; "I know. I always have felt since that you cannot like me, and I have been so grateful to you for keeping silence about that miserable, disgraceful episode in my life—no, no, look me in the face, Vane."

"I won't. Look in your watch's face," cried Vane, merrily, "and don't talk any more such stuff, old chap. We quarrelled, say, and it was like a fight, and we shook hands, and it was all over."

"With you, perhaps, but not with me," said Distin. "I am different. I'd have given anything to possess your frank, manly nature."

"Oh, I say, spare my blushes, old chap," cried Vane, laughing.

"Be serious a minute, Vane. It may be years before we meet again, but I must tell you now. You seem to have worked a change in me I can't understand, and I want you to promise me this—that you will write to me. I know you can never think of me as a friend, but—"

"Why can't I?" cried Vane, heartily. "I'll show you. Write? I should think I will, and bore you about all my new weathercock schemes. Dis, old chap, I'm such a dreamer that I've no time to see what people about me are like, and I've never seen you for what you really are till now we're going to say good-bye. I am glad you've talked to me like this."

Something very like a sob rose in Distin's throat as they stood, hand clasped in hand, but he was saved from breaking down.

"Beg pardon, sir," said the fly driver, "but we shan't never catch that train."

"Yes; half a sovereign for you, if you get me there," cried Distin, snatching open the fly, and leaping in; "good-bye, old chap!" he cried as Vane banged the door and he gripped hands, as the latter ran beside the fly, "mind and write—soon—good-bye—good-bye."

And Vane stood alone in the dusty road looking after the fly till it disappeared.

"Well!" he cried, "poor old Dis! Who'd have thought he was such a good fellow underneath all that sour crust. I *am* glad," and again as he walked slowly and thoughtfully back:—"I *am* glad."

" Vane stood in the dusty road, looking after the fly."

Chapter Thirty Seven.

Staunch Friends.

Time glided on, and it became Gilmore's turn to leave the rectory. Other pupils came to take the places of the two who had gone, but Macey said the new fellows, did not belong, and could not be expected to cotton to the old inhabitants.

"And I don't want 'em to," he said one morning, as he was poring over a book in the rectory study, "for this is a weary world, Weathercock."

"Eh? What's the matter?" cried Vane, wonderingly, as he looked across the table at the top of Macey's head, which was resting against his closed fists, so that the lad's face was parallel with the table. "Got a headache?"

"Horrid. It's all ache inside. I don't believe I've got an ounce of brains. I say, it ought to weigh pounds, oughtn't it?"

"Here, what's wrong?" said Vane. "Let me help you."

"Wish you would, but it's of no good, old fellow. I shall never pass my great-go when I get to college."

"Why?"

"Because I shall never pass the little one. I say, do I look like a fool?"

He raised his piteous face as he spoke, and Vane burst into a roar of laughter.

"Ah, it's all very well to laugh. That's the way with you clever chaps. I say, can't you invent a new kind of thing—a sort of patent oyster-knife to open stupid fellows' understanding? You should practice with it on me."

"Come round this side," said Vane, and Macey came dolefully round with the work on mathematics, over which he had been poring. "You don't want the oyster-knife."

"Oh, don't I, old fellow; you don't know."

"Yes, I do. You've got one; every fellow has, if he will only use it."

"Where abouts? What's it like—what is it?"

"Perseverance," said Vane. "Come on and let's grind this bit up."

They "ground" that bit up, and an hour after, Macey had a smile on his face. The "something attempted" was "something done."

"That's what I do like so in you, Vane," he cried.

"What?"

"You can do all sorts of things so well, and work so hard. Why you beat the busy bee all to bits, and are worth hives of them."

"Why?" said Vane, laughing.

"You never go about making a great buzz over your work, as much as to say: 'Hi! all of you look here and see what a busy bee I am,' and better still, old chap, you never sting."

"Ever hear anything of Mr Deering now, uncle?" said Vane, one morning, as he stood in his workshop, smiling over some of his models and schemes, the inventor being brought to his mind by the remark he had made when he was there, about even the attempts being educational.

"No, boy; nothing now, for some time; I only know that he has been very successful over his ventures; has large works, and is prospering mightily, but, like the rest of the world, he forgets those by whose help he has risen."

"Oh, I don't think he is that sort of man, uncle. Of course, he is horribly busy."

"A man ought not to be too busy to recollect those who held the ladder for him to climb, Vane," said the doctor, warmly. "You saved him when he was in the lowest of low water."

"Oh, nonsense, uncle, I only saw what a muddle his work-people had made, just as they did with our greenhouse, and besides, don't you remember it was settled that I was to carve—didn't we call it—my own way."

The doctor uttered a grunt.

"That's all very well," began the doctor, but Vane interrupted him.

"I say, uncle, I've been thinking very deeply about my going to college."

"Well, what about it. Time you went, eh?"

"No, uncle, and I don't think I should like to go. Of course, I know the value of the college education, and the position it gives a man; but it means three years' study—three years waiting to begin, and three years—"

"Well, sir, three years what?"

"Expense to you, uncle."

"Now, look here, Vane," said the doctor, sternly, "when I took you, a poor miserable little fatherless and motherless boy, to bring up—and precious ugly you were—I made up my mind to do my duty by you."

"And so you have, uncle, far more than I deserved," said Vane, merrily.

"Silence, sir," cried the doctor, sternly. "I say—"

But whatever it was, he did not say it, for something happened.

Strange coincidences often occur in everyday life. One thinks of writing to a friend, and a letter comes from that friend, or a person may have formed the subject of conversation, and that person appears.

Somehow, just as the doctor had assumed his sternest look, the door of Vane's little atelier was darkened, and Mr Deering stood therein, looking bright, cheery of aspect, and, in appearance, ten years younger than on the night when he upset the table, and the Little Manor House was within an inch of being burned down.

"Mrs Lee said I should find you here," he said. "Why, doctor, how well you look. I'll be bound to say you never take much of your own physic. Glad to see you again, old fellow," he cried, shaking hands very warmly. "But, I beg your pardon, I did not know you were engaged with a stranger. Will you introduce me?"

"Oh, I say, Mr Deering," cried Vane.

"It is! The same voice grown gruff. The weathercock must want oiling. Seriously, though, my dear boy, you have grown wonderfully. It's this Greythorpe air."

The doctor welcomed his old friend fairly enough, but a certain amount of constraint would show, and Deering evidently saw it, but he made no sign, and they went into the house, where Aunt Hannah met them in the drawing-room, looking a little flustered, consequent upon an encounter with Martha in the kitchen, that lady having declared that it would be impossible to make any further preparations for the dinner, even if a dozen gentlemen had arrived, instead of one.

"Ah, my dear Mrs Lee," said Deering, "and I have never kept my word about the refurnishing of this drawing-room. What a scene we had that night, and how time has gone since!"

Vane looked on curiously all the rest of that day, and could not help feeling troubled to see what an effort both his uncle and aunt made to be cordial to their guest, while being such simple, straightforward people, the more they tried, the more artificial and constrained they grew.

Deering ignored everything, and chatted away in the heartiest manner; declared that it was a glorious treat to come down in the country; walked in the garden, and admired the doctor's flowers and fruit, and bees, and made himself perfectly at home, saying that he had come down uninvited for a week's rest.

Vane began at last to feel angry and annoyed; but seizing his opportunity, the doctor whispered:—

"Don't forget, boy, that he is my guest. Prosperity has spoiled him, but I am not entertaining the successful inventor; I am only thinking of my old school-fellow whom I helped as a friend."

"All right, uncle, I'll be civil to him."

Six days glided slowly by, during which Deering monopolised the whole of everybody's time. He had the pony-carriage out, and made Vane borrow Miller Round's boat and row him up the river, and fish with him, returning at night to eat the doctor and Mrs Lee's excellent dinner, and drink the doctor's best port.

And now the sixth day—the evening—had arrived, and Aunt Hannah had said to Vane:—

"I am so glad, my dear. To-morrow, he goes back to town."

"And a jolly good job too, aunt!" cried Vane.

"Yes, my dear, but do be a little more particular what you say."

They were seated all together in the drawing-room, with Deering in the best of spirits, when all of a sudden, he exclaimed:—

"This is the sixth day! How time goes in your pleasant home, and I've not said a word yet about the business upon which I came. Well, I must make up for it now. Ready, Vane?"

"Ready for what, sir,—game at chess?"

"No, boy, work, business; you are rapidly growing into a man. I want help badly and the time has arrived. I've come down to settle what we arranged for about my young partner."

Had a shell fallen in the little drawing-room, no one could have looked more surprised.

Deering had kept his word.

In the course of the next morning a long and serious conversation ensued, which resulted evidently in Deering's disappointment on the doctor's declining to agree to the proposal.

"But, it is so quixotic of you, Lee," cried Deering, angrily.

"Wrong," replied the doctor, smiling in his old school-fellow's face; "the quixotism is on your side in making so big a proposal on Vane's behalf."

"But you are standing in the boy's light."

"Not at all. I believe I am doing what is best for him. He is far too young to undertake so responsible a position."

"Nonsense!"

"I think it sense," said the doctor, firmly. "Vane shall go to a large civil engineer's firm as pupil, and if, some years hence, matters seem to fit, make your proposition again about a partnership, and then we shall see."

Deering had to be content with this arrangement, and within the year Vane left Greythorpe, reluctantly enough, to enter upon his new career with an eminent firm in Great George Street, Westminster.

But he soon found plenty of change, and three years later, long after the rector's other pupils had taken flight, Vane found himself busy surveying in Brazil, and assisting in the opening out of that vast country.

It was hard but delightful work, full at times of excitement and adventure, till upon one unlucky day he was stricken down by malarious fever on the shores of one of the rivers.

Fortunately for him it happened there, and not hundreds of miles away in the interior, where in all probability for want of help his life would have been sacrificed.

His companions, however, got him on board a boat, and by easy stages he was taken down to Rio, where he awoke from his feverish dream, weak as a child, wasted almost to nothing, into what appeared to him another dream, for he was in a pleasantly-shaded bedroom, with someone seated beside him, holding his hand, and gazing eagerly into his wandering eyes.

"Vane," he said, in a low, excited whisper; "do you know me."

"Distin!" said Vane feebly, as he gazed in the handsome dark face of the gentleman bending over him.

"Hah!" was ejaculated with a sigh of content; "you'll get over it now; but I've been horribly afraid for days."

"What's been the matter?" said Vane, feebly. "Am I at the rectory? Where's Mr Syme? And my uncle?"

"Stop; don't talk now."

Vane was silent for a time; then memory reasserted itself. He was not at Greythorpe, but in Brazil.

"Why, I was taken ill up the river. Have you been nursing me?"

"Yes, for weeks," said Distin, with a smile.

"Where am I?"

"At Rio. In my house. I am head here of my father's mercantile business."

"But—"

"No, no, don't talk."

"I must ask this: How did I get here?"

"I heard that you were ill, and had you brought home that's all. I was told that the overseer with the surveying expedition was brought down ill—dying, they said, and then I heard that his name was Vane Lee. Can it be old Weathercock? I said; and I went and found that it was, and—well, you know the rest."

"Then I have you to thank for saving my life."

"Well," said Distin, "you saved mine. There, don't talk; I won't. I want to go and write to the doctor that you are mending now. By-and-by, when you are better, we must have plenty of talks about the old Lincolnshire days."

Distin was holding Vane's hands as he spoke, and his voice was cheery, though the tears were in his eyes.

"And so," whispered Vane, thoughtfully, "I owe you my life."

"I owe you almost more than that," said Distin, huskily. "Vane, old chap, I've often longed for us to meet again."

It was a curious result after their early life. Vane often corresponded with Gilmore and Macey, but somehow he and Distin became the staunchest friends.

"I can't understand it even now," Vane said to him one day when they were back in England, and had run down to the old place again. "Fancy you and I being companions here."

"The wind has changed, old Weathercock," cried Distin, merrily. Then, seriously: "No, I'll tell you, Vane; there was some little good in me, and you made it grow."

The End.